The Otherworld series is
"PURE DELIGHT."
(*New York Times* bestselling author MaryJanice Davidson)

PRAISE FOR

DRAGON WYTCH

"Action and sexy sensuality make this book hot to the touch."   —*Romantic Times* (four stars)

"Ms. Galenorn has a great gift for spinning a compelling story. The supernatural action is a great blend of both fresh and familiar, the characters are each charming in their own way, the heroine's love life is scorching, and the worlds they all live in are well-defined."   —*Darque Reviews*

"This is the kind of series that even those who do not care for the supernatural will find a very good read."
—*Affaire de Coeur*

"Ms. Galenorn writes spellbinding stories that keep you on the edge of your seat as well as reaching for a cold glass of water. This is one series where I cannot wait to see what happens next!"   —*Coffee Time Romance*

"If you're looking for an out-of-this-world enchanting tale of magic and passion, *Dragon Wytch* is the story for you. I will be recommending this wickedly bewitching tale to everyone I know!"   —DarkAngelReviews.com

continued . . .

"I absolutely loved it!"   —*Fresh Fiction*

"Yasmine Galenorn has created another winner. . . . *Changeling* is a can't-miss read destined to hold a special place on your keeper shelf."   —*Romance Reviews Today*

PRAISE FOR

Witchling

"Reminiscent of Laurell K. Hamilton with a lighter touch . . . a delightful new series that simmers with fun and magic."

—Mary Jo Putney,
New York Times bestselling author of *A Distant Magic*

"The first in an engrossing new series . . . a whimsical reminder of fantasy's importance in everyday life."

—*Publishers Weekly*

"*Witchling* is pure delight . . . a great heroine, designer gear, dead guys, and Seattle precipitation!"

—MaryJanice Davidson,
New York Times bestselling author of *Fish Out of Water*

"*Witchling* is one sexy, fantastic paranormal-mystery-romantic read."

—Terese Ramin, author of *Shotgun Honeymoon*

"Galenorn's kick-butt Fae ramp up the action in a wyrd world gone awry . . . I loved it!"

—Patricia Rice, author of *Mystic Rider*

"A fun read, filled with surprise and enchantment."

—Linda Winstead Jones,
author of *Bride by Command*

DEMON MISTRESS

YASMINE GALENORN

BERKLEY BOOKS, NEW YORK

THE BERKLEY PUBLISHING GROUP
Published by the Penguin Group
Penguin Group (USA) Inc.
375 Hudson Street, New York, New York 10014, USA
Penguin Group (Canada), 90 Eglinton Avenue East, Suite 700, Toronto, Ontario M4P 2Y3, Canada
(a division of Pearson Penguin Canada Inc.)
Penguin Books Ltd., 80 Strand, London WC2R 0RL, England
Penguin Group Ireland, 25 St. Stephen's Green, Dublin 2, Ireland (a division of Penguin Books Ltd.)
Penguin Group (Australia), 250 Camberwell Road, Camberwell, Victoria 3124, Australia
(a division of Pearson Australia Group Pty. Ltd.)
Penguin Books India Pvt. Ltd., 11 Community Centre, Panchsheel Park, New Delhi—110 017, India
Penguin Group (NZ), 67 Apollo Drive, Rosedale, North Shore 0632, New Zealand
(a division of Pearson New Zealand Ltd.)
Penguin Books (South Africa) (Pty.) Ltd., 24 Sturdee Avenue, Rosebank, Johannesburg 2196,
South Africa

Penguin Books Ltd., Registered Offices: 80 Strand, London WC2R 0RL, England

This is a work of fiction. Names, characters, places, and incidents either are the product of the author's imagination or are used fictitiously, and any resemblance to actual persons, living or dead, business establishments, events, or locales is entirely coincidental. The publisher does not have any control over and does not assume any responsibility for author or third-party websites or their content.

DEMON MISTRESS

A Berkley Book / published by arrangement with the author

PRINTING HISTORY
Berkley edition / June 2009

Copyright © 2009 by Yasmine Galenorn.
Excerpt from *Bone Magic* by Yasmine Galenorn copyright © 2010 by Yasmine Galenorn.
Cover art by Tony Mauro. Cover design by Rita Frangie.

ISBN: 978-0-425-22864-7

BERKLEY®
Berkley Books are published by The Berkley Publishing Group,
a division of Penguin Group (USA) Inc.,
375 Hudson Street, New York, New York 10014.
BERKLEY® is a registered trademark of Penguin Group (USA) Inc.
The "B" design is a trademark of Penguin Group (USA) Inc.

PRINTED IN THE UNITED STATES OF AMERICA

10 9 8 7 6 5 4 3 2 1

Dedicated to my husband, Samwise,
my favorite geek and chiphead,
who also happens to be
one of the most gorgeous nerds in the world.

ACKNOWLEDGMENTS

Thank you to my agent, Meredith Bernstein, and to my editor, Kate Seaver—the best team I could have. To Tony, the most talented cover artist ever. To my Witchy Chicks—thanks, ladies, for being such a great support system. To my little "Galenorn Gurlz," who offer me their unconditional love. Most reverent devotion to Ukko, Rauni, Mielikki, and Tapio, my spiritual guardians. A reverent nod to Pele, the embodiment of island passion and tropical fire.

Thank you to my readers, both old and new. Your support helps keep us writers in ink and fuels our love of storytelling, and believe me, I appreciate each and every wonderful note you send, whether it be via MySpace, e-mail, or snail mail. You can find me on the net at Galenorn En/Visions (www.galenorn.com) and at MySpace (www.myspace.com/yasmine galenorn). If you write to me via snail mail (see website for address or write via publisher), please enclose a stamped, self-addressed envelope with your letter if you would like a reply. Promo goodies are available; see my site for info.

Be nice to nerds. Chances are you'll end up working for one.

—CHARLES J. SYKES

Only two things are infinite, the universe and human stupidity, and I'm not sure about the former.

—ALBERT EINSTEIN

CHAPTER 1

"Could you at least wait until I open the window to shake that thing?" Iris shot me a nasty look as I yanked the braided rug off the floor and started beating it against the wall. "I can barely breathe, there's so much dust."

Chagrined, I dropped the rug to the floor and gave her a sheepish look. Dust didn't bother me, and sometimes I forgot other people had to breathe. "Sorry," I said. "Open the window, and I'll shake it outside."

Rolling her eyes, she lifted the sash and pushed it up as far as she could. I took over, finishing the job. A wash of warm summer air filtered through the open window along with the sounds of horns honking, blaring music, and laughter from a gang of street kids who were smoking weed in the back alley behind the Wayfarer. The air had a happy-go-lucky feel to it, a stir of excitement, like a street party about to spontaneously erupt.

I leaned over the sill, waving to one of the boys who was staring up at me. His name was Chester, but he went by Chit, and he and his buddies had become a fixture around the bar over the past few months. Too young to come in, they hung around out back, and every now and then I'd make sure they got a good meal from the grill. They were good kids—a little at loose ends, but they never caused much trouble, and they weren't gangbangers or druggies. In fact, they kept some of the less desirable elements from hanging out in the alleys.

Chit waved back. "Yo, Menolly! What's shakin', babe?"

I grinned. I was far, far older than he, although I didn't look it. But like a number of the younger FBH men I'd met, he flirted with every woman who looked under forty, especially if they were Fae. And though I was only half-Fae, and a vampire to boot, he treated me like I was just another one of the locals.

"Just getting around to some long-overdue cleaning," I called down to him, waving again before I turned back to Iris, who was poking around an old-world trunk that had been hiding in a corner of the room.

Since I now owned the entire building the Wayfarer Bar & Grill resided in, I decided it was time to clear out some of the rooms over the bar and turn them into a paying resource. My sisters and I could furnish them, rent them out to Otherworld visitors, and make a nice chunk of change.

Even though we were back on the Court and Crown's payroll, money was still going out faster than it was coming in. Especially since we were paying Tim Winthrop for the computer work he was doing for the Supe Community.

The Wayfarer's second story held ten rooms, two of them bathrooms. And it looked like all of them had remained untouched for years. Piles of junk and thick layers of dust permeated the entire story. Iris and I'd finished one room, but it had taken us two nights to sort through the boxes filled with newspaper and old clothes.

I stretched, arching my back, and shook my head. "What a mess."

The room had obviously been turned into a storage room, probably by Jocko, who wasn't the cleanest bartender the Wayfarer had ever seen. Unfortunately, the diminutive giant had met an untimely end at the hand of Bad Ass Luke, a demon from the Subterranean Realms.

Jocko had lived in one of the Otherworld Intelligence Agency's designated apartments in the city, and I was pretty sure he'd never slept at the bar. We hadn't found any giant-sized clothes hanging around. At least not yet. But it was obvious that *someone* from Otherworld had stayed here at one time, because she'd left a bunch of her things here. I recognized the weave on a couple of tunics. They certainly hadn't been made over here Earthside.

Iris snorted. "*Mess* is certainly the word, isn't it? Now, if you'll get your albino butt over here, I could use some help moving this trunk." Hands on her hips, she nodded to the wooden chest she'd uncovered from beneath a pile of newspapers.

Shaken out of my reverie, I lifted the trunk with one hand and effortlessly carried it to the center of the room. Being a vampire had its perks, and extraordinary strength was one of them. I wasn't all that much taller than Iris—skimming five one, I towered over her by a mere thirteen inches—but I could have easily lifted a creature five times her weight.

"Where on Earth are your sisters? I thought they were going to help."

The Talon-haltija—Finnish house sprite—brushed a stray cobweb off her forehead, leaving a smudge from the grime that had embedded itself in her hands. Her ankle-length golden hair had been pulled into a long ponytail, and she'd carefully woven it into a thick chignon to get it out of the way. Iris was wearing a pair of denim shorts and a red and white gingham sleeveless blouse, with the ends tied together under her breasts. A pair of blue Keds completed her country-maid ensemble.

I grinned. "They are helping, in their own *special* ways. Camille's at the store buying more cleaning supplies and dinner. Delilah's out scrounging up a pickup so we can haul away some of this junk." I'd left running the bar to Chrysandra for the evening. She knew where I was, and she was my best waitress. Luke was bartending, and he'd take care of any jerks that stumbled in. Tavah, as usual, was guarding the portal in the basement.

"*Special* my foot," Iris mumbled, but she flashed me a brilliantly white smile. She had good teeth, that was for sure. "Let's see what this old chest holds. Probably dead mice, with our luck."

"If it does, don't tell Delilah. She'd want to play with them." I knelt beside her, examining the lock. "Looks like we need a skeleton key if you don't want me to bust it open."

"Forget about keys," Iris said. She leaned over and deftly inserted a bobby pin into the oversized hole, then whispered a soft chant. Within seconds, the latch clicked. I gave her a long look, and she shrugged.

"What? Simple locks I can pop. Dead bolts, not so much. Life is easier when you don't have to worry about locks and bars."

"I would have to agree," I said, opening the lid. As it softly creaked, the faint odor of cedar rose to fill the air. Even though I didn't need to breathe, that didn't mean I couldn't smell—at least when I chose to—and I allowed the aroma to filter through my senses. Mingled with the fragrance of tobacco and frankincense, the scent was dusty, like an old library thick with leather and heavy oak furniture. It reminded me of our parlor, back home in Otherworld.

Iris peeked over the edge. "Pay dirt!"

I glanced into the trunk's belly. No dead mice. No gems or jewels, either, but there were clothes and several books and what looked like a music box. I slowly lifted the box out of the soft cushion of dresses in which it had been nestled. The wood was definitely harvested from Otherworld.

"Arnikcah," I said, peering closely at it. "This comes from OW."

"I figured as much," Iris said, leaning over to examine the box.

Wood from an arnikcah tree was hard, dark, and rich, with a natural luster that shimmered when polished. Easy to spot by its rich burgundy tones, the color rested somewhere between mahogany and cherry.

The box was fastened by a silver hinge, and I flipped it open, gently raising the lid. A small peridot cabochon, inset on the underside of the lid, flashed as the sound of tinkling notes fluttered out. Not panpipes, but a silver flute, sounding the song of woodland birds at the close of sunset.

Iris closed her eyes, listening to the melody. After a moment, it stopped, and she bit her lip. "That's beautiful."

"Yes, it is." I examined the contents of the music box. "My mother had a box similar to this one. Father gave it to her. I don't know what happened to it, though. Camille would know, if anybody does. The tune's a common one, used to lull children to sleep."

The inside of the music box had been lined with a rich, velvety brocade. I'd seen it used in the skirts of women who belonged to the Court and Crown. A deep plum, the cloth had absorbed the scent of the arnikcah wood.

I shuddered, finding myself unaccountably sad as I touched the glowing gem fastened to the underside of the lid. Once more, the melody began to play, lightly trilling through the dusty room. I closed my eyes, transported back to the long summer nights of my youth when I would dance in a meadow as Camille sang her spells to the Moon, and Delilah chased fireflies in her kitten form. We'd come a long way from those days.

Iris peered into the box. "There's a locket inside."

I gently set the box onto the floor and picked up the heart-shaped locket. Silver, embossed with a scrollwork of roses and vines, the heart sprang open as I touched the hinge, revealing a picture and a lock of hair. The photo was definitely Earthside in nature, and was of an elf. A man. The lock of hair was so pale it was platinum. No dye had ever touched these tresses. I held it out to Iris.

She closed her fist around the hair and squinted. "Elf, by the feel. What a pretty pendant. I wonder who it belongs to."

"I haven't the faintest idea," I said. "What else is in the trunk?"

Iris lifted out the books and the pile of clothes. The books were obviously written Earthside: *The Idiot's Guide to Living Earthside* and *American English for Elves.*

The clothing had belonged to a woman. A tunic, several pair of leggings, a belt and jacket, a brassiere. I held up the undergarment. Whoever owned this had small breasts. The cloth was elf-weave, that much I recognized.

Beneath the clothes, in the bottom of the trunk, we found a journal. I opened it to the first page. The inscription read "Sabele," written in a scrolling hand. The name was in English, but the rest of the journal was in Melosealfôr, a rare and beautiful Crypto language from Otherworld. I could recognize it but not read it. But Camille could.

"This looks like a diary," Iris said, flipping through it. "I wonder . . ." She stood up and poked around the room, rooting under the towering piles of debris. "Hey! There's a bed here, and a dresser in the corner. Want to make a bet this was a bedroom, perhaps for whoever owned this locket and diary?"

I stared at the piles of old magazines, newspapers, and faded liquor boxes. "Let's clear away all this trash. Just haul it into the next room for now. We'll see what we find beneath it." As I replaced the music box and clothes within the trunk, laughter echoed down the hall from the stairs, and within seconds, my sister Camille stood at the door, two of her men in tow.

"Pizza!" Camille entered the room, gingerly stepping over a rolled-up rug. As usual, she was dressed to impress, in a black velvet skirt, a plum bustier, and stilettos. Morio was right behind her, carrying five pizza boxes, and behind him, Smoky towered over everybody, looking bemused but not entirely thrilled to be tagging along.

Iris jumped up and wiped her hands on her shorts. "I'm so hungry I could eat a horse."

"Hush, or Smoky might oblige," Camille said, wrinkling her nose as she gave the dragon a playful look.

He might look like six foot four of man flesh with silver hair down to his ankles, but when he transformed, he was all dragon under that snow white veneer. He ate horses, cows, and the occasional goat. On the hoof. He joked about eating humans, too, but none of us took him seriously, although I suspected there might be the occasional missing person we could attribute to him. Whatever the case, Smoky wasn't just a dragon who could take human form. He was also my sister's husband. *One* of her husbands.

Morio, a Japanese youkai-kitsune—fox demon, loosely translated—was her other husband. He wasn't nearly as tall as Smoky, but he was good-looking in a sleek, lithe way, with a ponytail that hung to his shoulders and the faintest hint of a goatee and thin mustache.

Camille had a third lover. Trillian, a Svartan, had been missing too long for comfort, and I knew she was worried about him.

"You just hush about my eating habits, woman," Smoky said, gently patting her shoulder. He indulged behaviors in her that would earn most people a one-way ticket to crispy critter land. Love was supposed to be blind, but I had the feeling in Smoky's case, he'd come to accept that he'd better develop patience with my sister or end up miserable.

I frowned at the pizzas. I'd give a lot to be able to eat pizza. Or anything, actually. My ever-present diet of blood kept me going, but I wasn't particularly thrilled with it. All salt, no sweets.

Morio's eyes gleamed as he pulled out a thermos and handed it to me.

"I'm not thirsty," I said. Bottled blood wasn't exactly a taste treat. Kind of like generic beer. It did the trick, but in no way or form could you call it haute cuisine. When I wasn't hungry, I left it alone.

"Just drink," he said.

I cocked my head. "What are you up to?" But when I opened the thermos, the blood didn't smell like blood. Instead it smelled like . . . pineapple? I hesitantly took a sip. If I ingested anything but blood, I'd get horrible cramps.

But to my shock and delight, though it was blood that flowed down my throat, all I could taste were coconut milk and pineapple juice. I stared at the thermos, then at him. "By the gods, you did it!"

"Yes, I did," he said, a victorious grin spreading across his face. "I finally figured out the spell. I thought piña colada might be a nice change for a first try."

Morio had been working on a spell for some time that would allow me to taste foods I'd left behind when I died.

"Well, it worked!" I laughed and perched on the open windowsill, one knee pulled up to my chest as I leaned back against the frame. As I drank, my taste buds doing a Snoopy dance, it occurred to me that this was the first time in over twelve years that I'd tasted something other than blood.

"I could kiss you for this."

"Go ahead," Camille said with a wink. "He's good."

Snorting, I set down the thermos and wiped my mouth carefully. More often than not, I ended up with a few spatters around my lips, and I preferred not to look like some blood-crazed monster.

"With all due respect to your darling husband, I think I'll leave his kisses for you. Not really my type," I said, winking at Morio. "No offense intended."

"None taken," he said, grinning. "Next time we'll try for some sort of soup flavor. What's your poison?"

"Hmm . . . beef vegetable would hit the spot."

Happier than I'd been in a while, I glanced around the room. "While you guys eat your pizza, I'll start clearing some of this junk out of here. Iris and I found something curious. Don't trash anything that looks like it might have belonged in a bedroom or to an elf."

I piled a stack of magazines in a box and carried them out, dumping them into the room across the hall. Smoky ignored the pizza and pitched in, helping me, as did Morio. Iris and Camille perched on a bench, digging into the Hawaiian-style pie.

As we worked, Camille alternated between eating and filling me in on what I'd missed during the day. With the summer solstice so close, the time in which I could be awake and active had been severely curtailed. I was down to around eight hours per night between sunrise and sunset. I'd sure be happy to see autumn and winter again. It sucked having to be in bed by five thirty in the morning.

"We finally got the wedding invitation from Jason and Tim. They're holding it during the night just so you and Erin can make it." She picked up another slice and held it overhead, letting the strings of mozzarella trail into her mouth.

"I'm glad they're finally getting hitched. They make a good couple."

Tim had won my respect a hundred times over when I'd had to turn his best friend, Erin. I'd sworn never to sire another vampire, but Erin would have died otherwise, and she made the choice. That's how I ended up with a middle-aged human vampire daughter. Tim was her best friend. He'd come through when Erin and I had needed him most, and my respect for him had soared.

"By the way," I said, "Erin's selling the Scarlet Harlot to Tim. She can't work there during the day, so he's taking over. He'll open a computer consulting business on the side, now that he's graduated from college."

"I know. He told me," Camille said. "I'll be sad to see Cleo Blanco fade away, but then again, I never did think he made a very convincing woman. He's much better-looking as a man. Although, he did a good job lip-synching to Marilyn Monroe's songs."

She licked her fingers and then added, "Oh, yeah, Wade called shortly before we left home. He said he has something he needs to talk to you about. I told him to drop by the bar, so he'll be over in a bit."

Shit. I didn't want to talk to Wade. We'd been arguing a lot lately, and distance definitely helped the heart grow fonder in this case. Whether it was the summer heat or the overdose of sleep, I didn't know, but we'd been getting on each other's nerves, and the problem wasn't showing any signs of easing up.

"Great," I mumbled. "Smoky, can you help me carry this rug? I can lift it, but it's so long it's unwieldy for one person."

Smoky obligingly propped one end of the rolled-up Persian rug on his shoulder, and I did likewise to the other. We carted it across the hall and tossed it onto the ever-growing pile of debris.

"Where's Delilah? We need to get some of this crap out of here before we end up with a fire. One stray spark, and this place would go up like a match." I kicked at the rug, and it shifted.

"Patience, patience," Smoky said. "Let me cast a frost spell in here. I can saturate everything with a layer of moisture and make it harder to burn."

I groaned. "And turn it into a breeding ground for mold. Oh, go ahead. At least I won't worry so much about fire then."

An hour later, we'd cleared the bedroom of everything that didn't seem to belong there. We'd uncovered a bed, dresser, trunk, writing desk, bookshelf, and rocking chair. Everything pointed to the original occupant as being a female elf.

"Who lived here?" Camille asked, picking over the remains of the second pizza. Smoky and Morio had settled into eating, and I could see that the other three pies were about to become history.

I shrugged. "I haven't the faintest idea. Nobody at the OIA filled me in on whoever held the job before Jocko."

Iris sat in the rocking chair, rubbing her hand over one of the polished arms. "Would the OIA have that information if you asked them?"

Camille shook her head. "Chances are, even though the organization's back up and running, that most of the files were lost during the civil war."

I had to agree with her. "Yeah. Most of the personnel have either been fired or arrested, depending on their loyalty to Lethesanar. Except, interestingly enough, the director of the Otherworld Intelligence Agency. Father told us he was a double agent, but I didn't know whether or not to believe it. Damned if the information wasn't correct, though."

"Jocko's dead. *He* can't very well help us," Camille said. "Any of your waitresses might know?"

"Doubtful, but that gives me an idea." I jumped up and headed for the door. "I'll be right back. Meanwhile, you guys search the room and see what's in the closets and in that desk. Look for whatever you can find. Check under the mattress, too."

I hurried down the stairs. While Chrysandra and Luke had come to work for me after Jocko's death, there was still one person who remembered the gentle giant. Peder, the daytime bouncer, had been around during Jocko's time. I flipped through the address book that we kept behind the counter and then picked up the phone, punching in his number.

Like Jocko, Peder was a giant. But where Jocko had been the runt of his family, Peder was smack in the middle of being height-weight proportionate for his race. After three rings, he picked up.

"Yef?" His English was still limited, and his accent was atrocious, but I knew Calouk, the common dialect used by the more uncouth members of Otherworld, and I switched to it immediately.

"Peder, this is Menolly," I said, my lips tripping over the rough words as I translated my thoughts into Calouk. "I know you worked for Jocko, but do you by any chance remember who was the bartender before him? Did an elfin woman run the bar? Her name would have been—"

"Sabele," he said. "Yeah, Sabele was the bartender before Jocko. She went home to OW, though. She vanished one day. Never said nuthin'."

Vanished? That seemed odd, considering the locket and diary left behind. "What do you mean, vanished?"

"She quit. That's what Jocko told me when he came here."

That didn't ring true. I was fairly certain Peder wouldn't lie to me, but that didn't mean that what he said was accurate. Giants weren't the brightest bulbs in the socket, and Peder wasn't on the gifted end of the spectrum.

"Are you certain? I found a few of her personal things upstairs while cleaning out one of the rooms. Items I doubt she would have left behind."

"That's what Jocko told me. He said . . . he said the OIA told him that Sabele deserted her post. She was really nice, though. I liked her. She never made fun of me."

His tone told me that, like Jocko, Peder was sensitive to ridicule. Giants were surprisingly emotional, not like trolls or ogres. Oh sure, they were oafs, but they could be caring oafs.

"Do you know if she had any friends around here? A boyfriend, maybe? Or a brother?" The image of the male elf's face from the picture in the locket drifted to mind.

"Boyfriend? Yeah, she had a boyfriend. He used to come into the bar a lot. I thought they went back to OW together and got married. Lemme think . . ." After a moment, Peder sighed. "All I can remember is that his first name was Harish. And her family name was Olahava. That help you any?"

"Yeah," I said, jotting down the two names. "More than you know. Thanks, Peder. And by the way, you're doing a good job. I appreciate it." Everybody needed strokes sometimes. Even giants.

"Thanks, boss," he said. I could hear the glee in his voice.

As I replaced the receiver, the door opened, and I looked up as Wade wandered into the room. His shocking bleached-blond hair was even whiter, thanks to a dose of peroxide, and he'd given up the glasses he used to hide behind. He was wearing a pair of PVC jeans—gods know where he got hold of those—and a white T-shirt. A thick, shiny black patent leather belt studded with metal grommets rode low on his hips. I blinked. When had he gone punk?

A psychiatrist until he'd been bitten and turned, Wade Stevens was the leader of Vampires Anonymous, a support group for the newly undead. He'd become my first vampire friend when my sister Camille insisted I join the group.

Lately, though, he'd been on edge and snippy, and I had no intention of wasting the energy to find out why. I had enough problems to deal with, without adding a moody vampire to the list. Anyway, I wasn't the coddling type. His mother did enough of that. In fact, his mother was one of the primary reasons I'd stopped dating him. A vampire herself, she was the perfect antidote to any attraction I'd felt for Wade.

He leaned across the bar. "We need to talk."

"I'm busy," I muttered. Avoidance wasn't my usual MO, but I had no intention of ruining my mood. "Can we do this later?"

"No. We need to talk *now*," he said, his eyes shifting toward red.

Whoa. Touchy, touchy.

"Fine. In the back, where the customers won't overhear us." I led him into the office and closed the door behind us. "All right, what's so damned important that it can't wait for a few hours? Or days?"

I waited, but he remained silent. Irritated, I started to push past him, intending on returning to the bar, but he stopped me, barring my way with his arm.

"Fine. I'll just tell you straight out, because I don't know how else to do this. I've thought this over and over for the past few weeks, but there's no way to get around it. I have to put some distance between us, or you're going to ruin any chance I have of becoming regent of the Northwest Vampire Dominion."

I stared at him, unable to believe what I was hearing. "You've got to be joking."

"No." He waved me silent. "I'm asking you to quietly withdraw from Vampires Anonymous. Don't show up at the meetings. And don't contact me in public . . . keep all of our communications in private. You've become a liability to me, Menolly. And to the group."

CHAPTER 2

I stared at him. *Liability?* Who the fuck was he kidding?

"You have to be joking. What happened to our plans? You know the ones. Where I'm supposed to be your *second*, if you won? And what about all the big talk about creating an underground vampire police force to corral the rogue vamps? Did all of those plans suddenly go up in smoke?"

Wade avoided my gaze. "I know, I know. But face facts. Your presence at the VA has divided the entire group. Half the members want you dead, the other half worships you like a goddess. But in the larger vampire community, your name's become synonymous with *troublemaker*. Menolly, you'll cost me votes that I can't afford to lose."

His voice dropped an octave, and he slammed his hand against the wall next to me. "If I don't win the position of regent, Terrance will. And then everything we've worked for will go straight down the toilet."

I stared at him, wondering where he'd found this new, unpleasant side of himself. Wade was usually mild, soft-spoken. What had happened? But in my heart, I knew the answer. Ever since the Earthside vampires started coming out of the closet along with the other Supes, they'd begun to hive off into regions, choosing leaders to represent them. The regency for the Northwest Dominion was up for grabs, and Wade wanted it. He wanted it so bad he could taste it.

"Fine." I slammed the door open so hard one of the hinges broke. "Then leave. I won't bother you or your fucking group again. You can go to hell, for all I care. Just make sure to take that battle-axe of a mother with you."

The look of surprise that washed across his face made me feel good. I hoped I'd hurt his feelings. *Bad.* Nobody used me, then dumped me when I became inconvenient. And the sooner sucker boy found that out, the better.

"Menolly, don't be this way." Wade spoke softly, but he could have melted into tears, and I wouldn't give a damn.

"Don't be *what* way? You kick me out of the group, you tell me you don't want to be seen with me, and you expect me to smile and play nice? Get real." I pointed to the door. "I told you to get out."

"I knew you were going to be pissed," he said, looking irritated. "Please try to understand. This is my chance to make a difference as the dominions take shape. I know we talked about you being my *second*, but that was before all the fallout over you staking Dredge. When you killed him, it sent a shock wave through the vamp community that still refuses to settle."

Disgusted, I gave a little hiss and narrowed my eyes. "Idiot. Dredge was a monster, and he would have destroyed *every* possibility for vampires to live among FBHs without being hunted down and staked. What I did was harder than anything you'll ever have to do. You know exactly what he put me through. Do you realize how fucking painful it was to relive my own torture, rape, and murder in order to sever the ties that bound me to my sire?"

"Yeah, I know—"

"Like hell you do!" I cut him off, so angry that I shoved him away so he wasn't standing so near me. "Go through one-tenth of what I endured, and then look me in the eyes and tell me what I did was unjustified. But you couldn't take it, could you, *boy*? You'd end up crawling on your belly, sucking Dredge's cock, begging him to spare you. You would have curled up in his court just to stop the torture." I didn't care who heard me now. There was no wiggle room when it came to discussing Dredge. Not for me.

Wade's eyes flashed red. He leaned forward, staring down at me, his long lashes fluttering against his pale skin. "Don't be an ass. I *know* what you went through. And I know you *had* to kill him. But Menolly, be logical. If I don't win, Terrance will. And Terrance is another Dredge in the making. He wants to bring the mystique of fear back into being a vampire."

Terrance, the owner of the Fangtabula, was an old-school vamp. Badass and arrogant, he thought nothing of using mortals for his private feeding station, then tossing them out when they were dry. But he was a Boy Scout compared to Dredge.

"Bullshit." I stared past him. As much as I hated to admit it, I knew he was right. I had become a controversy, a division among the vamps. I weighed down his campaign, unless he chose to stand by my side and defend me. And he could do it—if he wanted to. But Wade didn't like being the bad guy. Wade wanted to win on his charm, not his ability to lead.

I felt the bloody tears well up and willed them away. I wouldn't let him make me cry. "Damn you. I've done one hell of a lot for Vampires Anonymous, and to be shoved aside like this is a fucking slap in the face."

"Menolly—"

"Don't *Menolly* me. If you had any real balls, Terrance wouldn't have gained the foothold he has now. But you don't like confrontation, and you're still trying to please everybody, even though you know you can't do it. If you'd taken Terrance out when he started showing signs of being a troublemaker, we wouldn't be facing this problem."

Wade grabbed me by the shoulders.

I slowly reached up and took hold of his wrist, squeezing hard enough to feel the bones shift. "Take your hands off of me, or I'll toss you across the fucking room." My fangs extended as anger clouded my senses.

He abruptly let go. I shoved him again, just enough to give him the message that I was serious.

His gaze never left my face as he steadied himself.

"I agree that you've done a remarkable job for Vampires Anonymous, but don't ever lose track of the fact that the group is *my* baby. I started it, I built it into what it is today. There have been others who've put just as much time into it as you, if not more. Sassy Branson for one. Now, can't we keep this civil?" He leaned down, his lips a hairsbreadth from mine.

I let out a low hiss. "Don't you go all red-eye toward me." No breath, no whisper of air passed between us.

His gaze lingered on my face. "I thought you liked men who take charge. You're certainly spending enough time with that incubus. And he's still a *breather*, demon spawn or not." And then Wade was kissing me, pushing me hard against the door.

Without so much as a second thought, I kneed him in the groin, and he shuddered, backing away. While a kick in the balls didn't hurt vamps the same way it hurt FBH men, it still smarted.

"Touch me again, and I'll stake you. First you kick me to the curb, and then you try to kiss me? No more. I rescind my invitation. Wade Stevens, you're no longer welcome in my home. You may not pass through my door. And think twice about darkening my bar again." I couldn't prevent him from visiting the bar—it was a public venue—but I could make certain he never came inside our house again.

He actually had the nerve to look shocked. "Menolly—don't! We'll figure out something—"

"Too late. *Get. Out. Now.* If I have to, I'll call Tavah to help me, and we'll take you down. You can't stand against both of us." The bloodlust pounded in my ears. I wanted to hunt, to seek, to tear something apart. "You'd better go. I don't know how much longer I can hold myself in check."

He took one last look at me and then, smart enough to recognize my breaking point, vanished in a blur. I was walking on the razor's edge, I was stronger than he was, and he knew it.

I tried to gather my wits. So that's where we were at. Wade had betrayed me for political reasons. He'd broken our friendship for personal gain, and while I understood his desire to ascend to the regency, I also had the suspicion he was overreacting to play a part in front of his buddies. He'd always wanted to be the good cop. And to do so, he'd had to make me the bad cop. *Typical man.*

I sidled out to the bar. The smell of sweat and booze rose to overwhelm me. The sound of heartbeats drummed out a pulsing tattoo, threatening to send me into a feeding frenzy. I motioned to Luke.

He took one look at me and immediately nodded toward the door. "You need to hunt."

Luke was a werewolf. He understood instinct, especially since he didn't live with a pack, the way most of the werewolves did. A lone wolf, he was on his own, and he had to remain alert. Luke had never told me what made him break with his pack, but I'd checked, and he had no criminal record, though the scar running down the side of his face told me he'd seen trouble in his past.

"Yeah. Really bad. Can you tell Camille I'll be back in a little bit? If I don't get myself outside, I'm going to explode, and that would not be a good thing. And if Wade comes back, tell him I said to get the fuck out of my bar and stay out."

Luke was good at reading between the lines. He didn't ask questions, just threw his bartender's rag over his shoulder, then headed toward the stairs. I gave him one backward glance, then slipped out the door.

Moving so fast no one would notice me, I passed by the alley behind the Wayfarer. I didn't want to put Chit and his posse in danger. No, I knew exactly where to go.

When I hunted, I tracked the lowlifes: the rapists and druggies and pimps and pushers that haunted the Seattle night. If I *had* to drink from an innocent, I made sure that I never took more than they could spare, and I wiped their memories, leaving only a pleasant suggestion that they'd been out for a long walk and needed a little nap and a good steak to refresh themselves.

The city proper was sweating with the scents of gasoline fumes and heat rising from the pavement and the mingled perfume from over a half-million people. I slipped through the back alleys, crossing from neighborhood to neighborhood until I reached the Central District, a high-crime area that I frequented during my hunts. I almost always found somebody to stalk and seldom went away hungry.

Closing my eyes, I sent out feelers as the city moved around me. There—down a nearby alley. A rumble of excitement filtered out from a group of gangbangers getting ready for a brawl.

Used to be the Crips and the Bloods controlled the Seattle streets, but lately a new set of gangs had moved into town. The Zeets, named for their hold on the infamous Z-fen market—the current date-rape drug of choice used primarily by pimps to keep their stables in line because it was so highly addictive—kept a tight fist on the drug trade. And the Wings, an Asian-based gang, had taken over the protection racket.

I zeroed in on the group. Ten or eleven, they were from the Zeets. The energy of drug-enhanced testosterone raced through them like a line of sparks. I slipped through the shadows, pressing close to the brick buildings that lined the passage. As I approached the end of the alley, it opened into a dead-end space. I listened to the snippets of conversation that floated out.

"They're gonna cream their pants when we get done with them—"

"Dude, give me that shit. My turn—"

"So I walked in and found Lana fuckin' some asshole she met at school. She'll never do that again."

"What'd you do to her, dude?"

"Gave her a beating she'll never forget—"

"We ready? My old lady's been bitchin' about too many late nights—"

I turned my attention to the man who had beat up his girlfriend. He'd do. He was tall, lithe, with a long braid that hung halfway down his back. His beard and mustache were blond, but his eyes were so dark they were almost black. He was wearing a blue wife-beater and a pair of cargo pants covered with chains. I noticed he had a lead pipe sticking out of one deep pocket on the side of his pants. *Oh yeah*, he'd do just fine.

I stared at him, focusing on him, willing him to stay behind. Old-school vamps used the trick a lot, but I usually didn't bother. It felt a little like cheating, but tonight I didn't care. He'd crossed the line in my book when he bragged about beating his mate.

"I'll catch up in a minute," he said as the others moved off down the alley. As they disappeared, my quarry looked around nervously, as if he wasn't sure why the hell he'd stayed behind. He shivered. I could feel his tension from where I stood. As he moved to follow his buddies, I stepped out of the shadows, blocking his path.

"Going somewhere?" I asked softly, my head down so he couldn't see the crimson light of my eyes.

"Get out of my way, bitch," he said, with a hint of contempt.

I raised my head and smiled, my fangs fully extended.

"What the—" He backed up a step.

"Oh baby, don't run away. I promise, I won't hurt you like you did your girlfriend." And then, giving a little hiss, I began to walk toward him, steady strides that played into the fear spreading across his face. Oh yeah, some days being a vampire felt good. The power to intimidate, the power to bring someone so cocky, so sure he was king of world, to his knees rippled through me. It was a better high than any drug could offer.

He backed up another step, then turned to run, racing toward the wire fence that blocked the end of the alley. I let him go for a few yards, then closed the gap between us in two leaps, landing in front of him.

"Who are you? What do you want?" My man backed away, his voice quivering. "You aren't human, are you?"

"Only half," I whispered. "Or at least I *was* half-human. Before I died."

"Vampire!" Recognition filled his face, and he tried to squirm around me.

"Not so fast, *boy*. Recess is over." I grabbed him by the collar, slamming him against the wall. *"Look at me,"* I said.

He obeyed, fear clouding his eyes.

"Tell me your name."

"Jake."

"Okay, Jake. I want you to tell me, did you really hurt your girlfriend?"

He nodded, unable to stop himself. "Yeah, yeah . . ."

"Did you rough her up?"

Again the unwilling nod. "Yeah."

"Did you bruise her? Make her bleed?"

"Yeah. Yeah."

"And *why* did you do that?" I wanted him to say it. I wanted to hear his story. It made it easier to do what I had to do.

"She wanted to leave me. She said I roughed her up too much. She found another guy." His voice was strangled, low, and shaking. I could smell the fear rolling off of him.

"So you taught her a lesson? I bet you enjoyed it, too, didn't you? You strike me as the kind of man who enjoys knocking his women around. So, what did you do to her lover?" Cat and mouse. Like Delilah, I played with my food before I ate.

He closed his eyes. "Sliced him up. Killed him. Made her help me get rid of the body."

"I thought as much," I said. "You're all the same. Pathetic lowlife scum." A wave of distaste rushed through me. If I let him go, he'd continue leeching off of society, and he'd end up killing his girl. He'd kill her if she tried to leave, and he'd end up killing her even if she stayed. Women who were caught in an abuser's trap usually didn't get away so easily.

"What are you going to do to me?" he asked, his breath ragged. "I don't want to die. Don't kill me. Please?"

"How many times has your girlfriend begged you not to hurt her? How many times did you go ahead and mess her up, anyway?" I whispered in his ear, nibbling on the lobe.

He mumbled something, but I ignored it, leaning in to bite him on the neck. As my fangs slid through the flesh, the rich taste of blood welled up, and my restlessness turned to euphoria. I moaned softly, sucking harder, drawing the blood out of his veins, then began lapping the running stream, shuddering as it trickled down my throat.

Jake groaned, his cock growing hard behind his pants as

he rubbed against me. I ignored his erection until he wrapped his arms around me, pressing his neck against my lips.

"Don't stop," he begged me. "Don't stop, please . . ."

My desire vanished. I pulled away, staring at the man who was now on his knees in front of me, still rapt in the throes of my charm. Disgusted with him and annoyed with myself, I leaned down. "Listen. I want you to go to the Fangtabula. You know where that is?"

He nodded.

"Good. Go tell them you want to be a blood whore. Tell them you like it rough."

Jake struggled to his feet. As he stumbled off, I knew that I was sending him to his death. He'd go straight to the club, all right. He was too enthralled to disobey me. And Terrance's thugs would let him in. Before morning, there'd be one less scuzzball in the world.

Somehow, the thought didn't please me as much as I wanted it to. Because for every Jake I got rid of, there were a dozen more to take his place. Satiated, done for the night, I turned and went back to the bar.

My name is Menolly D'Artigo, and I'm a vampire. I'm also half-Fae and half-human. My sisters and I work for the OIA, the Otherworld Intelligence Agency. We were transferred Earthside to keep us out of trouble, but that's when our problems really blossomed. You see, we promptly discovered that a demon lord from deep in the Subterranean Realms—Shadow Wing—plans on breaking through the portals that separate the different realms. He intends to lead an army of his demons to raze both Earth and Otherworld to the ground and set himself up as king of the land.

My sisters and I are on the front line of the battle. For a while, we were fighting alone, but we've been slowly gathering allies. The newly returned Queens of Fae—Earthside—are on our side. In a way.

The elfin Queen, as well as the new Queen of our homeland—Y'Elestrial—are backing us up as much as they can.

And we've gathered together members of the Earthside Supe Community and have their pledges of support.

But the fact is that no matter how many allies we count in our ranks, the enemy numbers in the thousands. And demons aren't easy to kill. Bullets bounce off, they're hooked on uranium, so radiation's like a fix. Even bombs can't wipe them out all that easily.

So here we stand, the brains of the resistance, trying to figure out how to save two worlds, one monster at a time. As a career move, this sucks.

Camille, my oldest sister, is a Moon witch whose magic goes astray too often for comfort. And now she's delving into death magic, thanks to her youkai husband. Delilah, the second-born, is a two-faced Were, meaning she turns into a golden tabby when the Moon is full or when we're squabbling. But she's also recently discovered a second Were form, that of a black panther.

And me? As I said, I'm Menolly D'Artigo. I was an acrobat-slash-spy for the OIA until I fell off the ceiling and got caught by the most sadistic vampire who ever walked the realms. But I had the last laugh and sent a stake through Dredge's heart. Which is a big no-no among vampires. Frowned-on behavior or not, it felt good. When Dredge realized he was toast at my hands, well, that was the best day of my second life.

So here we are, a small vanguard against a violent threat against all of Fae and humankind. Unfortunately, with friends like us, the world sure doesn't need any more enemies!

CHAPTER 3

By the time I got back to the Wayfarer, my anger at Wade had retreated to a low boil, just enough to keep a grudge aflame but not enough to do anything about it. I gave Luke a thumbs-up and headed upstairs. Camille gave me a quick once-over and motioned to her chest. I glanced down at my shirt and grimaced. I'd been sloppy. Blood splattered my top.

"Excuse me for a moment," I said, darting back down the stairs to the back storeroom, where I kept extra clothing. I slid out of the bloody shirt and pulled on a deep indigo turtleneck, checked my jeans to make sure they were still clean, and headed back upstairs.

Once there, I whispered to Camille, "Is my face clean?" I couldn't look in a mirror to check, and it was hard to tell by feel.

She nodded. "As a whistle."

"Thanks," I said, sitting on the bench near the bed, one leg folded under me. "Good job," I said, looking around. Most of the junk had been cleared out, and it was now apparent this room had been a bedroom. And then, because I knew I had to tell her, I added, "Wade kicked me out of the VA group."

"Because of Dredge?" Camille sighed. "I wondered if they were going to. Fickle bastards."

"I get it. I really do, but I'm so pissed that Wade didn't even *try* to find another solution that I rescinded his invitation to our house. Don't extend it again unless I agree, okay?"

"Sure." Camille scooted over next to me and took my hand. Once again, I realized how completely she'd accepted my transformation. She never blinked, never grimaced, never gave any sign that my death and rebirth had changed her feelings for me. Delilah was still struggling, and I didn't hold it against her. Kitten was a lot more uncertain about her place in life than Camille was. I squeezed Camille's hand, gently, and gave her a grateful smile.

"Thanks," I said, after a moment. "For being a wonderful big sister."

"That's what I'm here for," she said, then after another moment, motioned to the room. "So, what are we looking for?"

"The woman who lived here was named Sabele, and she was the bartender before Jocko. The OIA apparently decided she went AWOL and ran home to her family. I'm not so sure. For one thing, Iris and I found her music box and journal. Did she show you?"

Iris shook her head from over in the corner. "Didn't have time. We barely were finished carting out all the trash by the time you came back."

"I'm sorry I wasn't here to help." I glanced at Camille. "You can read Melosealfôr, right?"

She nodded. "Yeah, why?"

"That's what she wrote her journal in," I said, hopping up to retrieve the diary. I handed it to her. "What do you think?"

She glanced through it. "You say she was an elf?"

"That's what Peder says. And the clothing backs it up."

"Hmm . . . that's odd." A curious look spread across her face.

"What?"

"It's just that Melosealfôr is a Crypto language. While a number of elves understand a few words, few actually use it on any regular basis. Mostly Cryptos like unicorns, centaurs, dryads, and naiads speak Melosealfôr, along with all Moon witches pledged to the Coterie of the Moon Mother, but the language isn't common." She began to flip through the journal. "You say she vanished?"

"That's what Peder says. I doubt if she'd leave her journal behind—or this." I opened the music box and carefully lifted out the necklace, flipping open the locket to show her the photo and the lock of hair.

"Her boyfriend?" Camille frowned, stopping near the back of the journal. She skimmed over a paragraph, then flipped forward a few pages, hunting for something. I watched as she ran her fingers over the delicate calligraphy. "Okay, this is kind of creepy."

"What?" I put the locket down.

"This," she tapped her finger on one passage. "She's talking about being afraid to walk home alone. That she was followed by 'that man' again. A few pages back, she wrote that she had the feeling she was being watched." After a moment, she placed the book on the bench and shook her head.

"Sounds like she had some trouble on her hands. Any mention of whoever it was who was following her?" I had a nagging feeling that the OIA had never bothered to find out what had really happened to Sabele. They'd just assumed she ran off. And maybe they'd assumed wrong.

Camille shrugged. "I don't know. I'll read through the whole journal by tomorrow night. Maybe I'll be able to tell you then. Meanwhile, there's another man mentioned here. Elf, I think, by the name of—"

"Harish?" At her surprised look, I added, "Peder remembered her boyfriend's name. If you can figure out where he might be, so much the better. Her family name was Olahava." I suddenly wanted to know what had happened to her. Was she off somewhere having lots of cute little elf babies, or had something bad happened? "What do you think about tracking her down?"

Camille smiled. "She's gotten under your skin. I can tell. Okay, fine with me, and Delilah loves playing chase. It's the cat in her."

I glanced at the clock. Almost midnight. "You should be

getting home. Take Iris with you. She looks beat." The Talon-haltija had curled up on the bed and was softly dozing.

"Right. By the way, while you were out, Delilah called. She found a truck we can borrow tomorrow afternoon. We'll come down and clear out the junk from the other room while you're sleeping. She's at home with Maggie right now." Camille stood up, brushing off the back of her dress. She hefted the journal in her hand. "You've got me curious. And that can only mean one thing. We're in for trouble."

I flashed her a smile. "Aren't we always knee-deep in a dunghill? I've had enough cleaning for one night. I'll follow you down and give Luke a hand at the bar."

With a laugh, she motioned to Smoky and Morio and gently roused Iris from her slumber. As they headed out the door, I followed. Vampire or not, there were times I was incredibly grateful for my family—both blood kin and extended.

It was five minutes past one when the door opened, and Chase Johnson wandered in. Head of the Faerie-Human Crime Scene Investigations unit and chief of detectives, he was also my sister Delilah's on-again, off-again boyfriend. I didn't give them a snowball's chance in hell to make it in the long run, but they were determined to try.

Their relationship was one for the *Jerry Springer Show.* I only say that because unfortunately, Delilah had forced me to sit through way too many episodes during her late-night trash-TV binges. But I watched the show with her because it gave us time together.

Chase sidled up to the bar. Last time he'd paid a late-night visit to the Wayfarer, he'd been covered in blood, and we'd been off and running on the hunt for Dredge. This time, however, he looked reasonably clean and relatively calm. He glanced around the room, then settled himself on a barstool.

"Club soda, no ice," he said. "Have you seen Turnabout Willy lately?"

I snorted. Turnabout Willy was all human. Perfectly fine when he was sober, when he drank he thought he was Superman. He'd never put himself in enough danger for the courts to lock him up. At least not yet. But Chase worried about him. Why, I didn't understand and hadn't asked.

"Willy hasn't been in for about a week. I think he's back on the wagon, but he'll fall off again. He always does. Just wait and see."

"That's what concerns me. He's going to go on a bender one of these days and convince himself he can fly. I'm not looking forward to getting a call that he took a nosedive off one of the downtown skyscrapers." Chase toyed with the soda. "Listen, I didn't come here just to ask about Willy."

"No shit, Sherlock. What do you want?" I gave him a toothy grin. Chase and I butted heads a lot, but we'd developed a healthy respect for each other.

"I've got a question for you."

I wiped the counter with a clean rag. The Wayfarer was still fairly packed, but everybody looked happy. Chrysandra was the best waitress I had. I leaned over the counter.

"Sure thing. What's up?" I said, refilling his glass.

"I've got a problem, and I wondered if you'd look into it. I'd ask Delilah—she's the PI, after all—but this is more along your alley." He glanced across the bar at me, his dark gaze meeting mine. It used to be that Chase wouldn't even look at me. Now we were comfortable around one another. More or less.

"What's going on?"

He shrugged. "I'm not sure if it's actually anything or not, but here's the deal. We took a missing person report a couple days ago. Now, normally, I wouldn't think twice about bringing this to your attention, but the info came through the FH-CSI tip line, and the person who's missing is a vampire."

I stared at him. "Who made the report?" Vampires seldom ever approached the authorities about anything. Chase was right to be concerned.

"Don't know. The line's set up to provide anonymity. It was a woman's voice, though. We couldn't get a trace on the number. She had call block. Anyway, have you heard of the Clockwork Club?"

"I *know* of it," I said. "I've never been invited to their meetings."

The Clockwork Club was the opposite of the Fangtabula. A classy, upscale vampire hangout, they didn't allow blood whores or vamping on the premises. Bottled blood only, and only blood taken from volunteers.

The club reeked of old money. The members had been among the blue-blooded crowd during their life. They ignored both the old-school vamps as well as the sloppier newborns who hadn't learned how to cope. Elitist and determined to keep it that way, membership was by invitation only. From what I knew, the club's roster stood at under two hundred along the entire West Coast. There were three branches: one in Seattle, one in Portland, and one in San Francisco.

"A member of theirs, a female vamp, disappeared five nights ago. She hasn't been seen or heard from since she vanished. Apparently, she managed to pass in society."

A few vamps struggled to hide their undead status to their friends and family. Some of them managed, at least for a while. Our friend Sassy Branson had kept up her charade for well over three years now. I didn't consider it a healthy choice, but some vampires took longer than others to learn how to let go of their old lives. Hell, I wasn't one to talk. Look at how long I'd carried the scars from Dredge before confronting him.

"What happened? You sure she didn't walk into the sun? You know the suicide rate among vampires is astronomical compared to other Supes."

Chase shook his head. "No. The woman who left the tip was positive that there's foul play involved. She told us the name of the girl and her husband. The couple lives here in Seattle. Claudette Kerston was twenty-one at her death. She's been a vampire for seven years. Apparently, she has a full life, if that's what you call it. She's married. Her husband's still alive. I checked her out. Apparently, the Social Security office had no idea she was dead." He arched his eyebrows.

"You outed her." I shook my head. Vamps who passed caused a lot of problems in terms of record keeping once they were found out.

"Inadvertently. I didn't do it on purpose. I had a talk with her husband. Sure enough, he knew she was a vampire, and

he helped her hide the fact. Social Security and the IRS are
going to be breathing down his neck, but there's nothing I can
do about that."

He grinned, then shrugged. "What can I say? They broke
the law. Anything a vampire earns after death is subject to
taxation, and you know as well as I do that there are some
very wealthy vamps who went to their deaths as paupers. It
would seem walking among the undead is a good way to earn
a living."

I gave him that one. "It has its perks. Especially when you
consider the lack of need for food or certain other amenities
and the ability to charm money out of anybody. That's why
the regional dominions are forming—to serve as liaisons to
the government for the vampire community."

"Whatever the case," Chase continued, "her husband's
worried sick. He told me that Claudette always comes home
on time. He showed me what the girl's been keeping herself
busy with."

"You mean she's not just sitting around soaking up the at-
mosphere?" If she was a member of the Clockwork Club, she
had no reason to work or do anything she didn't want to. Nobody got invited who didn't have a few million tucked away.

"Old money, inherited from her father, so no, she didn't
need a job. But she's writing a book. A guide for new vampires. To me, it looks well-thought-out. I don't think she's a
flake or particularly bloodthirsty. In fact, if Claudette were
alive, I'd mark the case as suspicious because there's no reason I can find for her to want to disappear. At least not on her
own."

Chase frowned and toyed with his glass, staring at the end
of his right pinky finger, which was missing its tip. The finger
had healed, but the inner scars were still there. The Chase we
knew now was less obstinate, more thoughtful, and more than
willing to go the extra mile in the fight against Shadow Wing
and his cronies.

"You think her husband's telling the truth about them being happy?" This case just screamed of a husband staking his
wife and then reporting her missing. If they'd tried to scam
the government, he couldn't very well come out and say what

he'd done. And if she's the one who had the money, then declaring her missing would eventually net him big bucks.

The courts were still hung up on whether killing a vampire was murder or not. The conservative factions wanted to declare the undead personae non grata without any rights. The liberals wanted full rights for all vampires and Supes. It was a hot debate right now, and not likely to be tied up neatly with a pretty bow.

"You know, you'd think so, but all my instincts tell me he's on the up-and-up." Chase usually didn't give people the benefit of the doubt, but this time he seemed genuinely convinced that the guy was telling the truth. "What do you say, will you look into it? Ask around? You'll get better results than I will."

"You're spot-on there," I said. "Most vamps don't like the cops." Whereas I might actually be able to sniff out anything suspicious. Especially if I hit Sassy Branson up for info on the Clockwork Club and its members. I leaned on the counter.

"So will you?" he asked. "Check it out?"

"Sure, why not? If you'll do something for me." I gave him a toothy grin. "Another missing person case. Or rather, a *possible* missing person. An elf named Sabele Olahava had my job, right before Jocko took over. She vanished, and the OIA claimed that she disappeared back to Otherworld. We're thinking, maybe not so much."

Chase jotted down her name in the notebook he kept in his pocket. "Sabele . . . Sabele . . . I think I actually met her a couple of times. Right around the time we were pulling together the FH-CSI." He paused, squinting. "That's right, I remember her. Ultrathin. Kind of pretty, but pale. Most elves seem to be pale and thin. You think something might have happened to her?"

"We're not sure, but would you check your records? See if anything was going on back then around the Wayfarer? See if she made any complaints? Camille's going to translate her diary fully tomorrow, but from what we can tell, it sounds as though she might have had a stalker."

I slapped the counter with my bar rag. "Okay, I need to close up, so you need to get your butt out the door. You people frown on bars keeping their doors open past two A.M., you know."

He snorted. "*You people?* I assume you're talking about the cops? Frankly, if I had it my way, the bars would close at midnight. Too many drunks on the road as it is." Pushing himself off his stool, he adjusted his jacket and headed for the door. "I'll see you Sunday. Delilah invited me over for dinner."

I quickly slipped out from behind the bar and glided over to him, gingerly touching his arm with my fingertips. "Just so we understand each other, Chase. You make sure you don't pull any more crap like you did with Erika. Play it straight and honest with Delilah, and we'll get along just fine. Now, I promise I'll call you when I find out anything about Claudette. And if you find anything on Sabele, phone us first thing."

He nodded, leaving without another word. I smiled, satisfied. I still scared the crap out of him. And I considered that a *very* good thing.

CHAPTER 4

~⋙❈⋘~

I was almost done closing the bar when Nerissa poked her head in. A golden goddess, she was a member of the Rainier Puma Pride, and a werepuma. I'd seen her transform once, marveling at the beauty that had started as human and ended up as a big cat. She was lithe and supple, and when she raced across the Puma Pride's land under the feral Moon, I could only stand and gawk, amazed that such an incredible woman could be my lover.

Nerissa worked for the Department of Social and Health Services, helping place troubled children who fell under the state's care into foster homes. And she looked like she'd had a long, hard day by the weary look in her eyes.

Slipping out from behind the bar, I met her near the door. She leaned down and brushed my lips with hers. *Soft.* Her skin was *so* soft, and she smelled like a warm, dusky meadow. A flame stirred in my belly as she let out a low growl, wrapping her arms around my waist as she pulled me so close that I could feel the pulse of the blood in her veins. I opened my lips to her tongue, and she lingered, gently forcing me back against the door.

Aroused, I flipped her around, pinned her against the wall,

my hand slipping up beneath her shirt to caress her silken skin. As my fingers trailed up to her breasts, she slid her legs apart, and I pressed my knee between them, knowing only too well what waited beneath the linen material.

I reached around her to lock the door. A light flashed in her eyes as I motioned toward the back. In my office there was a daybed, and by the time we reached it, she'd stripped off her shirt and was working on her pants. I was out of my jeans and turtleneck in seconds flat, and we were on each other like bunnies in heat. I dipped my head to trail kisses down her breasts, down the center of her muscled stomach, down to the lovely thatch of golden hair that told me she was, indeed, a natural blonde.

Her thighs tensed as I slid between them, tonguing her with gentle, circling strokes. Within seconds, I'd cajoled her into a quick, hard orgasm. We hadn't been together for about a week, and Nerissa was sexual in a way I couldn't ever imagine being. I loved the connection, but sex, for her—as it was for my sister Camille—was on par with food. Necessary for survival.

She gasped, shaking her head as she laughed. "I'm dizzy. I was so damned horny, I couldn't wait to get over here."

I sat back, grinning, as she propped herself up on her elbows. "Only too glad to help."

"Now, it's your turn," she whispered, staring into my eyes. I shivered as she ran her fingers lightly over my body. Even now, I was sensitive about the scars that covered me from head to toe, but when Nerissa made love to me, it was as if they didn't exist, as if Dredge had never touched me. She'd won my confidence and my trust, and I gave neither freely.

She slid her fingers between my legs, her fingertips barely grazing my skin as they fluttered quickly against the white-hot fire that was building in my stomach.

I fought the urge to drag her down to the floor and press my teeth into that bronzed neck of hers. At first, I'd been terrified of losing control, but over the months, I'd discovered that I *could* focus, could enjoy the passion without letting the predator take over. Blood and sex were intermingled for me and always would be, but I'd vowed never to taste Nerissa's blood. She'd offered, but I refused.

Leaning down, she took one of my nipples in her mouth, sucking so hard that if I were human, it would have hurt like hell. But the sensation just drove me on, and I let out a low moan, leaning my head back and closing my eyes.

"Come on, baby, let go," she said, lifting her head. "Give it up. Give up the control."

Even as I fought back the thirst, I felt myself coming—a wave rolling in to swallow me whole, to send me reeling down the rabbit hole. I gave myself over to trust and let the orgasm carry me outside of myself, into the realm where there was no blood, no body, only sensations and souls mingling.

"Menolly? You okay?" Her voice was soft, leading me back.

I sat up and rested my head on her shoulder. "Better than okay. I needed you, too. Had a bad day, of sorts. I'm surprised to see you so late, though. You've got a long ride home tonight. Or, are you staying at our place?"

She wrapped her arm around me, and the steady thump of her heartbeat lulled me into a state of peace, rather than seduced me in. Lucky I fed earlier, I thought. We sprawled together, just holding one another, for a good ten minutes, before Nerissa let go of me and sat up, reaching for her shirt.

"Shit. I need to talk to you about something," she said, her expression falling.

"Just don't tell me that you don't want to be seen with me. Been there, done that tonight, and I'm not taking it too well." I draped her pants over a nearby chair and began to get dressed in my own clothes.

She cocked her head. "Who the hell said *that* to your face? Is he still alive? And if he is, tell me who it is, so I can go rip his throat out."

I shrugged as I zipped up my jeans. Wade's betrayal had hit deeper than I thought. "Wade," I mumbled. "He kicked me out of Vampires Anonymous. Apparently he's convinced that associating with me will jeopardize his chances of snaring the regent's position for the NW Vampire Dominion. Fuck him. Or not. And would you believe he tried to put the moves on me, after he cut me off? I can't believe he did that. The sleaze."

Nerissa leaned against the counter, a frown on her face. "You think he's slipping more into the predator side of his nature? That seems out of character with what you've told me about him."

I jerked my head up. It couldn't be true. Wade, of all vampires? Turning into a badass?

"No," I said quickly. Too quickly. I caught the panic in my voice. "At least, I don't think so."

The geeky glasses had vanished, yes. And sure, he was wearing a shiny replica of Jim Morrison's pants. But moving into the shadows? I shook my head.

"I know he's worried that Terrance will win. And if Terrance prevails, all the work the VA club's done over the past few years goes down the drain. Maybe I overreacted. Wade's just facing reality. As much as I hate to admit it, he's right. I'm a liability now. I'm *controversial*." It stung even more to admit I could see his side of things, but I couldn't deny reality.

"Shit," she said. "I'm sorry." She held out one hand, and I took it, just lightly holding her fingers.

"So that's my news. What did you want to tell me?"

She rolled her eyes. "Oh, life just gets better and better. The Council of Elders held a meeting tonight and asked me to attend. I came directly here afterward. You know, right, that since Zachary's going to be in a wheelchair for the rest of the summer, and since his bid for City Council is pretty much toast, Venus the Moon Child is serious about wanting me to run in his place?"

"Right, but I also thought the COE had debated shelving the idea for a while because you're so against outing yourself as a Supe." Nerissa was in the closet about being a Were. Passing had helped her career over the years.

"Yeah, I thought the issue was off the table, too, but apparently not. The council met again and discussed it at length. Venus thinks it will be good for the community. And if the state fires me when I come out, we can slam them with a lawsuit under the new anti-Supe discrimination laws going into effect. When the government scrambled to give Earthside Fae rights, they had to extend the same to the Weres. So if I come out now, theoretically they can't touch my job." She fidgeted.

The Fae first. Supes second. Vampires—maybe sometime in the future. The government had never been known for an equity-for-all stance. I gazed into her eyes. Flickering indecision stared back at me.

"You don't want to run, do you?"

Nerissa shook her head. "I never did. I don't want the responsibility. The campaign will eat up all my free time. I won't have a moment to myself, especially if I keep working, and I plan to keep working. I like my job too much to give it up. And that means . . ." She glanced up at me. "I won't have much time for my friends. *Or lovers.*"

I blinked. "You aren't walking down Wade's road, are you?"

"Not at all," she said, and by the tone in her voice and the strained look in her eyes, I believed her. "If they told me to break off with you just because you're a vampire, I'd tell the council to screw itself. Venus knows we're lovers, and he's okay with it. And Venus practically rules the Puma Pride at this point. No, the problem is that if I accept the challenge, I'll have to spend every spare moment campaigning. By the time you get up for the night, I'll be exhausted. And I don't have the luxury of getting by with just three or four hours of sleep."

Her eyes brimmed with tears. I leaned over as she sat there, pants in one hand, her other hand clenched in a fist, and kissed the salty drops away.

"Why do it, then?" I asked, but I already knew the answer. She was a member of the Puma Pride. She had an obligation to her tribe members. She owed them allegiance. And sometimes—as with our fight against the demons—the greater good came before personal desire.

She opened her mouth to speak, but I brushed my fingers across her lips.

"Don't even bother," I whispered. "I understand."

I gently backed away and slipped into my boots, zipping

them up after checking to make sure the stilettos were still firmly in place. I went through a lot of heels, considering how much I put my footwear through, what with all the fighting and running I did.

"You know that I care about you. You know that I love being with you. And you know that I don't expect anything from you."

She ducked her head, a faint smile emerging to light up her face. "Yeah. I feel the same. Which means we're *perfect* for each other, and we'll probably end up growing old together."

The thought crossed my mind that I'd live long, long after she died, if I wanted to, but I chose to keep quiet. No sense bringing more gloom and doom to the conversation.

"I'm going to have to put my own life on hold. The Council of Elders wants an answer tomorrow. At least they gave me the *illusion* of free choice." She picked up her handbag and slipped the strap over her shoulder.

"Out of curiosity, what happens if you refuse?" I had no idea how the politics in her Pride worked. All I knew was that most Weres were big on honor and respecting their elders.

"They'd slowly cut me out of everything that matters. I'd find myself living on the periphery. I'd be part of the Pride in name only. Eventually I'd end up leaving. Hell, the only reason Zach's still there is because he's *on* the Council of Elders. Venus backs him up, so the others have grudgingly kept him in the loop. But once you spurn the council, it's only a matter of time until you find yourself alone and ignored." With a pause, she raised her head. "I'm not ready to leave that all behind."

"I get it," I said. And I did. She finished dressing in silence, and I walked her to the door. "We'll do what we can. I can come out and visit you more often. I can be there when you get home, maybe once a week. We'll figure something out."

When she didn't answer, I slowly hovered up to gaze at her, eye level, and planted a gentle kiss on her lips. "It's not like we won't ever see each other. And listen—we're free agents. I know you. You're sexual, like Camille. If you need Venus, or anyone else . . . I have no problem."

"The same goes for you, I hope you know. I'm not the jealous type. At least . . ." Nerissa leaned against the doorframe and ran her perfectly polished nail down my cheek. "I've been thinking. I don't want to lose you, Menolly. Men come and go, but you're my *girlfriend*. So . . . how about we go exclusive—meaning no other *women*?"

Feeling oddly cherished, I smiled. That kind of exclusivity I could live with. "No other women, it is."

"Good. I'm going home, and I'm going to tell Venus I'll run for City Council. And then I'm going to hope like hell I lose the election." With a toothy grin, she vanished into the night.

As the door swung shut behind her, I thought about her situation. It wasn't so different than the one my sisters and I were facing. We had obligations we didn't want to fulfill, but we did because it was our duty and our destiny.

And as much as I was going to miss Nerissa coming over two or three times a week, I respected her decision. She was loyal to her community.

Yes, I thought, arming the security system and locking the door behind me. Nerissa was a woman after my own heart. And that's why I wouldn't make waves. I headed down the silent street toward the parking lot where I'd left my Jaguar, feeling unaccountably lucky.

CHAPTER 5

~∞~

Rather than go straight home, I decided to pay a visit to Sassy Branson and see what I could find out about Claudette and the Clockwork Club. Morning was still a good three hours away, and Sassy never minded me popping in on her, especially since my daughter, Erin, lived with her.

Erin. Now there was a minefield. Even as a child, I'd never pictured myself becoming a mother, but here I was, barely into adulthood myself, with a middle-aged daughter for whom I was responsible.

Sassy lived in a mansion in the Green Lake area. Set back on two acres, the house was huge, and it was fully paid off, thanks to Sassy's well-to-do late husband. The fact that Sassy had been a lesbian, albeit hiding in the closet during her marriage, had apparently never bothered him. Both husband and wife had led separate yet comfortable lives while married.

A moment after I punched the intercom on the gate, Janet's ever-present voice rang out. I told her who I was and waited as the gates swung wide.

Janet was Sassy's assistant, housekeeper, and long-time friend, all rolled into one. Once I'd learned about Sassy's sexual preferences, I'd wondered if Janet had ever been her lover, but in the intervening months it became clear that Janet walked the straight and narrow. But the woman had taken care of Sassy since Sassy was sixteen, and she was as loyal as they came.

And Janet was waiting for me at the door when I scrambled out of my Jag and dashed up the stairs. Her dowager's hump matched Julia Child's. Janet was just as proper and funny as Child, too, and actually looked a lot like the grande dame of French cooking.

"Miss Menolly, welcome. Miss Sassy is waiting in the parlor." Her voice was gravelly, but her smile was warm.

"Is Erin with her?" I asked, eager to see my daughter.

Janet nodded and headed toward the kitchen while I peeked around the door into the parlor. Erin and Sassy were sitting at the chess table, playing a game. Sassy was dressed in Chanel, as usual, and reeked of the same perfume. Not a hair dared step out of place on her elegantly coiffured head.

Erin, on the other hand, was not—and had never been—a girly girl. But Sassy had decided that during her stay, Erin wouldn't be allowed to wear her old flannel shirts nor the baggy jeans she loved so much. And Sassy always got her way. Erin sported a linen pantsuit, looking slightly uncomfortable.

My daughter had lost her tan and was rapidly approaching the near-albino stage every light-skinned vampire eventually reached. Dark-skinned vamps stayed that way, but any artificially heightened skin tones disappeared.

"Boo!" I said, entering the room.

Erin leapt to her feet, then dropped into a deep curtsy. She'd learn to control her urge toward obeisance eventually, but during their first years, nearly all vampires genuflected if their sires were present. I would have with Dredge, if he'd stuck around after turning me. I would have hated every minute of it, but I'd have done it because it wouldn't have been possible *not* to acknowledge him.

"Hey, how's it going?" I motioned for her to sit down again, then parked myself on the opposite sofa.

"Sassy's been helping me learn how to control my glamour." Erin still didn't sound like herself. That, too, was to be expected. She was my child now, and a natural eagerness to please overrode her personality. Add to that, Erin had been president of the Faerie Watchers Club before I turned her, so she had that whole Fae fangirl thing going, too.

"Very good. That's an important lesson, Erin. You must learn to control yourself around breathers, and that includes controlling how you manipulate them. Practice hard for me, okay?"

I hated speaking to her like she was a child, but that's what the situation required. She was young, very young to her new form, and the wonder of discovering her new abilities could easily turn into abuse. Vampires who weren't trained took a turn toward the predator really fast. The last thing I wanted was to have to stake my daughter. I glanced at Sassy, who was staring at Erin with pride in her eyes.

"Erin's doing a marvelous job," she said. "She's making remarkable progress—a real quick study. Erin, why don't you go to your room for a while? Watch TV or talk on the Internet or whatever you like until sunrise."

Erin obeyed without question, murmuring her good nights. I'd invested Sassy with the authority to direct her, and until I revoked it, Erin treated Sassy as her guardian when I wasn't around.

As soon as Erin had ducked out of the room, Sassy turned back to me, concern filling her eyes. "I heard about what happened between you and Wade. I'm so sorry, my dear. He told me what he was planning before he talked to you, and I tried to talk him out of it. Surely there must be another way to address the problem." She leaned forward and almost imperceptibly touched my hand.

I frowned. Like I'd suspected, Wade had been here first. No doubt he wanted to line up her support.

"You sure you don't want me to leave and take Erin with me? Associating with me isn't likely to win you any friends right now." A cheap shot, true. But petty or not, Wade's about-face had hit a nerve that wouldn't stop aching.

Sassy snorted. "My dear, aren't you forgetting something? *I also staked my own sire.* And I reminded Wade of that. I'm just not as high-profile as you are, and since I keep my nature undercover, only the vamp community and a very few Supes know I even exist on the flip side. But I've decided I'm tired of hiding in the closet. I'm outing myself as a vampire, I'm speaking out about Takiya, my sire."

Impressed, I smiled at her. "I think it's time, Sassy. Stand up and be your true self."

"Menolly," she hesitated, glancing at me, a nervous twitch fluttering at her eyebrow. "There's something else I need to speak to you about."

I held her gaze. I knew perfectly well what she wanted to talk to me about. I'd felt the subject hanging between us for months now, every time I walked into Sassy's house. "I think I know what it is, and if I'm right, I've suspected it for weeks. But I decided to wait until you were ready to talk about it. It's Erin, right? You're falling for her?"

Sassy shrugged, giving me a rueful smile. "*We're* falling for *each other*. God knows, I didn't plan on it. Good heavens, I would never have even looked in her direction but . . . we've talked so much in the past weeks. We get along so well. We're close to the same age—I'm a bit older but not by that much. Everything fits."

"I know, but she's still so young to the life—"

"Menolly, I give you my word. I won't push her into anything. But last night, Erin came clean with me. She says she's always favored women, but she's never had the courage to stand up and say so. Her family wouldn't accept her if she had, and they meant a great deal to her. Now, there's nothing to lose. If they wouldn't accept her as a lesbian, they sure aren't going to accept it when she tells them she's a vampire. And she's *going* to tell them."

I nodded. I'd suspected for weeks now that Sassy and Erin liked each other in more than a friendly way. The idea of them hooking up didn't bother me, but I was worried Erin wasn't ready to handle a relationship. Coming out of the grave was harder than coming out of the closet. Stick both in the works at once, and you were asking for trouble.

"Just so long as you don't send her into overload. Erin has a lot to learn about her new life, and I'd hate to see her lose direction because she was focused on a relationship instead of gaining control over her growing abilities. I have Dredge's blood in me, and he was *very* powerful. Probably one of the most powerful vampires who ever walked the worlds. And my bloodline is half-Fae, so Erin's going to have some interesting fallout from her lineage." I sighed. "How far has it gone? I know that sounds nosy, but—"

Sassy inclined her head gracefully. "Being her sire, you have every right to ask. We haven't . . . done anything. We talk a lot. I'll abide by whatever you wish, but if you want me to keep things on a platonic basis forever, then I have to ask you to find her another place to live. I know that's not fair—"

I laughed. "Not fair? You opened your house to her and took her in. You've given your time and energy to helping her. How many other vampires would have done the same for me? No, Sassy, I'm in your debt. I think, though, if you can just keep things on a platonic level for another year, it would be best. I'm not saying don't talk or hold hands but . . . leave it at that for now?"

Sassy nodded. "I promise. Erin will remain here, we'll be good, and you won't be disappointed." She gave me a subtle wink. "And you—how is the lovely young Were you're dating?"

If I could have blushed, I would have. I didn't broadcast my love life like Camille. It wasn't that I was uncomfortable with my sexual choices or shy. It was just that they were a private part of my life—like when I fed.

"We're taking an enforced break, but not because we want to. Her Pride has decided she should run for the City Council seat that Zachary was vying for. He still has a long way to go toward healing and needs to focus on regaining his strength." I leaned back and stared at the ceiling. An intricate chandelier illuminated the room, a vision of dragonflies in stained glass. "Tiffany?"

She nodded. "With the production stamp included. My late husband's mother owned it, and she gave it to us as a wedding present because I admired it. She was a formidable woman, but fair." She paused, her voice catching. After a moment, she shrugged. "Margaret was a good mother-in-law.

She never chided us for choosing not to have more children after our daughter drowned."

I'd never asked Sassy about her daughter, not wanting to pry, but the older woman seemed to want to talk. "What was her name?"

Sassy looked up at me, surprise washing across her face. "I've never told you much about her, have I?"

I shook my head. "No, and I never felt right about asking."

Janet entered the room then, with two goblets filled with blood. I didn't ask Sassy where she got her bottled blood—it just didn't seem appropriate. I accepted one of the flutes and nodded gravely to the older woman. Janet refused to be treated like a friend by Sassy's buddies. She had a strong sense of propriety and showed no interest in joining the conversation.

"Thank you, Janet. If you'll adjust the curtains, then you can attend to whatever you like for an hour or two. Just be back around four." Sassy spoke affectionately to her. If it bothered Janet that Sassy was a vampire, she didn't show it. After the housekeeper left, Sassy turned back to me.

"She's seen you through most of your life, hasn't she?" I swirled the drink. It wasn't animal blood, that was for sure.

Sassy ducked her head, smiling. "Yes, she has. I never, ever tried to put the bite on her, even when I was hungry. I hate to think about the day she passes. I'm so very much going to want to bring her over to our side, but I refuse to do so. I've already told her that I won't do it, but I'll be by her side till the end. Janet has cancer, you see. A slow, progressive brain tumor. She's dying, Menolly, and in about a year, I'll lose her." Bloody tears welled up in her eyes. "She's been closer to me than anybody—my family, my friends, even my late husband. Janet's . . . a part of me."

"But you won't bring her over," I said.

I wondered how she'd feel when Janet was slipping away. I'd sworn never to sire another vampire until I was faced with Erin's imminent death and her pleas to live. I'd broken down, turned her, and now, here we were. But I kept my mouth shut. Sassy would have to face her conscience at the end and then live with whatever choice she made.

"No." Sassy took a sip of the blood and daintily wiped her mouth with a crimson napkin. "Menolly, I miss hunting. For the past six months I've bought my blood from the blood bank. There's a new one, you know, downtown. They're paying street kids for blood and selling it to vamps. Gives the kids a little money, and they keep a record so nobody gets depleted. Wade's responsible for that little enterprise."

I stared at the goblet of crimson fire. "Why haven't you gone hunting?"

Sassy cleared her throat. I looked up at her. She held my gaze.

"I've started to enjoy it too much. I'm slipping. Just a little, Menolly, but it scares me silly. That's why Erin's good for me. She reminds me of how important training is. Helping her, helps me." She hesitated, then continued. "I want you to promise me something. I don't have any family, so consider it payment for helping Erin. Down the line."

I knew what she was going to ask, because I'd made Camille promise me the same thing. "*If* the time comes, I promise you. I'll be quick. You won't suffer, and you won't make anybody else suffer."

With a nod, Sassy relaxed and leaned back in her chair. "Thank you. That sets my mind at ease. Now, about my daughter. She was beautiful. Her hair was the same golden blonde as Delilah's. And she was so tiny and yet so strong. Abby had the kind of self-confidence that comes naturally, and there wasn't a mean bone in her body. Abigail was my saving grace. She gave me a reason to bury myself under customs and mores. I loved her more than anything, Menolly. I would have died for her." She hung her head and once again, a catch entered her voice.

"When she was five, we went to Ocean Shores on vacation. We were walking on the beach—Janet and Abby and I. Johan was off in a meeting somewhere. He had a conference call or something. Anyway, I decided to catch some sun, and I fell asleep on the blanket. The next thing I knew, Janet was screaming. I woke up to see her racing into the water. Abby had gone to play at the edge of the waves when the tide started to come in. The waves caught her."

I squeezed my eyes shut to give her privacy in her pain.

"Abby was pulled into a riptide, and before Janet could reach her, she was gone. Just like that. The lifeguards were on the scene within minutes, but we didn't find her body till the next day when she washed back up onshore."

Sassy let out a long, measured sigh, and I knew she was practicing the exercises I'd taught her. Sometimes, when the emotion grew too intense, it helped to force the lungs to move, to take a breath even though the oxygen was unneeded. To hold it, count away the panic or fear or anger, then let it go slowly.

"What happened?"

"The light of my life died that day. Johan and I managed to get through it. Janet was terribly broken up and blamed herself, but it wasn't her fault. I should have been awake. I should have been watching my daughter." Crimson tears began to streak down her cheeks. "I spent the rest of my life avoiding the memories. And I've spent the years since my death trying to make up for it by helping others."

There wasn't anything I could say to help. Sassy dashed at her cheeks with a brilliant red handkerchief. After a moment, she composed herself. "On to other things. Why did you come tonight? There's something else, isn't there?"

Startled, I remembered my original reason for dropping by. "Yeah, I need information about the Clockwork Club, if you have it. And I need to know if you are acquainted with a woman named Claudette Kerston."

She snorted. "The Clockwork Club? They invited me to join, but they're not my style. Take out your notebook. They're a peculiar group, and you'll want to remember what I tell you." And with that, the mood lightened, and she began telling me about the most elite vampire country club in the nation.

CHAPTER 6

The faint stirring of sunset brought me out of my slumber. I blinked, sitting up abruptly and throwing the covers back before I quite realized where I was. I never needed blankets. I didn't get cold, but I felt too vulnerable sleeping naked without at least a sheet covering me.

I stretched and yawned. Even after twelve years of death, I still yawned out of instinct. The oxygen wasn't necessary, but it had been so ingrained in my persona for almost sixty years of life that I still hadn't shaken the habit.

Sometimes, when I yawned, a particularly odd, hollow feeling rushed through me as the air passed into my body and lungs without flooding me with the relief each breath brought to a living person. The air molecules rushed through my veins, trying to find a hold, trying to stimulate blood cells, but there was no catch, no recognition. I let out the breath, slowly, in a long stream, and my lungs fell silent again.

So many reflexes that were imprinted on behavior and thought became invisible, until they took on a new meaning after death.

As I pushed my way out of the bed, the secret passage to my lair opened from up the stairs, and Delilah and Camille came traipsing down. Camille was carrying Sabele's journal.

"Good, you're awake. Iris wants you to help her with Maggie."

Sometimes one of them would come down to wait for me to wake up, but they knew enough to stay away from the bed, out of the danger range. When I woke, instinct took over, and it was easy to hurt someone who'd gotten too close.

"So anything earthshaking happen while I slept?" Unlike someone just taking a nap, if the demons broke in and set fire to the world while I was sleeping, I wouldn't know about it until the sun set.

"I translated Sabele's diary," Camille said, sprawling across my bed on her stomach, bending her knees into the air and crossing her ankles. The stilettos on her shoes looked dangerously sharp. "And I have to tell you, she was one fascinating elf. She was also being stalked by some creep."

Delilah handed me my jeans, and I shimmied into them. When it came to jeans, my theory was the tighter the better. Nothing screwed with my circulation anymore. Of course, if I couldn't fight in them, they weren't worth the denim from which they were made, but other than that, I liked them snug.

"Unrequited love?" I asked, sliding a silk turtleneck over my head.

"You should wear a tank top. It's so warm out," Delilah said.

I shook my head. "Not ready for it. Not yet. Besides, the hot and cold don't affect me." Free of my sire or not, I still felt self-conscious about the kaleidoscope of patterns Dredge had etched on my body with his long nails and a dagger. I hadn't reached the point where I felt comfortable wearing revealing clothing. I leaned over to fasten my granny boots.

"Unrequited love?" Camille repeated. "No, oddly enough. You'd think so, but this guy—where's the page?" She flipped through the diary. "Right, here it is. The guy's name was Harold Young. He went to the University of Washington, apparently. Harold was following Sabele around, but he never made a move to ask her for a date or anything like that. Sabele was getting spooked. Then, for five nights in a row he trailed her home. The sixth day . . . well, the diary's blank. It ended there."

I glanced up at her from lacing my boots, and as I lifted my head, one of my braids managed to get itself hooked on the fringe of my bedspread, the thin threads tangling with the ivory beads that decorated my cornrows. Delilah hurried over as I tried to tug myself free.

"Here, you're going to rip the spread if you aren't careful."

As she unwound the threads from my coppery hair, a playful glint began to grow in her eyes. She stared at the strings, fixated. Oh shit, I knew what that meant.

"Let go of my hair and back away slowly," I said, quickly grabbing for my braid in her hand. "I've got it."

She quivered for a moment, breathing quickly, and then reached out again, her eyes glazed over. Within the blink of an eye and a whirlwind of color, I had a golden tabby hanging from my braids, wrestling them with all the glee of a kid in a candy store.

"Hey! You little sh—" I tried to shake her off, but my braid was still tangled in the threads. Delilah tightened her grip on the hair.

Camille raced over and scooped her up, getting a nice little swipe on her arm for doing so. I decided that I could buy a new bedspread and ripped the fringe off the edge, tearing the material in the process. But it freed me. I turned to find Camille holding Delilah up above her head, her hands wrapped around our sister's furry tummy. Delilah plaintively yowled and squirmed, her eyes wide, toes splayed, tufts of fur sticking out from between them.

"You free?" Camille asked.

I nodded, and she tossed Kitten on my bed. Delilah promptly zoomed off across the room and up the stairs on a manic quest for—well, for whatever cats were aiming for when they did that. I'd asked her about it once but only got a burst of laughter in reply.

"Well, hell. That was not exactly the way I planned to start my night," I said, examining the ruined spread. "It's not too bad. Maybe Iris can mend it for me when she has some extra time."

Camille finished untangling the fringe from my hair and gave me the once-over. "You ever think about a different hairstyle? Your hair used to be so pretty when you wore it long and curly."

"Just why do you think I wear it this way?" I asked. "Think about it. When I'm fighting, it's out of my way. When I'm hunting, I don't get blood on it. And . . . well, generally, I think it's kind of cool."

"Yeah, well at least take it out once in awhile to wash it. I can braid it again for you." She tossed the fringe in the trash basket. "Just sticking your head under the shower and hoping the shampoo makes it through those tight braids isn't exactly sanitary."

I stared at her, bemused by the bizarre turn in conversation. "I'm *dead*, Camille. You really think I'm all that sanitary to be around?"

"I dunno. Aren't you?" She frowned. "Actually, I never think about it anymore. Dead to me means rotting and in the dirt, or covered with blood from a fight you're not walking away from. Since you don't fit either category, I've taken you out of the *Dead Zone* and stuck you somewhere in the *Creatures of the Night* category."

I let out a laugh. "That is the most whacked-out thing you've said today." I glanced at the stairs. "You think Delilah's going to be back down here soon?"

"I don't know. Depends on whether she got distracted."

"Eh, well." I motioned for her to follow me. "Let's head upstairs. So you said the man who was following Sabele was named *Harold*?" I'd been wondering if maybe Sabele's boyfriend had been up to no good, but his name was Harish.

Camille followed me up the stairs, turning off the light at the top. We slipped out from behind the bookcase that covered the secret entrance to my lair, into the kitchen, only to find Iris, sitting on a short stool, leaning over Maggie with a frustrated look on her face.

"Please, little one, eat your dinner—" She glanced up as we entered the kitchen. "I'm so glad you're here. Maybe you can get her to eat."

"What's wrong?" I leaned over Maggie just in time for the baby gargoyle to screw up her face and let out a series of angst-ridden *moophs*. I held out my arms, but Maggie, who usually came lurching my way the minute she saw me, just sat there, sniffling.

"She doesn't want to eat her dinner. She wants her cream drink. But she has to eat some solid food. We're supposed to wean her soon." Iris sighed, pushing the dish of ground lamb and vegetables toward Maggie again, who promptly shoved it away, pouting.

We were weaning her off the cream, sugar, cinnamon, and sage drink that had made up the bulk of her diet until recently. The book on woodland gargoyles said she was ready for her secondary food stage—ground meat with herbs and vegetables twice a day, and the drink—which simulated mother gargoyle milk—once a day. Eventually, we'd bring her mice to hunt and teach her how to fend for herself.

Iris offered Maggie the lamb again. This time, the calico fuzzball scooped up a handful of the ground meat mixture but instead of eating it, she sent it sailing my direction, hitting me square in the face.

"Thank you," I said, grimacing as Iris handed me a towel. I wiped the meat off my face. *"Trolls on a stick,* why don't we just give her the bowl of cream? We can't let her go hungry, and it's obvious she's not going to eat her dinner tonight."

"No," Camille broke in. "She'll be perfectly fine if she misses one meal, and she *has* to learn how to eat meat. She needs it to support those growing bones and wings. She can just go without her dinner tonight."

Iris sighed. "You're right. I'm going to take her into my bedroom and put her down for the night."

As Iris left the room with the wailing Maggie, Camille and I sat down at the kitchen table. "Where were we?" she asked.

"You were going to tell me about this Harold fellow mentioned in the diary. Do you think he had anything to do with the elf boyfriend?"

"Oh, that's right! No, not in any way, shape, or form. Harish, her boyfriend, is apparently over here on a long-term assignment for Queen Asteria. He's a technomage learning all he can about Earthside technology so he can take the information home and find a way to make it mesh with the elfin magic."

"You think he's still around?" I leaned my elbows on the table and reached out to play with one of the toothpicks sitting in a crystal container.

"I can find out." Delilah poked her head into the kitchen from the hallway. She slipped in and opened the refrigerator, pouring herself a glass of milk and slicing off a piece of apple pie. "Sorry about that back there," she said with a grin. "Your head's just a whirlwind of temptation to a cat, you know."

Camille pulled out a chair for her. "Yeah, we know."

"As I said, Tim and I can comb the Supe Community rolls and see if we find any mention of a male elf named Harish. It shouldn't take more than a few minutes using the search function."

"Good idea," Camille said. "If that fails, we'll ask Morgaine if she knows of any. The Triple Threat keep an active eye on the local OW elf and Fae population."

Delilah let out a snort so loud that milk sprayed out of her nose. "One of these days they're going to whip your butt for that. And you're not gonna be able to grovel low enough or fast enough."

Some time back, Camille had begun referring to the three Queens of Earthside Fae as the *Triple Threat*. So far, Titania, Aeval, and Morgaine hadn't caught wind of it.

"Eh, if they do, Camille can just send a lightning bolt their way using the horn of the Black Unicorn. That'll fry them," I said, slapping the table. "Come on, time's wasting. I don't have long during the summer, so let's get busy."

Just then, Iris reappeared. "She's down for the night. I hope." She glanced at the clock. "I've got a date tonight, so I won't be home to watch her."

"Bruce?" Camille asked.

"Oh yes, he'll be here in an hour or so."

I cleared my throat. "You really like Bruce, don't you?"

She blushed. "Yes, I do. He might be a leprechaun, but he's a good soul. Even if he does have too much blarney in him. We're celebrating tonight."

"What, did a new beer come out?" I liked Bruce, but I had to admit, I wasn't all that happy that Iris had a life on the side. If she ever decided to run off and get married, I didn't know what we'd do.

Iris flashed me a withering stare as she finished putting the dishes in the dishwasher. "*No.* And don't you go being so snide about my boyfriend. Bruce got hired on by the University of Washington. He'll be teaching Irish history and Celtic mythology. It's temporary—one semester only, starting in the fall. Their usual professor is taking a mini sabbatical to have a baby."

Delilah swallowed the last of her pie. "You think you can be a little nicer to the guy? He's a sweetheart, and funny as hell."

"I get it, I get it," I said. "And I'm sorry. I just keep thinking you're going to elope and move out. And trust me, *none* of us want that."

With a laugh as clear as a mountain stream, Iris shook her head. "Oh my stars, is that why you always ignore Bruce? He thought you didn't like his kind! Menolly, you most of all should know that you girls are my family now. If Bruce and I get married, we'll just have to build a little cottage out back and live here. I'm pledged to fight at your side in this war against Shadow Wing. I won't let you down."

Touched by her loyalty, I felt like a heel. "I'm sorry. Truly. Please, give Bruce my apologies. Go out and celebrate. We'll find a babysitter for Maggie."

At that moment, the polished spikes of quartz that formed a circle on a side table began to glow. It let out a loud hum that made me cringe, it was so grating. Camille's wards had been breached. An intruder was on the land—one who wasn't looking out for our best interests.

"Shit, we've got trouble," Delilah said.

"Oh for Pete's sake. This would happen *now*, just when I need to get ready," Iris muttered, glaring at the crystals. She yanked off her apron.

Camille jumped up. "Who's going out to check? Morio and Smoky are both out, and I have no idea where Roz and Vanzir disappeared to.

"You wait here, we'll let you know if we need you. I'll go first," I said, "since I can move silently. Kitten, you want to shadow me in cat form?"

As I made for the door, Delilah quickly shifted form and padded along behind me. Camille headed into the living room to grab her silver dagger, along with Delilah's, and stand ready. Iris took off for her bedroom to sit with Maggie.

I softly opened the back door, leaning out into the warm night. The stars were glowing overhead, and the Moon was still visible in the sky, waxing and golden. The trees swayed in the lazy breeze, their dark silhouettes fluttering against the indigo sky. I listened, letting the night flow around me, sorting out what was normal and what didn't belong.

Our home was an old Victorian, three stories high, not including my basement lair, on a patch of acreage in the Belles-Faire District of Seattle. Our property was wild and overgrown, and a path through the woods led down to Birchwater Pond, where we held midnight rituals and sunrise rites on the holy days. The house proper was in an open patch, with a few huge shade trees around it, and gardens dotted the large meadow-like yard: Camille's herb garden, Iris's kitchen garden, and several heady flower gardens that I could never view under the light to see the true color of the blooms.

As I stood there, waiting, a noise caught my attention. Barely audible at first, it grew as we waited. It was coming from the path leading to the pond, and I slipped down the steps and through the shadows, heading in its direction. Delilah followed me in her cat form, blending into the low-growing bushes so well that the only way I knew she was there was by the heat coming off her body.

I wove through the yard, wishing that my ability to turn into a bat was in full order, but I hadn't mastered it yet, no matter how hard I tried. Once I was in the air in the mouse-angel form, I tended to waver and get caught on the updrafts and gusts that swept by. The power was more of a hindrance than anything.

As I approached the trail mouth leading into the trees, the noise took on shape and form. A rustling of leaves, the sound of gnashing teeth. One with the trees, I passed like a shadow myself, barely grazing the ground as I hurried along.

The noise grew; it veered to my right, off of the path in the forest proper. I gauged the undergrowth. Vampire or not, I could still break twigs and limbs if I stepped on them wrong. I leapt up to one of the firs, clinging to the trunk. I'd been an acrobat when I was alive—a spy who could cling to ceilings, who could find any foothold in the wall as long as my human heritage didn't kick in and send me sliding to the ground below. Most of the time, it worked. The one time I needed it to work, it didn't, which was why I was a vampire now. But becoming *vampyr* had honed my skills.

I slipped from trunk to trunk, easily skimming along branches, leaping from tree to tree. The woods here were tightly interwoven, the trees grew close to one another, and it was easy for me to make my way toward the noise while avoiding the forest floor.

A clearing ahead promised to reveal what had broken through the wards. Or at least I hoped I was on the right track and not just chasing down Speedo, the neighborhood basset hound. As I clung to one of the giant cedars that overlooked the grassy opening, my worries about being on the wrong path vanished. But what I saw wasn't what I hoped for.

In the clearing, leaning over a log, was a squat, short man. His skin was leathery, the color of old mold, and it sagged in folds on his face. His face was covered with carbuncles and pasty white nodules that threatened to burst with every motion his jaw made. He was chewing on something, and as I squinted, narrowing my focus to get a better look, I realized there was a dead possum on the tree trunk. Mr. Ugly was ripping at the slippery flesh with jagged teeth, broken and yellow.

A ghoul. My stomach turned. We had a ghoul on the property. Which meant that somewhere near here there had to be a necromancer raising the dead. Not exactly the most desirable neighbor we could hope for.

Ghouls were tricky. If you didn't destroy them entirely,

they'd keep fighting until they were so much mush. Fire was good, but I didn't use fire. I could knock him down in seconds flat, but until we found a way to permanently put him on disable, whatever was left would just keep coming at us. And worse, the necromancer would be able to track his abomination to our land.

I glanced down. Delilah was hiding in the bushes below, staring at the ghoul intently. She glanced up at me. I slowly shimmied down the tree, making certain not to attract the ghoul's attention.

"Delilah," I whispered, so low I wasn't sure she'd picked up on it till she nodded her head. "Go back and tell Camille and Iris we have a ghoul out here. Camille should bring the horn—if she still has firepower in it. We need to fully burn every piece of this creepshow once we take him down. I'm going to stay and keep an eye on him. Maybe try to pin him."

Again, she bobbed her head, then took off toward the house. I turned my attention back to the ghoul. Play time, I thought, as the sickening sound of his jaws ripping at the possum's sinews bombarded my ears. My hearing was exceptionally keen, and I could tune out noises when I wanted, but right now I had to keep myself alert and focused.

I gauged the distance between us, then gathered myself and sprang. The ghoul didn't hear me until I landed about two feet behind him. He jerked up his head as I arced my leg to the side and whipped it across his back, sending him sprawling as well as leaving a nasty cut from the heel of my boot. Granny boots were handy in more ways than one, I thought, especially high-heeled granny boots.

The ghoul grunted—most couldn't talk, let alone scream— as he lurched forward over the trunk and landed square atop the possum's corpse. I couldn't really kill him. He was already dead. But maybe I could knock him out of commission till Camille got her butt out here with that unicorn horn.

He started to get up again. Ghouls, like zombies, would keep on going and going, until they were destroyed. Kind of like a demented Energizer Bunny. However, the real problem with ghouls was that, unlike zombies, they still had some sort of reasoning going on in their heads. They weren't brilliant, but they were aware enough to take orders. I wasn't sure what caused the distinction—it had to be some twist to the magic used to raise them—but there it was. This dude wasn't just going to be a pile of shambling flesh.

As he pushed himself to his feet, I kicked him in the backside again and landed atop him, grimacing at the smell that wafted up. Overripe, by about a year, I'd guess. I grabbed hold of his head and twisted, breaking his neck. It wouldn't kill him, but the more limbs I could disable, the harder it would be for him to attack us. And then it hit me—he'd still function without a head, but he wouldn't be able to see us. Or at least it *should* work that way.

I twisted, hard, not wanting to have to use my teeth to sever the flesh, but if need be, I'd do it. I was stronger than he was, by a long shot, so even though it might take a little while, I could rip him apart, limb from limb.

Unfortunately, as I was focused on carving up our new friend, I wasn't paying attention to what was going on behind me. A hefty kick to my back knocked me off balance.

I went down but immediately tucked and rolled, flipping onto my feet again à la Bruce Lee. As I whirled around, I found myself staring into the face of a tall man wearing a leather jacket. He was sporting a bushy head of hair down to his shoulders, and an even bushier beard. Think ZZ Top, only muscle-bound and not so friendly looking.

Fangs extended, eyes crimson and burning, I dropped into fighting stance, ready to take him out.

He smiled softly and pulled out a long wooden stake, pointing it directly at me. "You *really* want to take me on? Fight me, and I'll dust you so fast you won't have time to blink those beautiful bloody eyes of yours. Now, step away from the ghoul, or you'll find yourself a pretty shish kebab. Your choice. What's it going to be?"

CHAPTER 7

I stared at him, gauging how serious he was. He *looked* pretty damned serious. After a moment, I said, "Who the fuck are you, and what are you and your damned ghoul doing on our land?"

Mr. Nefarious blinked and then shrugged. "Call me Wilbur. As to who I am, I'm a necromancer, that's my ghoul, and I'll thank you to leave him in one piece. He wandered off before I realized he was gone and—oh Christ, lady. You *broke* him."

I glanced over at the ghoul, who was standing again, his head listing precariously to the left, a lopsided, brainless grin on his face. I'd done a tidy job of crushing the vertebrae at the base of his neck. He looked rather pathetic, actually.

I turned back to Wilbur. "Put the stake away. Your ghoul was on our land, he set off our wards. What do you expect? You let your toys run around without a leash, they're going to get hurt. *Wilbur*, you say?" I shook my head. Just what we needed. A necromancer named after a pig who was best friends with a spider. "Where you from, Wilbur?"

He blinked. "I moved in down the street a few months ago. The old London house. I keep to myself, and usually keep him on a tight leash." Here, he jerked his head toward the ghoul. "But now and then, accidents happen." He lowered the stake, keeping an eye on me as he did so. "You and your sisters are pretty damned famous. I figured that Martin would head here; your whole place shines like a Kmart blue-light special."

A noise on the path made us both turn. He raised his spike again, then lowered it as Delilah and Camille came racing down the path. I waited till they reached us, both looking confused as they took in the situation.

"Girls, meet our new neighbor, Wilbur. Wilbur's a necromancer. Wilbur owns the ghoul, whose name is Martin. Apparently, Martin got away from him."

"Martin?" Camille was holding the unicorn horn. She promptly stuffed it in her pocket, but not before I noticed that Wilbur's gaze had fastened on it.

Mental note: Watch this dude, I thought. Necromancers weren't all that trustworthy to begin with, and if he had any sense of how powerful her weapon was, he might just set about trying to swipe it.

Delilah cleared her throat. "Wilbur? You an FBH?"

He blinked. "Well, that's rude. But yes, I am. Name's Wilbur Folkes, and I live down the street."

"How long have you been a necromancer?" Camille asked, her eyes never leaving his face.

Wilbur shrugged. "A few years, more or less. I need to get back to the lab. I've got some potions on the stove and don't want them to curdle. Now, if you'd let me take my ghoul, I'll try to make sure he doesn't bother you again. I just hope I can fix his neck," he said with a bit of a snarl.

I stood aside as he muttered something under his breath. Martin obediently shuffled over to Wilbur's side.

Still suspicious, I turned to the others. "I'll just make sure Wilbur and Martin find their way back to the road." They nodded, and I led the pair through the woods to the edge of the road.

Wilbur had apparently had enough of our conversation, and Martin could only grunt, so I kept my mouth shut, deciding the less that he knew about us, the better. We were only a five-minute walk from the edge of the road, as the crow flies, and Wilbur was pretty light on his feet for such a big man. He darted over tree roots, around trees and bushes without hesitation. When we reached the road, Wilbur silently yanked Martin across the street by one arm, none too gently. I watched as they headed down the pavement, and before long, I saw them turn in to what was, indeed, the old London house.

Delilah and Camille were gone by the time I reached the spot where I'd tackled the ghoul, and I sped back to the house. They were waiting for me as I burst into the kitchen, both looking alternately amused and confused.

"You tell Iris yet?" I asked.

"Yes they did, and it sounds peculiar to me, let me tell you that. But I need to be getting ready for my date. Bruce will be here shortly." Iris headed toward her bedroom.

"So," I said, floating gently into the air where I felt the most comfortable. "What do you make of our new neighbor?"

"I think we're going to end up in court someday," Delilah said. "Judge Judy, no less."

"Heaven forbid," Camille said. "I don't trust him. I don't like the look of him, and I'll tell you this right now: He's been practicing necromancy a lot longer than 'a few years.' That man has a tremendous amount of power, and he reeks of death." She stared at the table. "I should know. Morio and I are starting to delve deeper into bone magic. The path is a shadowy one, and the deeper you go, the darker it gets."

Delilah glanced at me. I gently shook my head. Camille was doing what she needed to do. The Hags of Fate had decreed whatever role Morio was to play in her life, other than that of husband and protector. It wasn't up to us to question her or him, or their choices.

"You think Wilbur's lying about anything?" I trusted Camille's instinct. It was a lot more reliable than her Moon magic.

"Oh, he's telling the truth about his name and the fact that he's an FBH. But there's a lot hidden behind that thicket of fur he calls a beard. I don't pick up any strong demonic aura, but anybody who's raising the dead and creating ghouls has to be doing something shady."

"Great, just one more thing to concern ourselves with. I'm losing track all over the place of what the hell we're—oh that's right. Kitten, call Tim and check on Harish?" I frowned, trying to remember what we'd been talking about before the wards had interrupted us.

Camille poured herself a glass of wine, then searched out a package of Oreos. She settled in at the table while Delilah picked up the phone.

"Hey Jason, is Tim there?" Kitten leaned against the wall as she talked. Athletic, Delilah was tall—an inch over six feet. Her shoulder-length blonde shag was starting to grow out. After a moment of silence, Tim must have come on the line, because she said, "Listen, I know you're up to your ears with wedding plans, but can you run a quick check for me off the Supe Community files? I don't have the full roll call on my computer, and we need to find out if there's an elf from OW registered. His first name is Harish; I don't know his surname. Yes, that's right . . . H-a-r-i-s-h . . . Thanks, call me when you find out."

As she hung up, I asked, "So when are Tim and Jason getting married? I know we got an invitation the other day, but I forgot to look at it."

Camille crossed to the bulletin board where we kept notes and messages and removed a creamy-colored envelope from the pushpin that had been holding it there. She handed it to me. I opened the flap and slid out the thick, textured paper. Beautiful work, I thought. The paper had to be handmade. As I opened the invitation, a rich calligraphy announced:

Mr. & Mrs. Simon and Virginia Winthrop cordially request the pleasure of your company at the wedding of their son, Timothy Vincent Winthrop, to Jason Alfonso Binds, son of Mrs. Petti-Anne Binds.

We would love for you to join us at Woodbriar Park on the 19th day of June at 9:30 P.M., as Timothy and Jason pledge their lasting love and commitment under

*the stars. The Reverend Monica Trent, a pastor from
the United Worlds Church, will be presiding. Reception
and late-night buffet in the park to follow.*

Attire: Semiformal

*Gifts: In lieu of gifts, the couple is asking that you make
donations to the Harvest of Gold Food Bank.*

A handwritten note had been included, indicating that the
invitation extended to Camille's husbands, Chase, and guests,
should Iris and I choose to attend with dates.

"Are we all going? What about Iris?" I smiled softly. Tim
and Jason had been together for several years. They had a
solid relationship, and it was nice to see them formalizing it.
A part of me loved the ritual and pageantry of weddings.

"Of course we're going. I asked Roz to watch Maggie that
night, and he agreed." Camille grinned at her.

I blinked. "Roz? Rozurial is back?"

An incubus, Rozurial had been helping us for some time
against the demon menace. He was a mercenary, a bounty
hunter, totally unethical when it came to women, and just
about as gorgeous as you could ever hope to want in a man.
He was also a good friend. We'd made out a little, but I hadn't
let it go any further than that. So far. About three weeks back,
Queen Asteria had called Roz back to Elqaneve—the elfin
city—for some brief mission she wanted him to complete.

"Yeah. He showed up last night." Delilah frowned.

My mood lightened, and I realized just how much I'd
missed Roz's irreverent nature. The phone rang, and I reached
for the receiver. "Probably Tim," I said. But it wasn't. It was
Chase. "Listen, I have some news about the Clockwork Club
and Claudette. But I imagine you called to talk to Delilah?"

"No. Put me on speaker, please." He let out a long sigh,
and I knew that whatever the news was, it wasn't good.

I punched the speaker button and replaced the receiver.
"Go ahead."

"I need the three of you to get over here right now. We've
got a problem." He sounded unusually tense.

"What's wrong?" Delilah asked, a look of concern washing over her.

"I've got two dead bodies with no possible reason why they should be dead. But they are. Both of them are Fae—one's from OW, one is Earthside-born." He coughed. "Can you be here in half an hour?"

I glanced at Delilah and Camille, who both nodded. "We'll be there," I said. As I punched the speaker button to hang up, Iris entered the room. My jaw dropped.

Iris had always been pretty, but tonight she'd taken it to a whole new level. Her hair was glowing, woven into a plaited chignon, and a beaded, low-cut halter dress the color of the evening sky showed off her figure. The crowning effect was a sparkling gold and black shawl draped around her shoulders.

"Oh my gods, you look stunning!" Camille stared at her. "Bruce is going to be panting in his boots when he gets a glimpse of you."

"Iris, you're gorgeous," I said. "But we need a sitter for Maggie stat, because Chase just called. He needs us over there."

Iris grinned. "Not to worry," she said, staring over our shoulders. "We have company."

I glanced around. Roz had just walked in the door.

"Roz, you're on Maggie duty tonight. Bruce just called. The limo's on its way up the driveway." Iris checked her purse. "I have money, my keys, and my cell phone. If the world ends, you can call me. Otherwise, I may not be home till dawn." She blew us a kiss and headed out the door, squeezing past Roz, who gave her a long glance over his shoulder as he let loose with a low wolf whistle.

Iris stopped in her tracks, turned, and said, "Excuse me?"

Roz just grinned. "Can't blame me, can you? You want to blow off your date and go out with me?"

Though he was laughing, I knew that he meant it. You could dress him up in a black leather duster and stick a miniature Uzi in his hand, but beneath all the curly long hair and weapons lay the heart of a sex fiend. A very pleasant and helpful sex fiend, but a sex fiend nonetheless.

Iris just fluttered her lashes, blew him a kiss, and sailed out the door.

"Damn, the woman's looking sharp tonight," he muttered before turning around. Camille let out a snort, and Delilah began whistling an aimless tune. Roz narrowed his eyes. "*What?* None of *you* will sleep with me, no matter how much I beg. And you—" he pointed to Camille. "Your husband's a maniac, so don't you dare tell him I said that."

She saluted and gave him a snarky grin. "Aye, aye, Cap'n Lovegun."

A few months back, Smoky had dragged Rozurial out into the front yard and pulverized him after he noticed Roz copping a feel off Camille's ass. The resulting bruises had not been pretty. After that, Roz made sure he kept his mitts away from Camille, except when she needed help.

"Come on. We have to book. Roz, you're on babysitting detail. Maggie's in bed. Check in on her a couple of times. We'll be down at the FH-CSI. Dead body problem." I planted a quick kiss on his nose. "There, consider yourself kissed, so quit whining. And don't eat us out of house and home."

As we grabbed our purses and keys and headed out the door, Roz sputtered behind us. Delilah and Camille fell into peals of giggles as we headed for Camille's car. As Camille coaxed the engine to life, I glanced out the window at the stars. Dead bodies and ghouls notwithstanding, summer over Earthside could be lovely—if a little cool in the Seattle area. I just wished I could see it all in the daytime for once, I thought, as we sped through the musky night.

CHAPTER 8

The FH-CSI building was located right on the edge of the Belles-Faire District in north Seattle, on Thatcher Avenue. The building was large, made of concrete, and illuminated by ground lights that encircled the perimeter. It appeared to be a single story, but there were actually three floors hidden below-ground, including an arsenal, an incarceration unit for the rogue denizens of OW, and a morgue and laboratory. The law enforcement headquarters, offices, and the medical unit were on the main floor.

The grounds surrounding the Faerie-Human Crime Scene Investigations building were landscaped with low shrubs and flowerbeds. There were no large trees nor hedges for escapees to hide behind or for disgruntled gang members to use. The Freedom's Angels, a group of Earthborn FBH supremacists, had grown in number, especially after the Earthside Supes and Fae began swarming out of the closet. There had been a few very ugly, very bloody incidents, thanks to the gang, and I had the feeling we hadn't seen the last of them.

We parked under one of the streetlights and headed into the building. Two burly armed and armored security guards were keeping watch at the doors, both Fae recently sent over from Queen Tanaquar. Y'Elestrial was slowly regrouping after the recent civil war, and our father was the new Queen's chief advisor.

Camille leaned close and whispered, "They both wield powerful magic as well as beefcake. I can feel their energy signatures from here."

Delilah nodded. "Me, too, and I'm no witch."

I tried to concentrate on the men, but all I could sense was the pulse of their hearts, the sound of blood swishing through their veins. If they'd been demonic or undead, I would have sensed something. But regular magic—powerful or not—was usually beyond my ability to home in on.

As we passed through the outer entrance, the guards eyed us, but apparently we didn't pose a danger by whatever criteria they were using, and they let us by without so much as a *Who are you?*

The entrance opened into a wide foyer. To the left was the station proper, through a set of bulletproof double glass doors. Straight ahead and slightly to the right was a staircase leading down. The elevators were directly in front of us. We turned to the left and pushed through the doors.

The room was bustling. Dispatch was busy. The number of officers from Otherworld had doubled in the past month alone.

Yugi, a Swedish empath, had been promoted to Chase's second-in-command. He was leaning over the shoulder of an elf who looked barely old enough for his voice to change, but he was probably older than all of us. By the looks of things, the elf was trying to get the hang of using the computer.

Yugi glanced up, smiling when he caught sight of us. "Hey, girls. The chief is in his office. He told me to pass you through stat." Just then the phone rang, and Yugi grabbed it, motioning for Officer Re'ael—as the elf's name tag read—to continue fiddling with the terminal.

"Yeah? Where? Okay, let me patch you through to the chief." Yugi punched a button on the phone as we filed through the cubicles toward the back of the building.

Delilah frowned. "I used to love coming here, but ever since Erika, I feel uncomfortable. Every time Chase's office comes in sight, I cringe." She'd caught Chase dipping his wick in another woman's inkwell not all that long ago, right on his desk. The fallout hadn't been pretty.

"Eh, he's learned his lesson. Next time, he'll ask first," I said, trying to be helpful. Chase could be stupid at times, but he learned from his mistakes.

We followed the maze of cubicles to the back wall that sported three doors and an opening to a hallway. One of the doors had Chase's name stenciled on it. Blinds covered the half window, but they were open. We trailed in on Delilah's heels.

Chase was taking notes as he listened to whoever was on the other end of the phone. He waved his pencil in the air, motioning for us to sit. After a moment, he grunted something to the caller and then hung up.

"Shit. I wanted to talk to you about those bodies, but we've got another problem. Come on—we've got an emergency on our hands." He grabbed his suit jacket, swinging it over the neatly pressed powder blue shirt he was wearing. I noticed a picture on his desk of a golden tabby, prominently displayed. Delilah. For some reason it made me smile that he kept a picture of her in Were form.

"What's up?" Delilah said.

He checked his gun in his shoulder holster and then hastily scribbled something on a piece of paper. "Who's driving?"

"I am," Camille said.

He tossed her the note. "There's the address. Come on, we don't have all day," he added, hustling out of the room. We followed. "We're headed to the Avalon Dance Club. Heard of it?" Without waiting for an answer, he raced on. "Some monster is attacking the dancers. The caller said it looked like a bizarre squid, of all things."

"Squid? You have to be kidding. In a nightclub?" I snorted, but the serious look on Chase's face stopped me. I could smell the stress and sweat rolling off of him. He'd had beef tacos for lunch again, that much I could tell, and he was worried. Hints of fear lingered in the droplets of perspiration.

"That's what she said. Meet me there. Don't screw around—it sounded like a brawl going on in the background. People are getting hurt."

He stopped at Yugi's desk. "Send a squad car and an ambulance to the Avalon Dance Club. Tell them to wait for us before they head in. We don't know what we're up against, and I don't want the men falling into a trap."

We jogged toward the door and slammed out into the balmy night. Chase veered for his squad car, Delilah running with him.

Camille and I raced to her Lexus. She revved the engine and floored it, screeching out of the parking lot behind Chase. I opened the passenger window. Chase had given each of us a flashing light, and I slapped it atop the speeding Lexus. As it caught hold, we sped through the night, the stoplights shifting to let us through at our approach.

The Avalon Dance Club was run by a group of Earthside Fae. A typical nightclub, it catered mainly to Fae, though the Faerie Maids were ever present, hoping to get laid and loved by one of their obsessions. The club was in the heart of the Belles-Faire District, and the station wasn't all that far away from it.

Chase made a sharp turn into the parking lot. The club had been a restaurant at one time, probably some franchise from one of the bigger chains that had gone belly-up, and parking was plentiful.

Camille gave the wheel a smooth turn and followed him in. As we jumped out of the car, she glanced at me. "Is it wrong that I'm actually happy to be heading into a fight again?"

I returned her smile. "You run with the Hunt. How can you help but love the chase? We're all predators, Camille. You, Delilah, me. Even Chase. Smoky hunts for his dinner. Morio's a demon child. Vanzir's a demon who hunts in people's dreams. Rozurial chases passion. Everything alive—and sometimes even the dead—hunts in one respect or another. The quest gives us a reason to live. You know that."

She nodded, patting her pocket. "I brought the horn, just in case."

"Let's go. There they are." I pointed to Chase and Delilah, who were motioning for us to hurry. We swung in beside them. Chase took a deep breath as the backup prowl car pulled into the lot.

"Nice to see they're on the ball," Chase muttered under his breath, opening the door to the club. He flipped open his walkie-talkie. "Car eighty-two, stay where you are in the parking lot until I call for you. Copy?"

The intercom crackled out with, "Copy, Chief."

As we entered the club, a volley of screams and shouts erupted from the room beyond the foyer. The coat-check girl had vanished, and we rushed into the main dance hall.

The Avalon was an old building. Its low, dark ceilings had been retrofitted with a long series of mirrors reflecting the dancers below. The colors du jour were royal purple and silver, and an updated disco ball twirled from the central ceiling. The music had stopped. The stage was now the scene of a massacre. As far as I could count, six members of the band were down. I couldn't see blood, but they didn't look very healthy.

Everywhere I looked, patrons were shoving and pushing to get out the side exits. But something appeared to be barring the doors, though in the semidarkness it was difficult to make out what the creatures were. They didn't seem to emanate body heat. Undead, maybe? Oh shit, that's *just* what we needed.

A woman near the front was clawing at something near one of the tables. I headed in her direction while Delilah and Camille took on whatever was barring the exits. What the hell were we up against?

As I raced toward the woman, I saw she was grappling with some creature—and damn it to hell, the thing *did* look like a squid. It writhed around her, tentacles encircling her waist and throat.

She beat at it, trying to get it off, but as I approached, the thing let out a hiss and lifted her up, tossing her across the room like I might toss a rock. She sailed through the air to land with a deadly thump on the floor near the stage.

Mr. Tentacles—who was still no more than a sooty silhouette—whirled around, one giant eye glimmering with white-hot fire. The closer I got, the more I realized that this was no ocean dweller. The tentacles seemed to work just fine on the floor, and they shrouded a razor-sharp beak. The spiked protrusion seemed more apt for drilling rather than eating.

"Okay, you bastard. Come on, let's see what you've got," I said, moving into position. Holding out two fingers, I motioned to it. "Come on, you butt-ugly bastard. Come to Mama."

The monster moved forward, propelling itself with its tentacles, reminding me of the cartoons where the octopus ran on tiptoe. But this was no cartoon, and these things were deadly.

I couldn't get a reading on it at first, and then as it approached, I was slammed by the sensation that only one species could produce. Demonkin.

"Shit! Demon!" I shouted as it lashed out with a tentacle. I dodged as the dusky black arm came swiping by. Instead of suction cups, it was covered with tiny, razor-sharp barbs. Youch! That sucker could do some real damage.

I backed away to regroup. Eight—no, ten—tentacles full of what were essentially serrated fishhooks? *No, thank you.*

As it slid toward me, it glided a few inches above the floor.

Okay. Not good.

Again, I jumped out of reach. The back of my knees brushed against a table, and with one hand I shoved it out of the way. The marbled bench went flying across the room and shattered. Too bad. I had no time for subtleties.

Gauging my position, with a sudden burst of speed I launched myself in the air, boot slamming against the rounded head of the demon. But my foot stopped short an inch or so from the actual creature, sending a shock wave through my body. Damn—I felt like I'd just smashed into a brick wall. What sounded like a thunderbolt ripped the air, and I went sailing backward to land across the broken table.

What the fuck?

Slightly stunned, I leapt to my feet. I could tell I'd bruised a hip, but bruises would heal within the hour. Just one of the perks of being a vampire. Nothing had been broken, nothing punctured.

Should I try again? I decided to come at the creature from another angle, and once more, found myself flying across the room. As I landed, Delilah screamed, and I pushed myself off the floor and headed in her direction, stopping cold when I saw her.

She was covered with blood. Camille had dragged her away from another one of the shadow monsters. Kneeling by Kitten's side, she started shaking her, just as Vanzir and Smoky raced through the doors.

Smoky let out a shout, and a cold snap filled the air, sending waves of frost through the room. Instantly, the temperature plummeted a good thirty degrees but didn't seem to affect the creeping cruds at all.

Vanzir muttered, "Oh shit," before shouting, "They're bathed in shadow—try light. Blast them with as much light as you can muster!"

Light? I didn't have a light, and I didn't think he was talking about flipping on the overheads. Camille let go of Delilah and pulled out the crystal unicorn horn. She gave me a wild-eyed look.

"You have to get out of here," she mouthed.

I didn't ask questions. I just booked for the entrance. The doors had barely closed behind me when a huge flash from inside the club sent me reeling and startled all the patrons who were hovering around the police car and ambulance.

There'd been no heat—she hadn't used fire—but whatever it was would have fried me in ten seconds flat if I'd been in the room with her. Sunlight in a can. Or a horn, rather.

I raced over to the officers, who were taking statements from the dazed crowd. Marquette, an OW Fae, and Brooks, a new FBH recruit, glanced at me. "Boss need us?"

"You better wait out here. But call several more ambulances. There are quite a few casualties. Make certain we have Otherworld medics on hand; it looks like only the Fae have been hurt."

While they radioed for help, I headed back to the building. The light had vanished, leaving no residue behind. The dance floor was almost empty, and there was no sign of the Demonkin. Camille and Chase knelt beside Delilah, while Smoky and Vanzir tended to those who had been hurt in the fight.

"What happened? Did you kill them?" I tried to ignore the smell of blood rising from Delilah's wounds. On closer inspection, they looked superficial, though jagged. Most likely, she'd gotten in the way of one of those barbed tentacles. "You need to get those tended to, or they'll scar."

"Menolly's right," Chase said, but Delilah shook her head.

"No. Look—they're already healing. Great Mother Bast, what the hell's going on? I know we heal fast, but this is ridiculous."

She was right. As we watched, the sides of the wounds quickly began to knit together. A moment later, and we couldn't see any sign of where they'd been. Our father's blood gave us healing powers that were far and above an FBH's, but this was abnormal, even for us.

"What the—" I stopped as Sharah and Mallen burst through the door, equipment in hand. Behind them came several teams of medics, in training for the FH-CSI.

Sharah made her way over to us as Mallen began directing rescue efforts. "What happened? What were you fighting?" She glanced down at Delilah, who by now was getting to her feet. "*Great Aeondel*, are you okay? Where did all that blood come from?"

"I got sideswiped by a deranged squid," Delilah said, resulting in a snort from Camille. "The cuts healed up immediately. I'm a little woozy, though."

Sharah's expression took on a vaguely skeptical look. "Deranged squid?" she asked, her voice remaining neutral.

"She means *Demonkin*." Vanzir joined us. A dream chaser demon, Vanzir had defected to our side and had voluntarily placed himself under our control through the Ritual of Subjugation, a painful and binding trial. His life was in our hands for as long as he lived and wherever he went. He looked like a shorter, younger David Bowie during his Ziggy Stardust days, with platinum short spiky hair and eyes that shone with an alien light. He had the whole punk, heroin-chic thing going on.

"I *knew* I smelled demon scent." I glanced up at him. "I tried to attack it but damn . . . You happen to know what those things are?"

"No more than you. I've never seen anything quite that . . . odd." He shook his head. "Did you manage to hit the one attacking you?"

I grunted. "No, and I can't figure out why. I was set to make contact, but the creature had some sort of force field around it. I landed my foot against the barrier, and it slammed me back on my ass." I shrugged. "Anybody else make a direct hit?"

Delilah looked at the others. They all shook their heads.

"Apparently not," she said, "but I can tell you this. When that thing was attacking me, I felt something squirming around in my mind. Like a swarm of beetles." She shivered. "In fact, for a moment, I thought . . ."

"Yes?" I encouraged her gently.

Delilah squinted and rubbed her head. "I can't remember what I was going to say. But it felt like it was drilling into my skull, into my very soul."

I groaned. "Great. A soul sucker. Just what we need. You think they're in cahoots with Shadow Wing? He's a Soul Eater."

"A Soul Eater's so powerful he wouldn't leave anybody alive. But that doesn't mean there isn't a connection." Vanzir frowned.

"These creatures don't seem to be his usual MO. Shadow Wing usually sends Degath Squads or powerful spies like Karvanak the Rāksasa. I can't imagine him sending monsters like these, but maybe I'm wrong." Camille frowned. "We'd better figure out what these things are right away."

Just then, Mallen joined us.

"Five dead, and not a mark on them," he said, his face ashen. "Two of the wounded managed to live. Both of the survivors are barely conscious. We're taking them in. What the hell went on here? I can't figure out what's wrong with them or why the others died."

Chase spoke up. He'd remained surprisingly quiet until now. "Whatever these monsters are, I want them found and destroyed. I also want to know why they're attacking the Fae and not humans."

"We should put in a call to a Corpse Talker," I said. "Since the dead are Fae, she might be able to provide some sort of lead."

"Good idea," Sharah said. "I can make arrangements. We've got one on standby."

Chase shuddered. "Oh wonderful. Just what I want to witness. Another bloody fast-food fest. But if you think it will help, get her into the morgue as soon as possible. We've already got two Fae on ice who seem to follow the same pattern we've got here. No wounds, no reason why they should be dead. Let's get moving."

Sharah nodded. She turned to me. "Will you be the liaison? Corpse Talkers don't like elves, and Camille shouldn't really get near them. The chance for a magical implosion is far too great."

Witches and Corpse Talkers kept a wide berth from one another. Some component of their magical makeup didn't mesh, and if their energy fields touched, the very real chance existed that we'd be on the receiving end of a very nasty explosion of some sort.

I glanced at Delilah. She'd toughened up quite a bit over the past few months, but she was still too squeamish to play liaison. She'd stand witness, but she probably couldn't keep it together if she had to be up close and personal with the Corpse Talker. They were creepy enough when viewed from a distance. Something about their aura gave off a major 'Do *not* turn your back' energy.

"Sure thing," I said, as we headed out into the night. Overhead, a lazy string of clouds rolled past the Moon. It was barely eleven o'clock yet, and the Moon Mother hadn't set. She'd sink into slumber around two thirty in the morning. The golden orb was growing toward full, and I knew both Delilah and Camille were feeling the siren song of her call. Three nights before the solstice she'd be full and ripe, and her energy would stay strong through Litha. Oh yes, the Summer

King was ushering in a wild ride for the Weres and any Fae ruled by the Moon Mother.

"Let's get this show on the road." I headed toward Camille's car. "We'll meet you at the morgue, Chase. We need to find out where these demons are coming from and put a stop to them before they kill again."

CHAPTER 9

When we arrived back at the FH-CSI building, Sharah, Mallen, and their trainees had already set up the bodies down in the morgue. The situation felt all wrong. None of the victims showed any signs of injury, there was no blood, no reason they should be dead. But they were.

The survivors were under strict watch in the intensive care unit upstairs, but the medics were having a difficult time figuring out how to help them. Tiggs, an officer, was still clinging to a thin shred of awareness. The other—Yancy—was fading. And nobody knew why. Sharah had called for an experienced healer from Elqaneve, but she wouldn't be here for a few hours.

As we gathered around the stainless steel tables holding the bodies of the fallen, it occurred to me that I was as dead as the victims. The only difference between them and me was that I'd undergone a little tweak before I died. A simple infusion straight from Dredge's vein and *bingo* . . . I existed among the walking dead. By all rights, I should be dust now, a blip in history.

Camille planted herself in the corner, well away from the tables. When the Corpse Talker arrived, we didn't want any accidents. Smoky stood by her side. Delilah sat in a chair near them, her legs folded in the lotus position, a notebook in her lap to take notes with. Vanzir planted himself next to her.

Chase and I waited near the bodies. His face was stark and weathered.

A few minutes later, Sharah entered the room, leading the Corpse Talker behind her. No one even knew what race of Fae they branched off of, or what they looked like. The Corpse Talkers hid themselves in an underground city in Otherworld, rumored to be deep within the forests of Darkynwyrd.

Only their women ventured out into the world, and only their women became Corpse Talkers. A few had gone mad, their powers shifting in violent and twisted ways. They wandered through OW, feared and avoided. But the majority hired themselves out to those who sought the truth from the dead.

She was cloaked in the garments of her profession. A cowled robe as indigo as the deep ocean covered her completely, and the gloves she wore showed long, slender fingers beneath the cloth. The hood cloaked her face from view, although a slight twinkle of pale gray flickered from within the shadowed hollow.

Her eyes, I thought. We already knew she wouldn't give us her name, so we didn't even ask.

She glanced from body to body—seven all told—and her voice echoed out of the folds of her hood. "Where do you wish me to begin?"

Chase shrugged, so I pointed to the nearest body. The man had been a half-breed, perhaps half-Svartan, half-Fae. Whatever the case, he'd been gloriously handsome when he was alive, but now he lay silent on the metal slab. Still beautiful, but not for long.

The Corpse Talker leaned over him. Her cowl shrouded her actions, but we knew what she was doing. As she kissed him deeply, sucking in all that remained of his soul, a faint bluish tinge rose from his body. I could hear her murmuring, coaxing the spirit to enter her body and speak through her. An ancient ritual as old as the Fae themselves, the rites of the speakers for the dead never failed to amaze me.

After a moment, she raised her head. "Ask."

I sucked on my lip, trying to think of the best questions. If we were lucky, we'd get two or three answers from each body. If not—as few as one. Or none. I decided to start with the most obvious. "What killed you?"

A raspy breath emerged from the Corpse Talker, and then, in a voice as dry as old parchment, she said, "Squid . . . it was horrible."

Delilah shuddered. "She's right. They're terrifying."

I motioned for her to be quiet. "Let me finish before the soul disappears for good." I turned back to the Corpse Talker. "Where are your wounds? We can't find them. *How* did you die?"

Again, a shudder, then the whistling voice. "Sucked dry—"

Before the soul could finish, the Corpse Talker shuddered, and we lost the connection. I motioned for her to move to the next body. We didn't have long from first contact. Once the souls were free from the bodies, they began the journey to their ancestors. Then the game was up, and we wouldn't have a chance to summon them again until the festival of Samhain. Unless, that is, the soul rested uneasy and journeyed to the Netherworld instead of the Land of the Silver Falls.

The Corpse Talker kissed the second body. I glanced over at Chase. From what Camille had told me, the first time he encountered one of the speakers for the dead, he'd almost fainted. This time, he seemed to be keeping it together.

As the transfer of soul essence took place, I became aware that Camille was faintly singing. She was barely mouthing the words, but I could catch the tune. It was a rhyme we'd chanted as children for protection.

> *Lips to lips, mouth to mouth,*
> *Comes the speaker of the shrouds.*
> *Suck in the spirit, speak the words,*
> *Let secrets of the dead be heard.*

The second victim was as unhelpful as the first. The only question he was able to answer was "How did you die?"

"Don't know . . . was there, then . . . eating at me . . ."

I frowned and glanced over at the others, who looked as puzzled as I did. The soul vanished before I could ask what it meant. The Corpse Talker moved to the third victim, who was gone, and the fourth, who also had joined her ancestors. The fifth, however, gave us a little more to go on.

"What killed you?" I asked after the ritual kiss.

In the same rustling voice all spirits used, the Corpse Talker said, "Demon. A demon. I could smell it. I was so afraid . . ."

I stared at the body. This man had realized it had been a demon. "How did you die?"

"Something entered my mind and ate away at me until it broke through the silver cord that tethered me to my body."

Delilah had mentioned feeling like there was something crawling around in her brain. Could it have been looking for her cord?

Curious as to how the man had recognized it as a demon, I asked, "What were you when you were alive? What did you do?"

"I worked in Y'Vaiylestar as a seer for the Court and Crown. They sent me over Earthside to do research . . ." His voice began to fade. "Mother—" was the last word he said, and then he vanished, and I knew that he'd gone to his ancestors. Grateful his mother had come for him, I rested my hand lightly on his.

After a moment we led the Corpse Talker to the two victims Chase had called us about, but they, too, had vanished to the Land of the Silver Falls. The Corpse Talker stood silent, then turned to Sharah, who nodded.

"Come with me," she said. "I'll take you to a place where you can wait until I . . . procure your payment."

As they headed out the door, Chase shuddered. "All of their hearts?"

Camille shook her head. "Only of those whose souls she actually touched. It's the rite. Communion with the dead through the consumption of the heart."

"Why not of those who she couldn't reach?" he asked.

"Keeps them honest," I said with a short laugh. "Prevents deception. Or maybe they have no interest in the hearts of those who were already gone. I don't know, and I doubt anybody knows the answer."

Chase frowned, then pushed it aside. "So what did we find out? The last one seemed to know we were up against demons. And he said that it ate him up?"

I nodded. "My bet is that the thing sucks souls dry."

At that moment, Sharah entered the room, carrying a pan and several opaque plastic bags. "I'm going to excise their hearts. I suggest you leave unless you want to watch me prepare dinner for our guest." She had a faint look of disgust on her face. Elves didn't like Corpse Talkers and vice versa, but she'd do what was necessary.

Chase was at the door in a flash. "Come on, let's check on the survivors."

We followed.

As she brushed past Sharah, Camille laid a gentle hand on her shoulder, and the elf gave her a brave smile. Sharah's job had turned out to be incredibly bloody compared to what she could be doing at home in Elqaneve. Though she was Queen Asteria's niece, she chose to stick it out here for the greater good.

One of the survivors was fading fast, his vital signs dropping even as we stood by his bed. The other drifted in and out of consciousness, barely coherent.

"It's in my mind," he whispered. "I can feel it . . ."

"Whatever we're dealing with is still feeding on their life energy," I said.

Vanzir spoke up. "It's probably trying to spawn as much fear as possible. Fear spurs on adrenaline, meaning more energy."

"He's right," Camille said.

"Okay," Chase said. "So we have a passel of demons that can get inside your mind and feed on it, then can drain you of your life without a scratch. But why did Delilah show wounds?"

"I'll bet you all of their victims were wounded for a bit. Sympathetic magic. They knew they were being attacked, so their bodies showed it. Why the wounds healed, I don't know. When Delilah shook the one attacking her, her wounds healed up almost instantly." I frowned.

"They only need to manifest wounds until they gain control," Vanzir said. "I'll bet you anything these two are still under attack. The demons are still here."

I whirled around to Chase. "If the demons are here, why aren't the alarms sounding?"

Smoky spoke up. "Want to make a bet it's because the demons are on one of the astral realms? They have to be. If they were on the physical plane, we'd know it—one way or another." He turned to Chase. "Are your magical sensors regulated to alert you to astral presences?"

Chase blanched. "I don't know; nobody ever suggested it, and I sure as hell wouldn't have thought of it. The OIA installed them when we set up the unit. When they were disrupted during the vampire fiasco, the OIA couldn't reset them, so I had to ask a couple of my men from Otherworld to work on them. I'm not sure what they did to fix the system."

"Crap. You can bet they're not geared toward astral intruders," I said. "The victim downstairs said the demon ate away the silver cord that bound him to his body. That cord, for humans and Fae, exists within the astral realms. So yeah, the demons are still here, on the astral plane, feeding on them. Shit, shit, shit." I bit my lip. What the hell were we going to do now?

"Can we attack them? Can you?" Chase glanced at the silent men, his face taking on a pensive expression.

"Not without knowing what kind of demon they are," I said. "The danger's pretty damned high, and fighting on the astral realm isn't exactly a cakewalk. Neither is getting there."

"So, we have to figure out what kind of demons we're dealing with, how they got loose in the city, and what the fuck to do about them," Chase said. "Preferably before anybody else gets killed."

Just then, Delilah's cell phone rang. She moved off to the side to answer the call.

Chase glanced at her, then turned to me. "By the way, I looked up the girl you asked about—the elf. She did file a report with the police, but it was a couple of years ago. Said some guy was following her. I remember assigning an officer to go talk to the man in question, but nothing much happened.

The guy denied it, said it was coincidence, that he'd just happened to be in the same area as she was. Since Sabele never called in again, we just closed the case."

"Let me guess. Harold Young."

"Yeah, Harold Young. How did you know that? He was a freshman at the UW. I can give you his last known address. If I remember right, he's the youngest son of some local millionaire." His gaze darted to his watch. "Now, you mentioned you had some information on the Clockwork Club and Claudette? Might as well tell me while we're waiting for Delilah."

"The Clockwork Club is an old-money vampire club, almost impossible to get into if you don't know someone already in it. Apparently, the club's been in existence since the 1700s, so it's just now emerging into the light. From what I can tell, there aren't any horrendous rituals or rites that go on there; they just keep to themselves, like most exclusive clubs."

Delilah flipped her phone shut. "What are we talking about?"

"The Clockwork Club," I said. "Chase is hunting for a vampire who disappeared not long ago. She belonged to an exclusive vampire club, has been in the closet, is still married, and suddenly vanished. No signs point to suicide or to her husband staking her."

"So any chance you can get through the doors to ask them about Claudette?" Chase asked.

I pressed my lips together and shrugged. "I can try. My source hooked me up with the name of a member who happens to really like the Fae. I'll see if I can spring myself an invitation to a social night there, but I can't promise anything."

"Tim called," Delilah said. "He found our boy, Harish. I have the address right here." She held up her notebook. "It's still early enough. What say we pay a visit and see if Sabele married him and is off somewhere, making babies?"

"Sounds good," I said. "Come on, let's roll."

CHAPTER 10

Smoky and Vanzir opted out of our jaunt to visit Harish, so it was just Camille, Delilah, and me. We wound through the streets, heading over toward the area in which Siobhan, our selkie friend, lived. The Fae had taken over the north side of Discovery Park in the past year, buying up land there, renting houses and condos. I had the suspicion that the big boom in the past few months was due to the Fae Queens reestablishing their domain. All of a sudden, neighborhoods surrounding parks, lakes, and wetland areas had taken on a decidedly "Faerie Land" feel to them.

As we drove through Discovery Park, the trees graced both sides of the road, overshadowing us and blocking the view. The park was a friendly one. Delilah and Camille often came here to walk and think and talk to the nature devas. I missed that, but since I'd been turned into a vampire, the nature spirits weren't comfortable around me, and I didn't like making them wary. So I chose to keep myself aloof unless they came out to play on their own. So many humans mixed up the Fae, elves, and nature devas, lumping us all together, even though we were three distinct races.

Nature devas were part Fae, part plant, and they lived only

to serve their species. Blackberry devas were huge and crept across the land, gobbling up space even as did their thickets. Tree devas could be a thousand years old, and while they weren't exactly the Ents of Tolkien's world, they did shepherd their charges and keep watch over what the two- and four-leggeds did within the boundaries of their woodlands. Flower sprites were often perky, almost chatty, except for a select few like the bluebell spirits, who could be deadly if you intruded on their land.

Camille turned left off Fortieth onto Lawtonwood Road, then followed it until we hit Cramer Street, where we made another left. A few blocks down, and we pulled up in front of a large house. Camille turned off the ignition.

I glanced at the house. The lights were blazing. "Shall we?"

"Lead on," Camille said. "You and Iris discovered Sabele's trunk. Did you bring her necklace and the lock of hair?"

I nodded, patting my pocket. For some reason, I'd taken to carrying her locket in a little box with me. I'd grown concerned over the elf and couldn't pinpoint why. "What about her diary? I don't suppose you have that with you?"

She shook her head. "No, but I've got a pretty good memory. I know what to ask."

The path leading to the house was cobblestone. The yard was neatly tended, almost to the point of where it felt too tidy. I glanced around, looking for any sign of disorder, any sign of the wildness that a lot of Fae households possessed. Our own yard was a profusion of plants and grasses and mossy patches, but Harish apparently either hired a gardener or he was obsessive about keeping things neat.

The house was the same way. The siding sparkled with a suspicious lack of dirt for being in an area that only had sixty-some clear days a year, with the rest overcast and—often—drizzly or pouring. Everything looked perfect. I knocked on the door as Camille and Delilah flanked my sides.

After a moment, the door opened a crack, and a lithe young man peered out. He was an elf, all right, but he was an elf who wore glasses and who had apparently decided that the *Miami Vice* costumers had it right. He looked like a pretty boy, a platinum blond version of Don Johnson. He gave us the once-over and opened the door a bit wider.

"Yes, may I help you?" Neutral tone. Not friendly, not unfriendly.

"Are you Harish?"

"Yes," he said, the door edging open a few more inches. "What do you want?"

"We're looking for Sabele Olahava," I said slowly. "We thought you might know where she is."

That stopped him cold. The bored affectation washed off his face; the expression behind it was stark and bleak.

"She's not here," he said, starting to close the door.

"Wait—please. We need to know where she is. Can you just give us ten minutes?" Delilah stepped up, at her most winsome.

Harish looked at her for a moment, then let out a long sigh. "Very well. But I'm not inviting you in—not with her along," he said, pointing to me. "I'll come out on the porch and sit with you."

"How rude—" Delilah started to say, but I touched her arm and shook my head. He was just protecting his home, and he had every right to be concerned.

"He's right," I said. "It's *so* not a good idea to invite strange vampires into your house—not at all." I turned back to him. "Fair enough. Shall we sit on the porch?"

We settled on the covered porch, with Delilah still glaring at him, but I wasn't offended. Harish would take a great chance by inviting me into his house, and he knew it. I knew it. If it made him uncomfortable, then he had every right to keep me outside. It would have been the same if I'd opened the door to some big bruiser I didn't know.

"I'm Menolly D'Artigo, and these are my sisters, Camille and Delilah."

After we sat down, he let out another sigh and leaned back against the railing, pushing the cuffed sleeves of his summer blazer up his arms. "Why are you asking about Sabele?"

"She used to tend bar at the Wayfarer. I'm the new owner. I took over when Jocko was murdered." I kept my gaze fixed on him.

His eyebrow jumped a little. "I haven't thought of that bar in a while. Since Sabele disappeared, I can't bring myself to go past it."

"Disappeared?" Camille leaned in. "When? We thought she might be here, married to you."

His expression did jump then. *"Married?* Why the hell would you think that? We were engaged, but apparently she couldn't stomach the thought of marrying me. She left in the night without saying good-bye. I spent a year mourning, then a year wondering what I did wrong. This past year I've finally managed to shove her rejection out of my mind, and now here you are, dredging it up again."

I glanced at Camille, who was watching him closely. Our glamour didn't work on elves the same way it worked on FBHs, so we couldn't compel him to tell the truth, but elves weren't all that good at lying, either. They fudged the truth just fine, and obfuscated facts they didn't want you to know. But lying—it wasn't really inherent within their nature.

"Her diary said you were engaged," Camille said. "She was very much in love with you, according to what she wrote."

Harish paled, and for the first time, emotion broke through the composed facade he'd erected. "Diary?" His voice fell to a whisper. "You found her diary? Sabele never let anyone touch that journal. She'd never leave it behind."

"That's what we were thinking," I said, slowly withdrawing the box with the locket and curl of hair from my pocket. I opened it and handed it to him. "Do you recognize this?"

As the elf slowly lifted the locket by its chain, his expression went from worried to broken. "I gave her this the week before she vanished. It was an engagement gift. And the hair—it's her mother's. She'd *never, ever* let this out of her possession. Her mother died shortly after she first came over Earthside. Her father sent her a lock of her mother's hair, since she couldn't go home for the funeral rites."

"You really thought she would leave without telling you?" I asked, hating to pry. But something had happened, and I wanted to get to the bottom of it. "Why would she do that? You were engaged."

"Yes," he said quietly, fingering the locket. "We were planning a big wedding back in Elqaneve. When I gave her the locket, she put my picture in it and said she'd treasure it always," he said, his voice catching. In the light shimmering down from the sconce by the door, I could see that his eyes were a pale blue, and they shone with tears. "Then, not long after that, she disappeared."

"But you tried to find her?" Delilah leaned forward, her voice breathless. She had recently discovered the Brontë sisters, when Camille had cajoled her into reading *Jane Eyre* and *Wuthering Heights*, and that sparked off a flurry of old tragic love stories. Lately, romance movies had replaced *Jerry Springer* every Friday night.

"Of course I tried," he said. "What did you *think*? That I just chalked it up to *Oops, lost my fiancée* and moved on without scouring the city for her? Don't add insult to my pain, please."

"Sorry," Delilah murmured.

Harish shrugged. "No, I'm sorry. I still miss her, to be honest. I say I'm over her, I say that after three years I've chalked it up to fate, but . . . the truth is, I miss her every day. And every day I wonder if she's off living a wonderful life somewhere. Even though I'm still bitter, I hope that she's happy."

"Tell us what happened," I said gently.

With a sigh, he said, "The last time I saw her, we had a little spat—nothing major but enough that Sabele stormed out after dinner. She was like that—high-tempered. I loved it about her, usually. Anyway, I felt bad about it, and the next morning, I called to apologize. She wasn't home, so I left a message saying I was sorry and asking if she would please come over that night. She called back after I left for work and said she'd be here by ten P.M."

"And she never showed up?" Camille bit her lip and glanced at me. This wasn't easy on him—that much we could tell. He really did look haunted.

Harish shook his head. "No. I called the bar, but they said she'd left for the evening. I had no reason to disbelieve them. Later, when she still didn't show up, I went over to the bar and walked home by the path she usually took to my house. But there was no sign of her."

"Did you contact the police? The FH-CSI?" It would be the next logical move, but with Sabele an OIA agent, Harish might have been instructed not to, I thought. My hunch was right.

"No. I called her several times the next morning but got no answer. When the bar opened, I was right there, waiting, but instead of Sabele, an agent from the OIA was there. He refused to let me into her room and told me to keep quiet, that they were looking into matters. He said that if anything had gone wrong, I could endanger her by going to the cops. So I did what I was told and waited. After a few days, the agent showed up at my house. He told me that Sabele had gone AWOL—that she went home."

"Did you check with her father?"

"I couldn't leave right away, I had some pressing deadlines, and as much as I wanted to, I couldn't just drop everything. Three days later, I crossed over." He shook his head. "I went home to Elqaneve looking for her, but when I arrived at her house, her father had moved. He didn't leave a forwarding address. His neighbors said he'd moved some months before, so I assumed Sabele went to his new place. The only conclusion I could come up with was that she was hiding from me, that she couldn't bring herself to tell me she didn't want to get married. So I decided to let her go, since that's what she seemed to want."

Camille let out a long breath. "Did you ask if she'd taken her things from the Wayfarer?"

Harish shrugged. "Yeah, but the new owner—Jocko—was very particular. He wouldn't allow me upstairs. Nobody else had seen her around. I dropped in every night for weeks hoping to find someone who'd seen her go, who might know why she left. But it's like she never existed."

I pushed myself up, pacing back and forth on the flagstone in front of the stairs. "Something doesn't add up. Wouldn't her father come to look for her if he hadn't heard from her for a while?"

"You don't know her family," the elf said. He stood. "I

apologize for my rude behavior earlier. I'd like it very much if you'd all come in and have something to drink." Pausing, he bit his lip as he looked at me. "I mean . . ."

"Don't sweat it," I said. "I'm not thirsty, and trust me, I won't take advantage of your invitation. I never hunt anybody who doesn't deserve it. When we leave, you can rescind your invitation; it will help you sleep better, and I won't take offense."

We followed him into his house. Our house was large, but his was spacious. An open floor design, one-story ranch style, the house rambled across the property. His living room overlooked the water. Even though the inlet was a block or two away, the view remained unobstructed and breathtaking. The house was tastefully furnished if a little boring. I kept my mouth shut, but Delilah, as usual, blurted out the first thing that came into her fluffy little head.

"You certainly like beige," she said, then clapped her hand to her mouth. "I'm sorry—I didn't mean . . ."

"Not a problem. I'm not the most adventurous of men," Harish said, motioning to the big oak dining table. "Please, sit down." As we took our places, he slipped into a chair and toyed with the locket. "Her father wasn't supportive when she joined the OIA. In fact, he strongly disapproved. Sabele told me that the day she signed up, he actually said to her, 'If you get yourself killed, I'm not going to bother looking for your body, and I won't enter your name onto the scrolls of the ancestors.' In effect, that would mean her soul would be doomed to wander in the Netherworld until she could be put to rest."

"Harsh," Camille said, glancing at Delilah and me. Our father had been proud as peaches when we joined the OIA. He'd supported every choice we made. Well, almost every choice. He'd been pissed out of his mind when Camille got herself involved with Trillian.

I frowned. "Did he just hate the service, or was he unhappy that she chose to align herself with the Fae rather than Queen Asteria's court?"

While some elves served the OIA, there was a strong divide in the elfin community between the purists and those who didn't mind stepping outside the box. Elves weren't as open to other races as most of the Fae were.

Harish shrugged. "I think her father's a pacifist. He disapproves of all military service. He wanted her to become a priestess in the temple of Araylia, the goddess of healing. But Sabele liked adventure. She never could stand the thought of being shut up in a temple, quietly living out her life serving others." He bit his lip. "Can I offer you something to drink? To eat?"

Delilah and Camille accepted lemonade.

"No, thank you." I politely declined. "So you're telling us that until tonight, you thought she just skipped out on the relationship?"

The pain in his eyes was fresh and new, as if we'd ripped open a wound that had never quite healed. "That's precisely what I thought. You think something happened to her, don't you?" He set a tray on the table, containing glasses, a pitcher of lemonade, and a plate of oatmeal cookies. "That's why you're here?"

I leaned back, stretching out my legs. "We weren't sure, but now . . . now I think that we should assume something happened to her. Why the OIA said she went home confounds me, but they might have not wanted to admit they didn't know where one of their agents went."

"Did you know anything about the man who was stalking her?" Camille asked, leaning in.

Harish blinked. Twice. "Stalking her? Someone was stalking her?"

I hesitated on my next question. If Harish thought Harold might have done something to Sabele, there was no telling what he might do. But we had to know everything he could tell us. I decided to take the risk. Elves tended to be pretty even-keeled.

"Did she ever mention somebody by the name of Harold Young?"

The elf slowly sat back in his chair, a suspicious look on his face. "Harold Young? I know that name. Sabele mentioned him a couple of times. She said he gave her the creeps. He came into the bar on a regular basis. But I just thought . . ."

His voice dropped to a strangled whisper. "I just thought he was some obnoxious customer and told her to ignore him."

"Did you know she filed a police report, naming him as a stalker? The cops talked to him briefly, he denied it, and since they never heard from her again, they closed the case."

Again, the deer-in-the-headlights look. "No. She didn't tell me she went to the police. Why didn't I take her more seriously? Do you think this guy did something?" He stared at the floor. "I told her she was overreacting when she mentioned him to me. What if he really did want to hurt her? I betrayed her by not believing her."

I didn't know what to say. Delilah and Camille were as tongue-tied as me. After another moment of uncomfortable silence, I cleared my throat.

"Don't second-guess yourself. There's no way of knowing, sometimes. And we aren't *positive* that she fell prey to harm. It just *looks* likely."

"Can you find out? I can pay for your time," he mumbled. "Whatever it takes."

Delilah was about to say something when I stepped in. We needed the money, true, but I didn't want him to feel like we were ghouls, feeding on the dead. "Listen, we'll take a look around. If it appears that this is going to be cost-intensive, we'll talk money then. Delilah's a professional PI, so we're already off to a head start. For now, the best help you can give us is to tell us everything you remember. Where her favorite hangouts were, what she liked to do, anything you can remember about this Harold guy. Can you get us a dossier by morning?"

Harish let out a soft sigh. "Of course. Give me your address, and I'll have it sent over tomorrow." He stood up, looking far older than when he'd first opened the door. "Thank you. I'm praying you find out that she just got bored with me and actually did go home. But you know . . ."

"What?" Camille said.

"I've always had a feeling that something was wrong. I couldn't shake it, but it seemed . . . well . . . like I was overreacting. I finally just pushed it away and chalked it up to a wounded ego."

"One last question," I asked. "Do you know why Sabele wrote her journal entries in Melosealfôr? It's an unusual language for most people to speak, let alone write."

Harish gave me a soft smile. "When we were young, we were friends with a unicorn. Not one of the Dahns Unicorns, but one from the Golden Wood. He taught us the spoken version, and the sprite he traveled with taught us to write in it. Sabele and I used it as a secret language for many years, a way to keep our thoughts private. I guess she still thought of it as a way to keep the world out of her business."

"Thank you," I said, my stomach dropping at the sadness in his gaze.

"We'll be going, then. Here's my card," Delilah said, handing him her business card as we headed for the door. "I wrote our home phone number and cell numbers on the back. Please, get everything together as soon as you can. You can send the information to the Wayfarer or down to the Indigo Crescent bookstore that Camille owns, or to my office, which is just above the store."

And with that, we said good-bye and headed back to the car.

It was after midnight by the time we got home. As Camille slowly pulled into the yard, I glanced at the wards. Linked to the crystals in our kitchen, they glowed, soft rings of large quartz crystal spikes embedded into the ground. Their ivory light showed all was well. No ghouls for the moment, at least.

As we entered the kitchen, we found Iris sitting in the rocking chair by the stove. Her eyelashes were heavy with tears, and her makeup was streaked. She was clutching a tissue in her hand, and her beautiful dress lay in a pile on the floor. She'd changed into her bathrobe, and her hair flowed down her shoulders.

Rozurial was fixing her a cup of tea. He glanced at us and shook his head, an angry look on his face. Camille and Delilah hurried over to her, while I took the tea from Rozurial and carried it to her chair.

"What happened?" Delilah asked, brushing back a wayward strand of the long, golden locks that Iris was so proud of.

Iris flushed. "Bruce happened. A bunch of his buddies showed up at the restaurant and got us kicked out. Bruce didn't seem to care, so they all decided to go to a bar. I didn't want to go, but they complained I was being a party pooper, so I went along. Once we were there—it was Clancy's Pub— Bruce's friend Hans vomited all over me. That was *after* he tried to cop a feel. I slapped him in the face when he groped me. He threw up on me, and that damned Bruce just laughed at the whole thing. I was so embarrassed. I just wanted to fall through the floor."

The pain in her voice made me want to do a little leprechaun hunting. My fingers itched to find the little creep and smack him around for hurting Iris's feelings. I forced myself to remain calm.

"What did you do?"

"What could I do? I told Bruce I was leaving, and instead of trying to get me to stay, he just let out a belly laugh. Yes, he was drunk, but did he have to be so cruel?" She started to cry again, and I saw red.

"You want me to have a talk with him?"

Iris sniffed and blew her nose. She shook her head. "Not with those fangs out, you don't," she said.

I hadn't realized my fangs were extended and did my best to rein myself in. "Sorry. I won't put the bite on him. I promise."

Camille picked up the dress, wincing as the smell of stale, alcohol-ridden puke wafted up to assault us all. "I'll see if I can get the stain out. We'll have it dry-cleaned if need be." She headed toward the laundry room.

Delilah patted Iris's hand and gave her a kiss on the cheek. "Men can be so damned frustrating. I was ready to kill Chase over Erika."

Roz settled in at the table with a cup of tea and a turkey sandwich. "We're not all like that, Iris. Now me, I've never, ever been rude to a lady."

"No, you just seduce them and then dash out the back

when they aren't looking," I said, glancing at him. But when he grinned at me, I couldn't help grinning back.

"Of course. That's my job, love. You know that. But I do my best to leave them happy and without heartbreak." Without his duster, he was just like every other curly headed pretty boy, though he had that slightly psycho edge that gave his eyes a dangerous appeal. He was wearing black jeans, a black mesh wife-beater, and a matching Australian hat that looked like it was straight out of *Crocodile Dundee*. It looked good on him, too.

Iris wiped her eyes. "I suppose I'm foolish to cry over this. But it was supposed to be a special night, and look what happened. I just . . . I had hopes . . ." Her voice trailed off as she rubbed the bridge of her nose between her eyes. "I have such a headache. Thank you for the tea, Rozurial."

He pushed back his chair and knelt by her side. "Don't give up on him yet, pretty wench. Bruce is a good sort beneath that loutish exterior. Tomorrow, give him a nasty tongue-lashing, and I'll bet you anything he toes the mark from now on." Leaning forward, he brushed her lips with a kiss, and she blushed but didn't protest. "You are far too lovely inside and far too pretty on the outside to be alone for long. Give him a second chance, and if he screws that up, I'll thrash him for you myself."

I was about to say something when the wards went off again, chiming and flashing from their master table. Camille came racing in, her hands covered with soapsuds. "Damn, something broke through again."

"The ghoul?" Delilah asked.

I shrugged. "I don't know, but we're not going to find out by standing here. Roz, stay with Iris and Maggie, while we go find out if we need to kick some butt."

CHAPTER 11

I was tired of sneaking around. I didn't care who it was; if they set off the alarms, they weren't welcome here, and I'd whale on their backside.

"Come on, we're not pussyfooting around this time." I slammed open the kitchen door and, with Camille and Delilah following me, headed into the backyard. The Moon was still up, though she was on her way to setting for the night, and the yard was awash in her glow.

"Where should we look?" That's one thing the wards couldn't tell us—where the breach had occurred. Camille and Morio were working on a fix for that, but for now we'd have to hunt down our intruder.

"Wherever we sense trouble." Camille clattered down the steps behind me. It had been a long night already, and I could tell both she and Delilah were feeling strained. "Let's split up. I'll head toward the gardens. Delilah, you take the path toward Birchwater Pond. Menolly, why don't you head toward the southwest corner of the acreage?"

"Sounds good to me," I said, heading to the left of the house.

We hadn't done much with the overgrown thicket that sat

in the southwest corner of our lot. In fact, we'd made the decision to leave it wild for the nature spirits and animals to forage in. Now, scotch broom overran part of the area, and a giant blackberry bush was making inroads in its grasp for conquest, its vines budding thick with blossoms. The grass here was knee-high and lush. Twin oaks rose out of the thicket of broom, their trunks hidden by the brush. The rain made everything grow thick here, and Camille said the plant spirits were thriving.

As I gingerly pushed aside a nasty bramble vine that drooped across the faintly delineated trail, a spider dropped down from a branch overhead. Startled, I brushed her aside. The orb weavers here were large and striped, but they weren't venomous. Not that poison would affect me.

Ever since our encounter with the werespiders, Delilah had become squeamish about arachnids. Camille wasn't fond of them either, but she hadn't developed an outright fear yet.

As for myself, I kind of liked the little creatures. They were tenacious, persistently reweaving their webs when they were struck down, patiently waiting for their catch. They drank blood—well, blood and body fluids—and I drank blood. They were feared among a large section of the population. So were vampires. We had quite a bit in common, this spider and I.

I made sure the *Argiope* found her way onto a nearby leaf and continued making inroads onto the thicket of scrub brush and overgrown ferns. The faint marks of the trail ended at the edge of a patch of broom. The plants were huge, towering seven feet high, with brilliant flowers that glimmered golden in the moonlight. The scotch broom made a crackling sound as seed pods exploded, scattering the next generation to the winds.

Ducking between two of the giant weeds, I pushed my way through the labyrinth of grayish green stalks. Not sure where I was headed, I tried to follow my instincts. And then, a few yards into the patch, I sensed something ahead. Or rather, I heard it. A heartbeat. And scent—the scent of delfalia flowers. And delfalia flowers were only found in Otherworld.

I crept forward, searching for the source of the sound. And then in the darkness of the shaded copse of broom I saw the outline of a heat source. Bipedal, could be human, could be Fae or elfin. I slid forward, silent as the night. What the hell was going on? Where had he come from? At that moment, I noticed that the twin oak trunks were glowing. Or rather, there was a glow *between* them. A portal. We had a freakin' rogue portal on our land!

Holy shit, that's probably how the bloatworgle had found its way onto our land a few weeks ago. And who the hell was here now? I squinted, trying to get a better look at our visitor. Whoever he was, he wasn't friendly, or the wards wouldn't have started to sound.

A few steps closer, and I stopped short. He was Fae, that much was clear, and he was dressed in blue and gold, the colors of Y'Elestrial. One of the old guard? Our deposed queen was still on the run with a handful of supporters, and reports of massacres and skirmishes filtered through on a regular basis, according to our father, who now had access to all the inside information. But what was the man doing here? Had he come to assassinate us? Lethesanar must really hate our family by now. Not only had our father and aunt been instrumental in her downfall, but my sisters and I'd switched sides.

Whoever he was, I couldn't let him return through that portal without finding out why he was here. I bided my time till he looked away, then leapt, swiftly grabbing him around the neck.

"Who the hell are you, and what are you doing on our land?" I pressed my knee into the small of his back. "Answer me, because with one move, I could break your back with my knee. And I don't think you'd want that, would you?"

He sputtered, struggling against me. I decided to take the most expedient route and brought my fist down on his head, promptly knocking him unconscious. Then I slung him—and the bag he was carrying—over my shoulder and headed back to the house.

Camille saw me as she emerged from the flower and vegetable gardens. "Who's that?"

"I don't know, but I found him near the twin oaks. By the

way, the scotch broom is hiding a portal between the two trees. We're going to have to ask Queen Tanaquar or Queen Asteria for someone to stand guard. We can't have strangers hopping onto our land whenever they feel like it, especially since we don't know where it leads." I nodded to the house. "Get some rope and a gag. If he uses magic, we don't want him casting voice-activated spells."

Without a word, she ran ahead, dashing up the stairs to the porch. After a moment, she returned, Rozurial in tow, along with a loop of rope over her shoulder and a clean cotton dish towel.

"I figured Roz could watch the portal for us the rest of the night," she said.

"Good. Help me tie him up, and then I'll show Roz where it is." While Rozurial and Camille held the man's arms and legs together, I made sure he was secure, then twisted the towel into a thick rope and gagged him, making sure he wouldn't choke.

After he was firmly bound, I carried him over to the shed we'd recently retrofitted into a studio for Roz, Vanzir, and our cousin Shamas. Better not to have questionable visitors in the main house. I unceremoniously dumped him on the sofa. When Camille gave me a queer look, I shrugged.

"Hey, he set off the wards, he's probably dangerous, and I don't feel like being nice to somebody who's out to kill us."

"Gotcha," she said. "Go on. I can watch him. Show Roz where the portal is. Tomorrow we'll figure out what to do about it." She waved me out.

With a glance back at the shed, I led Roz toward the back end of the property. He stared at the thicket as we approached.

"Lovely. You ever hear of hedge clippers? A Weedwacker, perhaps? Even a goat would make a nice dent in the jungle you've got going here." He shook his head. "Nature freaks. You're all just a bunch of tree huggers." The fact that he was smiling when he said it kept me from shoving him face-first into the undergrowth.

"Camille and Iris want to let it grow wild for the plant devas, and frankly, I think it makes a nice change compared to the meticulously manicured lawns around here. Beauty bark sucks. I've never understood the desire to turn nature into a nice, tidy piece of art. Even back in Otherworld—the City of Seers, for example—they tend to overprune anything that even remotely threatens to get out of hand."

I parted the scotch broom to let Roz slide through. The cuts and scrapes I got from the various thorns and branches didn't bother me, but even though Rozurial was an incubus, he could still be injured.

He slipped through the opening, and we made our way between the bushes that crowded together. After a few moments, we stood in front of the oak portal.

"I wonder where it leads," he said.

"I'd like to know the answer to that myself. But if I go through and there happens to be sunlight on the other side . . . the results wouldn't be pretty. You want to take a peek for me?" I thought about pushing my hand through. That alone would tell me whether it was safe or not, but before I could try it out, Roz stepped through the portal and vanished.

I waited. One minute. Two minutes. An owl hooted softly in the distance as I stood there tapping one finger against my arm. Three minutes. I was beginning to get a little worried. Suppose Roz had stepped into a trap? Or worse? There were some places in Otherworld that made the Subterranean Realms look like a picnic in the park. Four minutes. Where the fuck was he? Maybe I should just bite the bullet and go through?

Just as I was about to steel myself for a potentially deadly and quick end, Roz came bounding back through the portal.

"Where the hell were you? I was worried you'd gotten yourself knocked off." I didn't like admitting how nervous I'd been; it conflicted with my image.

Roz draped one arm over my shoulder, a risky proposition. He knew I wasn't comfortable being touched, but then again, we'd had a few kiss-and-tell sessions, and I couldn't just switch on-off depending on my mood.

I steeled myself against his touch. His pulse was warm and heady with sexual energy and blood. The combo could be a lethal one, depending on the vampire in question. But he was an incubus and could afford to take a few chances.

"You were worried about me? How sweet," he murmured, leaning down to nuzzle my neck.

Shivering, I squirmed, bending my neck sideways so he couldn't nibble on it. "Stop it," I whispered. "Not now. We've got more important things to talk about than your penis and its whims."

"You'd love my . . . whims . . . if you'd just give me a chance," Roz said, his voice as slick as satin sheets. "Come on. You know we'd rock together."

That was the problem. He was right, and I knew it. But I also knew that I wasn't sure if I wanted to start up a second relationship. While Roz might be casual with humans and the other Fae he seduced, he had the potential to drag me deep into his world. And I just wasn't ready to fall into lust with him.

"If you don't stop, I'm not going to play tongue twister with you anymore." I pushed him away and crossed my arms, pointedly waiting.

He cleared his throat and gave me an *Eh—what can you do?* shrug. "All right, all right. I'll be good. The portal leads to the Windwillow Valley, as far as I can tell. No goblins, no bloody bands waiting there. I had a quick look-see, and I think it opens out near the Wyvern Ocean."

"That would place it near the northwestern boundaries of the valley, then. Near the Silofel Plains." I hadn't been there, but I remembered my geography lessons. "Did you see anybody there? Unicorns, maybe?"

Roz shook his head. "No. No one, which frankly perplexes me. The man who came through, you're sure he's trouble? Because not many of the Fae hang out in the Windwillow Valley except for those who live in synch with the Cryptos there. It's a wild place, unfriendly to most civilized politics, although I hear the King of the Dahns Unicorns keeps a strict court in Dahnsburg."

"He was wearing the colors of Y'Elestrial," I said, biting my lip. This didn't make sense. I was about to head back to the studio and our unexpected visitor when Delilah's scream cut through the night.

"Holy shit, that's Delilah. Leave the portal for now!"

We raced back through the patch of broom, shoving it aside and trampling all the young seedlings as we ran. As we burst out into the main yard, we could see Kitten near the trailhead across the lawn. She was grappling with something, and it looked suspiciously like an inky squid.

"Crap—it's one of those demons. That's what set off the wards! Come on, we have to get her away from it. The damn thing's hovering between the astral and the physical. We can't fight it right now."

I dashed across the yard, Roz matching my strides. He leapt ahead of me and suddenly vanished from sight. I skidded to a stop, looking around wildly. Where the hell had he gone now? But Delilah's cries startled me out of my bewilderment.

The creature had hold of her with its tentacles, and one was making its way toward her head. Crap! That couldn't be good. I raced in, trying to land a kick, but—as in the Avalon Club—I found myself bouncing off an invisible force field, and I went flying back.

As I leapt up again, I noticed something going on near Delilah's head. The creature's tentacle that was headed toward her skull was fighting with something I couldn't see. Roz! It had to be Roz!

Desperate to help, I tried to figure out what I could do. Then it occurred to me: I couldn't touch *it*, but I *could* get hold of my sister. I leapt into the fray, diving behind Delilah. I wrapped my arms around her waist and pulled. The demon struggled to hang on, but I had the advantage of being fully on the physical, and I managed to wrest Delilah from its tentacles. They gave way with a loud sucking sound.

Delilah was bleeding a little. I tossed her over my shoulder and raced away from the creature.

"Menolly, get behind the bush and close your eyes!"

Camille's voice rang out across the yard. I didn't ask why; I just did what she said. As we landed behind a thick bracken fern that was at least three feet high, I pressed myself to the ground next to Kitten and closed my eyes.

A loud crack sounded, like thunder, and I could feel my back singe as a wave of light rolled over me. I held perfectly still as it passed over us and dissipated.

"It's gone," Rozurial said, stepping out of whatever twilight zone he'd been in and offering me his hand.

For once, I accepted, wearily struggling to my feet. The light had left me feeling weak. I didn't even want to think about what it might have done if I'd been standing out in the open. Delilah moaned, and we helped her up, but she was having trouble standing.

"It was the same one . . . the demon that attacked me in the club," she said when she was able to speak. "I could feel it trying to get inside my head. I think it has some sort of homing tail on me. There was a weird sense of connection there." She rubbed her temples. "Damn, I have a massive headache."

"How the hell did it find you?" I asked. "And if the demon was the threat that broke our wards, then that man—"

"Was sent here from Y'Elestrial, all right, but from Queen Tanaquar," Camille said, stalking over to glare at me. "We managed to hogtie the assistant to the chief advisor of the Court and Crown. And boy, is he pissed."

CHAPTER 12

The chief advisor of the Court and Crown was our father, and so the man tied up in the shed was . . . *our father's assistant.*

"Oh shit!" Since I'd been the one to coldcock him, I raced on ahead to explain. Father was going to be *so* pissed at us, and me especially. He'd always been on my back to think things through, to find all the facts I could before acting. Even as a child, I'd been impulsive, if introverted.

I skidded into the studio to find the man sitting on the sofa, arms folded across his chest. He stared at me, anger dripping off him like icicles off the eaves on a cold winter morning.

Camille had untied him, but I had the feeling that wouldn't exactly make up for the lump on his head or the rope burns that were showing on his wrists. I'd made sure he couldn't get out of the knots.

Normally, I wouldn't give a shit. Sometimes we made mistakes; sometimes someone got roughed up who shouldn't have, but we were fighting demons, and I'd rather be safe than sorry. But we were talking Court and Crown here. Tanaquar was paying us again. We couldn't afford to lose her money or her goodwill. Too much depended on gathering as many allies as possible.

Camille had dropped into a curtsy. The same with Delilah, though it looked a little silly when she did so in jeans. I settled for a simple bow at the waist. Honor and protocol were expected. Back in Otherworld, Lethesanar had expected her subjects to grovel on the ground. At least Tanaquar wasn't that power mad, and she'd done away with a number of the stringent Court regulations when she ripped the crown from the Opium Eater's head.

I kept my mouth shut while we waited. Again: protocol.

"I see you haven't forgotten *all* your manners," he said, his voice a low growl. As he stood, shaking out the wrinkles from where I'd roughed up his outfit, he motioned for us to stand. "Get up. Do you mind telling me why you attacked me?"

I glanced wildly at Camille, but she pressed her lips together. I was the one in the hot seat this time, and she quietly eased back a few steps, leaving me to face him. Hell, I didn't even know his name. Father must have mentioned it at some point, but for the life of me, nothing came to mind.

"Honorable . . . Assistant . . ."

"Forgotten already? My name is Yssak ob Shishana." He stood, waiting, hands folded across his chest.

I cleared my throat. "Honorable Assistant Yssak, I am *so* sorry. I never would have knocked you out if I'd known you were our father's assistant. I thought you might be on Lethesanar's side, come to finish us off. You know, of course, we had a death threat on our heads." I blinked and gazed up at him.

Yssak arched his eyebrows, and he visibly relaxed. Maybe I could pull this off without getting us all in the doghouse, after all.

He was a striking man, really. Not gorgeous, not even terribly handsome, but he had an interesting face: craggy and full of lines worn from battle, not age. His hair was blond and caught back in a braid like our father always wore, plaited with ribbons the color of his uniform. He was tall but not overly so. In fact, he was almost ordinary, yet if I'd passed him on the street, I'd have looked twice, because beneath the simple exterior, the man exuded power. I could smell it—like pheromones from sex or fear.

He sucked in a long breath, then let it out in a slow stream. "I suppose I can see how you might jump to conclusions, given the demonic threat you're facing and the mood of the prior queen toward your family."

"There's more," Camille said softly, moving to stand beside me. "The wards on our property were breached a short while ago. We were out hunting for the cause. Menolly came upon you before we found the real intruder—a demon we haven't been able to identify, who we can't seem to fight."

I gave her a grateful smile. Just because Yssak worked for our father didn't mean we were home free when it came to slipups like this. Father was tougher on us than any of our bosses.

Delilah had slumped onto the sofa. She looked pale.

"Excuse me, Honorable Assistant, but our sister was attacked by the creature. May I tend to her?" I hated standing on formality, but again—protocol. Father had drilled it into us from birth. Breaking free of his patterns when we were in the actual presence of the Court and Crown would be like having teeth pulled. Not so much fun to contemplate.

Yssak blinked. "Why didn't you say so before? Good heavens, girl, I'm irritated, yes, but I wouldn't have made you wait if you'd asked. Your father would have my head if I put one of his daughters in danger."

He stood back as Camille and I knelt by her side.

"Are you okay, honey?" Camille took her hand, then felt for her pulse. She turned a worried look on me. "It's rapid, way too fast. Shit, did that thing get its tentacles linked into her silver cord? I can't read her signature, I'm too close to her."

Roz pushed her aside. He tipped Delilah's chin up, gazing into her eyes. Delilah murmured something soft. Roz whipped around. "Damn the gods—that thing is still attached to her. Her energy is being slowly siphoned off."

"Can you take us onto the astral where we can fight it?" Camille asked. "Smoky can carry me over."

"Smoky's much more powerful than I am," Roz said. "I can't erect enough of a barrier to carry all of you during the transfer. But I can go find him. He's out at his barrow." Without so much as a blink, he vanished onto the Ionyc Sea.

Camille motioned to me. "Bring blankets. We have to keep her warm. Brandy or port, too—anything to keep her strength going. *Hell, hell, hell.* We have to find out what the fuck those things are and how to fight them."

Yssak hurried over to my side. "How may I assist? Tell me."

Frantic, I shook my head. "I don't know. I don't know. Stay with Camille while I go get the blankets and booze."

He nodded—one curt bob of the head—and took up guard duty while I raced out of the shed, galloping back toward the house. Times like this, I didn't mind being a vampire. My increased speed meant I could summon help a lot faster than either of my sisters.

I burst into the house to find Iris standing watch with Maggie, keeping her eye on the door. She was armed with her wand. Iris might be short, but she sure as hell could wreak a buttload of damage with that silver and crystal contraption.

I was relieved to find Vanzir there, too.

He frowned. "What's going on?"

"Those fucking demons—one has hold of Delilah's silver cord. It's the same one that attacked her earlier. The beast must have traced her through the astral or something, because she's losing energy. Iris, get me a warm blanket and some brandy or port." I turned back to Vanzir. "We have to find out what they are and how to kill them, or we're going to be in a world of hurt."

Vanzir laid a gentle hand on my arm, startling me. He seldom touched any of us. I stopped, staring at him.

"I know what they are," he said. "That's where I went—to do some research."

I paused. "Go on."

"It comes from an ancient race of demons found mainly Earthside, on the astral plane. Summoned thousands of years ago by the great sorcerers of a culture that predated Sumer, they're known as the Karsetii." Vanzir looked pale. When a demon pales—especially one who has seen and done what Vanzir has—you know you're in trouble.

"You don't look so hot." I glanced over at Iris, who had just returned with the blanket and a bottle of brandy. She handed them to me. "Stay with Maggie, Iris. We'll be back in a few minutes." Motioning to Vanzir, I headed toward the back door. I could run faster alone, though. "Meet me at the studio. Pronto." And then, I was off.

Roz hadn't returned yet by the time I reached the studio, so I helped Camille arrange the blanket over Delilah and fed her some brandy. She didn't want it—she was conscious but seemed woozy—but we made her drink it.

"I wish her twin could help. She's on the spirit plane," Camille said.

"Yeah, but the spirit plane isn't the same as the astral. Arial might not be able to cross over to the astral that easily." The name still sounded strange on my tongue. We'd only recently discovered that Delilah had a twin who died at birth. Apparently her twin had been a wereleopard and was watching over her. The emergence of Delilah's panther form might be connected to Arial, or maybe not. We weren't clear on the whole situation yet, and Father only begrudgingly talked about it. Even then, he told us as little as he could get away with.

Vanzir showed up just as Kitten finally let me give her a shot of the amber liquor. He took one look at her and pressed his lips together.

Camille quickly introduced him to Yssak. "Vanzir works with us now."

Yssak nodded. "So I have heard." Turning to Vanzir, he said, "You're a brave creature to undergo the Ritual of Subjugation."

"Whatever," Vanzir mumbled. "I was just telling Menolly that I found out what the demons are."

Camille caught her breath. "Thank the gods. Finally, some good news. What are they? How do we kill them? Do you think they're aligned with Shadow Wing?"

"You may not think it such good news when I tell you what I know. They're Karsetii, a race of demons spawned in the astral planes. They get most of their sustenance from people."

"You aren't talking about spirit demons, are you?" Camille asked.

I glanced at her. "Good thinking. Spirit demons are very, very bad. But they *can* be hit from the physical plane if we use silver."

Vanzir shook his head. "No, though they're similar in nature. But Karsetii are worse than spirit demons. They're also known as *demons from the deep*, and until now, no one's spotted one since well over two thousand years ago." He let out a long sigh.

Holy shit. Then the creature was probably pretty damned hungry. "*Two thousand years?* Then it must be Shadow Wing's doing—"

"Not so fast," he said. "Unlike typical spirit demons, the Karsetii don't live in the Subterranean Realms. I've never heard of them over there. Carter, one of my friends, is an expert on demonology. He's a demon himself and he confines his interests to the study of the Demonkin. I went to him. He's convinced it can't be Shadow Wing summoning them, because the Karsetii refuse to obey any other demons."

Vanzir knelt beside Delilah and felt her pulse. "I can sense the creature attached to her. It's feeding off her. We have to keep her alive until we figure out how to destroy this thing."

"So the demon isn't part of a Degath Squad?" I almost wished it was. We could take down the Hell Scouts, though they were getting harder to handle each time.

"No." He shook his head. "They aren't part of the Hell Scouts, and they don't make alliances or allegiances. They live on their own terms. And like I said, Carter combed his records—he's got them all on computer now—and hasn't come up with a verified sighting in two thousand years."

I tapped my finger against the table. "How do we kill it and free her?"

"That's the part you aren't going to like. You can't touch it from the physical plane. You have to be on the astral in order to kill it."

"Great." Camille paced over to the window, then turned back, leaning over the sofa to softly brush Delilah's bangs out of her face. "So we have to travel to the astral plane to hack it to pieces. And then figure out how the hell it got here."

"There's more." Vanzir lifted his head, staring at me with

wide-open eyes the color of . . . whatever color they were, it
wasn't one I had a name for.

"Tell us everything," I said.

"I don't know exactly *how* to kill it, for one thing. Nobody
does. It's been two thousand years since one of these creatures showed up to cause havoc. And for another, most likely
the demon attached to Delilah is just a sucker spawned off the
hive mother."

"Say what?" This did not sound promising.

"The demon that has hold of Delilah and the other demons
that killed the patrons of the Avalon Club are all just avatars
of the mother demon. There's only one Karsetii loose, but
she's like this giant hive that can spawn off incarnations of
herself. These shadows then travel out to seek nourishment,
which is absorbed by the mother. Even if we step out on the
astral and manage to vanquish the one that has hold of Delilah,
the demon will just re-form back as part of the mother."

"But if we send this one back to the hive, will Delilah be
okay?" I didn't care about the central motherfucker right now;
I wanted my sister free from this freakshow.

Vanzir hesitated. "I don't know," he said slowly. "But we
can try."

"Then let's figure out how to get over to the astral." As I
yanked off my jacket, Smoky and Rozurial bounded into the
room, fresh from the Ionyc Sea. Without so much as a pre-
amble, I motioned them over. "Come on, boys, we need to go
into the astral, demon hunting."

Smoky glanced at Delilah, then at me. "I can take two of
you. Camille and Menolly, you come with me."

Roz motioned to Vanzir. "I can probably get you safely
across, where I wouldn't chance it with the girls."

"I can make it on my own, it just takes me longer than it
does you or the dragon," Vanzir said.

"We don't have longer," I said. "Go with Roz."

Yssak tapped me on the shoulder. "What do you want me
to do?"

I pointed at the door. "Keep everybody out unless someone named Chase Johnson or Iris shows up. And guard

Delilah. We're going over physically. So you're her only protector over here on the solid side of things."

Yssak nodded and patted his dagger. Neither Smoky nor Vanzir asked who he was as we readied ourselves for the crossing.

Smoky spread out his arms, and Camille walked into the shelter of his left, while I hesitantly stepped into the umbrella of his right. While I liked Smoky well enough, I sure wasn't as entranced with him as my sister was.

As I slipped under his outstretched arm—the man was six four and towered over me—the musky scent of dragon hit me full-on. Just one more reminder that he wasn't human. You could slice and dice and rearrange the pieces, but in the end, the puzzle formed one huge-ass, fire-breathing, hot-blooded, white and silver reptile wannabe.

Smoky glanced down at me, almost as if he knew what I was thinking, and smiled softly. "Let's go take care of Delilah," he said.

As I huddled in the crook of his arm, staring across his chest at Camille, who looked right at home, I realized that except for going through the portals and being out of my body during my death, and again during the ritual when I broke my bonds to Dredge, my sire, I'd never really ventured out on the astral consciously. I was trapped in my body, though at times in my dreams it felt like I went wandering all over the world.

Camille slid one hand across Smoky's stomach to touch my own, which was firmly planted on his side in the least obtrusive place I could think of while still maintaining contact. She laced her fingers through mine, and I gazed into her eyes, grateful that she could read me so well.

"Don't be nervous—we're going over in body. You'll be fine," she said. "This is nothing compared to riding through the Ionyc Sea. It's no worse than stepping through a portal."

"Uh-huh." I didn't like relying on anybody else for my transportation, but we had no choice. And if she was right, well . . . I'd been through enough portals to know what to expect.

Smoky's aura began to hum. Even *I* could hear it, and I was about as head blind as one of half-Fae blood could get when it came to auras and energy signatures. Demonkin, I could sense, and other undead, and physical manifestations like the scent of fear or arousal or heat. But magic—be it Moon or dragon—was beyond me.

I shivered as the world began to fall away, deconstructing itself everywhere but within the shelter of Smoky's arms. Camille was wrong. It wasn't like crossing through a portal. Stepping into a portal was like planting yourself between two magnets that yanked body and soul apart and put them back together again somewhere else in the blink of an eye. In the portals, there was the briefest second of feeling like the world had torn itself apart and you with it. But this was different.

Everything outside the barrier that Smoky had erected was nebulous and insubstantial. The shed and Delilah and Yssak slowly faded out of view into a gray mist that sparkled with silver and white points of light, dew glistening on cloud banks.

And then we faded in somewhere else. The mist was still thick when Smoky opened his arms, and Camille and I stepped out of his shadow. It swirled around our ankles, our knees. Vague shapes in the distance resembled twisted, malformed trees.

"Where the hell are we?" I asked, hesitantly stepping forward. The ground—or whatever was under the mist—felt firm enough, but there was an ethereal feel to the air. I quickly turned, staring at Camille. "Can you breathe? Is there oxygen here for you? I can't even tell."

She gave me a slow nod. "Yes, it would seem so. This isn't . . . like the Ionyc Sea. I've been in-body on the astral plenty of times before, especially when I run with the Hunt. But . . . this is different. I don't know how to explain it. It's almost as if I don't need to breathe."

Smoky cleared his throat. "The astral planes are part of the Ionyc Lands, and all of them work on very different principles than Earth and Otherworld. We'll be fine as long as we don't step off into the sea. Or unless we hit a patch of rogue magic. Just keep your eyes open for anything that sparkles in an unusual way—especially containing red or orange swirls, which usually indicate sorcery. A number of the shadow sorcerers come to play here."

"Okay . . . so where's the creature—" My words drifted off as I noticed a dark shadow to our right. It was hard to tell how far away it was, considering the lack of perspective here on the astral, but it looked for all the world like the demon squids we'd been facing. Only here, we could clearly see what it looked like, and the sight didn't give me any comfort.

The thing was huge—far larger than it had appeared on the other side. Black, with a bulbous head that was so bumpy it reminded me of either a giant brain or a cauliflower. And two of its tentacles were attached to a silver cord that led to . . . crap! There was Delilah. She wasn't on the astral, but with the creature connected to her, she appeared in a wispy, ghostlike manner.

"There—it's sucking her life out of her!" I let out a low growl. "Let's rip it to shreds."

Just then, Rozurial and Vanzir appeared next to us. I motioned to Delilah, and they nodded as Camille and I moved forward.

"Wait—let me look for dangers first—"

Smoky's words were lost as we raced forward. Somebody was fucking with our sister, and that was enough for us. As we raced in, Camille prepped some sort of spell while I quickly calculated the best angle from which to attack the demon. I didn't want to hurt Delilah, so we had to detach it from her before we started whaling on its butt. That meant severing those tentacles that were sucking the energy out of her silver cord.

As if she'd been reading my mind, Camille sent a bolt of energy—much brighter on the astral than it usually was— toward the upper part of the demon's feelers. The bolt met its mark, and a brilliant flash severed the appendages from the giant mantle that protected the overstuffed head. As Delilah's cord retracted and she disappeared from sight, the Karsetii let out a loud shriek and smoothly turned to face us.

"Bring it on, girl," I whispered, waggling two fingers.

Apparently, the thing was listening. It veered away from Camille and headed directly toward me. I steeled myself for the impact and, as it swung one of its feelers in my direction, I raced forward and leapt in the air, kicking at its head. Unlike at the Avalon Club, this time I landed a hit. Score one for the home team!

My foot landed square under the giant eye, one round pupil swimming in a sea of white. The body of the Karsetii wasn't nearly as squishy as it looked. In fact, if I'd been alive, I probably would have broken my leg. As it was, I left a nice, tidy imprint on the thing's forehead.

It roared and lashed out again, this time catching me on the side as I dove for cover. A shock wave raced through my body and sent me into a spasm as I landed, rolled, and came up into a crouch.

Ignoring the pain, I called out to Camille, "Watch out for those tentacles. They land a nasty jolt that would probably drop you in your tracks!"

She nodded as she geared up for another spell. "Gotcha!"

Just then, Smoky came whistling by in his usual fashion, arms outstretched, fingernails turned talons, his ankle-length braid whipping itself out of the way. He scored a hit along the side of the demon, raking a foot-long gash into its side. The thing responded by smacking him with one of the short feelers that wiggled close to its head. Smoky yelled and went careening to the side, landing flat on his back.

"Oh shit," I whispered. Anything strong enough to knock the dragon off kilter had to be packing a real punch.

"I think the tentacles closer to the head have more juice," he said, leaping up and adjusting his trench. Amazing. Not a spot on him.

Roz raced to my side. "Let's see if technology works over here," he said, pulling out a nasty looking handgun.

"Holy crap, put that thing away—"

I was interrupted by a hail of bullets that went spraying toward the demon. They bounced off, as I'd expected, ricocheting every which way. Thank the gods none of us were in their path.

"Idiot! Put that thing away. You can't kill most demons with guns. You should know that!" Vanzir strode up and yanked the gun out of Roz's hand, tossing it on the ground.

"Vanzir's right. We aren't out to kill this one, anyway. It's just going to go home to the mothership until we can take care of the main creature." Camille let out a little growl. "I wish I could call on the lightning here, but it just doesn't work the same as it does on the flip side. The best I can do without Morio is to use energy bolts. If he was here, we could try death magic."

As she was talking, the big bruiser had started to cruise over our way, and now it lashed out with one of its tentacles, aiming directly for her head. There wasn't time to warn her, so I just leapt, grabbing her by the shoulders and rolling to the ground with her. We landed hard in the thick of the mist as it swirled up to coil around us. Camille let out a loud *"Oof"* as we hit the ground, her skirts tangling around my legs. Ms. Demon of the Deep's tentacle passed overhead without making contact.

As I scrambled to untangle myself from Camille's voluminous yards of chiffon, Vanzir moved forward, his eyes shifting through a kaleidoscopic array.

He spread his arms high, and from the palms of his hands glistening threads appeared, billowing in the astral breeze. Vanzir let out a low belly laugh as the threads grew in length, shooting toward the Karsetii demon like a swarm of bizarre neon worms. The look on his face was freaky-ass scary, and for the first time, I realized how glad I was that he was on our side.

"Oh great gods, look at him." Camille shuddered as I helped her up. "Can you see the threads?"

"Yeah," I said. "What the fuck are they?"

"I'm not sure but they're—holy hell, look at that. They've attached to the demon!" She backed up a step, her gaze riveted on the pair.

Vanzir's threads—still connected to his palms—had made contact with the Karsetii. They were burrowing into the creature's side just like the tentacles of the demon had burrowed into Delilah's silver cord. He let his head hang back and a look of sheer bliss swept over his face. Not good bliss, but dark, wild, feral bliss that made me both want to touch that energy and yet run like hell.

"He's feeding," Camille whispered. "Vanzir's a dream chaser. He feeds off dreams. He must be able to drain energy off astrally based creatures, as well."

"Whatever he's doing, it's working." Smoky pointed toward the Karsetii. "Look."

The demon was fading right before our eyes. The aura around it began to dissipate, and without warning, it vanished with a pop. Vanzir stumbled, falling as the shock of disconnection hit him.

"Are you all right?" I hurried to his side, kneeling to make sure he was okay. "Are you hurt?"

He shook his head. "No."

I extended a hand, and he stared at me for a moment, then accepted my help. As I pulled him to his feet, I caught a whiff of his scent. He looked on edge. "You sure you're okay?"

He leaned close. "You know what the scent of blood does to you, girl? This is my form of blood. Draining energy intoxicates me. We *all* have our triggers, babe. This is mine."

As he spoke, a wave of sexual tension burst through my shields, and I bit my lip as my fangs extended. He noticed and slowly licked his lips, a dangerous gleam filling his gaze.

I swallowed, trying to push back the thoughts starting to run through my head. I so did not need to get involved with a demon—at least not with a full-fledged bad-guy demon who was under our subjugation. But Vanzir held my attention, and with a slow smile that bordered on mockery, he blew me a kiss.

Turning my back on him, I strode over to where Camille and Smoky stood. "Let's get the fuck out of here before that thing comes back." Without another word, we crossed back to our home to see how Delilah was faring.

CHAPTER 13

~<>~

Yssak was exactly where he'd been when we left. He watched impassively as we stepped out of the astral. Delilah was huddled on the sofa, awake and looking scared.

I hurried to her side. "We chased it away for now. We have to find the hive mother that's spawning those beasts, though."

She shuddered and let out a sigh. "Will it come back after me? I feel so incredibly tired."

"What can we do?" I turned to the others. "Until we can find this thing, how do we protect her? It can break through the wards on the land. We can't see it even when it can see us. The Karsetii could easily sneak an attack on her before we can stop it. And when it retreats to the astral—like it did this time—we'll be helpless until we can get over there."

"I can think of one option," Camille said, frowning as she gently brushed Delilah's bangs out of the way. "It wouldn't be all that fun, but it will probably keep you safe for now."

"What is it?" Delilah sat up. "I don't want that thing in my head again. It feels like it's raping my soul." She burst into tears, and within seconds, a frightened, meowing golden tabby was shivering on the sofa in her place. I scooped her up and cuddled her as she snuggled close, hiding her head in the crook of my arm.

"Poor Kitten, you've had it rough tonight, haven't you? And shifting that quickly isn't going to help; I know it stings when you transform so fast." As I murmured gently to her, she finally began to purr. I scratched her ears for a bit, and Camille hunted through the shed till she found some spare cat food, which Delilah scarfed down. After about ten minutes, I felt the familiar hum in her body that told me she was about to shift again.

As soon as she'd changed back, Delilah gave us all a contrite smile. "I'm sorry. I'm just under a lot of stress, and having a demon rooting around in my mind didn't help."

I rested a hand on her shoulder. I knew exactly how she felt, thanks to Dredge. Violations like that didn't go away easily.

"What were you going to say?" Delilah asked Camille.

Camille shrugged. "I may be off base, but what about the warded room down at the Wayfarer? The one where we stashed Vanzir until we could perform the Ritual of Subjugation? Think for a moment. The room is barred to all astral, etheric, and demonic forces. If Vanzir couldn't get *out*, then the Karsetii shouldn't be able to get *in*."

"You might have something there." I'd forgotten about the panic room, as we'd taken to calling it.

Camille nodded, eager. "What do you say, Delilah? We could carry one of the sofas from the upper rooms down, make sure you have blankets, food, and some books. I know it's not the most appealing option, but it might keep you safe," she added.

Delilah let out a long sigh. She looked over at Vanzir. "On pain of the symbiont you wear around your neck, tell me this. Were you truly unable to break out or communicate with anybody in there?"

Vanzir's gaze flickered slightly, and I wondered what he was thinking. But all he said was, "I didn't really try, to be honest, but yes—the room muted my ability to sense anything outside of its walls. I doubt if the demons from the deep would be able to break through." He gave her a concerned smile. "It's creepy in there, though—I'll say that much for it. Very quiet. Made me feel like I was cut off from the world."

"I won't be able to help you out much once I lock myself in there," she said. "Laptops and cell phones won't work through the magical static. And I have to be out by Tuesday night. Wednesday's the full Moon, and if I'm locked up when she ripens, I'll go crazy."

I glanced at Camille. "That means we have to find out where this thing is from, why the hell it woke up after two thousand years, and then we have to kill it. All in just a couple of days. Do you think we can do it?"

Camille shrugged. "We've done the impossible before."

"Let's book. We'd better hurry before the creature comes back. Since it's got a trace on Delilah, she seems to have become its primary target."

Everybody moved then, even Yssak, who followed us back to the house.

Yssak looked cautiously around as he entered the kitchen.

"Never been Earthside, have you?" I asked, motioning to Iris. "Iris, please help Delilah gather up a backpack of clothes. Also some books, games, a blanket or two, pillow . . . let's see . . . water bottles and snacks. Oh, add toilet paper and soap to that list. The panic room at the Wayfarer has a small bathroom attached, but I don't think it's stocked with any supplies."

With a blink, Iris turned and sped out of the room, followed by Delilah. One thing I had to say about the sprite— she moved fast when need arose.

Yssak was staring at the refrigerator. "The box is humming."

"Yeah, well, it does that. We'll explain later. By the way, why did Father send you over here? We got so caught up with the demon that we forgot to ask." I grabbed my keys off the pegboard next to the phone.

He snapped to attention. "Your father sent me with news. First: It's believed that Lethesanar fled to the Southern Wastes, but no one knows for sure, so Lord Sephreh bids you be cautious. While it's doubtful the deposed queen would come through the portals, one never knows."

It was odd to hear our father called *Lord*. For so many years it had been *Captain* while he was in the Guard Des'Estar. Did this mean the three of us would be more acceptable to the nobility who flocked around the Court and Crown like vultures around a carcass?

"Good to know," I said, frowning. "The Southern Wastes are the perfect place for someone like Lethesanar to run to. She can hide there and disappear into the wasteland of scum suckers."

The vast desert, formed during an ancient war between the sorcerers' guilds and the cities, led by one powerful necromancer in particular, was rife with rogue magic. It attracted vile creatures and mercenaries looking to escape into violent anonymity. "What else do you have for us?"

"I have news for Camille."

Camille set down the bottle of water she was drinking from. "Is it from Trillian?" she asked, breathless. When Trillian had been commissioned to find our father, he was supposedly captured by a goblin brigade. Then we discovered the abduction was a ruse; Trillian was on a secret mission for Tanaquar.

Our father, who actually *had* been abducted by a group of skittish mountain Fae, escaped from the Goldensün. We'd expected Trillian to show up again once Father was safe, but he'd failed to surface. Now we were all worried. His soul statue was intact, but we hadn't heard a word from him, even though we knew he'd last been spotted in Darkynwyrd not all that long ago.

"No, but it's about him—an *unofficial* message." He gave her a long look that said, *Listen and don't try to second-guess me.*

"What is it?" Camille's hand fluttered to her throat, and I moved toward her, hoping that it wasn't bad news.

"Your father has sent me to instruct you that you are to journey to the Windwillow Valley shortly before the autumn equinox. Until then, forestall your worries."

Bewildered, she cocked her head. "And where does he want me to go once I reach the valley?"

"Travel to Dahnsburg." Yssak held up his hand before she could speak. "That's all I can tell you."

Camille sucked in a slow breath. "Thank you," she whispered.

"There's something more," Yssak said, looking at me again, his lips set in a grim fashion.

A lump lurched into my throat from my stomach. More? I really didn't want there to be more. More wasn't always better.

"What's going on?"

"This, I'm afraid, is bad news." He didn't look happy, but assistants—especially within the Court and Crown—were trained to be the bearer of news both good and bad, and so he straightened his shoulders and slicked back his hair.

"I'm sorry to have to be the one to tell you this. Your aunt Olanda was murdered by a sorcerer on a trip through Darkynwyrd. She was on her way to Y'Elestrial to see your father. Everyone was killed: your aunt, her attendants, and her guards. That's my primary reason for being here. Your father sent me to escort your cousin Shamas home for the funeral rites. Olanda te Tanu's husband and children must perform the Severing Ritual before the ceremony, which will take place on the dark Moon next."

"Oh no," Camille said, wincing. Aunt Olanda had been a sweet, if distant, woman. Father was closer to Aunt Rythwar, but Olanda had always been a warm presence in the background. We'd had little contact with her, but enough to know that she always tried to do the right thing.

"Do they know who did it?" I asked.

Yssak shook his head. "No, I'm afraid not. Her husband has hired someone to investigate, but so far, there aren't any leads."

"Camille, both you and Delilah should go to her funeral," I said. "Father will need our support. I'll stay home with Maggie and keep things running here. We can plan the trip next week. Yssak, please, have a seat while we contact Shamas."

"You're right. We should go," Camille murmured as she picked up the phone. "I'll call Chase and ask him to send Shamas home."

While she was on the phone, I motioned to Roz and Vanzir. "Vanzir, I want you to stay here. Guard Iris and Maggie while we're out. If Smoky or Morio drop in while we're gone, call us. Roz, come with us."

Vanzir gave me a curt nod and immediately went to the back door and locked it. "Don't forget to have Camille reset the wards before you leave," he said. "And—"

"Damn," Camille said, hanging up the phone.

"What's wrong? Couldn't you get hold of Chase?" Delilah asked.

"No, I just talked to him. He's sleeping at the station tonight, and he'll send Shamas right away. But that's not the problem. There's been another murder. An elf—female. Looks like she got hit just like the others. Chase had an interesting piece of information, though. Apparently the girl was found in the vicinity of Harold Young's house. Chase recognized the address from when he was checking on Sabele for us. Just something to keep in mind."

Interesting was right. What it meant, exactly, I didn't know. "Camille, do you mind if we take your Lexus? It will fit all of us, and you can crash at the Wayfarer for a bit while I check on a few things. Meanwhile, Roz, if you'd load Delilah's things into the car, I'd appreciate it."

Roz slid past, brushing up against me as he did so. I was still so keyed up from the battle that I shuddered and leaned toward him, my nipples stiffening as he pressed against me.

"I noticed the spark between you and Vanzir out there on the astral," he whispered. "Don't think I didn't see it. You're better off with me, and you know it. You know what to expect from me."

I could smell him. His blood was running hot, and for once, I bit back an automatic retort. He leaned down, slowly, and kissed the tip of my nose, laughed, then headed out the door. I didn't say a word. Not a word.

CHAPTER 14

By the time we got to the Wayfarer, the place was almost empty. It was nearly closing time. I could tell that Camille and Delilah were winding down. Considering we'd been through two battles already this evening, I was amazed they were even still on their feet. We had a lot of stamina—our half-Fae heritage ensured that—but even we had our limits.

Luke arched his eyebrows as the four of us walked in and he let out a low huff.

"Finally decided to show up?" he asked, winking. We'd developed a casual but comfortable friendship over the past few months, and I trusted the bar in his hands, as long as Tavah was guarding the portal.

"We're headed downstairs," I said. "I'll be back in a bit. If you close up before then, just lock the door on your way out."

He nodded as we vanished through the arch leading to the stairwell. As we clattered down the stairs, I could hear Tavah talking to someone.

The safe room—or panic room, depending on how you looked at it—was in the basement along with the portal. We'd hacked into the magical programming of the portal to prevent Lethesanar from finding out we'd stayed Earthside.

With the bitch queen off in the Southern Wastes, we no longer needed to worry, so the directional magic had been retuned to its normal destination, and legitimate OW visitors were once again flowing through the portal on a regular basis. And the Faerie Watchers Club was back in action to greet them, sans Erin as president. Henry Jeffries, a regular customer and part-time employee at the Indigo Crescent, had taken over the helm of the group.

Tavah was waving good-bye to an elf who was stepping into the portal. As we watched, a brilliant light flashed, and the elf quickly vanished in a flurry of sparkling dust. Faerie dust. I snorted. Literally.

"Everything okay?" I asked.

Tavah nodded. She was a vampire, too. Full Fae and not at all picky about her meals, though I'd bound her to a promise not to attack any of our guests. "Yeah, nothing out of the ordinary. No trolls, no goblins. Ever since the portal was reprogrammed back to Y'Elestrial and Queen Tanaquar set up guardians on the other end, we haven't had much trouble. A party of seven Svartans are scheduled to come through in about an hour. Thought you'd like to know."

Camille perked up, and Tavah shook her head. "Sorry, Camille, no Trillian listed among them."

"Figures," Camille muttered.

"Be sure to log their intended itinerary and length of stay. There's no telling how much that will help, but chances are they're going to be charming the pants off anybody they meet, and probably the money out of their pockets." I motioned to my sisters. "Come on, let's get you situated."

We headed down the dimly lit hallway to the safe room. The enclosure had been enchanted by Otherworld Intelligence Agency wizards when the Wayfarer was first retrofitted for OW use. From the most powerful sorcerers' groups around—at least on the right side of the law—the wizards had embedded the magic directly into the molecular structure of the walls. They had altered the makeup of the wood and metal, had fortified it to withstand attack from both physical and magical means. The Wayfarer might burn to the ground or blow up, but the room would be left standing. And no one could teleport in or out by any method we'd run across.

I unlocked the door and flipped on the light. There was no TV; this was a holding pen for enemies, not a hotel room. Television wouldn't work here, anyway. The magical wards interfered with reception. Neither could radio waves get through, nor cell phones. A regular telephone worked, but we didn't have one installed. Again, enemies don't need an outside line.

Delilah looked around and let out a sigh. "This is the drabbest place I've ever seen. Good gods, the walls are olive green, and the light looks like an interrogation lamp right out of a fifties film noir movie. How did Vanzir stand it?"

"He managed, and so will you. It's only going to be for a little while." Camille dropped an armful of Delilah's bags on the sofa. "You've got books, and I brought your laptop. You won't be able to get through to the Net here, but you can play games on it."

Roz glanced around as he unloaded the rest of Delilah's gear onto the floor. "Vanzir was telling the truth. There's no way I could jump out into the Ionyc Sea from here, either."

"Good," I said. "It's secure, then."

"Listen, I was thinking," Delilah said. "You need to call Tim and get the Supe Community rolls from him. Set up a phone tree and warn all the major Supe groups about the Karsetii. If that thing targets the Fae and elves, we need to make sure to warn everyone. Whatever good that will do. The demon's one big bad bitch."

"Good idea," I said. "I'll call him as soon as I go back upstairs." I spread a sheet over the sofa as Camille shook out a blanket and fluffed up a pillow.

Delilah set her laptop on the small table in the corner under the light, then crawled under the table to plug it in. She was covered with dust bunnies when she stood up again. She gave me a scathing look.

"Can't you at least clean this joint now and then?" She wandered into the bathroom. It was little more than a cubicle with a toilet, a shower, and a pedestal sink, but at least everything worked.

Camille tossed her a towel and some soap. "Here. I remembered to bring shampoo and conditioner, too, along with your favorites." She held up a big bag of crunchy Cheetos and a box of Hostess powdered-sugar donuts.

Delilah gave her a big grin. "You're the best big sister anybody could ask for, you know that?" She turned to me. "Can you let Chase know where I'm staying and why?"

"Yeah, but if he comes over to visit, he'll need to ask for me. I'm not telling Luke or Chrysandra what we're doing down here. They don't need to know. For one thing, it would put them in jeopardy. For another, we don't want to advertise your presence."

"Speaking of which, Chase is due over for dinner tomorrow night. Cancel for me, would you? Somehow I doubt if we'll be in the mood to sit around eating spaghetti." She sighed and sat down on the sofa. "At least it's comfortable, and the room has a good light and plenty of ventilation, but it's still a cage."

Camille kissed her softly on the forehead. "We know . . . we know. But this is for your own protection. If we don't have to worry about the demon getting at you, we can focus on hunting down and destroying the main hive mother. It won't be for long."

"Camille's right, Kitten." I stroked her hair. "The less we have to worry about you, the quicker we can get you out of here. Think of it like being kenneled for a night. Speaking of which, did you bring your litter box?"

"Damn it, I knew I forgot something," she said, her shoulders slumping.

"I'll get you one," I said as Camille and I headed for the door. "I'll be down in a while with a box, some litter, and something hot for you to eat."

As we shut the door and locked it, Camille turned to me. "I hate this."

"So do I, but what else can we do? That creepy crawler has her energy signature, and it's probably trying to track her right now. I just hope it doesn't openly attack my patrons if it manages to follow her scent here."

"At least it's almost closing time, and you won't have to

worry about that till tomorrow. I've got to get some sleep," Camille said as we headed up to the main floor. Luke was gone, and the bar was clean and closed for the night.

Camille yawned. "All right then, I'm going to crash on the cot upstairs, the one in Sabele's old room."

I nodded. "I've got some things I want to check out, and I've got to pick up a litter box for Delilah. Roz, stay here and guard Camille. And be careful, dude. Fingers in the wrong place, and you'll be nursing a broken nose again, and not from me."

He snorted. "Hey, my fingers are never in the wrong place. It's all a matter of timing." At Camille's scathing look, he held up his hands. "No problem, the timing isn't right tonight. You have nothing to worry about."

"Right," Camille said, but she grinned and wearily began climbing the stairs to the second floor. "Good night. Menolly, wake me before you head home so I can snag a ride with you."

I showed them how to set the security system, hoping to hell Roz would mind his manners. Smoky wasn't above cooking and eating his rivals. Even though the others made light of his threats, I knew him well enough now to know that he meant business when it came to my sister.

Before I left the bar, I called Chase at the FH-CSI building. Since he was sleeping there, he'd pick up.

"Chase? This is Menolly. Listen, I have a couple of quick questions."

Chase cleared his throat, sounding groggy. "I was sleeping, but sure. Go for it. It's only . . . what . . . three in the morning."

I had less than three hours to go before sunrise, which meant I had about two and a half hours before I had to be back to collect Camille and get home to my lair.

"What's Harold's address again? I want to run by there and check on things." I grabbed a pen and pad of paper from behind the counter.

"Why? What are you planning on doing?" Chase sounded suspicious.

I grinned at the phone. "Don't worry, I'm not going to put the bite on him just yet. I just want to see if I can sense anything going on. I promise, I'll leave him alive. And with all his blood."

Chase sighed but put me on hold. When he came back to the phone, he gave me the address. I jotted it down and tore the paper off, sticking it in the pocket of my jeans.

"By the way, Delilah is staying at the bar for now in the panic room. That demon that tried to latch onto her earlier at the club? Well, it tracked her down. When we arrived home, it attacked her again. We managed to drive it off, but we can't trust that she'll be okay unless she's in a place that's impervious to magic and astral creatures."

"Motherfucking son of a bitch." Chase cleared his throat. "So, will she be safe there?"

"Yeah, for now, but listen—we don't want to advertise her presence here. So if you want to visit her tomorrow, wait till after sunset when I come down to the bar. That way I can let you in without anybody being the wiser. Unless we catch this demon before dinner tomorrow night, consider dinner on hold until later." I glanced at the clock. "I'm going to take off. I also want to see if my contact is willing to front me a guest invitation to the Clockwork Club."

After a quick sign-off, I motioned to Roz, who was sitting in a booth, waiting for me to leave so he could lock up. He slid out from the seat and wandered over to the counter.

"I'm heading out." I swept my braids back from my face. "I shouldn't be running into trouble, but in case something happens, call Chase. He'll know where I've gone. And also Sassy Branson. Camille can check with her."

I glanced around the silent room. The Wayfarer had become like a home away from home for me. I loved my job here. Sure, it was a cover, but I got to meet people, I enjoyed the hustle of the bar, and it kept me in the various loops as far as information went.

Roz stopped me, his hand lightly covering my wrist. "A moment before you go. I won't take long."

"What is it?" I glanced up at him, at his long, dark, unruly hair that brushed the top of his shoulder blades, at the jet eyes gleaming against his pale skin. His lips were crooked, but in a playful manner, and he gazed at me, searching for something.

"I know you think I'm always just out for sex, and usually I am. I'm an incubus. It's what I *do*," he said.

I frowned. Where was he taking this, and why? And why now?

He leaned down so his words were a bare whisper. "Can't you feel the sparks between us? I don't want to deny my attraction for you anymore. And before you bring up Nerissa, I *know* she's your lover. I'm not looking to supplant her. I'll never be good for anyone that way again. Not as a one-and-only, not as a husband. Not even as a steady beau. If that were the case, I'd still be with Fraale, and you saw just how well that worked out."

Fraale was his ex-wife. Centuries ago, the gods played havoc with their lives, turning them into a succubus and an incubus. It tore apart their relationship, and while they still loved each other, Rozurial knew it was hopeless, while Fraale still kept her torch burning.

"I know." I deliberately let out a sigh. The situation just seemed to call for it. "And I'm sorry. You two . . . you belong together—"

"No, not now." He shook his head. "Not ever again. We've been through too much. With me out of the picture, she doesn't have to deal with the constant reminder of what we used to have. Of who I used to be. Of who *she* used to be. Much better to just leave the past in the past. You, of all people, should know that." He stepped closer, so we were bare inches apart.

I knew exactly what he was talking about. Before I'd been turned into a vampire, my own past had been hopeful, a life ahead of me that didn't include demons or walking among the dead or drinking blood.

But there was no going back. Even if by some miracle Roz or I happened to revert to our former states, we'd still carry the memories of what made us who we were in the present. We could never return to simpler times. The past was dead, and better it stay that way.

"I know. Trust me, I do know." I let my gaze linger on his and found myself wanting to reach up, to kiss him.

What would be the harm? Who would we hurt? Camille and Delilah weren't interested in Rozurial as a lover. Nerissa and I agreed to be exclusive in gender, not as lovers per se. Jareth—the only other man I'd touched since before Dredge— was back in Otherworld, in Aladril, the City of Seers. And sex with him had been more of a thank-you than anything else.

So why was I hesitating? Was I afraid I'd get hooked on the incubus? We'd kissed before, true, but it had been playful, almost buddy-buddy-like. This time, I knew it would be for real.

I listened to the clock tick away the seconds, then made my decision. I let myself hover a few inches off the ground and leaned in.

A shock wave ricocheted through me as he gathered me into his arms, his tongue seeking entrance. Every nerve in my body flared, burned by the wave of pure sex that emanated from his touch. The fire sparked off my own ravenous hunger to fuck, to feed, to drink deeply.

Rozurial's eyes deepened, the violent brown turning jet black as he held me. His hands weren't moving, and yet it felt like he was touching every inch of my body. As the kiss deepened, I fell—dark and wild—into the passion that swelled from his aura to encompass me.

Tumbling so deeply, I realized that this was why men feared incubi. One kiss, and their women would race off, following the holy grail of sex that promised to leave them exhausted and drained and satisfied in a way they'd never before managed to reach. Was this what Trillian had done to Camille? Was the Svartan charm as powerful as the kiss of an incubus? If so, I knew why my sister would never, ever walk away from him again.

And then Roz let go and gently pushed me back. He looked triumphant and delighted and thoroughly ready for more. But all he said was, "You have work to do before the dawn. This is just the start, my Menolly. You and I have an appointment to keep. We're both demons, creatures of the night, creatures of the blood. You drink it, and I stir it. Together, we'll rock the world."

With that, he pushed me out the door, and I heard him arm the security system. My stomach fluttered. Thirst parching my throat, I stood there, staring at the door, thinking I'd just opened my very own Pandora's box.

CHAPTER 15

❧❦❧

The streets were dry and dark. A warm front was drifting through, keeping the smog low and thick. The wind remained silent, and there was nothing to blow away the taste of exhaust and grit that filtered through the air.

I wasn't quite sure what I was looking for, but Chase's words had stuck in the back of my mind. They'd found the latest body near Harold Young's house, and Harold Young had been stalking Sabele.

One thing was for sure: Harold lived in a pricey neighborhood. When I was a block from his house, I slid out of Camille's Lexus, locked it, and headed out on foot. The sidewalks were empty, and most of the house lights were off. I might as well be a ghost or a character in some slumbering dream. As I silently passed through the maple-lined streets, keeping to the shadows, the soft whisper of leaves brushed against my shoulders, the only sign that I'd been there.

Reading the house numbers was problematic, especially with the Moon setting, but it took me mere seconds to glance at the mailboxes, and when I reached two houses away, I slowed.

Harold lived in one hell of a big house, but it wasn't as tidy as its neighbors, and several cars and a van lined the driveway that extended off the street toward the back of the house. I found the mailbox by the side of the road and glanced at the names, using a penlight to guide me. Harold Young, all right, along with a half-dozen other men's names. So Harold had roommates.

Slipping up on the lawn, I ducked behind one of the large fir trees that filled the double-wide lot. The house was three stories, and I noticed a light on in one of the upper floors. Hmm, somebody was awake, and I wanted to know who.

There wasn't a tree close enough to the window to climb. I could do the hover thing and probably remain unnoticed, but I decided to try my ability to turn into a bat. I wasn't proud of my skill. Some vampires mastered it, some never managed to get the hang of it, and some—like me—were fairly weak but could get ourselves aloft for a time. If there'd been a wind, I wouldn't have even bothered. Wind and me as a bat do not mix.

Closing my eyes, I tried to focus on the shift. Unlike Delilah's Were abilities, this wasn't a natural state for me, and it didn't come as easily. But after a moment, holding tightly to the image of a bat in my mind, I felt my body begin to transform. The change always freaked me out. I didn't like the way it felt. There wasn't any pain, but it just felt *wrong* and vulnerable.

A moment later I hovered in the air. Menolly the vampire, all right. Vampire *bat*. Stifling my impatience, I concentrated on winging my way up to the third-story window. I managed to ascend to the roof just outside the window. It was a steep incline, with a small overhang of eaves that dropped off to the ground below. As I held myself steady in front of the window, I peered in.

The room was lit, all right, but I was having trouble seeing. Bats certainly weren't blind, contrary to popular opinion, but I had better vision in my normal form. Frustrated, I landed gently on the roof, making certain I was at a place where I wouldn't go tumbling off, and gratefully let go of my winged form. Somehow, I didn't see flight as a regular activity in my future.

Once I'd shifted back, I reassured myself I was all in one piece, then flattened myself against the shingles as I peeked inside the room again. *Much better.* The light gave me a full view, and thankfully, the room was empty at the moment.

From where I was hiding, I could see a single bed—unmade. The sheets looked grungy. Dirty clothes littered the floor, along with a few take-out containers and a half-dozen textbooks. There were posters thumbtacked to the walls—mostly fantasy scenes—wizards and castles and Boris Vallejo chicks. I gazed at one of them, my attention caught by her voluptuous breasts and golden skin. She looked a lot like Nerissa, and boy did that make me hornier than hell.

Pulling my attention back to the matter at hand, on the dresser was a mishmash of personal effects: brush, comb, what looked like a razor, wallet, change, and other assorted pocket gear. The desk was covered with books and papers. *Frat boy.* Had to be. And this was probably a frat house, because no mother in her right mind would let her son keep a room this dirty.

And then I noticed a chart on the wall. It was squished in between a particularly busty Amazon and some engineering diagram. I squinted, trying to focus. The symbols on the paper looked vaguely familiar and stirred up some sort of warning bell in my gut, but they were drawn in pencil and hard to read from where I was perched.

I tested the window. Unlocked. People were stupid, I thought. Or maybe they were just too trusting. Nobody ever thought an intruder would manage to sneak in an upstairs window, but I—along with others like me—Fae, Supe, and human alike—proved them wrong time and again.

As silently as I could, I slid the window up and eased myself over the sill. So far, so good. Nobody seemed to notice. The door to the hallway was closed, so I snuck over to the poster to take a closer look.

As I approached it, a wave of energy lashed out and smacked me full-on. What the fuck? The attack continued the closer I got. And then it came into focus. I recognized a few of the symbols. They were summoning runes. Specifically: demon-summoning runes.

A stir outside the room caught my attention, and right before the door opened, I dove under the bed and froze. At least I didn't have to breathe—they wouldn't hear me panting. My luck extended to the fact that his sheet and bedspread were hanging over the edge, giving me protection in the shadows.

I scooted as far back as I could, and it was then that I noticed just how grungy the floor beneath the bed was: dirt, a dead French fry or two, and—*oh good gods*. Scattered among the dust bunnies and crumbs were several used condoms. At least they'd been tied like a balloon so they weren't leaking, but this was a new level of gross, even for me, and I knew my habits could be considered fairly nauseating by some. College boys, all right.

"Dude, I'm telling you, you gotta calm down." Dude number one was talking and, by judicious squirming around, I could peek out to see it was the guy in the Skechers.

"But shit, man, what we did—what *you* did . . ." Reebok Boy countered.

"She ain't gonna say a word, man. I spiked her drink. She was so high on Z-fen that she won't even remember it. And don't tell me you didn't have fun, 'cuz man, you were right in the middle of that fuckfest. Don't even *try* to tell me you didn't enjoy it." Skechers Dude moved enough for me to see he was wearing cargo pants and little else. "Besides," he said, his voice shifting. He sounded threatening rather than comforting now. "You came up with the idea. You wanted to make the H-Man happy."

There was a loud sigh, then Reebok Boy said, "Damn it. Yeah, I know. I know. I'm just having second thoughts now."

"Well, *don't*. Besides, it's over. And if she gives us any shit, well, we can always use fresh meat for the Big Man. Now, shut that damned window, Larry. It's your turn to keep watch over the soul stone, and you're late for guard duty." Skechers Dude headed out of the room, shutting the door behind him.

Soul stone? What the hell was a soul stone? Did he mean a soul *statue*? And if so, how did these two creeps get their hands on one? And why would he have to keep guard over it?

These guys were obviously living in their own demented little world, and I was itching to put them out of my misery. Rapists and I had bad chemistry. Or maybe they weren't wacko. Maybe they were just into some role-playing game, like World of Warcraft, although after the portals had opened, the RPGs had taken a bit of a hit. Real life suddenly became a lot more interesting to a lot of people.

Larry—Reebok Boy—cleared his throat, uttered a very succinct, "Fuck you, too, Duane," and shut the window. I was hoping that he would leave, so I could get out from under the bed, but he decided to change his clothes.

As he dropped his pants, I found myself at the perfect angle and unfortunately caught a good look at his dick, which was neither impressive nor lacking. But the sight of the used condoms was enough to squelch anything but the most analytical interest I might have in that portion of his anatomy. Larry wasn't wearing a shirt, but apparently he worked out. At least enough to have a decent six-pack. I managed to catch a glimpse of short, shaggy hair that looked like it hadn't been washed in days and of a bizarre tattoo on his left calf. As I stared at the squiggly black ink, I suddenly realized that I was looking at an intricate bindrune, made up of demonic runes.

Shit! What the fuck?

What the hell was he doing wearing that on his body? He was an FBH, that much was obvious, so it wasn't like he had demonic blood. At least, I couldn't sense any. Aware that I'd stumbled on a major headache in the making, I waited while he slid into a pair of black cargo pants and a black turtleneck. He jammed a black knit hat on his head and glanced around the room, suddenly pausing. I held still, wondering if he'd seen me, but he just grabbed up what looked like a Taser and then took off out the door, shutting it behind him.

As I slid out from under the bed and dusted myself off, I debated. I really wanted to know what the hell was going on here. Something sounded screwy, and I had the sinking feeling that date rape was the least of their fuckups. But the clock was reading close to three thirty, and I needed to get home in two hours. I either had to give up the idea of contacting Roman, the vampire Sassy had wangled a meeting with for me to find out about the Clockwork Club, or I had to give up on Harold and his housemates for the night.

I hesitated.

As much as I wanted to follow Larry, I'd never be able to come up with a good explanation for why I was prowling their halls, and I wasn't good at winging it. I could use my charm, yes, but with the hormones running wild, chances were Camille would be better suited toward a hunt-and-seek mission. I took a moment to photograph the demonic runes with my cell phone and then eased open the window, slipped out onto the roof, and closed it behind me. Within a few seconds, I was back on the sidewalk in front of the house and headed for the car. As usual, I had more questions than answers.

It was a short drive to Roman's home, which was yet another huge house. But this was no frat boy hangout. From what Sassy told me, Roman had inherited a sizable fortune from an old "uncle." Then she told me that the uncle had been Roman, reinventing himself, before it was safe for vamps to come out of the closet. So I expected an older man, perhaps a bit weather worn, when I rang the bell. A woman wearing a maid's uniform let me in. She was a vampire—that much I could tell right off the bat. But she wasn't very powerful, and she kept her eyes down as she led me into the living room.

Sassy had a mansion, but Roman's home might as well have been a palace, although it was too gaudy for my taste. There was so much frippery that I could barely make out the exquisite antiques beneath the froufrou that overwhelmed the joint. Every chair was overstuffed, every table overflowed with draping plants and lace doilies and baskets full of—well, I wasn't sure what they were full of, but they reminded me of a thrift store.

I cleared my throat, wondering if this was what the Clockwork Club members thought of as old money and good taste. If so, I'd never make it. Not that I really wanted to, other than to check out Claudette's disappearance.

There was nobody in sight, so I sidled over to the nearest

non-white chair and gingerly sat on the edge. Though in the dim light and clutter, no one could tell if I got it dirty.

I'd been sitting there for ten minutes when the door opened, and a shimmer slid into the room. A blur, really—faster than even *I* could see. A moment later, I jumped as Roman appeared by my side. He wasn't old, after all—at least not in looks. He looked to be around thirty-five or so, and he had long, dark hair, a beard, and the grayest eyes I'd ever seen. He was silent. Totally silent. And when I stood to greet him, he looked right through me.

Shivering—power rolled off the vampire like waves on the beach—I opted for a nod instead of shaking hands.

"Thank you for seeing me," I said, managing to find my voice. I'd thought Dredge was old, but this vampire was older.

He circled me, watching me—for what, I wasn't sure, but he was looking me over inch by inch, and I felt terribly uncomfortable. Roman's power was too reminiscent of Dredge's ability to command the room.

After a few moments, he retreated to the chair opposite the sofa and motioned for me to sit down again. Roman was wearing a pair of black linen trousers and a spotless white shirt, over which he had draped a jewel-toned patchwork smoking jacket, as flamboyant as his home and just as expensive. My first thought was Siegfried and Roy or Liberace, but I kept that little tidbit to myself. *Don't offend the man before you have a chance to ask him for a favor.*

He waited until I was seated before speaking. "Menolly," he said, his voice rolling over my name with a rich accent that I couldn't place. "Sassy said you might be paying me a visit. How nice to make your acquaintance. What might I do for you?"

No niceties, no chitchat—just down to business. Maybe he was okay, after all. I considered the best way to phrase my words but finally settled for, "I need your help to get me into the Clockwork Club for an evening. I'm not looking for membership; I'm not looking for trouble. I just need to ask some questions."

He pulled out a pack of miniature cigars and took one out of the box, tapping it on the table before lighting it. He leaned his head back and pursed his lips, letting a perfect O of smoke drift out of his mouth. I stared at him, wondering if he was inhaling the smoke with which he blew such exquisite rings.

After a moment, he lightly pinched the end of the cigar and set it in an ashtray, then regarded me silently, as if thinking. I was about ready to get up and leave when he said, "Perhaps. Sassy . . . has my trust, and I hers. If she had a reason for asking on your behalf, then it must be a good one. What do you need at the club?"

Truth will out, I thought, so might as well just tell him. "Claudette Kerston disappeared not long ago. She's a vampire, seemingly happy and well-adjusted, and she belongs to the Clockwork Club. And nobody has seen her for several days. Her friends and husband are worried."

He stood and walked toward the door. "Margaret will show you out." Without looking over his shoulder, he added, "Menolly—you won't find her there. Yes, she disappeared, but I give you my word—it's no use checking with the club, because you won't find any answers. She vanished as if the night swallowed her whole or the sun burnt her to ashes."

"How do you know?"

"Because her sire . . . her link to him broke. He felt her scream, and then . . . no more. Consider Claudette dead. For good, this time."

"Who's her sire?" For some reason, I needed to persist. Something about Roman fascinated me. He terrified me, too, but . . . he fascinated me.

"You ask too many questions. You are young; you will learn as you age. Your blood is strong, and your sire was a powerful creature." He paused at the door, his hand on the knob, then added, "Claudette was my daughter. I turned her. She is dead, believe me. Now, go in peace . . . this time." With that, he left the room.

For a moment, I stood, uncertain what to do, but then the maid reappeared and silently led me to the door. As I stepped out into the lightening sky, she glanced back at the voluminous hall behind her and whispered, "You are lucky. Not many who come seeking his lordship ever set foot back into the outside world again. I don't advise a return visit."

Before I could ask what she meant, she closed the door, and I heard the lock turn. I jogged back to the Lexus, wondering what the hell was going on. So many secrets, so many hidden agendas and power players and so much intrigue.

Worn out from the night, before I returned to the Wayfarer, I sped to the supermarket. Thank the gods for twenty-four-hour shopping. I grabbed a bag of kitty litter, a cat box, a couple of sandwiches, a box of donuts, and some chips. Delilah would have to be happy with that.

Roz helped me cart the slumbering Camille out to the car. I said a quick good-bye to Delilah and dropped off her supplies, then we sped home. I slipped into my secret lair only moments before the dawn's blush began to wake the world again. Too tired to take off my clothes, I crawled into bed, and as the sun began his ascent, I lost myself in the slumber that controls the walking dead.

CHAPTER 16

The sounds coming from the kitchen were loud and annoying as I waited impatiently for Iris to clear everyone out so I could emerge from my lair. Other than my sisters, Iris, and Smoky, no one knew that the entrance to my chambers lay behind the bookshelf near Maggie's kitchen playpen, and I wanted to keep it that way. Too many cooks spoiled the broth, and too many confidants increased the chance of blabbing to enemies. It was getting hard enough to keep secrets with as many people as we had trotting in and out of the house.

I pressed my ear against the wall. It sounded like Vanzir and Roz were shouting, and I started to wonder what the hell was going on. It occurred to me that maybe I should drill a peephole against the back of the bookshelf and keep it cloaked from back here. That way, when I needed to, I could open it to see what was going on. It would increase the danger of my lair being discovered, but with a little ingenuity, maybe we could cut the risk to a reasonable level.

After a moment, Iris's voice echoed through the kitchen. "Everybody out."

I heard Vanzir say, "We know she comes up somewhere near here. Why not just have this out in the open? We're all safe."

"That's bull hockey, and you know it," Iris countered. "You don't know exactly where the entrance is, and you're not going to."

"Out. Now." Iris's voice carried over the babble, and I heard the sound of chairs scooting on the floor and footsteps on tile. After a moment, she tapped on the bookcase.

"Safe to come out," she whispered, and I pushed open the shelf unit, which was on well-oiled hinges, and slipped into the kitchen, shutting the door tightly again. The door was heavy. While I was able to open it easily, my sisters and Iris had to expend a little sweat.

Camille was sitting at the table. Spread out, facedown cards and stacks of poker chips in front of each chair revealed there was a poker game going on. Iris was wearing a banker's cap along with her dirndl dress and looked absolutely charming, though a bit discombobulated.

"Thanks," I said. "I thought they'd never leave."

"The boys didn't want to chance me sneaking a peek at their cards," Iris said, winking. "I promised them I wouldn't look." A sly grin tipped the corner of her mouth, and her eyes twinkled. "I don't have to, anyway. I've got a straight flush."

"Why, you shark," I said. "Taking them to the cleaners?" Iris was a house sprite of many talents. We knew she was—or had been, at one time—a priestess of Undutar, the Finnish goddess of mists and ice. But she was also one hell of a fighter, and now, apparently, a damned good gambler.

"As always," she said. "I can bluff those boys under the table." She put two of her fingers in her mouth and let out a shrill whistle. "Come back in," she called.

I glanced at the clock. Ten past eight. The sun had set a few minutes ago, but sunrise would come all too soon. Once again, a longing for autumn and winter swept over me. One thing was for sure, I'd never move to Alaska, unless it was only for the dark half of the year.

As Vanzir, Roz, and Morio filed back in, a thought struck me. "Whatever happened with Yssak? Is he still around?"

Camille shook her head. "No, Shamas showed up, and the two of them returned to Otherworld. From what Iris said, our cousin is really torn up. He may have spent more time with

Aunt Rythwar, since she fostered him, but he loved his mother dearly. And Smoky's out at his barrow. Apparently he got himself into a tiff with Titania over Morgaine. He can't stand her, you know."

"Neither can I," I said. "I don't care if she is our ancestor. Morgaine is trouble waiting to happen. She just hasn't shown her true colors yet. And speaking of, why do we have to go to the summer solstice celebration? I have no interest in seeing the coronation."

"Are you serious? We have to keep tabs on what goes down in the Courts of the Three Queens. Things are strained enough between the Triple Threat and the OW Fae Queens. And don't forget, Father will be there, too. And Queen Asteria. We're obligated to show up. Besides, Delilah really wants to go."

"Delilah?" That didn't sound like Kitten.

"Yeah, I'm not sure why, though, but she's been all excited about it for the past couple of weeks. And I want to go." Camille gave me a look that said the matter was settled.

I shrugged. "All right, but I'm registering a protest."

Morio nodded. "You may not be best buddies, but Camille's right. It's vital that we all keep track of the courts. Ever since Camille helped Aeval emerge from the crystal and regain her throne as the Unseelie Queen, your fates have been tied to them. The ramifications of this rise to sovereignty are staggering, when you think about it. The Earthside governments are enchanted with having their *own* Fae. It gives them a one up on Otherworld—though I doubt if any politician would spell it out that clearly."

"Testosterone war," I grumbled. "*Mine's bigger than yours.* I know, I know. But I don't have to like it. Titania's all right. I don't trust Aeval, but at least she's got some common sense about her. But Morgaine . . ."

"Morgaine is a tornado waiting to touch down," Iris said. "She's going to be a handful as time goes on. And because she can claim kinship with you, you can't just outright deny her. Not without just cause."

"She's right," Camille said. "She's playing good cop–bad cop with us. Only we'll be the bad cops if we don't accept her gesture of friendship. I still think you're wrong, and that the rise of the queens is the best thing for Earth, but I'm not going to argue. I just hope Smoky doesn't cook her goose if she's out at his barrow along with Titania."

"Don't you mean *her raven*?" I grinned. "Now there's a thought. I wouldn't mind seeing him fry the whole lot of them, but especially her."

Camille frowned. "I grant you, Morgaine may be trouble, but I still think she'll pull through for us. It's obvious we're not going to agree, so let's leave it alone."

"Fine by me." I slid into a chair at the table. "This morning you slept all the way home. I wanted to leave you a note, but by the time we pulled into the driveway and Roz carried you in, sunrise was almost here, and I had to get downstairs." I motioned to Roz. "Did you fill them in on what I told you?"

He gave me a brief nod, studying his cards. "Yes, ma'am."

"Don't you *ma'am* me." I snorted.

Camille broke in. "We stopped by the bar as soon as we were up and out of here today, to let Delilah know what was going down. And Chase called. Another body. Now that Sharah knows what to look for, she confirmed yet another Karsetii attack."

"Shit. Body count is rising."

"Yeah. By the way, the two men who were hanging on by a thread? One of them died today. The other's still managing to fight the demon. I told Chase we'd drop by there later tonight and go over on the astral to try to dislodge the demon from the guy. Dunno what we'll do with him afterward."

"Hmm, we could stash him with Delilah, though I'm not thrilled with putting Kitten near the hands of a stranger." Even as the words came out of my mouth, I knew the idea wasn't an option.

"No. We have one safe room, and she stays in it. Alone." Camille shook her head. "We can disrupt the thing for now, but we can't possibly save everybody this creature is attacking."

"Well, it will buy him some time, at least." Buying time was about all we could do. "Did you find out anything about Harold today?"

"Yeah, we did. More than we really want to know." Camille opened her notebook and referred to her notes. "Morio and I did some sleuthing. From what we found out, Harold Young's house is listed as an official social organization at the school, but it's not a fraternity per se. Seems that the boys are all members of an exclusive, invitation-only fraternal order that most of their fathers were part of when they were in school. Harold's very wealthy uncle deeded him the house to share with his buddies."

That seemed odd to me. "His uncle? Not his father?"

"Looks that way. His father has money, too, but his uncle was the one who owned the house."

"Old money?"

"Blue-blood old," she said. "Now for the news you're just going to *love*. The group calls themselves Dante's Hellions."

"Dante? I don't think I'm liking this so far. Don't tell me they use Dante's *Inferno* as their bible?" I could just see a bunch of FBH kids using the book as their reference guide.

"Close." Morio stretched his arms over his head, draping his left around Camille's shoulders. She leaned toward him, and he stroked her hair with his hand. "From what we heard through the grapevine, they usually live up to the name. Those boys have been in a lot of trouble over the years."

The name rang a sinister alarm for me, too. I frowned. "I take it they're social misfits?"

"That's the understatement of the year," she said, frowning. "Of course, Delilah's better at finding out information than I am, but I can tell you this: All the boys who are part of the society are of genius level or above, they all congregate in the computer science department, and a majority of the group come from families who have roots in the Rosicrucian tradition."

The Rosicrucian order was esoteric, along the lines of the Freemasons. I thought about the chart of demonic runes on the wall. "I don't think these boys are Rosicrucians. Those runes weren't so much Hermetic as demonic. And I'm not talking the Seal of Solomon, either."

"From what Roz told us, I think you're right." Camille flipped through her notebook. "Which is why I've called and booked an appointment in forty-five minutes to talk to the boys in their house. I told them I'm an Otherworld reporter studying human educational habits. They think we're interested in writing a story and that I might be able to get it printed in a local Fae newsletter. We're due there at nine fifteen. I wanted you to come with us, so I told them that was the earliest we could make it. Morio's posing as my right-hand man, and you're going to be my photographer. Just avoid standing in front of any mirrors, or you'll give yourself away."

Morio smiled, his teeth brilliant white. While they weren't the needlelike shape they took when he was in his demonic form, they still looked ultrasharp. Now and then, the youkai in him really shone through.

"From what I could tell when I was helping Camille do the research, these dudes do not like fraternities." He smoothed the dark gray turtleneck across his flat abs and brushed a stray lock back from where it had escaped his mid-shoulder ponytail. His eyes glimmered, flickering between deep brown and brilliant topaz. It struck me that he was looking a little more feral than usual.

"Most of them were rejected by the Greek houses," he continued. "Everything we could find out points to the whole lot of them being outcasts. They aren't well-liked. Even the computer geeks, hardcore gamers, and fringe crowd steer clear of them."

"Wonderful. Sounds like quite the crowd. We already know that Harold was stalking Sabele. And last night I overheard two boys, Larry and Duane, discussing the fact that they'd spiked a girl's drink with Z-fen and gang raped her. I wanted to tear their heads off but figured we needed them alive for the moment."

"Crap. We'll make sure they pay for that, no matter what else we do." Morio looked ready to kill.

"Consider them wiped. So, the plan is: We go in, see if they'll give us a tour of the house, play up to their egos. At their age, testosterone's going to be running high." Camille grinned.

"That ought to do it." I drifted slowly up toward the ceiling. "Say, Morio, you have any more of that blood that tastes like pineapple juice?"

He glanced up at me. "No, but I have one bottle of what should taste like strawberry nectar, and one that should taste like beef soup. I recommend heating the soup-flavored one."

Iris nodded to the refrigerator. "They're clearly labeled. Make sure you wash your dishes. I'm trying to train Delilah to clean her own litter box. The least you can do is wash your own bloody pans."

I hit the floor with a soft *thunk.* "Will do, Ms. Iris. I don't have time for anything now, but I'll grab a drink when I get home. If I'm to be your camerawoman, I need a camera."

"Use the camcorder," Camille said. "They think I work for one of the tabloids, so it stands to reason we won't have expensive equipment. I'm going to get dressed. Vanzir, you and Rozurial head over to the FH-CSI building and wait for us. We'll need your help, as well as Smoky's, to jump out on the astral."

As Morio followed her up the stairs, I motioned to Rozurial. "Come out on the back porch. I want to talk for a moment while they're getting ready."

I shut the door behind us and turned to Roz, who leaned against the built-in counter that was covered with flowerpots and gardening supplies. He was wearing a pair of black leather pants, form-fitting to a breathtaking degree, and a black tank. His hair hung free to his shoulders. He placed his hands on the counter behind him and spread his legs just enough to let me stand between them.

"We don't have long," I whispered, suddenly hungry for him. The kiss had echoed through my dreams. As I pressed between his legs, he wrapped his arms around me, enfolding me as he brought his head down and brushed his lips against mine. Once again, sparks flared, and his musky scent lured me in.

He played his lips against mine, teasing me, scraping his teeth gently against the skin as he very lightly flickered his tongue into my mouth. If I'd been alive, I would have been lost for good. He could have done anything he wanted with me, and I wouldn't put up a fuss. As it was, I was so horny that I thought I was going to scream.

I managed to pull myself away from him. "We have to go. But later—later . . ."

His dark eyes gleamed, and he gave me that sardonic smile. "Later, I'm going to lay you down and slide between those gorgeous legs of yours and make you come so hard you won't be able to breathe."

I laughed then. "I don't have to breathe, so no problem. But yes . . . I think I'm ready, Roz. I think I'm ready for you."

"Good," he said, brushing his lips across my forehead. "Because I've been ready for you since we first met."

And with that, we headed inside to grab our coats. As we left the house, Iris watching Maggie and waiting forlornly for her drunken sot of a leprechaun to call and apologize, my thoughts lingered on a certain curly haired incubus. Just what tricks could he teach me?

Vanzir and Roz took off before we could reach Camille's car. I shook my head as the pair disappeared from sight. "We've got some really odd bedfellows, you know?"

Camille grinned. "I have the feeling one of them is about to become a bedfellow for real." She let Morio take the driver's seat and rode shotgun. I sat in the back with the camera and a few other odds and ends.

As Morio backed out of the driveway, I ran over everything I'd seen the night before, in as much detail as I could. Camille listened, nodding periodically. When I came to the used condoms and dust bunnies, she let out a strangled "*Ewww*" and shuddered.

"Yeah, it was pretty gross," I said. "And I'm *used* to gross."

"I'm just glad we don't have to use condoms," Camille said, glancing over at Morio, who simply grinned and kept on driving. I could see the smile plastered across his face in the mirror.

"Does the shot you and Delilah got before we left wear off? I can just see you with a half-demon child . . . or a half-dragon."

"Dragons can't impregnate Fae, and the shot lasts until we

go home and take the antidote," she said. "But . . . I dunno, Morio, can I get pregnant from you? Theoretically?"

He arched one eyebrow, still smirking. "Yes. You can. I wouldn't object, but now isn't exactly the best time, considering the circumstances."

"There's no *best time* when it comes to me and children," she mumbled.

Morio pulled to the curb in front of the Hellions' house. I pointed out the window on the third floor. "That's Larry's bedroom."

Camille glanced at me. "Ready? They know that you and I are half-Fae, by the way. I decided they might be more interested in talking to us, and boy, did they bite when I mentioned it."

She slid out of the seat. As usual, Camille hadn't stinted when it came to dress. She'd done herself up royal, with a full chiffon skirt in a rich plum, a black and silver bustier that squeezed her boobs into an eye-popping display, lace gloves, and a lace shawl.

Morio was dressed in black jeans, a black mesh tank, and a leather jacket. He'd unleashed his hair, and it was sleek, shiny, and just ever so slightly waved. They made one hell of a couple. Actually, Camille looked good with all her men. They were all on the flamboyant side and fit together like a jigsaw puzzle.

I was still dressed in what I'd put on when I got up: indigo jeans, skintight, and a silk turtleneck in pale blue. The shirt hid my scars without appearing too warm. The heat—or cold—wouldn't bother me, but it helped me to pass when I went out in public. I was wearing a denim bolero jacket over the top and lace-up stiletto boots that came to my knee. Holding the camera in what I hoped looked like a professional manner, I followed Camille and Morio up the stairs to the front door.

I was glad that I was looking at my feet when the door opened, or I might have given something away. Because Larry was standing there, welcoming us in. When I heard his voice, I slapped on an impassive expression and glanced at him, but I might as well have not existed. He was staring at Camille's boobs with the look of a kid staring through a candy store window. Yep, she had some impressive weapons, all right.

"I'm Camille, the reporter? Here to speak with Harold Young?"

"Yeah, right . . . come on in." He ushered us into an extensive parlor. But size wasn't always everything. By the condition of the room, it was obvious that a pack of college boys lived there. Take-out containers lay strewn across the tables, a foosball table sat off to one corner, *Penthouse* posters covered the walls, and a flurry of books and papers covered most of one long table that looked like it had been swiped from a library.

Black velvet drapes covered the windows, making me cringe. They were covered with lint and dust. At least the guys hadn't shoved them in the washing machine, because they still looked to be in one piece, if a little ratty.

Larry motioned to the sofa. "Just dump all that stuff on the floor," he said. "You guys want a beer or something?"

Camille murmured a polite no, as did Morio. I shook my head and held up the camera. "Got to keep a steady hand," I said, trying for casual.

"Heh," Larry said, glancing at me for the first time. He started to look away, then stopped, his eyes flashing back to me. I froze. There was something in his expression that didn't track right. Almost like he recognized me. But that was impossible. I'd been careful to make sure I'd stayed hidden.

Camille glanced at him like she sensed something off, too, because she smoothly interjected, calling his attention back to herself. "Thank you for taking time out to talk to us. As I said, I'm Camille and this is Morio. And our camerawoman, Menolly." She glanced around. "Will Mr. Young be joining us? I understand he's the president of Dante's Hellions."

Larry's gaze flickered back to me for a second, but he returned his attention to Camille. "Yes, he'll be down in a few minutes. I'm Larry Andrews. I'll be sitting in on the interview, if you don't mind. Harold wanted me to."

"Not a problem," Camille said smoothly.

"So, you girls are from Otherworld, you said?" He might as well be drooling. I noticed that Camille, who usually didn't mind being stared at, was subtly reining in her glamour. Morio wasn't looking all too happy, either.

"Right," I said. "Camille and I came over Earthside a year or so ago in order to study the culture, particularly the educational structures. That's how we got the idea to do a story for the *Front Line*, the Fae newsletter we work for."

Larry looked at me again, and again there was the spark of recognition. I frowned. How the hell could he have seen me? I *knew* I'd stayed hidden the entire time I'd been in his room. Maybe I was just being paranoid.

At that moment, there was a movement at the entry to the parlor, and a gangly young man stood there. He was average height and must have been mid-twenties, with short-cropped hair and beard stubble the same color as mine. With black wire-framed glasses, torn jeans that looked all too expensive, and a T-shirt that read Fuck You, Too, he looked like the typical college geek. Except that his energy reeked of Demonkin.

I heard Camille gasp, then her hand fluttered to her throat, and she forced a smile as she stood. "Harold, I presume? Harold Young?"

He gave us the once-over and, with a thin smile that was anything but friendly, crossed to the sofa and held out his hand. Camille stared at it for a fraction of a second before taking it.

"Yeah, I'm Harold. You're Camille, the reporter?" His gaze slid over her in a sleazy, possessive manner.

"Uh . . . yeah." Camille tried to extricate herself from the handshake, but Harold wouldn't let go until she yanked her hand away. He folded his arms across his chest, smirking as she wiped her hand on her skirt. I didn't think she even realized she was doing it.

Morio bristled, and I slid a hand onto his arm. He sucked in a deep breath, then let it out slowly. Our little interaction didn't go unnoticed. Harold raked his gaze over Morio, and then he turned to me, ignoring the youkai.

"And you? You're Fae, too?"

I nodded. "The name's Menolly." I thrust my hand at him, wanting to see if I could pick up anything. I also wanted to give him a little taste of his own medicine. When he clasped my hand, I squeezed. Hard. He gasped and tried to let go, but I held on for a beat longer than necessary, squeezing again while flashing him a big smile. Oh yeah, this meeting was going hunky-dory, all right. Just like the meeting at the O.K. Corral.

Harold stared at his hand, then at me, and motioned for us to sit down again. He cautiously took a seat opposite in the chair that Larry had vacated. Larry sat next to him on the ottoman, and the hierarchy was clear. Harold was the big cheese, all right.

Camille pulled out her notebook and nodded to me. "If it's all right, Menolly's going to film you."

"No." Harold shook his head. "No film."

"All right, then." Camille frowned, motioning for me to put away the camcorder. "Will you tell me a little about the background of Dante's Hellions? Why and when did you start the organization?"

Harold let out a loud snort. "I didn't start it. My father belonged to it, and my uncle. I joined when I was a freshman."

"Why not one of the other fraternities?" Camille's eyes flashed, and I knew she was goading him. And she got a reaction, all right.

Harold let out a harsh laugh. "Because the sheep in this college are a bunch of idiots, and I have no intention on joining their fucking social clubs. I'm president of Dante's Hellions because the university is run by a bunch of imbeciles. Because when the big one goes down, we fully intend to be the ones left standing in our little corner of the globe."

He flashed us a dazzling grin, and in that smile, I saw the unmistakable signs of a predator. Harold Young was dangerous. And who knew what he'd been dabbling in over the years?

CHAPTER 17

Camille blinked and glanced at me. I gave her an impercep-
tible shake of the head. She swallowed and turned back to
Harold. "The big one? And that would be—?"

"End of the world, baby." He leaned toward her, way too
close. I had a bad feeling about this dude. He ignored boundaries. The thought of him following Sabele at night gave me
the creeps. And yet, she'd mentioned that it didn't feel sexual
with her. But whatever the reason, I now firmly believed he'd
been stalking her.

"I'm talking about the Apocalypse. About Ragnarok.
About end of the line, it's over, lights out." He let out a low
chuckle. "When it's all done, we intend to be the founding
fathers of the new order. Of course, we'll have to recruit a few
women. Can't birth a new race without the opposite sex, you
know." Again, his tone oozed over the words, making me
want to jump in the shower.

I could tell Camille's smile was forced, but hopefully this
bozo wouldn't pick up on it. He was so full of himself that he
probably didn't notice much beyond his own grandiose sense
of self.

"So you believe that civilization is going to collapse?" I

felt the need to intercede. He was too focused on Camille and not in a good way.

Harold's gaze flickered to me. He looked annoyed. "Better believe it, Red. We know the end is coming, and it's going to be bathed in fire, not ice."

As I stared into his eyes, looking beyond the arrogance, I began to see something that scared me shitless. He smelled like Demonkin because he'd been dealing with demons. He had that look: the glow in his eyes that read demon fire, the sense of entitlement . . . Was he in league with Shadow Wing? Or was he just another stupid dabbler who'd been playing around where he shouldn't have?

I stood up. "Excuse me; I have to make a call. I'll just step into the hall, if you don't mind."

Camille gave me a confused look, but I just smiled. Morio let out a slow breath. "Do you need company?" he said softly.

I shook my head. "No, why don't you stay here with Camille and the boys." No way in hell was I leaving my sister alone with these creeps. Harold and Larry might be human, but they were up to no good, and I didn't have any intention of putting her in danger.

I hurried into the hallway and pulled out my cell phone. Two rings, and Iris picked up. "Hey, listen. Call me in five minutes. We need to extricate ourselves from here before we get into trouble. And there's plenty of trouble afoot—we just need to figure out what."

Iris sucked in a deep breath. "There's more trouble than you think."

"What's going on?"

"Vanzir just called. He heard through that fiendish grapevine of his that a new general's moving into town to take Karvanak's place. In other words, there's another big bad on the loose." She fell silent.

"Thanks. We'll head out. Don't bother with the rescue call—I'll think of some excuse." I flipped my phone shut and stared at it for a moment. We were in trouble. We were in big trouble. Karvanak had been bad enough; the Rāksasa had nearly destroyed us and he had managed to kidnap and torture Chase. Shadow Wing wouldn't bother with small fries this time. No, we'd be facing something worse. That much I knew for certain.

I hurried back into the room where I found Harold on the floor, with Morio on top of him, his hands wrapped around the dork's throat. Camille was trying to pull Morio off of him, to no avail. Larry had moved toward the other side of the room, eyes wide.

"What the fuck is going on?"

Camille glanced up at me. "Morio decided to—"

"Camille, just shut the fuck up. *I'm* taking care of this, so back off," Morio said, letting go and standing up. He dusted off his hands and gave Harold a rough kick with his toe. "Get up. Now."

I blinked. Morio never spoke like that to my sister. But his eyes were shifting color. Any minute, and I had the feeling he'd be transforming into his full demonic form. And while he was on our side, that wasn't going to help us out right now.

"Everybody just chill, or I'll take matters into my own hands," I said.

Harold stood up, wincing as he rubbed his throat, his gaze glued on Morio. His eyes were flashing with a familiar psychotic twitch. He reminded me all too much of Dredge.

I stepped between him and Morio. "I'm not going to ask what happened, but that's enough." As Harold let out a snort, I turned on him and hissed, letting my fangs descend. He jumped, taking a quick step back.

"Thought you'd see things my way," I said. "This obviously wasn't the best idea. Let's just consider the story dead, and we'll let ourselves out. And you," I jabbed my finger against Harold's chest. "I strongly suggest you rethink whatever might be going through that little brain of yours. You're asking for a world of hurt, and you know nothing about what's really out there."

With that, I motioned for Morio and Camille to leave, then I backed out of the room. As soon as we were outside, I pushed them toward the car.

"Get in," I said. "We need to have a long talk. And Delilah needs to hear what Vanzir has to say, too."

"Bad news?" Morio said, his voice still thick with anger.

"Yeah. Bad news. We'll stop at the bar and pick her up, then head over to the FH-CSI building."

"Not a good idea," Camille said. "If the Karsetii is attacking one of the officers still, then it's going to be right there and might notice Delilah's presence. Remember—those things are all linked to the hive mother. If it senses her, chances are she'll spin off a second, and we'll be fighting two of them."

"Damn it. We need her. Okay, we have to get rid of this motherfucker so she can get back into action. We'll tell her in a while, then. Camille, if you can get in touch with Smoky, call him and have him meet us there. Vanzir called Iris with some bad news."

"Oh lovely. Just what we need." Camille sighed and stepped on the gas.

I leaned up between the front seats. "Meanwhile, what the fuck happened back there?"

Morio shrugged. "Harold put his hands on Camille."

"Since when do you fly into a fury over that?" Morio had never seemed terribly possessive, but now his eyes flashed again, and he let out a growl.

"She's now my *wife*. And no one touches my wife—or any woman I know—without her permission. Harold didn't ask for permission. Therefore, I put a stop to it." With another shrug, he looked out the window.

Subject closed. That's all she wrote, folks.

I glanced at Camille. "Harold was really stupid enough to try something in front of Morio?"

"Harold did more than try something. Morio had gone over to examine a painting on the wall, and Harold plopped his sorry ass down beside me, jammed his hand up my dress, and tried to slip a finger in my pussy. I knew he was a creep, but that little maneuver still took me by surprise."

"What? With Morio right there? Is he a total idiot?"

Camille rolled her eyes. "Harold Young not only reeks of Demonkin, but he's so freaking arrogant that he doesn't have any clue that people might try to stop him. I smacked him a good one, and that's when Morio landed on top of him. I thought you were going to kill him," she said softly, aiming her comment at Morio.

Morio shrugged. "If Menolly hadn't come in at that moment, I would have. He's worse than useless. The world is better off without his kind." He turned toward her, his gaze steadfast and cool. "You belong to Smoky, Trillian, and *me*. You are *not* a plaything to be manhandled, and no one will ever take advantage of you while I'm around."

I sat back, chewing on this new information. Harold had no sense of boundaries. Harold had attacked Camille, and if Morio hadn't been there, he and his buddy Larry would have tried to rape her. Not that they'd get all that far—not unless they had a weapon. But they would have tried.

Harold had stalked Sabele, and I now believed in my heart that she was dead. Larry and his buddy Duane had spiked some girl's drink with Z-fen, one of the most addictive date-rape drugs around, and then had themselves a messy little gang bang. The whole group seemed to be infested with a taint that was connected with some form of Demonkin energy. So what else had they done? And how far were they capable of taking their attacks?

As we pushed through the doors to the meeting room at the FH-CSI building, I wondered how many times we'd come here, how many times we'd met to strategize. How long could we hold out against the approaching tide of demons?

We had no hope to destroy Shadow Wing on his home turf—not now, maybe not ever. So we'd put up the fight here. We'd collect the spirit seals and hide them. We'd fight the demons. We'd guard the portals. And we'd never stop, because until Shadow Wing was dead, he'd never give up. Even when we had all of the spirit seals—the ones he hadn't managed to capture, that is—he'd be after us and after them. And if he ever discovered where they were, then Elqaneve and Queen Asteria would be in danger.

Chase and Yugi were sitting at the table. Sharah was standing behind them. Roz and Vanzir were waiting for us, and

Smoky appeared off the Ionyc Sea as we swept in. We slipped into our chairs.

"Delilah not coming?" Chase asked.

"Think," I said softly. "You really want her around here, where that mother of a demon is hanging out?"

He blinked. Once. Then he softly said, "I hear you. Not a problem. We've had two more attacks tonight while we were waiting for you. Guys brought them in. The victims are still alive and are in the medical unit, but unless we do something, this thing's going to just blow wide open. The Fae community will be a group of sitting ducks."

"Yeah, well hold onto your dick. We've got bigger problems than that," Vanzir said. He leaned forward, his elbows on the table, his eyes narrowed. He always looked right on the edge of taking a good swipe at somebody.

Even with Roz's warning, I realized that I actually found him attractive. We both lived on the edge. We were both vampires—I via the blood, Vanzir via soul energy. Roz I could groove with. Vanzir . . . I had a feeling we would understand one another on a gut level. No prettiness, no niceties . . . just sheer understanding.

"Tell everybody what you told Iris." I slid into the seat between him and Roz. Roz flashed me an impassive look, but he pursed his lips ever so slightly.

Vanzir glanced at me, then let out a long sigh. "Here's the deal. Shadow Wing's assigned somebody new to take Karvanak's place. The news is spreading like wildfire through the underground."

"Three questions: Who and what is he? Is he here yet? And did he make it here the same way you crossed over to Earthside?" I asked. When we'd first performed the Ritual of Subjugation, Vanzir had explained how he managed to slip Earthside unnoticed. He arrived via the astral plane. Few demons had the ability to shift through the astral like he did, other than incubi, succubi, and others who worked out on the astral.

"First, it's not a *he*. It's a she. And yes, she's here. Stacia. She's a lamia in her natural form, and she's a general, like

Karvanak. We don't know much beyond that, but given her nature, she's bound to be nasty."

"Great, a Greek demon this time," I muttered.

"Greek, Persian, who gives a fuck?" Chase tossed his pen on the table, along with his notebook. "How'd she get here?"

Vanzir squinted. "Could be someone over Earthside used a Demon Gate spell to let her in. Takes a damned high-powered wizard to gate in a demon that powerful."

"Since Demon Gates allow an FBH to control the demon—laughably, considering how little it takes to break that control—could it be another demon who did it?" I asked.

"A *demon* who can use a Demon Gate?" Morio straightened his shoulders. "Not good. But I didn't think demons could wield control over their own kind via magic."

"The majority—no," Vanzir said. "But there are a few, especially half-demon–half-human, who can manage that kind of magic without frying themselves."

"Shit. Then we're possibly facing a half-demon wizard on Shadow Wing's side? Just dandy," I said.

"Don't assume," Smoky said. "We need facts, not assumptions, or we could let ourselves in for trouble."

"What does this Stacia look like? In both her natural form and human?" Chase shifted in his chair, his right hand twitching.

Karvanak had captured him and tortured him, trying to blackmail us into giving him the fourth spirit seal. I still wasn't clear on what Chase had been through. He was reticent about discussing the subject, which I understood all too well. It had taken me twelve years to talk about what Dredge did to me the night he killed and turned me.

But whatever had gone on between the demon and the detective, it left Chase short most of his pinky finger, as well as making him a lot edgier. When it came to going up against the bad guys, Chase had always been a by-the-book guy. Now he was harder, more willing to go to the extreme.

Vanzir arched his eyebrows. "She's not a Penthouse Pet, that's for sure. At least not in her natural form. Lamias generally look like a giant anaconda with the torso and head of a human female. In human form, they're like sirens and can bewitch men with their song. So we know that much, but as to Stacia—the only other thing I found out is that, down in the Sub Realms, they call her the Bone Crusher."

Camille rubbed her temples. "This just gets better and better. We don't know where she's at or what she looks like when she's in human form?"

Vanzir shook his head. "Nope. Woefully lacking on info there. Sounds to me like Shadow Wing's been keeping her hidden. What she can do, what she looks like, where she is—there's just no information to be had right now."

"Delightful," she said. "We'd better pass this information to the Triple Threat and the Supe Community. She could wreak havoc in no time. Want to make a bet she's traveling with a bunch of snakes?"

"Snakes aren't a problem," I said. "Demons are."

"Snakes aren't a problem unless they're being controlled by a badass bitch," Camille countered. "There's a chance, given what she is, that she can summon them, and want to make a bet that if she can, they aren't going to be harmless little garter snakes but a bunch of pit vipers or cobras or something equally deadly?"

I had to give her that one. "Good point. Okay, so that's another thing on our list. First, figure out what she can do and where she's hiding. Then hunt her down and put her out of commission. Meanwhile, we've got to kill the Karsetii, or at least drive it back into hibernation, and we have to do so before the full Moon."

"Yeah," Camille said, "both Delilah and I will be useless when the Moon Mother goes ripe."

I thought for a moment. "You can't ask the Moon Mother to direct her Hunt the demon's way, can you?"

Camille blinked. "I never thought about that possibility." She bit her lip and then shook her head. "No. When I'm running with the Hunt . . . I can't even begin to explain. It's like being in the grip of a mania. The Moon Mother leads us where she will, and we have no choice but to follow. There's no thought, no planning, no coherency. Just the ecstasy of the chase."

I shrugged. "Eh, it was worth asking. Okay, count that idea out."

I toyed with the pen Chase had tossed on the table. "Then we just have to find the motherfucker and blast it out of existence before we've got a body count higher than a teen-slasher movie."

"Anything else we need to know?" Chase asked.

"Yeah." I grinned. "This is your lucky day, Chase. While we're tossing problems into the ring, we just came from Harold Young's house. For starters, two of the boys are into gang rape via Z-fen. And second, I suspect Harold and his cronies of killing Sabele. He's a fucking lunatic, and he's dangerous. I recognize the predator nature, and he's got it big-time."

"He's also tied in with the Demonkin, somehow. I'm not sure what the connection is, but his energy reeks of it." Camille frowned.

"Yeah. And considering the sleazy way he put the make on Camille—"

"What did you say?" Smoky slowly swiveled his head my way, and all I could see was angry dragon, not the man who sat calmly in the chair.

I struggled to keep from laughing as Roz shrank away.

Arching an eyebrow, I said, "Don't get your wings in a flurry. Morio took care of almost killing him. He would have finished the job, but I managed to intervene first. But that's not my main point. Yes, Harold got too touchy-feely with Camille, but last night I heard his buddies Larry and Duane discussing spiking some chick's drink with Z-fen and screwing her. They were far too proud of the act."

"Shit. Shit. Shit," Chase said. "Z-fen. That crap's everywhere. Cheap to make and so addictive that after a couple of doses, you're a fucking junkie. Why don't we just spike the water supply with it and hand over control to the pushers?"

"Yeah, well, the pimps use it to control their stables. We already know that." I sighed. "I guess we need to find out what connection Dante's Hellions have with the demons."

"Dante's Hellions?" Chase frowned. "Just how much have I missed out on?"

We brought him up to speed.

I jotted down a few notes for him. "The group is scary, and what's even worse is that they're smart. I get the feeling there's a minimum IQ level applicants have to meet to be offered membership."

"I'd hate to see what their hazing rituals are like," Camille said, shivering.

Smoky spoke up. "So we have three main focuses. One: Find and kill the Karsetii. Two: Figure out what's really going on with Harold and his crew—"

"And see if they had anything to do with Sabele's disappearance," I interjected.

"Right. And three: Start digging up information on Stacia."

I nodded. "That about sums it up. But don't forget that we also have to find and recover the fifth spirit seal. With a new general in town, we can't let down our guard for a moment. Karvanak was bad, but I have an uneasy feeling that the lamia is going to be far worse."

As I glanced at Vanzir, I found him studying my face. He didn't look away. "Is there *anything* else you can tell us about her?" I asked.

He blinked. "As I said, I couldn't dig up anything more. But the fact that her record is so cloaked doesn't bode well. Karvanak was bad, but he was also a hedonist. Who knows what this bitch is like?" His gaze lingered on my face.

I gave him a brief nod. "Okay, since we're here, we might as well begin with the Karsetii. If there are three victims still under attack and they're all here, maybe we can manage to trace the demon shadows attached to them back to the hive mother."

"Sounds good," Camille said, standing up. Morio and Smoky followed suit, as did Roz and Vanzir. "Roz, Smoky, we'll need you to take us over to the astral. Chase, you better stick around here on this one."

"Yeah," Chase said quietly. "I wouldn't have the faintest idea what to do once I was over there. I'll help Sharah keep an eye on the victims still under siege." He paused. "Good luck, guys. Go get the sucker. Delilah is depending on us, you know."

"We know." I headed for the door, a wave of foreboding sweeping over me. This was going to be one bitch of a fight, and how we would trace the hive mother down through the astral was still a question that I, at least, didn't have the answer to. "Believe me, we know."

CHAPTER 18

Once again, we filed into the medical wing of the building. We'd seen far too many bodies in the past few days, far too many victims. I just wanted to find the Karsetii and vaporize it. For twelve years now, I'd lived in a world of blood and death. When we came Earthside, I found myself hoping we'd be assigned to some rinky-dink post without any stress. Now I was realizing that the carnage had only just begun. The tide against us was swelling, the demons were knocking, and we couldn't bar the door much longer.

The victims, including Tiggs, the surviving officer, were all in one large room. Tiggs, an elf from Elqaneve, was deep in a coma and fading fast. The others were all Fae. Five victims still alive at this point. I'd lost track of how many dead.

I walked softly between the tables, thinking of their imminent deaths, of their life energy being siphoned off. Their souls would join the ancestors, but they shouldn't be dying yet. It wasn't their time. It wasn't their choice or a death forged out of honor.

I turned to the others. "Let's get the hell over there and kick the fuck out of this monster. We'll figure out how to deal with the demon when we're there."

Smoky nodded and stood back, holding out his arms. Camille and I gravitated toward him. Roz and Vanzir clasped hands. We looked at Chase and Sharah, who were staring gravely at us.

"If we don't come back . . . hell. If we don't come back for some reason, get your ass down to the bar and tell Tavah to send Delilah home to Otherworld immediately. Tell her what's going on. I guess that's it," I said.

He blinked. "You'll come back. The demon *can't* kill you all."

Camille sighed. "Look around you, Chase. The victims—they're all Fae—well, Fae and an elf. Face it. We're a blue-light special to the Karsetii. Smorgasbord on a stick. But with a little luck, this whole conversation is moot. At least we know what we're up against. Morio, stay here to protect them. We can't all take a chance on going."

Morio looked like he wanted to protest, but with a nod from Smoky, he accepted the charge and went over to stand by Sharah and Chase.

In the shelter of Smoky's arm, Camille reached across his stomach and took my hand as I slid into the nook on his other side. Camille took a deep breath and closed her eyes. I followed suit—the eyes, not the breath—as Smoky wrapped us in his voluminous trench. Within seconds we were shifting, traveling, and I could feel the icy chill that came with crossing layers of reality.

As we stepped onto the astral, Smoky opened his arms, and Camille and I spread out, her to the left, me to the right. Vanzir and Rozurial appeared a few yards away to the right. Roz left his gun in the holster this time, but he opened his duster and pulled out a scroll.

I frowned. "What's that?"

"Trace spell. If nothing else, we can put a trace on it and follow it back to the hive mother." He was about to say something else when Vanzir pointed off to our left. Three forms were there: the Karsetii clones. Two were feeding off two victims each, the third was feasting on three, including Tiggs.

"Greedy suckers, aren't they?" I watched them for a

moment. "They haven't noticed us yet. They must be intent on draining energy. I think Roz should cast the trace first. That way if they get away before we can land any blows, then at least we can follow them. And rather than try to kill them, let's just scare them off. It'll be easier to follow them that way than if they vaporize and reappear back at their central source."

"Good idea," Camille said, gesturing to Roz. "Go on."

He spoke in low tones in what sounded like Greek. After a moment, a small flash briefly flared and then died out. He squinted, staring at the demons. "I think it took."

Camille nodded. "Yes, I can see it in their auras. Now, how do we chase them home without getting ourselves killed?"

"Your handy-dandy light flare, how else?" I grinned at her. "Eventually you're going to cast that thing so many times you'll glow like the sun."

"Oh yeah, that would be lovely," she said. "Okay, get behind somebody and shelter yourself. I brought the horn, so I'll give them one hell of a blast." She thrust her hand in a side pocket that she'd had specially made in her skirt and pulled out the horn of the Black Beast. The crystal spire gleamed, sparkling with the gold and silver threads that wove ribbons through the polished spike. "Oh yeah, babe, get ready to rumble."

It occurred to me that my sister was starting to enjoy these battles a little more than was good for her, but hey—what could I say? I liked a good bloodletting myself. In fact, as I watched the others prepare, it occurred to me that no matter what happened, we'd never go back to our prior lives. We could never again be who we were before landing here, Earthside. If we won peace, would there be a place for us? Or would we have to retreat, to find other battles in other places where we were needed?

Shaking the thoughts out of my head, I looked up at Smoky, who opened his trench wide. "Step inside," he said with a lecherous grin. I stepped back, but he merely laughed. "Don't flatter yourself. I'm not making advances. Get inside my coat, and I'll protect you from the light."

Camille snorted. "Get thee hence, wench. My husband is offering protection. I advise you take it."

"*Hence wench*? You making a bad SCA video for You-Tube?"

"Don't knock the Society for Creative Anachronism. They have great clothes." She stuck her tongue out at me. "Just do it."

"Yeah, yeah." I stared up at the overgrown lizard and shook my head. But slide into the protection of Smoky's immaculate white trench coat, I did. He enclosed me in his arms, and I stood there, muffled from the world, my nostrils filled with the scent of his musk.

He really was a heady piece of ass, but he was also pompous and given to bouts of jealousy that I would never put up with. Camille bore it with a smile, and he indulged her more than he'd ever indulge anybody else. I decided *not* to bite him for the "Don't flatter yourself" comment.

"Yo, you freak-assed squids! Get your butts over here and put up a good fight."

As I stood there in the dark shadow of his protection, I heard Camille and winced. Why did she have to grab their attention? Why couldn't she just let loose and be done with it? There was a sudden flurry of movement—I could sense it even within the confines of Smoky's trench coat—and then a loud crash, like thunder.

A brilliant flash that almost blinded me, even through the heavy white material, and a howling gust of wind whipped by. Without thinking, I buried my head in Smoky's chest and felt him wrap his arms around me as he grunted with satisfaction.

"That's my girl," he whispered, and I realized he was talking about Camille. The light flared and then died, and he opened his coat. I stepped away and flashed him a half-assed smile. He gave me a quick nod, then turned his attention to Camille. "Are you all right, love?"

She laughed, her hair streaming in the astral wind that the flare of light had produced. "Oh, I'm better than all right," she said, and I realized she was high on the adrenaline rush of the magic that had lashed through her from the horn. "Roz, is the trace working?"

He closed his eyes and held out his hands. "It's working." With a sudden rush, he motioned for us. "We've got to book. They're on their way home, and we don't want to lose them." With a rush he was off, running like the wind.

Smoky and Vanzir were hot on his heels. Camille grabbed my hand, and we, too, were racing through the mists. Running on the astral was a whole new ball game. We were all fast in the physical world, but here, we sailed.

Camille quickly caught up to and passed Smoky and Vanzir, letting go of me so I could keep pace with them as she poured on the speed, matching Rozurial step for step. My jaw dropped as the ground passed beneath my feet. How the hell was she running so fast?

Of course! The Hunt! Camille was used to racing through the skies with the Moon Mother every month. She knew how to traverse the realm, even if she couldn't haul her ass over to it by herself. Under the full Moon, her goddess yanked her out onto the astral.

As the pair disappeared into the distance, Smoky grimaced. "We have to keep up. We can't let them get there alone, without backup."

"I can manage their speed, but you two might have trouble," Vanzir said.

"Not if I'm flying," Smoky said, and without warning, he shifted into his dragon self. As he unfolded into the gigantic beast he really was, I careened to the right to avoid being smacked around by his wings.

Without missing a beat, Smoky said, "Hop on." His milky white body undulated like a snake in the astral breeze.

I swallowed a brief flash of fear. He was huge. It was easy to forget just how intimidating he could be in his natural form.

"Come on, *love*," Vanzir said with a snort, grabbing me as he leapt onto Smoky's back. He yanked me aboard, in front of him, and wrapped his arms around my waist.

Smoky let out a low chuckle as his wings caught the updraft of the breeze, and we were suddenly aloft, soaring faster than I could imagine going. I'd never ridden on the back of a dragon. Hell, I'd never been in an airplane, either. Smoky could outfly my Jaguar any day.

As I stared down at the swirling mist that covered the astral plane, it struck me as absurd. Here I was, a vampire, riding on the back of my brother-in-law, a dragon, with a demon holding onto my waist, in pursuit of some whacked-out squid who slurped up people's life energy. I broke out laughing, but then the laughter died away as I remembered Delilah, locked up in the panic room to protect her, and the growing body count from the Karsetii.

Vanzir tightened his grip, and I felt his breath on my ear as he leaned in. "Two of a kind, babe. We're two of a kind," he said in a gravelly voice.

I knew he was taunting me, but I didn't answer. How could I? He was right. How could I argue over something that was so basically true?

Smoky dipped, gliding lower to the ground. Now we could see Rozurial and Camille racing across the mist-shrouded ground. They were single-minded machines, neither noticing us nor looking up. Forward they ran, keeping pace with one another. From here, I could see that Camille had a slightly crazed look on her face. The full Moon was coming up in a couple of days; she was probably already feeling the energy. Hunting prey on the astral must only increase the drive.

The touch of Vanzir's hands around my waist began to burn, as he pressed against me from behind. I couldn't help myself. I leaned back, leaned into his embrace as his lips sought my neck, sucking hard, biting, nipping at me.

"Oh Great Mother, this is not the time nor place," I said, trying to break free of whatever mania was sweeping over us.

"Don't let the energy worry you," Smoky's voice bellowed out. "You're just feeling the rush of Camille and Rozurial's hormones. They're both running so hot and heavy, they're leaving a trail of pheromones in the astral breeze. The only thing that anybody has to watch out for until we catch up with the Karsetii is if that incubus takes it in mind to play touchy-feely with my wife. Just ride the wave till we get there."

Dizzy, I tried to pry myself out of Vanzir's arms, but he gripped me tighter, his lips pressed against my neck, my shoulders, my cheeks. I twisted around, intending to push him away, but the vortex of color swirling in his eyes caught me short. I let out a short bark of surprise as he fastened his lips on mine, lifting me up and turning me around to face him.

As I straddled Smoky's back, pressing against his sides with my knees to keep my balance, Vanzir leaned forward, backing me up till I lay flush against Smoky's opalescent scales. Vanzir rested on top of me, his hips pressing against me between my legs, his lips kissing me so deeply that I felt myself falling. The passion built, threatening to engulf me. Suddenly worried, I felt for my fangs with the tip of my tongue, but they stayed retracted.

"They won't come down unless you want them to," Vanzir whispered. "When you fuck another demon—a real demon— you'll find it easier to keep control of your nature. And I won't automatically try to drain you like I normally would someone who isn't of demon heritage."

"You try to drain me, and that collar you wear beneath your neck will kill you immediately," I said, but he brushed aside my comment as his lips met mine again, and he pressed hard against me, his fingers reaching for my zipper.

I wanted him. I wanted to strip naked and fuck right there on Smoky's back, but we were headed into battle. We'd need all our energy, all our senses.

"No, we have to be ready for battle. We can't do this here—now. But later, I want you." I pushed against his chest, feeling his heartbeat. It wasn't like a normal pulse. As I gazed into Vanzir's eyes, his lip twitched, and he slowly extended his tongue and flicked my nose.

"I know," he said, smirking. "Don't you ever lie again about how you feel. We're both demons. Leave falsehoods for those who can't take what they want, who don't possess the power to tear life apart at the seams. We can share this together without worrying about stealing life from our partners."

As he eased up, I pulled away and stared into his eyes. "I thought you weren't into women," I said. "You know I'm with Nerissa."

"I also know you and Rozurial have something going on. As for you and women—so what? I'm like you. I pick my partners based on who I'm attracted to, not what equipment they come with." A veiled cloud passed over his face. "Karvanak wasn't my choice. He reamed me repeatedly. But he's dead now, and I hope he spiraled into oblivion. But just because he abused me, doesn't mean I don't fancy a pretty boy now and then."

And then I understood what he meant. We *were* two of a kind, on more than one level. We'd both been tortured at the hands of sadistic assholes. I'd probably had it worse—Dredge had forever shifted my nature, but that didn't mean that Vanzir wasn't sporting hidden scars. True, he'd been a demon already, but he'd also been trying to sublimate his instincts. Karvanak had used that against him.

I touched his hand gently. "We *are* alike. And yet . . . remember this: Most of our comrades have been through hell of one sort or another. Delilah didn't ask to be turned into a Death Maiden. Camille's always been the anchor for everybody else and their traumas, and one of her oath lovers is missing. Rozurial watched his family get torn apart by Dredge, and then the gods ripped his marriage to shreds. Even Chase—Karvanak gave him a taste of his torturous ways. We aren't that special, Vanzir. We just understand one another."

"Heads up!" Smoky's voice echoed over his shoulder. "Looks like the incubus and Camille found something!"

I swung around, once again straddling Smoky face forward. His sinuous neck bobbed to the side, giving us a bird's-eye view of something that struck a nasty, nasty chord in my gut.

The Karsetii clones were there, yes, aimed at a black portal that had a series of runes inscribed in blue flame across it. I recognized the runes; they were demonic, and the last place I'd seen them had been on a poster on Larry's wall.

"Shit—a demonic portal?" Who knew what else could get through that thing.

"Not just a portal," Vanzir said, his grip around my waist tightening. But the passion of moments before had vanished. He was all business now. "That's a Demon Gate."

"What the fuck? Who opened it?" I stared at the runes as they flickered in the astral breeze. Camille and Roz had stopped short and were staring at the thing from a distance as the Karsetii clones headed toward it.

"I don't know, but it wasn't cast right," Vanzir said. "This one . . . the runes are out of sequence. Whoever cast this is a fool. There's no control attached to it—no method for commanding whatever comes through."

"Then the Karsetii was summoned. But whoever did the summoning—"

"Whoever did the summoning," Vanzir said slowly, "has no control over the creatures they've commanded in. And the gate's still active and open."

"And who knows what's waiting for us on the other side."

Smoky grunted as we headed in for a landing. As we touched down, Vanzir and I leapt off and raced over to Camille and Roz. Smoky shimmered, and within a brilliant flash, he was standing there in all his glory. His hair automatically began to braid as we watched the Karsetii clones, who scurried for the Demon Gate. Bright light of any form seemed to bother them.

As they scooted through the gate, I studied the runes, paying particular attention to how a couple of them had been drawn. Whoever set this up had to have drawn them in blood with a quill pen; that's how a Demon Gate was usually set up. And usually, the canvas for the runes was dried skin from a sentient being—human if we were dealing with human wizards, Fae if we were dealing with Fae sorcerers.

Vanzir cocked his head. "Look. The rune on the left. That one usually calls out to the *creatures from the fires*, but it's off, just by a fraction of an inch."

"What's that mean?" Camille asked. "Morio and I haven't gotten far enough into our study of demonic magic for me to read them clearly."

"The curved line there—it's supposed to curve in, not out. The shift changes the meaning to *creatures from the depths*." Vanzir shook his head. "Sloppy work. Whoever did this is no first-rate wizard, I'll tell you that much."

And then I knew. I knew who'd drawn this. "I've seen this mistake before. On the poster on Larry's wall and on Larry's ankle. He has a tattoo of that rune. Harold and the Dante's

Hellions—they have to be the ones who summoned the Karsetii!"

Camille sputtered. "Dante's Hellions? So that's how come they smell of Demonkin! Why the hell are they summoning demons?"

"I don't know, but we'd better find out. Because even if we shut down this gate, chances are they'll just open up another one, and who knows what the fuck they're going to call in next time?"

As we stared at the Demon Gate, a low, rumbling noise filled the mists. My stomach flipped. "We've got trouble," I said. "Can you feel it coming?"

Vanzir and Camille nodded, and we all stepped back from the gate. We were just in time. As the rumbling increased, a huge Karsetii—four times the size of the ones we'd been fighting—appeared through the gate.

"It's Big Mama, folks. I think she's come to play ball."

Camille pulled out her unicorn horn. "Batter up," she said, just as the Karsetii swiveled her way and began barreling down on her.

CHAPTER 19

"Holy crap!" I leapt toward Camille as she stumbled back. "Move! Now!"

She spun around, racing like the wind away from the demon, which was careening at full tilt toward her. Either it sensed her magical energy or the energy of the horn. Whatever the case, it aimed itself at her, tentacles streaming behind it. No lumbering movements here. The thing sailed through the air like a real squid swimming through water.

Smoky was instantly on its tail, shifting into full dragon form again as he hurled himself at the creature. Rozurial pulled out a long silver sword and headed into the fray, with Vanzir on his heels. I decided to help Camille. She might be able to run faster than me out on the astral, but I was still stronger. I raced to the front of the squid and leapt in between them.

The Karsetii was rumbling at me, full throttle. I waited. It could ram me a good one, but it couldn't suck out any life energy from me because—guess what?—I didn't have any.

As it loomed large, slowing by a fraction of a second, I ducked and spun, kicking with every ounce of strength I had as it zoomed overhead. My foot met it square in the eye, and I heard a shriek. Even though the impact jarred me to the core, it wasn't as rough as hitting its incarnations. It occurred to me that perhaps they were part of the hive mother's defense; maybe the demon was more vulnerable in person than its "children" were.

The Karsetii let out another shriek. I rolled out from under it, arching my back to leap back to a standing position. Smoky was on it now, and he had the bulbous brain of the demon in his gigantic mouth, shaking it like a dog might shake a rat. I stepped back, both impressed and wary. Smoky in attack mode at any time was impressive, but when he was in full dragon form, whoa Mama, he was a mean sucker.

I heard Camille gasp, then she yelled, "Menolly, run like hell. I'm going to fry this thing with fire."

I ran. I ran so hard I almost tripped over Roz, who was darting around, looking for an opening in which to attack. Vanzir was just standing there, arms folded across his chest, watching the fight.

I raced past him, and he knocked me to the ground, shielding me with his body. I had the feeling the move wasn't entirely altruistic, but I wasn't complaining. Anything to keep me from becoming a crispy critter at the hands of my sister's wayward magic.

"Smoky—move!" Her voice echoed through the mists as she held up the horn. I gather he moved, because she let out some sort of incantation, and a heat wave ripped through the area. The Karsetii let out a piercing scream and—from my prone position—I saw a flaming ball of demon squid barreling through the Demon Gate. The gate pulsated then fell silent.

As I pushed myself to a sitting position, I saw that Camille was covered with soot and slime. She grimaced, and I realized that not only had she been blasted by fallout, she'd been burnt. I raced over to her, but Smoky was there first. She moaned as he lifted her into his arms.

"She's got burns on her arms and legs. They don't look life-threatening, but they probably hurt like hell, and they're going to need attention before she gets infected," he said.

"Take her back over. We're already at the FH-CSI. They'll

be able to treat her right there. Meanwhile," I glanced back at Roz. "Roz will have to shift me over."

"No. He's not that good at shielding. He can take Vanzir but not you. All of you wait here," Smoky said, then vanished with Camille.

I dropped to the ground. I wasn't tired, but all of this chaos had left me reeling. "I hate this. We don't know if the thing's dead—"

"It's not," Vanzir said. "But it's severely wounded."

"Great. So we've got a wounded demon on our tail. And we've got a group of college kids opening Demon Gates. And my sister's hurt . . . again." I glanced up at Roz, who held out his hand. I took it, and he pulled me to my feet.

"There's nothing you can do about it now," he said, moving closer. Vanzir just watched, a bemused look on his face.

I wasn't sure what to do. In the course of one day, I'd decided to sleep with both of them, and now what? It wasn't that I felt any sense of guilt or worry; if they got their noses in a snit, too bad. At this point, my heart belonged to Nerissa, if anybody. But how was I going to work this? Somehow Camille's bed seemed to expand with every addition of another lover. I wasn't sure I wanted *anybody* sharing my bed. I might share theirs, but I didn't want long commitments or ménages. One partner per session was more than enough for me.

Just then, Smoky stepped onto the astral again. "Come, Menolly. I'll take you over."

As I moved toward him, Roz and Vanzir vanished. Smoky stopped me. "We need to talk a moment now that they're gone."

"What's going on?" He sounded so serious that he had me worried.

"You are making a mistake if you sleep with the demon," he said.

"Which one?" I asked. "I'm a demon. Roz is a minor demon, too. And Vanzir—"

"I'm speaking of Vanzir. Rozurial is an incubus, and while I find him annoying, he's basically helpful and listens to reason. Vanzir may be bound to you and your sisters, but he's still wild. Think twice before opening yourself to him. The vulnerability may be more than you care to risk."

As he stared down at me, I saw a kindly streak flash through his eyes. Usually, Smoky treated Delilah and me like hangers-on. Oh, he was nice enough, but if it weren't for Camille, we knew very well he wouldn't be helping us. But *this* expression—it almost read as caring.

"Why are you telling me this? Why do you care?"

He laughed then, low and throaty. "You are my wife's sister. So now you are also *my sister*. Families matter to dragons. And so I protect my family—all of you. Come, Menolly. Let's get back to the infirmary and see how Camille is doing. I want her to stay safe, if she's to be the mother to my children."

"What?" I stared at him. "Camille can't interbreed with dragons!"

He grinned. "There are ways. Trust me, there are ways around the problem. But for now—no talk of it. She doesn't need anything else to worry about right now. That's for the future."

As he enfolded me in his arms, I was stunned at his little announcement, yet things were much clearer. Smoky had claimed Camille. He may not be her only lover or husband, but he took his claim seriously.

Delilah and I also had a claim on her. Therefore, since we were bound to Camille, we were bound to Smoky, and in a way I'd never expected him to accept. And Morio probably felt the same way—and Trillian, too, which is why he'd been helping us out. Feeling less alone, I closed my eyes as we shifted off the astral, back to Camille's side.

Camille was sitting on a table, wincing as Sharah tended to her burns. The red had faded somewhat, and I could see they were superficial but still painful.

"You won't scar, not if we get this ointment on and pump you full of tegot tincture," Sharah was saying. The tegot plant was a natural antibiotic that worked wonders on both Fae and mortal alike. "Meanwhile, you rest for twenty-four hours and stay out of trouble. You can't risk spreading the damage any further."

"But Menolly needs me—" Camille started to say.

"Stop," Morio said, his voice firm. "Delilah can help Menolly now that the Karsetii is gone. It might come back, but you can be sure it will take awhile to heal and regroup after what Roz told me you did to it."

"The fox is right," Smoky said, pushing through to her side. "You will rest tonight, and if you don't, I'll tie you up and leave you in bed."

"Like that would be anything new," Morio said, grinning. "But don't sweat it, Camille. We'll help Menolly, too. All of us."

"Not everyone. Someone has to stay home and protect Iris and Maggie and Camille, since she can't fight." I looked at the men standing there. "Morio, you stay with her. Smoky and Roz can shift over to the astral plane, and we may need their skills in that department. Vanzir knows Demonkin. So that leaves you on the sidelines this time."

Morio nodded. "No problem."

"Okay, first things first. We know that Harold Young is summoning demons. We've got to sneak into that place and see what they've got hidden in there." I glanced at the clock. Midnight. "We have time. Let's swing by the bar, grab Delilah, and head out. Harold won't be expecting us again, and with our luck, he and his buddies will be out partying."

"I'll see that Camille and Morio get home," Chase said. "Give Delilah a kiss for me."

Smoky, Vanzir, and Roz fell in behind me as we headed out the door. It was time to get some answers and start putting this puzzle together.

Delilah jumped a mile high when I unlocked the panic room door. She'd been lounging on the sofa, scarfing a bag of Cheetos and watching a DVD, Jack Black's *School of Rock*. Yeah, that was my Kitten, all right. She dusted her hands on her jeans, leaving a bright orange smudge, and broke into a wide grin.

"Did you get it? Can I come out?" She grabbed me and gave me a tight squeeze before I could disentangle myself.

"Well, we didn't kill it, but it's gone for now, because Camille fried its ass. But we've got work to do. Get your coat and come on." On the way, I filled her in on what was going down—or at least everything we knew.

"So, the Dante's Hellions are the ones responsible for the current mayhem," she said.

"Yeah. And they're real whack-jobs."

"How are we going to work this?" Delilah glanced back at the men. "No offense guys, but Menolly and I are a lot quieter than you are. We can sneak in, no problem, but you get to clunking around there, and we're going to have a mess on our hands."

Smoky harrumphed but remained silent. Roz sighed. Vanzir just snickered.

"Here's what we'll do." I parked the car a block away from the house. "You and I will sneak in. Meanwhile, the three of you . . . oh hell, we may need you to fight, but Delilah's right. We all can't sneak in there until we know what's on tap. Stay close to the house and keep an eye out for trouble." I didn't like splitting up, but Delilah was right. We'd never get in there with these three. The bickering alone was worse than a gaggle of geese.

"I don't like it," Roz said. "We've snuck into places before—like the place with the venidemons—"

"Excuse me," I said, "but you did not sneak into that house. From what I heard, you barged in, tore through the joint, and ended up alerting every creature that was there. For this operation, we require subtlety. You three remain on watch and use your common sense." I gave them a second look and shook my head. "Whatever scraps you can scare up between the lot of you."

We climbed out of the car and headed toward the frat house, keeping to the shadows. Somehow, Smoky managed to hide, even with his brilliant white clothes. Of course, the Moon was nearing full, splashing her light on everything and everybody around.

We skirted the house, looking for any way in from the

outside other than the front door. After a moment Roz pointed to the left side of the back porch. A door led beneath the porch steps. *Bingo.*

"Okay, you guys keep your eyes open and stay out of sight." I quietly opened the door and peeked in. The cubby-hole was about ten inches taller than me at its highest, right against the house. I motioned for Delilah to watch her head, then slipped into the opening. She followed suit and closed the door behind her.

While neither of us could actually see in the dark, our natures made us much more attuned to dim light. A splash of moonlight washed through the steps, and in the silver glow, the broken beams showed us the outline of another door, this one leading directly beneath the house.

I tugged at it. There was a padlock holding it shut. I was about to break it when Delilah held up her hand. She pulled out a playing card–sized case from her pocket and quickly picked the lock. Opening the door, I slipped through, and she followed me.

While I'd expected to find a typical crawl space, I hadn't counted on an opening in the floor that was obviously well-used. An attached ladder offered access, and I peeked down into the hole to find it led to a tunnel, approximately ten feet down. The tunnel appeared empty, so we scrambled down the rungs.

Two strings of Christmas tree lights ran along the passage, one near the ceiling, which was about seven feet high, and the other near the floor, which was compacted dirt that had been covered with wood planks.

I hesitated, motioning for Delilah to stand still, then listened as hard as I could. Delilah was listening, too; her ears had perked up, and her eyes were closed. She was probably smelling the air, too. Together we made a good team, though Camille with her sense of all things magical didn't hurt us any, either.

"You hear anything?" I whispered.

Delilah shook her head. "No. Nothing."

I nodded. "Okay, then. Let's get a move on." I cautiously made sure that I kept to the wooden boards. Who knew what was hiding in the crannies between them? Viro-mortis slimes made their home in the area. And there were other creatures— not all necessarily magical—that could pack a punch. Hobo spiders for one thing, and rats.

As we picked our way along the tunnel, I wondered how long this had been here. Harold may have taken over the house four or five years ago, but the tunnel itself—even the wood used to make the walkway—looked far older. The dirt walls were hardened, compacted in a way that only time could produce.

As if reading my mind, Delilah whispered, "I can sense age here. Age and . . . death. A lot of death." She shivered. "I don't like this, Menolly. There's been a lot of pain soaked into the land here. Camille could probably feel it more than I can, but it's so strong that it practically reeks."

I closed my eyes, trying to sense what she was talking about. Usually, I drew a blank, but this time a few things did filter in: energies I was familiar with. The scent of spilled blood—both old and fresh. The ripple of Demonkin energy in the air. The subtle flow of a breeze that told me we were headed for a large chamber where the air was circulating.

"Come on," I said, motioning to her. We descended along the sloping passage. I tried to estimate how far belowground we were. We had to be at least fifteen to twenty feet below the house, but I had the feeling we hadn't reached the bottom. How was the foundation staying put? Or was this like some cockeyed basement?

The tunnel came to a halt at a T. It turned to the left and then curved toward the right, spiraling down like a conch shell. I looked to the left and, remembering the layout of the house on the lot, figured that it would take us under the street in front of the house.

"Sewer?" Delilah whispered.

Of course! I motioned for her to stay put and jogged down the tunnel, only to find myself facing a door. I cautiously opened it just a crack, and sure enough, the smell of sewage filtered through. A glance toward the roof showed rungs lead- ing up to . . . yep . . . a manhole. So this part of the tunnel gave them access to the streets from below.

I hurried back to where Delilah was waiting and reported my findings to her.

"But why would they need it? Why not just use the front door?" she asked.

"Maybe they don't need to use it. Maybe whoever lived here before had some reason for it? It occurs to me that it would make the perfect way for a predator to come and go. Maybe a serial killer."

Delilah shivered. "I don't like that thought. This group is bad enough."

"Yeah, well, remember their families contained a number of members, all belonging to Dante's Hellions." I wondered how far back this whole setup went into Harold Young's family traditions. His uncle had owned the house and Harold had to learn those demonic rites from *somebody*. Somehow, I didn't think years of playing Dungeons & Dragons or Diablo had been of much use in that department.

I motioned to the right, and we headed down the spiral. Delilah reached out and touched my arm.

"One minute. My cell phone's on vibrate, and I'm getting a call. I can't believe it's working down here. They must have some sort of technical setup to receive calls belowground." She answered, speaking in low tones. "Yeah, we're fine. So far, so good." She quickly described where we were, and I realized that either Smoky or Roz had called her. After a moment she hung up. "Smoky. Wants to know why we haven't checked in."

"Oh good gods, he really *does* consider himself our big brother," I said, grimacing.

Delilah laughed softly. "Actually, I kind of like it."

"Yeah, you would." I flashed her a grin. "Okay, let's go find out what's at the end of these stairs."

We coiled downward, the tunnel now a true circular stairwell, the shaft dug straight out of the dirt. As we came to the end, I could see a metal door leading into what was probably another tunnel.

By now, I'd lost track of how far we were beneath the ground, but the airflow seemed fairly brisk, so the place had to be well-ventilated. I glanced up at the ceiling, looking for vents. Sure enough, running along the wall, spaced every ten feet or so on the way up, ran a series of ducts. Whoever had built this underground lair had been serious. And they must have had money.

I paused at the bottom of the stairs and quickly stepped back against the side of the wall. Delilah joined me. We waited, listening. In the distance, the faint cadence of voices rose and fell. I couldn't tell just how far away they were, but I was ready to assume they were up to no good and therefore worthy of caution. I pressed my ear against the door then, but nothing filtered in from directly on the other side. With a glance at Delilah, who nodded her head, I carefully turned the wheel and opened the door a whisper.

A silent wash of air rushed past us, and I peeked through. The tunnel I had been imagining wasn't there.

Instead, I found myself staring at the metal walls of an underground complex. Faint lights—like the Christmas tree ones, only round—ran along the ceiling in two strings. The corridor led straight ahead, and I could see doors spaced along the wall farther down.

Shit. We'd landed in something big, all right. Or something that had been big. It was hard to tell which. Whatever the case, the echo of voices from up ahead—faint but definite—told us that the place hadn't been abandoned. And whatever those voices were chanting gave me the creeps.

Delilah tapped me on the shoulder. She nodded to the hallway, and I shrugged. We'd come this far. We might as well take a look at what the Dante's Hellions were up to.

CHAPTER 20

The chanting was either in Latin or some other archaic language, and the sounds of medieval instruments joined in the harmony. As the music wove through the hallways, it pulled me in. The melody echoed through the halls like a haunted drumbeat, and the voices set me on edge.

Delilah leaned toward me, her breathing rapid and shallow. "I don't like this."

"Hold tight, Kitten. We can't afford for you to transform here," I whispered. "You'd bolt, and I'd never find you." She looked on the verge of shifting, and the thought of a twelve-pound golden tabby by my side didn't bode well for a fight. *Not* the best battle companion.

"I know. It's the music. I can feel it penetrating my body, like mist on an autumn night." She shivered.

I took hold of her hand and squeezed. She smiled faintly.

"Let's go just a little farther down the corridor and see what we can find out," I suggested.

There was nowhere to hide from here on out. We'd have to dart down the corridor and hope nobody saw us. I pointed to the first door on the left. "Let's try for that room. We can hide in there if we hear somebody coming." I just hoped the room was empty, or we'd be paying one hell of a surprise visit to somebody.

We dashed, racing silently for the door. I paused just long enough to press my ear to the steel but heard nothing. I swung the door open. As we stepped in, the darkness was so thick it clouded my sight, but at least I couldn't sense anybody else in here with us nor see any heat signatures. The room smelled musty, old, and unused.

I closed the door softly as Delilah slid in behind me and waited a beat . . . two beats. No sound. "You have a flashlight?"

She didn't answer, but within seconds, the pen-sized flashlight she kept on her keychain cut a swath into the darkness. It wasn't a regular-sized torch, by any stretch of the imagination, but it was stronger than the dime-store variety. We glanced around the room. So far, so good. Nobody stirring.

And then Delilah froze, her beam capturing the far wall in its glow. There were three sets of manacles on the walls, and a body hung from one set of manacles. The others were empty, but beneath an empty set lay a pile of dust and some clothing.

"Oh shit. Oh no," I said as we slowly approached. I knelt by the clothing, and Delilah flashed the light in my direction. Jeans, a pretty red blouse. Women's clothing, about a size eight. As I shifted the cloth around, ashes scattered from the folds of the material. I knew exactly what kind of ashes they were.

"Vampire. They had a vampire chained in here, and they dusted her." And I'd bet my fangs on who it had been.

I turned my attention to the other body. She was naked and long dead. Partially mummified, she'd been an elf. And she'd been petite, pretty, and in pain—that much was clear from the expression on her face. A few of her fingers were missing, roughly chopped off, and a gaping hole in her chest gave me the shivers. As I gazed at the weathered skin and features, my heart dropped.

"Oh great Bastus." Delilah must have been thinking along the same lines I had. "Sabele?"

I nodded. "We can't know for sure, not yet. But . . . yeah,

I think so. And that—" I pointed to the pile of ashes. "That was Claudette, the vampire Chase told me was missing. Dante's Hellions have just crossed the line from wing nuts to murderers." I examined Sabele's body. "They took her heart. It's missing."

Delilah winced. "Goddamn pricks. They aren't connected with the Corpse Talkers, do you think?"

"Unlikely." I slowly shook my head. "A number of demonic rituals call for body parts, especially the heart and blood. This is bad. *Really bad.* And considering what we've found, I think we need to get the hell out of here. We're treading in dangerous territory, and from the sound of that chanting, there are quite a few guys involved. Maybe they're just playing a record, but I don't want to find out without backup, even with my strength."

Delilah followed me to the door, where I peeked out before we slipped back down the hall. I wanted to take the remains with me, but that would alert the group that somebody had been here. Before we left, I used my cell phone to snap a couple of pictures, and then we were off. We lucked out on our way back up the passageway. Nobody heard us, nobody saw us.

As we slipped into the cubbyhole beneath the porch, fastened the padlock, and then emerged from the house, Smoky, Roz, and Vanzir were there, waiting. I pressed my finger to my lips and motioned toward the car. Talking could wait until we were home and all together. We'd want Camille in on this. Chase, too. We were dealing with FBHs. Murderers, yes, with connections to the Demonkin. But they were still human, and that meant we needed Chase's input.

On the way home, Delilah called Chase and asked him to meet us at the house. I could tell from the way she spoke, he'd been sleeping. The past couple of days had a been a blur of bodies and worry. The nights had felt unusually wearing, even for me, taken up with chasing the Karsetii and figuring out what the hell Harold and his crew were up to.

After she finished talking to Chase, Delilah put a call in to Iris, who apparently had also been in bed.

"We'll be home in twenty minutes or less. Can you make a snack? We're famished. And wake up Camille. We'll need to fill her in on what's going on."

I pressed on the gas pedal and felt Camille's engine roar to life, eating up the pavement. The Lexus had power, that was for sure.

"Iris is making a second dinner," Delilah said, licking her lips.

I grinned. All the Fae ate like fiends, at least as far as humans were concerned, and most of us never gained an ounce. I'd been forced to give up eating once I was turned, but I still missed the meals my mother had cooked for us. Even only being half-Fae, my sisters ran up one hell of a food bill, and I knew perfectly well that Camille wasn't above using her glamour to cadge a cutthroat price on prime steak or expensive berries from the butcher and grocer.

The wards were shining clear and unbroken as we headed up the drive. The house was ablaze with lights, a welcoming sight after our trip through Harold in Wonderland's house. Iris had lit the porch with Christmas lights, weaving a Faerie dance with their twinkling colors. Leave it to her to think of little touches like that. Their warmth was so different from the stark white lights of the tunnel.

As we trudged through the door, the smells of cooking blasted me. As we burst into the kitchen, where Camille sat in the rocking chair, her legs propped up and loosely bandaged, Iris was scurrying around, dressed in a sheer black nightgown with a light linen robe thrown over the top. Her hair was down, flowing around her ankles, and she was glowing. Hello, what did we have here? That was after-sex glow, if I was not mistaken.

The door to her bedroom, which was right off the kitchen, opened, and Bruce, the leprechaun, popped out to join us. He was a cutie, that was for sure: barely taller than Iris, lean, and with a shock of black hair that resembled polished onyx. His eyes were the brightest blue I'd ever seen, and he was wearing a short robe over what looked like satin pajama bottoms. Oho, so Iris and Bruce had made up their spat. I grinned at her, and she grinned back.

"What's for dinner?" Delilah said, not even noticing our guest.

Roz winked at Iris. "You little minx. You two-timing me?" he said, but he smiled as he waved to Bruce.

Smoky let out a harrumph. "Watch out, Bruce, or this one will try to muscle in on your territory." He thumbed toward Roz. "If he needs a good thrashing, just let me know. I'm always up for that job." Though he smiled, there was a look in the dragon's eyes that told me he wasn't joking.

The doorbell rang, and Delilah ran to answer it, returning with Chase. I motioned to the table. "Everybody make themselves comfortable. If you want food, raise your hand so Iris can see. We've got some things to discuss, and they aren't very pretty."

Everyone scrambled for a seat. Smoky and Morio sat next to Camille, while Delilah parked her butt on Chase's lap. Roz and Bruce were helping Iris pull together the quick spaghetti dinner she'd made, and I took my usual place, hovering slightly out of reach above the table. Vanzir and I were the only ones not eating, and he squatted near Maggie's playpen. She was nowhere to be seen—no doubt still asleep in Iris's room.

"Here's the deal," I said as they began passing around the platter of spaghetti and the French bread dripping with butter and Parmesan. Out of respect for me, Iris had forgone the garlic except for the barest whiff of it.

"Delilah and I found Sabele's body. And," I turned to Chase, "I found out what happened to Claudette. Harold's gang killed them both, or so it looks."

"Shit," Chase muttered, setting down his chunk of bread and reaching for his notebook.

"Eat. You can make notes later," Iris said, leaning over to tap him on the hand. She and Bruce were sitting on barstools that raised them high enough to the table so they weren't dwarfed by everyone else. Chase flashed her a smile, put away his pen, and picked up his fork.

We described our jaunt through the underground labyrinth. "Nobody built that complex in just the few years Harold's been living there," I said. "It's a lot older than that. We didn't have time to check out the rest of it, but I think there has to be a ritual chamber in there. They have to have someplace from which to summon the demons, but I'd like to know a little more before we go in."

"There's not much more we can do but just dive in feet-first," Camille said. "You can bet they aren't going to have the blueprints for a secret demon-gating chamber at City Hall. But . . . I wonder—Delilah, can you fire up your computer and see if you can find out anything on the house itself? If it's old, maybe there's information about who owned it before Harold's uncle? Something that will tell us who they were and if they were also involved with Dante's Hellions. Maybe a predecessor of the group?"

Delilah nodded, her mouth full. She'd taken the chair next to Chase as soon as the food was being doled out. One thing he'd learned quickly about Kitten: She was territorial of her food. If she offered to share, no problem, but until she'd made the offer, Camille never snagged a bite off her plate. Chase had learned the hard way, and I'd been there to witness the scratches he received for his trouble before Delilah could stop herself.

"That's a good idea," I said. "Chase, can you look into the records to see if any members of Dante's Hellions other than Harold have been arrested? Their parents, too. Especially their fathers and brothers."

"I can have that to you by tomorrow night at the latest," he said.

"Great. The more information we're armed with, the better." I thought for a moment. "Vanzir—can you get us in to speak with your demon friend Carter? I want to ask him if he knows about other demons unconnected to Shadow Wing who showed up over the past . . . say . . . one hundred years near Harold's house. Especially oddball ones."

He nodded. "I think he'd be willing. You want me to head out now?"

"No, wait till tomorrow." I frowned. "What else? Are we overlooking anything else?"

"How about a return visit to Harish? If we can pinpoint when Harold started hassling Sabele, maybe that will help?

And where did he meet Claudette? The Hellions sure wouldn't be given an invitation to the Clockwork Club." Camille sat up. "Chase, while you're at it, look into any other missing person reports of Fae or Supe women. Or even FBHs who live in the vicinity of Harold's house. Look back through the files for a number of years. The manacles on the wall do not bode well for the female population."

I snapped my fingers. "The girl—Larry and Duane were talking about spiking her drink. I wonder if we can trace her down."

"Probably not, unless someone went missing, but it gives us an idea of how they work. But the vampire—vampires aren't affected by drugs, and they only drink blood, so how'd they get hold of Claudette?" Chase bit into his bread, wiping the butter from his chin.

"There are ways to control us," I said. "Silver chains, garlic ropes . . . it can be done."

Camille let out a sigh. "We've got too many questions and not enough answers."

I glanced at the clock. It was nearing four A.M. Not enough time for me to go out on the prowl, and both Camille and Delilah were looking rough around the edges. "We'll have to take this up tomorrow. Delilah, even though we chased off the Karsetii, I think you should spend the rest of the night in the panic room—"

"No." She swallowed the last of her spaghetti and downed a glass of milk. "I'm not going to be locked up like some precious china statue. We have to take a stand somewhere, and I'm making mine here. You wounded it pretty bad. My guess is that the thing will have to regenerate before it comes back."

Camille cleared her throat. "We can't make her go."

We could—or rather, *I could*—but I wouldn't. I gave her a quiet nod. "All right, it's your choice, but sleep lightly."

"I'll stay with her," Chase said. "If anything happens, I'll wake Camille and . . ." He glanced at Morio and Smoky, both of whom were sitting by her side. "And you guys."

"I'd feel better if you had somebody in the room who could hop over to the astral without waiting. Vanzir, sleep right outside Delilah's door, if you would. We'll fix up a cot for you. That way Chase can alert you before he has to run all the way down to the second floor."

"No need for a cot," he said. "I'm fine with a sleeping bag."

"I've got one in my room," Delilah said. "It's got a lot of padding."

Once we had things sorted out, Bruce and Iris, both of whom had listened silently to the whole discussion, slipped away to her bedroom. Smoky gathered up Camille and carried her up to her room, followed by Morio. Delilah and Chase headed upstairs behind them, Vanzir swinging in behind.

Rozurial sat there, watching as the room emptied. After a moment, we were the only two left in the kitchen. I had hoped it would work out this way. I looked over at him. Without a word, he stood and took off his duster. He draped it over one of the chairs, then put his hat on the table.

He looked *so good*—not terribly tall, but dark curls draping down his back, his pale face dusky with the faintest shadow of stubble. His muscles gleamed under the black tank, and his jeans fit snugly around thighs that promised they could wrap around me like no one else's could.

Roz opened his arms, and I walked into his embrace as he leaned down, letting his lips linger against mine, holding me firmly.

"Take me," I whispered, wanting to wipe away the images of the dead Sabele and the ashes that had been Claudette. "Take me, carry me away from myself. Get me out of my head."

"My pleasure," he whispered. And he led me into the parlor.

Though Rozurial knew I was scarred, as I slipped out of my jeans and top, I wondered what he would say. Would he grimace in that polite, concerned manner that people had when they caught sight of the marks Dredge had carved into my skin? Would he still want me? I folded my jeans over the edge of the sofa and turned around, ready to get it over with if he suddenly changed his mind.

But there he was, staring at me, delight and desire playing across his face. He slowly licked his lips, a twinkle in his eye cluing me in to the fact that, *oh yes*—despite my scars— Rozurial was going to lay his hands on me. And I *wanted* his hands on me. I *wanted* him to touch me.

He took a step forward, then paused. "Is there anything I should know?" he said quietly. "I've never bedded a vampire before. And I've never . . . I don't know what triggers might bring up bad memories. Tell me what I shouldn't do. Then tell me what you want me to do."

His restraint surprised me. The scent of his pheromones was musky and overwhelming. I wanted to race across the room and straddle him, taking him down below me. I felt for my fangs, checking to see if they were extending, but all I felt were teeth. Normal teeth. Could it be that Vanzir was right? If I slept with demons, would it help me hold back my instincts to bite? I'd kissed Roz before, and I remembered wanting to drink from him, but something had shifted—something was different.

I thought over what he said. When I was with Nerissa, she knew instinctively what to do, and her instincts were very, very good. But I'd only been with one man since Dredge, and that had been during a ritual, so this was new territory for me. Almost as new as my very first time.

"Let me be on top until I'm comfortable with you," I said. "Don't ever hold my hands down. I can't let myself be bound."

"Okay," Roz said, gently moving another step toward me. "What about touching you? Anywhere off-limits?"

Tilting my head, I swallowed as he ran his gaze over me. "Don't trace over where he carved his name on me. Don't give it importance."

And I showed him, then, where Dredge had used one intensely sharp fingernail to write his name in my flesh across my mound of Venus. He'd laughed and said, "I own you. You belong to me," and I'd known that I'd never be free from him. The scar was eternal, and there was no way to get rid of it. If I'd been alive, perhaps plastic surgery, but it wouldn't work on me in vampire form. Nerissa had suggested a tattoo, and I was researching the idea to see how tattoos reacted on vampires.

Roz glanced at the scar, his gaze lingering for a moment before he shook his head. "He's dust and ashes, in the grips of his master. Nobody owns you now. No matter what scars you bear, no matter what world you walk in. You belong to yourself, Menolly. That's one of the things I love about you. You're a warrior. You don't flinch. You do what you need to, and you answer to no one."

And then he slid off his boots and drew his tank over his head. His chest gleamed with a thatch of curly dark hair running down the center, lightly dappling his abs. I had never seen him without a shirt, and his wide-set shoulders were honed, tight and rounded with muscle.

He reached for his belt buckle and shook his head when I would have helped him. "Let me undress for you." He unbuckled the silver latch and drew the belt out of the loops, the sound of leather sliding on denim sending a shiver through me. He dropped it next to his shirt. And then his fingers were on his fly, and he unzipped, pushing his jeans down his thighs to the floor before stepping out of them.

I found myself suddenly shy. If I could have blushed, I would have, but instead, I chanced a look out of the corner of my eye. Rozurial stood there, a bodybuilder without extremes, his V-waist perfectly balancing out his shoulders and thighs, and at that tip of that delicate V, his cock stood ready, at attention, thick and throbbing. Mesmerized, my gaze climbed to meet his eyes. Passion rolled off of him with the promise of sweet honey wine on a warm night.

"It's true what they say. Even *I* can feel it. No wonder men hate you." I could see it in his eyes. Women would throw themselves at his feet, legs open, welcoming him in. And they wouldn't regret it. "How many women have pined for you, after you left them?"

Roz shrugged. "I don't know. I won't lie to you. You know what I am. Over the past seven centuries I've had thousands of women. I've kissed them and fucked them and left them begging for more. I love women, Menolly," he said softly. "*All types of women.* Tall, short, thin, fat, young, old . . . it doesn't matter. I crave them. That's *what* I am. That's *who* I am. I have no choice; this is my nature. The only kind of women that I don't find attractive are those who are timid, who wait for a man to make them feel whole."

"I know. Just like . . . this is *my* nature." I opened my mouth slightly and willed my fangs to unfurl. He watched, unafraid, unmoving. "I drink blood. I charm and seduce my way into feeding on my dinner. Vanzir was right; all demons are takers, aren't they?"

"But we also give," Roz said, and then he was standing only a few inches away, his breath soft against my skin. "Let me give to you. And you . . . I want you to give yourself to me. Let's find out where this takes us?"

I nodded, then. He wrapped me in his arms, lifting me up, and my lips were fastened on his. I retracted my fangs and fully kissed him, my tongue sliding into his mouth as he pressed against me, his cock a rigid soldier. Roz lowered me to the ground, and the world blurred.

He darted across my body with his lips, butterfly kissing me as he swung around, lowering himself to let me fasten my mouth around him. I sucked deeply, the shaft of flesh sliding in and out between my lips, the taste of salt lingering in my mouth. As he moaned, a surge of power raced through me, and I licked harder, teasing the tip of his penis with my tongue as he forced himself to keep a steady pace.

Roz kissed my stomach, my chest, my nipples, between my thighs, his tongue cajoling me to fly. He was so different from Nerissa—not better, not worse—just different.

With a quick turn, he was suddenly above me, hands on my waist, flipping me over as he rolled beneath me. I climbed atop him, clasping his hands in my own to balance myself.

"Menolly," he whispered. "Ride me—ride me hard."

And so I did, my hips grinding down on him, as he thrust up to meet my descent. In silence, he bucked, raising me up, and I let my constant control slip away. I couldn't hurt him the way I could Nerissa—at least, not nearly so easily. My fangs stayed safely put. I closed my eyes as we rocked on the floor, my knees scraping the rug. And then, we were there—poised, ready for flight, and I realized that whatever else might be true, Rozurial and I were well-matched.

I shook away the thought and let myself slide, and the slide became a cascade, which became a raging river that raced to the edge, tumbling into the chasm. And for once, I let the current claim me without a fight.

CHAPTER 21

I shot to a sitting position, suddenly waking to sunset as the realization that someone was in the room with me filtered into my thoughts. Her heartbeat echoed with the continual pulse of the blood in her veins. Every scent was heightened, her phero-mones, her passion, the scent of the hamburger she'd had for lunch. A ravenous thirst welled up in my throat, and the crav-ing for blood swirled in my thoughts. I wanted to chase, to hunt, to—

"Hey, you're awake." Camille was sitting in the corner, reading the paper. She flashed me a big smile as I shook my-self out of my thoughts and forced myself to take a long breath, holding it for five beats as I slowly settled into myself. She must have heard me, because she said, "Thirsty? I'm sorry—I didn't know when you last drank, or I wouldn't have waited for you."

As I brought myself under control, I gave her a wan smile in return. "I should have had a drink before I slept this morn-ing. I'm sorry. I didn't mean to frighten you." I smiled. I'd been so occupied with Rozurial, I'd forgotten to take a drink before sleeping—something I always tried to remember. Because what had happened years before might just happen again if I wasn't careful.

A year after the OIA helped me regain my sanity, they decided that I'd developed enough self-control and allowed me to return home to live. Father wasn't pleased, but he'd allowed it. Where Delilah and he tiptoed around me, Camille accepted me back like nothing had happened. Or rather, like something had happened, but it was time to move on.

When I first returned home, none of us were used to all of the changes that were happening to me. Transitioning into a vampire takes time. Oh, the initial change is fairly quick, but learning the ropes can take years, especially when your sire's kicked you out into the world on your own.

One evening, Camille came in to see if I was up yet. She was standing right near the bed as I woke, thirsty and longing for the taste of blood in my mouth, and in my passion and thirst for blood, I didn't recognize her.

I grabbed her arm, dragging her toward me, raking the snowy white skin with my nails. As she screamed, I lowered myself to her wounds and began to suck hard, lapping at the sweet and salty taste of her life force.

"Menolly! Menolly!"

All it had taken were two cries to pull me out of my trance. The sight of her, bleeding and terror-stricken, stopped me short. Camille had saved me from killing the family. Camille had done her best to make me feel like part of the family still. And now, Camille was in my grasp, long gashes ragged and red on her arm and my chin was wet with her blood.

I dropped her wrist and slowly scooted back, cowering on my bed.

"Stake me. Just stake me now, before I hurt one of you." The smell of her blood was still calling me, but I pushed it away.

She wouldn't listen. "No. You can learn control. And I should have known better," she said, crossing the room to wrap a linen towel around her wounds. "Next time, I won't stand close enough for you to grab. How long do you need when you wake up?"

"What are you talking about?" I asked dully.

"How long do you need before you remember where you are?"

I thought about it, eyeing her closely. She looked nervous but not repulsed. And her expression told me she still loved me. "I don't know. A couple minutes. But I can't jump out of bed immediately. By the time I can stand up, I know where I am."

"So if I stay across the room, by the time you can get out of bed, you'll know it's me," she said as if it was all settled. "I'll tell everyone that the OIA let us know this would be safest. That way we don't have to explain how we found out."

I tried to protest, but she waved me off.

And from then on, nobody ever stood next to my bed when I was due to wake. And I'd never hurt anyone I loved again.

Camille still bore the scars from where I'd ripped her forearm, but she never used them against me. She told Father that she got them on the fence he erected to keep the deer out of the garden. The fence came down the next day. Delilah knew better, but Camille threatened to take away her catnip if she said anything. And to this day, Father still didn't know that I'd attacked Camille.

"How are your burns?" I asked.

She shrugged. "Healing. Most were superficial, and while they ache, I'll be fine. Sharah's tegot tincture works like a charm." As she spoke, she shifted her skirt so I could see her legs. They still looked bright pink, but she was healing up quickly. "Nerissa called," she added.

I glanced up at her, my heart thudding. I waited for a wave of guilt, but none came. What Roz and I'd done together didn't negate my feelings for Nerissa, just as I knew what she did with Venus the Moon Child or any other male lover wouldn't negate her feelings for me.

"What did she say?"

"She sends her love and wants to know if you can come

over to the compound a week from tonight. She's taking the next day off so you two can spend the entire night together." Camille's eyes were twinkling.

I grinned like an idiot. Nerissa never took a day off, and that she'd do so just to spend the entire night with me gave me a warm fuzzy feeling. Disconcerted—I didn't do warm fuzzy—I tried to brush it away, but I couldn't.

"She's a special woman," I said quietly.

"To take you on? I should say so." Camille rattled her paper and folded it into a square. "Andy Gambit is at it again."

"Shit, what's he written now?" I asked as I shimmied into a pair of jeans and a loose, long-sleeved, rose-colored blouse.

The *Seattle Tattler* was a rag, yellow journalism at its best, but since they often printed stories that included the Fae and Supes as primary targets, we subscribed and read it on a regular basis. Andy Gambit was, by far, the worst reporter on the staff. He was always taking potshots, at us in particular. His goal in life seemed to be focused on becoming one of the big-time paparazzi, but somehow he never quite crossed over to the level of the brightest and best busybodies of the world.

Camille gave me a long look. "You really want to know? It isn't pretty. In fact, it's a slam against all vampires. Hell, Weres, too."

"Oh wonderful. What has that prick got stuck in his craw now?" Knowing Andy, it could be anything.

Camille twisted her mouth in that peculiar way she had whenever something had set sour with her. She handed the paper to me. "Read it and weep."

I glanced at the headline. "Freedom's Angels Spread the Word: The Sordid Sex Secrets of Supes and Vamps." Uh-oh. I settled down to read as Camille made my bed and picked up my dirty clothes, tossing them in the hamper.

In a shocking revelation the Freedom's Angels, the premier moral compass group, have revealed new and sordid secrets about the creatures of the night. Dr. Shawn Little, a psychologist who volunteers his spare time to helping the group, has this to say about the

Earthborn who might contemplate entering into an intimate relationship with one of the demonic beings:

"Before ever letting one of the unnaturals touch you, bear in mind that if you enter into intimate relations with a vampire, you are—in essence—committing an act of necrophilia. We realize that the law doesn't see it our way, but morally, you are doing nothing more than having sex with a dead body that's been demonically reanimated.

"And should you decide to strike up a relationship with a Were creature, you are committing an act of bestiality. We urge all of the true Earthborn to resist any such temptations, to keep themselves pure, and not defile the temple of their body by cavorting with these unnatural creatures."

In related news, the Freedom's Angels have applied for recognition as an official nonprofit religious organization. They plan on erecting a temple that can hold ten thousand worshippers in Nevada. The church will be called the Brotherhood of the Earthborn and construction is expected to be finished before the year is out, regardless of the government conspiracy to cover up the truths revealed by the founders of the organization.

"Holy shit." I stared at the paper. "Why am I not surprised? They actually think they can attract enough people to fill that place?"

"Of course they can," Camille said, shaking her head. "We're fairly safe here, but there are plenty of people out there who think we all rode in on the train straight from Hel's domain. And they'd like nothing more than to drive us out again. Either that or stick us on top of a pyre and light the match."

"Hmm . . . wonder if they'll try to set up halfway houses for the blood whores. I wouldn't object if it were some other religion. Some *sane* religion."

While the ultra–right-wing Christians thought we were straight from the devil's lair, most of the mainstream denominations had found ways to coexist with us in a quiet truce.

Vampires had it harder than the Supes and Fae, definitely. The church's stance on the Fae and Supes had grown to encompass them as *beings of the universe* . . . a phrase now used by a number of religions as a catchall term instead of *humanity*. Vampires, though, they were still nebulous about. But mostly, as long as we didn't stir up too much trouble, the mainstream churches were content to live and let us live.

"So you and Roz sure had yourself a party this morning," Camille said as I tossed the paper on my desk and headed for the stairs. I stopped, turning around. She had a telltale smirk on her face.

"I should have known you'd find out," I said. "Yes, we had sex, and yes, it was good, and yes, he's all that incubi are cracked up to be. More so." And then, because I couldn't help it—and I knew she'd understand—I whispered, "He's got stamina, that's for sure."

She giggled. "So, you prefer Nerissa or him?"

"Apples and oranges. Or should I say, type O and type A. Can't really compare the two. And I'm not planning on giving up one for the other, nor am I planning on making a playdate with both of them at the same time, Ms. Harem Keeper." I sat down on the stairs. If she knew, the whole house probably knew. "Did Roz tell you?"

"Not at first." Camille shook her head. "I could smell sex in the parlor the minute I walked in there. His pheromones are extremely potent, and when Smoky came in, he was positive that Roz had just put the make on me and that I was trying to protect him. It took a lot to convince my hothead that Rozurial had *not* overstepped his boundaries with me. I finally made him fess up for his own safety."

Oh good gods. That overgrown lizard jumped to conclusions a lot, as did Chase. Only Smoky was a lot more dangerous than Chase. "Great. I suppose everybody knows by now?"

"Um . . . yeah. The arguing was pretty loud until I convinced Rozurial that to avoid a major pounding, he'd better come clean. He's very discreet, by the way. I was surprised. But by then, everybody was in the parlor trying to calm Smoky down. Sometimes I think he needs a good dose of elephant tranqs." But she was laughing as she said it.

"I guess he was just looking out for you," I said, even though I knew better. Smoky *owned* Camille. Granted, he'd accepted that he was on a time-share with Morio and Trillian, but that was the extent of his generosity. In Smoky's eyes, Camille was *his*, no two ways about it. "Okay, everybody knows we slept together. So nobody should be surprised when I don't talk about it, right? I'm just not comfortable spouting off about my love life to anybody but you and Kitten. And Iris."

She was about to answer when there was a commotion from above. We rushed upstairs, pausing to make sure the kitchen was empty before slipping through the entrance to my lair. From the sounds of things, something was going on in the living room.

Vanzir, Roz, Delilah, and Morio were scurrying around, and it looked like they were grabbing weapons. Iris was holding Maggie, and Smoky was nowhere to be seen. As Roz plastered a warm kiss on my forehead, nobody said a word, much to my relief. I gave him a quick kiss in return.

"What's going on?"

"A group of ghouls is tearing up the Wedgewood Cemetery." Morio slipped the strap of his bag over his head. "Chase called. He needs our help. Get moving!"

The Wedgewood Cemetery was next to the Salish Ranch Park, where we'd routed two dubba-trolls earlier in the year. It seemed to be a magnet for beasties. There was a gorgeous glassed-in arboretum in the park that was a sitting duck target for destruction.

"Ghouls?" I thought about Wilbur and his ghoul, Martin. "Think our new neighbor has anything to do with this?"

"I dunno," Delilah said, "but we'd better get moving, because there are picnickers still in the park, and you can just imagine what kind of field day those creatures will have. Not quite like having ants heading toward the basket. Picnic, my ass—a gory, bloody picnic!"

I glanced outside. The sun had set, but it was still light enough for strollers and skateboarders and teenagers to be hanging out. "Well, hell. Let's get a move on. Where's Smoky?"

"He took off for his barrow. He's trying to keep peace with the Triple Threat. Come on, we'll take your car and mine." Camille grabbed her keys. "Kitten, you and Roz ride with Menolly and fill her in on what we learned today. Vanzir, you and Morio ride with me."

"Wait a minute! What about your burns?"

"They're fine—no open sores, so I'm going." She gave me that look that told me it was useless to argue.

And so we were off, after I planted a quick kiss on Maggie's head.

On the way there, Roz sat in back, politely silent to the point of making me want to smack him, while Delilah detailed what they'd found out while I slept.

"Vanzir has Carter checking on other demonic activity. Carter told him to drop by with us tonight. We'll stop there after we take care of these ghouls."

Somehow, going to meet our indentured demon's buddy didn't sound all that comforting, but I let it pass. Carter was probably no worse than Vanzir, and he was providing us with information.

"What about you? Did you find anything out about Harold's house?"

She nodded. "The house is well over a hundred years old. It belonged to a Dr. Grout at first, who was a widower. He had a daughter, Lily, and the girl married Trent Young, a moneyed young man fresh over from England. Trent bought the house from the old man, who vanished somewhere. I couldn't find out anything else about him. As it so happens, Trent belonged to a rather scary lodge while back in England—the Eighth Circle."

"Eighth Circle," I said. "Let me guess—the eighth circle as in Dante's nine circles of hell?"

Delilah nodded. "One and the same. The lodge was said to be steeped in sorcery. Even more interesting, immediately upon settling in the U.S., Trent established a private club that he named Dante's Hellions."

"The same Dante's Hellions that Harold belongs to?"

"It looks that way."

So Dante's Hellions was a lot older than we thought. "I take it Trent Young is related to Harold Young?"

"Yeah," she said. "Trent is Harold's great-grandfather. Lily and Trent had two sons. One of them—Rutger—took over the house when the couple moved into a smaller place in the early forties. He was in his early twenties."

"What was going on with the club?"

"I think they were running it as a secret society. Rutger took over as president of the order shortly after he married a woman named Amanda. They had four children. Two daughters and two sons—Jackson and Orrin."

"Let me guess. One of their boys is Harold's father."

"Right. Jackson. By the time Harold hit middle school, his grandmother died, and his grandfather—Rutger—followed shortly after. Rutger left the house to Harold's uncle Orrin. Interestingly enough, the old man declined to leave Jackson and his sisters any inheritance."

"I wonder why."

"Don't know, but Rutger left the bulk of his estate to Orrin, except for a large trust fund he'd set up for Harold. Jackson ended up inheriting *his* money from his *maternal* grandmother. Orrin lived in the house until Harold started college. Then he moved into a condo and signed the deed over to Harold, who turned the mansion into the frat house you see today."

Delilah gave me a satisfied smirk.

"You were a busy bee today. So tell me, what else did you find out about Dante's Hellions through the years?"

I glanced out the window. We were about ten minutes away from the Salish Ranch Park, which straddled the boundary line that divided the Belles-Faire District from the central Seattle urban area. The park was adjacent to the Wedgewood Cemetery where, apparently, our ghouls were having a rousing good time.

"I can't find any mention of it after Orrin took over the house. Either it went underground or just fell off the radar until Harold decided to revive it."

She sighed. "Harold has been a severe disappointment to

his parents, failing not only to get into Yale, Princeton, or any other Ivy League college because of his personality, not his grades. He also managed to get himself in trouble a number of times."

"And Chase—did he do the background checks on the boys living there?"

"Yeah, I was talking to him when dispatch interrupted with the news about the ghouls. He'll fill us in on what he found after we take out the undead crew."

She pointed to the parking lot that served for both the cemetery and the park. "There—there's a spot near the gates."

I swung in, my Jag smoothly rolling to a stop as Camille pulled in on my left in her Lexus. We headed across the lawn. The cemetery's labyrinth of cobblestone paths was lit by a string of gas-lantern replicas, but in reality they were as up-to-date as Delilah's laptop. The lamps added a serene, peaceful sense to the somber environment.

The cemetery was still open, but it looked like most of the patrons—those still with breath in their lungs—had fled. The dead inhabitants remained dead, or at least I hoped so. If there was a necromancer somewhere around dabbling in resurrection, then we were all in trouble.

Chase strode over to meet us. He'd brought backup, and most of the officers were Fae or elfin.

"What have you got for us?" I asked.

"Ghouls. Apparently one of the picnickers was a house sprite and recognized them. He's the one who called in. He said there were quite a few." Chase motioned to the officers. "What do they need? What kills ghouls? And what's the difference between a wight and a ghoul? None of my men seem to know much about the undead."

I frowned. We'd fought more wights than I cared to remember not long ago, but ghouls . . . ghouls were just nasty. "Wights eat both spirit and body. Ghouls devour flesh only, but they're cunning, and until you torch them or tear them from limb to limb, they'll continue to fight. Even a severed arm can attack until you chop it up."

"Delightful," Chase said, and his tone perfectly mimicked Camille's. I started to laugh, and he frowned. "What?"

"Nothing. I think we're rubbing off on you. Okay, to kill a ghoul, silver always works, but it has to be big silver. No silver dimes, if they even still make them, no silver spoons. Silver as in big whopping silver. The metal sucks out the magical energy they've been infused with. As for other weapons, you can smash them with a hammer. Maces work. But to thoroughly destroy them, you really need a blade to cut them into little pieces."

"What about magic?" he asked, looking decidedly queasy.

"Fire works, magical or not. Ice, not so much, unless it freezes them solid so they can't move. Most other spells won't do any good. Oh, lightning works. They can't drown, and they *can* live without air, so strangling really isn't an option. But if you cut or twist off their head, they can't see what they're doing, so they make easy targets to pound on until they're fully . . . dead. Again."

Chase stared at me like I was a psycho.

"What? You *asked*." Why did I always have the feeling he thought I was going to change into a three-headed people eater or something equally monstrous?

"I know, I know." He shook his head. "I'm just amazed by the variety of ways you come up with to destroy people. Or *things*. Things that shouldn't be walking around. What about you? Can you drain their blood?"

I grimaced. "What do you think I am, a syringe? First— just *so* unappetizing. Do you have any idea of what those things taste like?"

He grimaced. "No, and I don't want to find out."

"Fine, but their blood tastes like dirt and feces and worms, so no, thank you. Second: Whatever blood most of them had when they first died is long gone. Dried up. Think bag of walking bones with decaying flesh. I have no stomach for drinking the liquids that form when they decompose. How about you?"

That did the trick, because he abruptly shut up and returned to Delilah's side.

"Grab whatever you can to give them a good thrashing. Tasers won't do the trick; if you use lightning or electricity, you need to fry them to a crisp with it, not tickle their funny bones," I called out behind him.

As we hurried along the path, we saw several teens who either hadn't heard the commotion or had ignored it. Chase sent one of his men over to firmly escort them out of the cemetery. We rounded the path, which wound through a patch of weeping willows, all old as sin and heavy with their long streamers of lacework leaves. I ducked under one of the strands as the sounds of growling came from up ahead.

As we rounded the corner, I stopped, motioning for the others to put the brakes on. Up ahead, in a pack that looked to be close to twenty members strong, hunched a group of ghouls.

They stank to high heaven. Some were long dead, others were still ripe and fresh. From where we stood, none of them looked like they'd been enchanted to last for the duration. No, they were castaways, raised for battle. Or for havoc. Ghouls like Martin—who belonged to Wilbur, our neighbor—were more resilient.

The ghouls who had their backs to us slowly turned. I groaned. They'd been feasting, and their dinner of choice was an older gentleman, thoroughly gutted by now. Camille sucked in a breath, while Kitten whispered something under hers. Chase cleared his throat, apparently waiting for me.

"Okay, we're going in. Just remember—they'll fight until you tear them apart. You can't just take an arm off, or a leg. They'll fight until they're in little pieces, or unless somebody casts a spell to negate their enchantment. And unless Morio's got one of those hidden in that handy bag of his, we're about to put on a show, folks." I glanced at him, not expecting anything, but still, a quiver of hope ran through me.

But Morio just laughed. "No such luck. But I've got a silver blade, and so does Camille."

"Then in for the fight. And be careful. They'll gnaw on any body part they can get hold of." As I tried to gauge their strength, it occurred to me that for once, it would be nice to fight an opponent who wasn't a pile of rotting flesh, or at least one who used deodorant. And then, pushing whimsy out of my mind, I moved in. It was time to rumble.

CHAPTER 22

As I jockeyed for a better position, the ghouls moved forward as a pack. I motioned for the others to spread out. Delilah and Chase moved to the right, Camille, Morio, and Vanzir to the left. Roz and I held center ground.

The ghouls paused, then mirrored our strategy, except there were a lot more of them than there were of us. How lovely to have a choice, I thought dryly as I tried to pick out the strongest of the group. Roz and I were best suited to attacking the ones with the most muscle. Luck held; the biggest brutes were coming right at us.

I heard the others suck in their breaths as our opponents drew close. And then—in that fraction of a second when all is silent in battle, when the lines have been drawn and all that you wait for is the final signal—I readied myself and sprang, Roz right on my heels.

Shouts rose as the others moved in, but all I could see were the two ghouls rushing toward me. Or, at least, shambling as fast as they could. Their flesh clung to bone like empty burlap sacks on a tree. Mold festered off the decay, oozing with carbuncles, the pus-laden boils giving their faces a lumpy look.

"You need some Clearasil," I muttered as I took a swing

for the biggest. He towered over me, even with his slumped shoulders and unbalanced gait.

I punched for the gut, hoping to double him over to where I could reach his head. With dead things, I could twist off their heads if I tried hard enough. Not pleasant, but it helped deflect their ability to situate their enemies. Then somebody with a blade could come in and hack them to bits.

The ghoul let out a low roar—the closest it would ever get to a shout—and I leapt for it, grimacing as my arms found purchase around his neck. He reeled backward from my sudden pounce as I managed to throw him off balance. I knocked him to the ground and swung around behind his head, pushing him by the shoulders to a sitting position. I couldn't very well get at his neck if he was prone. He pawed at me, struggling to get away, but this was one area in which I held the advantage: I was a lot stronger than he was.

I maneuvered myself to where I was holding his chin in my left hand, the back of his neck in my right. With a sharp jerk to the left, the sound of bones breaking echoed in my ears, but I wasn't done yet. Ghouls could get along just fine with broken necks. No, I had to tear off his head.

I pushed harder, hearing the rip of decaying flesh, and then I saw muscle—no longer firm and supple but spongy and ripe—and I poured on the sweat, twisting as the neck bones shattered. Within seconds, I was squatting there with the ghoul's head in my hands. The eyes blinked at me in surprise, but they didn't feel pain.

"Gross," I muttered, tossing the head far from the body. "Need a blade here!"

Morio raced over, his sword drawn. As the ghoul flailed blindly, Morio darted in and out, hacking away. I left him to finish the job, glancing around to see how everyone else was doing.

Delilah and Chase were working together, pounding on one of the ghouls, while a second opponent pawed at Chase. It looked to me like the creature had gotten in a few solid swipes. We'd have to make sure everybody was treated; wounds from the undead, especially ghouls and zombies, became infected quickly.

Camille was holding a ball of energy in her hands, and as one of the ghouls descended on her, she danced to the side and, instead of targeting him, sent the ball directly into the midst of the pack where it would do the most damage. I quickly turned, covering my eyes as it landed with a loud explosion. The smell of singed flesh filled the air, and Camille began to cough.

At that moment, there was a loud screech as a large bird swept down, aiming not for us but for one of the scorched ghouls. Oh crap, a vularapture—an undead vulture. They were far more dangerous than the ghouls. We definitely had a full-fledged necromancer in the area; one who could do some serious damage. Luckily for us, vularaptures weren't picky about their meals.

I darted a glance toward Vanzir, who was making quick work of his second ghoul. He had a methodical look on his face and went about it in a rough, if effective, manner. With one hand, he grabbed the ghoul's throat, and with the other, he grabbed its hair and yanked. Hard. I hadn't realized he was that powerful, because he pulled the freakin' ghoul's head right off the shoulders, the bones snapping like twigs. Of course, the ghoul might have had osteoporosis when she had been alive, making her bones brittle. The thought held an odd comfort for me.

Roz, on the other hand, was charging in with a deadly looking blade. He sliced and diced his way through the ghoul in front of him and turned to help Chase, knocking aside the one trying to gnaw on the detective's elbow.

"Thanks, man!" Chase called to him, dodging another swipe from the ghoul in front of him.

Delilah raised her dagger. The blade gleamed with a menacing blue tint. Not only had our father given us each a silver long knife, but recently, Delilah's had spoken to her, telling her its name, which meant that the two were bonded now.

"Lysanthra!" Delilah's voice echoed through the evening twilight, startling a nearby bird perched in a tree.

As I watched, the stars began to peek out against that tinge that straddles the line between blue and gray. For a moment, it looked like a silver light streaked down from one of the distant suns to strike the tip of the blade, but it couldn't be. She laughed, then plunged the blade into the ghoul that she and Chase were fighting. There was a split second where everything seemed to pause, and then the ghoul mumbled something and fell in its tracks.

What the—? *It had to be the silver of the blade,* I thought, watching as Roz took over slicing up the ghoul while Delilah and Chase moved on to the next one. I turned back to assess the battle.

Camille's spell had dropped three of them. Yay, her! She smelled a little singed around the edges herself, but at least she was still on her feet, and she hadn't burned herself like before. Vanzir was taking care of yet another ghoul, and it looked like we'd gone through over half the pack.

I dove in to another one, this one weaker than the first and easier to handle. I figured, *Why mess with something that works?* and once again went for the head-off trick. Another moment, and I was onto a third, while Morio went into cleanup mode for me.

We—along with Chase's men—cleared a path through the pack without injuries on our part, although Chase had sustained a few wounds he'd need to have checked out.

As I stood there, surveying the carnage, I noticed there was one last ghoul, but he was over by an azalea bush, crouching as if in fear. Ghouls tended to be emotionally challenged when it came to fear, so his actions made me pause. Hell, he was making it easy for me. I headed over, intending to dispatch him back to the grave, when I stopped short.

Martin. Martin the ghoul. *Wonderful.* Was our neighbor Wilbur behind all of this? I grunted as the others made their way to my side.

"What's wrong—oh shit," Delilah said. "That's Martin, isn't it?"

"Yeah, that's him, but he's not talking." I shook my head, trying to decide whether to put him out of our misery or leave him be.

He wasn't trying to attack us, and if he'd been feasting on the old man, I couldn't see any signs of it. No fresh blood on the face, no questionable matter staining his shirt. In fact, he was dressed quite conservatively in what looked like a faded pinstripe suit, and his neck appeared to have been fixed from when I'd broken it. Wilbur had welded a nice smooth steel collar around it, with a brace up the back of the neck to keep his head straight. Joy, a dandy and Frankenstein's monster, all rolled into one.

"Wait—don't hurt him!" The voice reached my ears faintly, and I spun around. There, running through the veil of dusk descending around us, was Wilbur. Wilbur the necromancer.

Chase looked confused. "Shouldn't we take care of this thing?" he asked, pointing to Martin.

"His name is Martin, and he belongs to our neighbor." I gave him a look that said, *I know, I know.*

"Oh, got it. Great. That explains everything." Chase let out a huff of exasperation and motioned to his men. "Clean up that mess, and be careful. Some of those . . . things . . . might still have some life in them."

"Wait a second," I said. "We might get a little help here." As Wilbur joined us, a worried expression on his face, I pointed to Martin. "You in the habit of losing that thing all the time?"

He stared at me, his concern turning to disinterest. "Martin has a habit of wandering off, yes. I try to keep him out of trouble, though . . ." His voice trailed off as he looked around. "What the hell happened here? Who owns all these ghouls?"

"We thought you might be able to tell us," I said. "Since you're a necromancer, and you have a sprightly ghoul of your own, we thought you might know who brought the rest of the gang back to life. Nice repair on the neck, by the way."

Wilbur grunted. "I had to do something after you got done with him." He glanced at the strange ghouls and shook his head. "I have no idea where these came from. They look crudely raised, though. Have you checked the cemetery for empty graves?"

Chase moaned. "Not grave robbers, too?"

"How else do you think necromancers get their dead to make ghouls and zombies from?" Wilbur seemed to be enjoying himself now. "Martin here willed his body to science.

I just happened to work at the laboratory that claimed him. They decided they couldn't use him and were going to bury his remains, so I volunteered to do the job. Martin was a transient—a bum. No one to care, no one to grieve for him. So I made him my pet."

"Do you recognize any energy signatures around here? If you do, please tell us," Delilah said. "We can use the help."

"And why should I help you?" Wilbur asked. "First you break my ghoul's neck, then you act like I'm the scum of the Earth—oh, don't try to lie to me," he added when Camille started to protest. "I know full well what you three think of me." He glanced at her again. "Well, the other two. You—you're an oddball. I can't figure your energy out, *witch*. Anyway, give me one good reason why I should help you guys out."

"Because I said so," Vanzir said, stepping forward. "I'm a demon. I could slip into your dreams and suck out your life force without blinking an eye."

"Down boy," Delilah muttered. Vanzir glared at her. "Sorry—I meant, stop it, Vanzir."

Before anybody else decided to play jack the testosterone, I stepped in. "Enough. Listen, all of you. We're facing some dangerous people. First, we've got a Karsetii demon roaming the astral, hunting the Fae. Actually, it will prey on *anybody* who works heavy magic." I emphasized the word *anybody*, and Wilbur paled. "Then we find a pack of wild ghouls on the loose. Somebody had to raise them, and according to Wilbur, here, they did a sloppy job in the process. Which indicates either a half-assed necromancer or some imbecile who has no idea what he's doing. I'm tending to guess the latter, given our discovery over at Harold's."

"Harold?" Wilbur asked.

"We have a bunch of stupid frat boys summoning demons and killing Fae and Supe women. I'm wondering if they aren't responsible for these ghouls, too." I sidled over to him. "You didn't by chance go to college around here?"

Wilbur shook his head. "College? I didn't even finish high school. I spent a number of years in the marines, down in South America. That's where I learned necromancy. In the jungle."

Shamanic death magic. He *was* experienced. If he'd been taught by a native tribe rather than learning the more ceremonial forms of necromancy, chances are he lived closer to the spirit world and had an easier time working his magic. Shamans tended to be far more powerful than most witches or sorcerers.

Morio whistled, low and through his teeth. "Heavy magic, then."

Wilbur shrugged. "The only kind I'm interested in." He turned back to me. "You said there's a bunch of kids dabbling in this? Not a good thing."

"Any chance you can give us some ideas of why anybody would raise ghouls, other than . . . well . . . for fun?" I leaned against a nearby headstone. Camille and Morio sat on the grass. Roz and Vanzir stood at my side.

Chase motioned to his men. "Take a look through the cemetery. See if we have any signs of desecrated graves. And these remains . . . bag them carefully, and then we burn the whole lot. We do *not* tell the families about this, just fill in the graves and keep it quiet." He stood near Rozurial. Delilah crouched at his feet, squatting on her heels.

"Why would somebody want to raise a bunch of ghouls? An army, I suppose—a band of fighters. They make excellent killing machines."

"Why did you raise your ghoul?" I stared at him. He was one of the oddest FBHs I'd ever met.

"Me? I raised Martin to be my assistant. He can understand rudimentary commands, he's handy to have around, and he doesn't talk my ear off." Wilbur shrugged. "There's not much use for this many ghouls unless you're trying to hurt somebody or unless you just want to practice your skills. Could be the result of a magical lesson."

Camille clapped her hand to her mouth. "Hey, back in Otherworld, down in the Southern Wastes, remember how there are pockets of rogue magic from when the sorcerers warred? Sometimes that happens in places where a lot of volatile spells were used. Do you suppose somebody was out here practicing magic, and the residue spontaneously caused the ghouls to rise?"

Wilbur frowned. "I've never heard of that happening before, but then I don't talk much with other necromancers."

"It might be possible," Morio said. "There are some places in the world where magic is part of the land itself. That happens from long and/or heavy use of magic in one area. But why this cemetery? Remember, it's the one that attracted those dubba-trolls we fought."

Grateful he didn't add anything about the trolls coming through a rogue portal—at least not in front of Wilbur—I considered the possibility. "You guys might be on to something. What makes this cemetery so special, though? Is Harold's place anywhere near here?"

Delilah frowned. "There's something . . . let's go back to the cars. I need to check something I left in my backpack."

Leaving Chase's crew to clean up, we headed back to the parking lot, Wilbur towing his ghoul behind him. Martin came compliantly, ignoring everything but his master, whom he regarded with puppy dog eyes.

I winced as a thought ran through my head, but I decided not to go there. *Not anywhere near there.*

When we got to the cars, Delilah dug through her purse, which she'd stashed under the seat, and pulled out a map. She spread it out on the hood as Chase held a flashlight. We all gathered around.

Delilah tapped an ink-stained mark on the paper. "That's where Harold lives. And this . . ." She sketched a line directly north. "This is where the Wedgewood Cemetery is. If you expand it in the other direction, this line also passes over . . . the Wayfarer." She glanced up. "I think this cemetery is built on a ley line."

"Which means there's a whole lot of energy waiting here to be tapped," Camille said. "I wonder . . ." She glanced at Wilbur and shook her head. "It'll save for later."

Ley lines were invisible chains of energy—a lot like a fault line—that ran through both Earthside and Otherworld. They connected places in a magical line, and any magic performed over a ley line was likely to be far more powerful than anywhere else. And then, as I stared at the map, I knew what

Camille had been about to say. Two of the rogue portals were also on this ley line.

Were all the portals connected by a series of leys, or were only the rogue ones popping up on them? And were all rogue portals connected to ley lines? Another mystery to explore, once Wilbur left us alone.

"Which means that Harold and his crew may be coming out here to perform ceremonies. Or that the energy they're raising is traveling through the ley and stirring up the bodies. Hmmm . . . I wonder. Chase, have your men check the exact whereabouts of the graves that have been disturbed and get back to us ASAP." I glanced at Wilbur, who looked mildly confused.

"It would seem that Martin might have been pulled here by the energy of the line, but that's a long way to travel from our neck of the woods." I frowned.

"I can explain that," he said. "I was taking him out for a walk, and he got off his leash." He held up a cobalt blue leash. It was then that I noticed that Martin's handy steel collar had a ring hanging off the back. The leash's clasp was bent, and it looked like someone had pulled really hard on it.

"Leash? You walk him on a leash like a *dog*?" Now there was a visual I could do without. The thought of the dapperly dressed dead man prancing along like a poodle on the end of a bright blue leash made me want to laugh. Or puke. And when you're a vampire, puking is not recommended.

Wilbur looked at me. "You're strong. Can you bend this back into shape for me?" He held out the leash.

Feeling like I was in the middle of some surreal Monty Python movie, I silently took the leash, bent the clasp into shape, or at least as good a shape as it was going to get, and handed it back to him without a word. Then I turned and motioned toward the cars.

"Let's get a move on. We've got a meeting with . . . Vanzir's friend, right?"

Vanzir nodded. "Yeah, but we'd better drop over to the FH-CSI to get his wounds looked at." He nodded to Chase.

Delilah grabbed Chase's arm and looked at the bite marks near the elbow where the ghoul had managed to rip through the cloth of his shirt and chomp down on him. No flesh was missing, but there was one hell of a bruise forming around the wound.

"Yeah, it's already turning red, and red means infection." She sighed.

Chase cleared his throat. "I have to get back to the station. I do have a job, you know. I promise—I'll have Sharah look at it the minute I get there. You guys go do what you need to do." He kissed Delilah soundly on the lips. "Call you later, sweetheart," he added as he jogged off toward the group of squad cars.

Wilbur flashed us an awkward smile, as if the expression was foreign to him, and said, "I'm headed out, too. I need to get Martin home. It's time to watch *Seinfeld*."

That did it. I tried to clear my throat, but a bubble of laughter broke through, and I let out a loud snort. "You've got to be kidding. You and the ghoul watch reruns of *Seinfeld* together? What the hell kind of freakshow world do you live in?"

Wilbur stared at me, his eyes flashing darkly. "You're one to talk. You live with your sisters and a bunch of men in one big house, you're out bashing ghouls in the middle of the night, you run a bar, and you're a vampire. You drink blood, for God's sake. Throwing stones ought to be the last thing on your list of to-do items."

Frowning, I tried to get hold of myself. But the thought of Wilbur and Martin sitting there watching *Seinfeld* was too precious. "Does he wear his leash while you're watching TV, or is he house-trained?"

"Menolly," Rozurial said, a scowl creasing his forehead. "You really shouldn't be such a bitch. He did help us out with information."

I coughed so hard that a dribble of blood oozed down my chin, and I suddenly realized what I must look like. As Wilbur silently marched away, leading Martin behind him on the leash, I raced after them.

"I'm sorry. I'm sorry—there's just been so much tension . . ."

He shook his head. "Excuses. Tension's no excuse for behaving so rudely."

So our necromancer was cultured, even though he looked like a mountain man and was a dropout. I glanced up at him, deciding to eat crow.

"I apologize. It was uncouth of me to spout off like that. You and Martin . . ." I fought for control and forced a smile. "You and Martin have a good evening, and thank you again for your help."

He looked skeptical but mumbled something that sounded like a vague acceptance and left, looking mildly disgusted.

"I think we'll be asking Iris to bake a lot of cookies to send his way," Camille said, giving me a shake of the head. "Menolly, sometimes you have to learn to keep your mouth shut. I love you, but you aren't the most diplomatic person in the world."

"You've got that right," I said, feeling let down and vaguely guilty.

"Can we get a move on?" Vanzir broke in. "Carter's waiting for us, and I don't want to make him mad by showing up too late."

"Yeah, yeah," I said, heading toward my car. "The last thing we need is for another demon to be angry at us."

As we headed out of the parking lot, I decided that maybe I should spend some time with Sassy Branson. She was, after all, the doyenne of the vampire set. If anybody could help me learn a few manners, it would be Sally.

CHAPTER 23

Carter's place was a little basement apartment-slash-shop along Broadway, near where the junkies congregated. A metal railing kept passersby from falling into the cement shaft. I peeked over the rail to look at the steps leading down to the demon's hangout. I had the feeling that if Carter hadn't been who he was, the stairwell would have been packed with street-walkers and addicts, using the cover to keep their transactions semiprivate. But a palpable energy buzzed around the steps, warning, *Stay away, or I'll eat you.*

Vanzir glanced around, but the walkway on our side of the street was devoid of people. A hooker leaned against a brick building on the opposite corner, dressed in a sequined mini-dress and platform boots. She looked bored, out of some retro seventies go-go act.

I wondered how old she was; she could have been thirty, she might have been fifty. How long had she been at it, and how many times had she tried to get out of the business? She sure didn't look happy. It occurred to me that we should give her one of Lindsey Cartridge's cards from the Green Goddess Women's Shelter. While they primarily focused on helping women get out of abusive marriages and relationships, they also worked in concert with Reclamation, a group dedicated to helping women who wanted out of "the life."

Three primer-splotched hot rods zoomed past, speeding. Bored teens, no doubt. I glanced at my Jaguar, parked right next to Carter's place.

"You think it's safe to leave our cars sitting unattended around here? The neighborhood looks kind of seedy," I said.

Vanzir nodded. "Yeah, no problem. Carter paid a witch to cast a spell out to—and including—the parking spaces in front of his place. No thieves, no muggers. They get within ten feet of the circle and freak. If you ever see somebody suddenly look really uncomfortable and cross the street, you can be sure they're up to no good."

"Hmm," Delilah said. "Where can we buy one of those for our home? If we could get one that encompassed the entire property . . ."

"You'd pay an arm and a leg. He has to have it reinforced on a monthly basis, and believe me, his witch ain't cheap," Vanzir said. "And her magic works. Every time." He winked at Camille, but it still sounded like a slam.

Camille arched one eyebrow. "Ease it back, dream boy. A tad bit passive-aggressive, you think?"

He stared at her for a moment, then sniggered. "You're good. You catch on quick." He thumbed toward the door. "Let's go."

Vanzir led us down the stairs and knocked four times on the door. After a moment, a small click echoed through the air as the door swung open. We followed the demon inside.

I'd never been in a demon's lair before and wasn't sure exactly what to expect, but whatever my preconceptions were, they weren't what Carter had going on. The room was large, with several doors leading back into the rest of the apartment. It was dark; the windows that lined the top of the wall were blacked out. No wonder I hadn't noticed them as we headed down the stairs.

A mellow glow from a dim lamp set off the gold and red upholstery that covered the sofa and wing chair. The coffee and end tables were rich walnut, and the furniture had the same feel as the furnishings in older vampires' lairs. Most of it looked decades old. I had the feeling Carter had been over Earthside for a long, long time, at least by human reckoning.

The walls were covered with tapestries that depicted wars and battle scenes, and one entire wall was taken up with bookshelves that were filled from top to bottom with books of all shapes and sizes. Our demon was literate, that much was clear.

A desk sat to the right of a side door, facing so that its occupant could see when anybody entered or left the building. And behind the desk—also dark walnut—sat an unassuming man who looked to be in his early thirties. He had wavy hair the same color as mine, and his eyes were like Vanzir's, a whirl of colors that were impossible to name. Only this demon had two spiked horns curling out of his head, one on each side, reminding me of those on an impala, curved back, regal, and polished to a high sheen. He was meticulously groomed, even though his hair looked messy at first glance. But it was a deliberate mess, no doubt held in place by plenty of hair spray.

As he stood and walked around the side of the desk, I saw that he was using a cane. His right knee was in a brace. "Welcome. I assume Vanzir has told you that I'm Carter." Sweeping his arm graciously, he motioned to the sofa. "Won't you have a seat, please?"

Carter was wearing a burgundy smoking jacket over a pair of spotless black trousers. We were dressed in blood, dirt, and, no doubt, ghoul innards. "Are you sure? We might accidentally stain your upholstery."

He laughed, his voice musical. "Don't worry about it. I have the cleaners in every month or two. I receive a number of guests who don't even *understand* the concept of taking a shower."

We settled onto the sofa and chairs that were spread throughout the room, and Carter snapped his fingers. A lovely young woman, delicate and thin and possibly part Chinese, slipped into the room. She waited silently.

"Kim, bring us some tea, please. And," he glanced at me, "a goblet of warmed blood." When I started to protest, he waved me down. "Nonsense. My hospitality will never be called into question. Not while I'm alive."

He slid into the chair nearest me and leaned back, resting his cane against the arm of the wooden frame. "Vanzir leads me to believe you're facing a Karsetii demon." He sounded almost eager.

I glanced at the others. Camille gave me a slight nod. "Yeah. We drove off the hive mother, but I don't trust that she's gone for good. We think we know who's summoning her, though, and we're wondering if you might have any records indicating demonic activity around a certain area of Seattle going back, oh—say one hundred years or so?"

Carter gazed in my eyes. He looked old behind that youngish face, and a little bit tired. "I arrived here when Seattle was young. I came in from the East Coast and started a printing company. Ran a couple of the very first newspapers in town, then decided to fade away and reinvent myself as someone new. Naturally, the populace wouldn't have looked too kindly on me if they'd found out I was a demon."

"Then you've been here for a long time," I said. Carter fascinated me. I knew he was Demonkin, but he didn't feel like any other demon I'd ever met—Vanzir and Rozurial included. I wondered just what type he was, but it seemed rude to ask.

"Yes, I've watched the city grow and evolve. My company was located in the Seattle Underground before she was underground." Carter flashed me a dazzling smile. Good teeth, that was for sure. "I'm able to cloak my horns when I know a stranger's coming, but I generally don't speak to many people and have since then grown used to a life of solitude."

"What do you do now to support yourself?" Morio leaned back, eying Carter closely. I watched the fox demon; he seemed wary but not closed off. Morio had good instincts, and I trusted them.

"I run an Internet research business. I'm a virtual research assistant for a number of college professors and scientists. I make a good wage that more than pays my bills. No one bothers me."

Just then, the lovely Kim returned, bearing a tray filled with cups, saucers, and a pot of tea. She had remembered to add a goblet of blood, and I accepted it rather self-consciously. I didn't really like drinking in front of others because I knew it made some people queasy, but I didn't want to appear churlish. I sniffed at the blood. Fresh. My fangs began to extend as the hunger in my stomach grew, and I quickly took a sip, forcing myself to center again.

As Kim handed out the teacups, I watched Carter watch her. At first, I'd thought she was his maid, but there was more going on there than just a master-servant relationship. He was gentle when he spoke with her, and gracious, even though his manner was quietly imperative.

As she finished, he said, "Thank you. Go to bed now and sleep safe."

She ducked her head to him, then just as silently backed out of the room. I cocked my head, curious.

"You wonder what she's doing here, don't you?" Carter said.

Startled, I nodded. "Yeah, actually. She's human?"

"Human, yes, but only half. Her mother was a demon—a succubus, but a weak one. Her father was human. Kim's mother had no use for the child and was in the process of selling her on the open market when I happened to notice. Kim is twenty-two now, so this was . . . oh . . . twenty-one years ago or so. Several of the demons bidding for her were . . . distasteful. I knew she'd have a short, miserable life with them, so I outbid them, bought her, and brought her here."

Everyone stared at him. Morio was nodding. Camille and Delilah both looked a little shocked. Rozurial just listened.

"Were you planning on keeping her?" I asked.

"No, not really." He shook his head. "At first I was planning to leave her on the doorstep of a church, but then I realized that her half-demon nature would doom her if they tried to bring her up human. She'd either end up in a mental institution or she'd end up in jail. So I hired a nanny and brought her up myself. I look on her like she's my own daughter. Kim is mute; she's never spoken a word, and we don't know why. The healer I engaged thinks it might be some genetic mutation that occurred from her mixed parentage. She knows sign language, though, and she can hear without a problem. I keep encouraging her to go away to college, but she prefers to stay home and take care of the apartment."

Kim looked old enough to be his wife, but if he harbored such thoughts about her, they weren't apparent.

"What area do you want information about? The city as a whole, or one specific neighborhood?" Carter finished his tea and rose, crossing to the bookshelf where he pored through titles until he found a large leather-bound book. He opened it, setting it on the coffee table. The book was an atlas, filled with holograms. Maps of the city. Magical, no doubt.

I gave him the cross streets nearest Harold's house. That was as much as Carter needed to know for the moment. He seemed on the up-and-up, though I wondered why he'd chosen to live Earthside, and why for so long, but you never knew. With demons, you just couldn't take unnecessary risks.

Carter glanced at the map, tracing routes with his fingertip. Then he stopped, looked at the page with a peculiar frown, and limped over to a filing cabinet that stood next to his desk. He shuffled through a thick row of neatly lined files, withdrew a folder, and carried it back to his chair. He handed it to me.

"I think this might contain the information you're looking for," he said, pressing his lips together grimly. "I have the feeling you're looking for a particular name, and you're likely to find it in there."

As I spread the file folder on my knees and opened it, Camille and Delilah peered over my shoulders. The folder was filled with neatly typed reports, old newspaper clippings—some from the *Seattle Tattler*, I noticed—and a few scattered photographs. I began to shuffle through the pages.

Two pictures of what looked like a red-eyed, horned troll rustling through what appeared to be a corner park. A blurry photograph that looked reminiscent of the ghouls we'd met in the cemetery, only they were crossing through a backyard, and—hello? What was this? A picture of Harold's house, complete with a dark cloud overhead. Only that cloud was no cloud. It was some sort of demonic haze. Even though the picture was dated as being taken twenty years ago, I could still feel the aura flicker off the photograph.

I slowly handed the picture to Camille and picked up the

thick sheaf of reports. As I flipped through them, I saw that they were each documented by date, address, and type of encounter. There were seven pages with Harold's address on it, and the dates went back to around 1920. The reports ranged from mild demonic auras being sensed to a period during the 1960s where there was a surge of power spikes noted by whoever had been keeping track of this project. Which brought me to . . .

"Carter, why do you have all this? All these reports?"

His gaze flickered my way, and the mild demeanor fell away. I found myself gazing into a swirling pool of colors, falling quickly as he sucked me in. For the first time since my early days as a vampire, I found myself gasping for breath as I tried to push his energy back. It swept over me like a wave, dragging me like a riptide, compelling me to follow. I had to go to him. I stood, taking a hesitant, unwilling step forward, and then found Morio and Camille standing between the demon and me.

"Pull it in, dude, or lose it," Camille said. "I can feel what you're doing, and you do it again—to any of us—and you're dead."

"Don't toy with me, little girl," he said in a neutral tone. "You don't have the power to stop me." But the drive to obey was gone, and Carter was back to the mild-mannered demon we'd first met.

"What the fuck was that about?" I raised my hand, wanting to strike at him. The last person to force me to do anything was dust and ashes now. "I don't like being forced. Get it? And don't ever, ever underestimate us. *We're stronger than we look.*"

Carter held up his hand. "Enough with the histrionics. I have no intention of making you do anything. I'm just answering your question. Let it be enough that I watch. I observe. I keep the records. *And I fly beneath Shadow Wing's radar.* Do you understand?"

I didn't, not fully, but what I did understand from his little display was that he wasn't one of Shadow Wing's puppets. No, he was a lot older than I'd first thought, and his power rivaled the strongest vampire's I'd ever met. And yet he sat here, in a dingy apartment in a bad neighborhood of Seattle, with a foster daughter named Kim and a brace on his leg. There was far more to Carter than met the eye, but he wasn't going to reveal his secrets easily. And for some reason, he was helping us.

I picked up the reports. "Can we get copies of these?"

He stood and held out his hand. "Give them to me."

I handed them over, and he limped gracefully over to an all-in-one machine on his desk. As he copied the documents, I watched him, trying to figure out what the hell he was and why he was helping us. One look at Vanzir told me that if he knew, he wasn't going to volunteer the information. We could make him tell us, and if needed, we would, but later, and *only* if necessary. Those with great power needed to use it wisely, or it turned into abuse. And we had the power of life and death over Vanzir.

Carter returned with a packet of papers. "Here. Take them and use them however you need to. Be cautious. Evil walks in many guises, and not all that seems evil is out to kill you. But paranoia is your best friend right now."

Vanzir, as if heeding an unspoken comment, rose. "I think that's all we can do here."

"Do we have everything we need? How do we identify some of these creatures mentioned in the reports?" I flipped through them, unable to decipher half the creatures that had been reported by name.

"Do you need to know more than the fact that demon activity over that particular neighborhood has been the highest of any area in Seattle on a consistent basis for almost a hundred years? I advise you to check your missing person reports over the years and see how many women headed out for a walk in nearby neighborhoods and never made it home during those decades. Use your wits," Carter said, standing. "Sometimes all you need to know is that something is happening, rather than the details."

He escorted us to the door, and we found ourselves on the sidewalk again, politely but swiftly dismissed.

I turned to Vanzir. He raised his chin slightly, daring me to ask what I wanted to ask. As I glanced around the streets, a cool breeze washed through, and I heard the murmur of whispers caught in it. There were eyes and ears in the night, and not all of them friendly.

"Let's head out," I said. "We'll meet at the bar to discuss what we've found."

Without a word, we split up and drove off, but Carter stuck in my mind for a long time after that.

As we gathered in my office at the Wayfarer, Luke knocked at the door. I motioned everyone to be quiet as I called him in. Werewolves had extraordinary hearing. He didn't need to find himself privy to what we were discussing. The bar rag hung at a lazy angle over his shoulder, but I could tell he was on edge. He must be feeling the pull of the Moon as she rode toward full, too?

"What's up?" Luke wasn't in the habit of interrupting me if he thought I was busy, so something must have happened.

"Trouble, boss." He motioned toward the front of the bar. "Freedom's Angels out there, harassing the Faerie Maids."

Oh shit. The last thing I needed was a group of self-appointed moral watchdogs in my bar hounding my customers. I turned to Camille. "Call Chase and get him over here." As I followed Luke out to the bar, I could hear the arguments in progress.

There were three of them. They looked a lot like bikers at first glance, but the leather jackets were Value-Mart specials, the blue jeans were new and hadn't been broken in yet, and the stubble on their faces was about ten hours old. The smell of paper dust and toner and stale office air clung to them like a cloud of old cigar smoke. These men weren't thugs, but they wanted people to think they were. They might have seen a few scuffles, but I'd bet my right fang that none of them had been in an outright fight. *Yet.*

The group was hassling two of the Faerie Maids who were drinking at one of the tables up front. The girls might be dressed to attract, but that wasn't a crime. At least not in *my* bar. And while the Faerie Maids were notoriously stingy with their orders and were lousy tippers, they were still my regulars.

"Have we got a problem here, *gentlemen*?" I sauntered up to the trio and insinuated myself between them and the girls. "Because I'd hate to see anybody in *my* bar feel threatened."

One of the men—apparently the leader—stepped forward, leaning down so that he was breathing stale beer breath in my face. Apparently they hadn't heard that a vampire owned the Wayfarer, because otherwise he wouldn't have been so stupid.

Luke immediately shoved him back, then folded his arms as he stood beside me. I could feel him quivering, and the scent of wolf lingered directly beneath the surface. We were close enough to the full Moon that the stress was taxing him. Werewolves were generally hotheads, anyway. I glanced at him.

"Luke, you need to go home for the night. I can take care of this myself."

"I'm not leaving you—" His eyes flashed dangerously and began shifting color.

"Yes, you will. I'm your boss; I'm ordering you to go home." I unmasked my glamour and stared at the werewolf. Luke stared back, but only for a second. I was alpha in the bar. I was his boss.

He lowered his eyes. "Okay, but I don't like this." Stalking over to the bar, he slapped the rag on the counter and strode toward the back. I assumed he was leaving by the back exit to avoid bumping into the Freedom's Angels and setting off a fight. The moment he was out of sight, I turned back to the men.

"What the hell do you want?"

"Listen, little lady, maybe you should think about finding a job somewhere else. Hanging out with this riffraff can't be good for your . . ." He stopped and gave me the once-over. "Wait, did you say you're the owner?" With a glance at the others, he shook his head. "No, that can't be right. I heard the owner is a—"

I opened my mouth, letting my fangs extend, and gave him a wickedly gleeful grin. "What? A vampire, perhaps? You got that right, bud. Now what the fuck do you want in my bar, and why are you bothering these women? Or do I even need to ask?"

Mr. Tough Guy straightened his shoulders and stuck his thumbs through the belt loops on his jeans, giving me a patronizing look. "You're a vampire? But you're just an itty-bitty thing. We're here to stake a claim for the Earthborn and lead the stray sheep back to clarity. This is our city and our world, and we're determined to keep it that way."

"Holy crap. Do you really *believe* the garbage you're spouting?" Camille's voice echoed from the door to my office, and I realized that Luke had clued them in on what was going down.

"I can take care of this," I said, but before I could say another word, Rozurial and Vanzir were flanking me, with Morio, Camille, and Delilah spreading out to form a semicircle.

"Got an idea," I said, jabbing my finger into the leader's chest and sending him stumbling back against his buddies with one tiny shove. "You get your sorry asses out of here before I throw you out. And if I ever see you near my bar again, I'll have you arrested. And if *that* doesn't work, I'll pay a visit to you in the middle of the night when you're asleep and make sure you leave my bar alone."

Eyes wide, he and his buddies backed up. His voice took on a threatening tone. "You *are* a freak. You and all your kind. And we don't like freaks."

"And I don't like repeat offenders," Chase said as he stepped through the door with two officers at his back. "Toby, I've told you before, you're crossing the line, and you're going to end up in jail."

I glanced over at Chase. "Toby?"

"Toby and the boys here work for White Castle Insurers. They apparently haven't thought through what being arrested for a hate crime can do to their employment histories." Chase was calm and collected as he swiftly nodded for me to step back. "I can take it from here. Let's keep this all on the right side of the law."

Oh, he was good, I thought, watching as his men shuffled the suddenly complacent trio out the door. Chase turned back at the door. "By the way, Turnabout Willy showed up, safe and sound. He was off visiting his sister." As the door swung shut behind him, I retracted my fangs and turned to the others.

"Thanks for the backup. I had to send Luke home—"

"Yeah, he was a stone's throw away from shifting," Delilah said. "It was so strong in his aura I almost changed over myself. As it is, I have a strong desire to shift into panther form and go maul those idiots."

"Idiots? Maybe," I said. "But remember, members of that group have killed before, and they'll do it again."

"There are more dangerous anti-Fae groups than the Freedom's Angels," Vanzir said. "They might not be as flashy, but the League for Untainted Humanity is far more deadly. Nobody's ever managed to prove it, though. I've got a few friends who keep an eye on them."

I turned to Vanzir. Once again, he surprised me. "Just how many demon friends do you have over here?"

He blinked. He couldn't refuse to answer direct questions, thanks to the soul binder that had merged with his body during the Ritual of Subjugation.

"I don't know off the top of my head, but at least fifty to sixty. Nobody knows how many are in the network. The double blind is for everyone's protection," he added, his eyes flashing. He did not want to tell me this—that much was apparent.

"Network? What network?" Camille frowned. "I thought you just knew a few demons who were hanging out over here."

Vanzir let out a low hiss. "All right, I'll tell you, but it could get me killed if I'm not careful, just so you know. I've stumbled onto a network of demons who've managed to get themselves Earthside. They've been working in concert against Shadow Wing. A resistance is slowly growing, but they can't stay in the Subterranean Realms. The danger is too great."

While we already knew some demons objected to Shadow Wing's plans, we hadn't known they were setting up an active resistance. But this was not the place to discuss the Demonkin, nor much else, if we wanted it kept secret.

Just then Chase came back through the door. "They shouldn't bother you anymore. If they do, just give me a call. Those three are relatively harmless, but there are others who aren't. Just keep your eyes peeled for a while," he said. "I've got to get some sleep. I've been on duty eighteen hours, and I need a break. What are you doing?"

Camille broke in. "I think we're headed back to Harold's. I was looking over the reports Carter gave us, and it looks like a great deal of demonic activity has been centered around that house over the past eighty years. Evidence of Demon Gate spells have been found a number of times."

I grimaced. "Great. *Demons R Us.*"

"That's about the size of it," she said, twisting a curl of her hair. "Chase, would you have one of your men look through your records to find out the number of women who've gone missing around that area over the past fifty years or more? Anybody who was last seen walking in the area, headed toward the area, who never made it to her destination?"

Chase nodded. "Will do," he said. "Be careful."

Delilah moved forward and planted a soft kiss on his cheek. "We promise," she said. "Go home and sleep."

As the detective headed into the night, I looked at the others. "I guess it's come down to this. We've run out of options. We have to go back in that place and see what we can find."

There was nothing more to say. I told Chrysandra to watch the bar for the rest of the night, and we took off, back to the home of Dante's Hellions.

CHAPTER 24

As we headed back to Harold's place, I glanced at the sky. The Moon Mother was nearing full, and we had to take care of things tonight. Otherwise, Camille and Delilah would be helpless. Not to mention, the full Moon brought with her so much power for Fae and Supes that it would attract the Karsetii back through the Demon Gate. I was sure of it. I usually didn't have premonitions, but this I knew.

"When we get there, we sneak in the way Delilah and I did before, but we *all* go. We can't take any chances. Delilah and I heard a lot of voices in there, and we need all the bodies we can get on our side. If they catch us, well . . . it's not like that hasn't happened before. We'll deal with it when it happens."

On the way to Harold's for the second time in as many nights, I worried. It was one thing when we were going up against the demons themselves, but these were humans, easy to kill, easy to harm, and easy to bring the wrath of the community down on our heads if we made any mistakes.

Just what were we going to tell Harold's parents if we had to take him out? *Mr. and Mrs. Young, I know this sounds shocking, but your son was the leader of a demonic cult who's been kidnapping and murdering Fae women.* Even if we could prove it, I had my doubts that they'd be on our side, given what we'd just learned about the history of the house. It sounded like Dante's Hellions had been around a long, long time.

Our run-in with the Freedom's Angels hadn't helped my mood any. Right now, I wasn't feeling all too charitable toward my mother's side of the family tree. Demons, I could deal with. Ghouls and wights and beasties that went bump in the night—all occupational hazards. But evil seemed too conniving in humans—too easy to hide, too easy to put a facade over.

We parked a few houses down and slid through the shadows. The lights were still on; it was barely eleven P.M., but we didn't have time to wait. The yard was empty except for a big-assed van. The boys were out, or they were summoning up another demonic playmate or hooked up to their computers playing War World or one of the other online games.

Apparently they hadn't discovered that we'd infiltrated their underground labyrinth, because the entrance looked the same as it had the night before. Once again, Delilah picked the padlock, and I took the lead, motioning for Roz to fall in behind me, then Delilah, Camille, Morio, and lastly—watching our backs—Vanzir.

We climbed down the ladder, then followed the tunnels, silently creeping through the dim passage, retracing our route. The only sounds were the distant rise and fall of voices, the sounds of small creatures creeping through the dark—rats and cockroaches and shrews—as they crossed through the shadowy passage, surrounded by the compact walls of earth.

There was a feel to the night that only those of us who routinely lived under the Moon could fully grasp. A sense of camaraderie. We were the silent partners of the world, the lurkers who went about life with the veil of secrecy forever shrouding our footsteps. Those who lived by the day were noisy, their actions visible in the light. Unfortunately, the night not only sheltered the mystical creatures but also the dregs: the serial killers and rapists and those who specialized in shooting others in the back.

We made it to the door that led into the underground

complex. I held a finger to my lips, motioning for the others to stop fidgeting. Pressing my ear against the door, I listened. At first, all I could hear were the shallow breaths of the others behind me, but then, as I focused my attention, their breathing dropped away. I could still hear the rats and cockroaches, but they, too, disappeared as I narrowed my attention further.

And then, there it was: the low chanting again, coming from the distance. Only it was deeper than before, more concentrated. I needed Camille to see if she could sense any magical energy coming from it, but for that, we'd have to enter the complex itself. I listened again for the sound of anybody lurking on the other side but could sense nothing.

Motioning everybody back down the tunnel a few feet, in low whispers I told them what I'd heard. "We'll head for the room Delilah and I found the bodies in. We can hide in there—"

"Remember, I've got an invisibility spell," Morio said. "It's not foolproof, and it doesn't cloak sound or scent, but a couple of us can use it from there to scout out what's going on down the hall."

"Great idea." I actually found myself patting him on the back, relieved. At least we had some semblance of a plan. It seemed like our main method was to rush in, beat the enemy senseless, and hope we didn't get hurt. Maybe others were more adept at this saving-the-world gig, but I had the feeling we'd forever remain the Three Stooges plus of the he-man set.

I cautiously opened the door, peering out into the hall. Nobody, but the chanting echoed through the empty corridor, an eerie backdrop as we slunk through the hall toward our destination. The room was still unlocked, and as I opened the door, I could see Sabele's body still hanging there. Suddenly furious, I slipped in and motioned to the others. They silently filed in, stopping short as they saw the getup on the wall. Camille walked slowly over to the body, her fingers brushing the leathery skin.

"What the hell did they do to her?" she whispered.

"I told you: They ripped out her heart and chopped off her fingers. They're a fucking bunch of sadists."

All my worry over what Harold's parents might say took a nosedive out the window as I stared at Sabele, wondering how long they'd let her hang there. Had they killed her there or somewhere else? Had she been awake when they'd done the deed? Had they violated her, fed on her fear, laughed at her cries? Flashbacks to my own night of terror at Dredge's hands flickered through my mind like an old movie. No matter that he was dust and ashes, no matter that I'd broken the bond, some memories were too horrendous to ever forget.

Camille brushed her hand across Sabele's face, gently stroking the wisps of hair that remained attached to the mummy back away from her eyes. "Sleep deep. Sleep and go to your ancestors, my friend. Sleep the sleep of the ancients, dream the dreams of the divine. Go and rest."

A faint whisper of wind blew through the room, and I shivered, not from the chill, but from the sense that Sabele was there, listening. Was she trapped? Did her spirit wander the halls of the damned, waiting for release?

Morio ran his hand down Camille's back, and she shuddered. He leaned close and gently kissed her shoulder, then her ear, before turning to me.

"Who do you want to send on the scout mission? Whoever it is has to move silently and preferably have as little scent as possible," he said, setting his bag down on the floor.

"I'll go," I said. "Will your spell work on a vampire?"

"I don't see why not. I can enchant two with the spell, so do you want to take someone else?"

I shook my head. I'd thought about taking Delilah, but too much chaos if we got separated. Better and easier to keep track of just myself.

"No, I can move faster than most of you, and I'm silent. What do I have to remember about the spell?" I looked at my boots. Heeled, but they were my working boots. I'd covered the bottom of the heels with a rubber compound so they made no noise. Some of my boots tapped nicely on the floor, comforting me as I walked, reminding me I was still alive, but I'd learned quickly that in our new gig as demon hunters, I needed the advantage of the silence I'd been gifted with when I was turned into a vampire.

"If you bump into someone, they'll feel you. If you make noise, they can hear you. If you attack someone, the spell vanishes. It's a spell aimed solely for reconnaissance. As a matter of fact, there are a few invisibility spells that will work during a fight, but they're hard to learn, and usually only the most adept sorcerers and witches can work them."

"How long will it last?"

He shrugged. "Hard to say; it varies with the recipient. But I think you should have about ten minutes, maybe fifteen if you're lucky. When you're invisible, you won't be able to see yourself, so you should have a pretty good clue when you start being able to see your hands and body again that the magic is fading."

I gave him a short nod. "I'm ready. Let's get this show on the road and find out just what we're up against."

He stood, spread-legged, his feet solidly against the floor. As he raised his head, his dark eyes glowed with a topaz ring, and I could see his demonic nature flicker to the surface. Morio took three deep breaths as a palpable energy rose around him, twisting and turning like a vortex of sinuous fire. He reached out and put his hands on my shoulders.

I couldn't understand the words, but as the chant flowed from between his lips, my body began to shift. It was almost like walking through a portal, but instead of everything around me becoming hazy, *I* felt nebulous, as if I was suddenly looking through a camera at the world around me. I glanced down and realized that I could no longer see my hands. Or my feet. Or any part of me.

"Okay, that's freaky," I said.

Delilah jumped. "Yeah, especially for us. You just vanished—all of you."

"Okay, I'm headed out then. I'll tap three times on the door when I return. Here's hoping the big blow doesn't start before I get back. The last thing we need is to be split up." I listened at the door again. Nothing sounded in the hallway save for the chanting that seemed to be an endless loop. Idly, I wondered if they'd taped it and just played it over and over again.

I slipped out and closed the door behind me. Nobody in

the hall. Keeping to the side, swerving around the doors that might suddenly open to reveal someone, I hustled my ass down the corridor. I could move far faster than any of the others, except perhaps Vanzir and Roz. And so I followed the thread of music and voices that called from the distance.

As I neared the end of the corridor, I saw a staircase going down. Next to the stairwell, a large bay window took up a good share of the wall, and as I pressed against it, what I saw made me jump back.

The staircase led into an amphitheater. The walls were painted black with gold trim. Tiers of shelves lined the walls, holding at least a hundred brass candelabras. Within each flickered three ivory candles. On one wall hung a stretched skin. I could tell it was human skin from the shape, and runes were drawn in blood on it. *The key to opening the Demon Gate,* I thought.

A large flat stone of black marble rested in the center of the room, and to either side of the altar, a seven-foot-tall blood-red pillar candle illuminated the stone. A ring of cloaked figures surrounded the altar, each in a gray robe belted with a red, black, and gold braided sash. At the head of the altar, one of the figures held a long sword, serrated and brutal.

But what caught my eye was the figure chained to the altar. Naked except for a wisp of a sheer scarf that was draped across her stomach, her long golden hair flowing across the marble, a delicate elf was manacled by her hands and feet. She was screaming, but the chanting drowned her out. I glanced up behind the figure with the sword and saw a black void forming in the air behind him. A Demon Gate! Holy crap . . . they were opening another Demon Gate!

I turned to race back for help. Unfortunately, I'd been so focused on what was unfolding in the amphitheater that I hadn't been paying attention to what was going on right behind me, and I ran into yet another cloaked figure. *Morio was right,* I thought. I might be invisible, but I still took up space. The thud as I accidentally knocked the man down was real enough, as was the fact that I ended up tangled in his robe and sprawled across him with a loud "Oof."

Holy hell, this was bad—real bad. As I scrambled to my

feet, he grabbed for me—for air, rather—and managed to get hold of my braids. He yanked, and I snarled, reflexively smacking him a good one. As my hand landed on his cheek, I saw a ripple shiver through the air as I began to shimmer back into sight. Oh fuck. I'd just attacked him, and now he could see me.

"What the fu—" The voice was oddly familiar, and I yanked his hood back, revealing Duane. Oh delightful. One miscreant I could do without. "Who the hell are you?"

He reached to grapple with me, but I hauled back and punched him a good one, slamming my fist against his jaw. I heard the bones break as he passed out. A quick glance around the hall told me that he hadn't been alone. Another cloaked figure was running toward the wall, shouting. At first I wondered why he wasn't just running away, but then a blaring siren filled the hall, and I knew what he'd been doing. At first I thought it was a fire alarm, but then I saw the lights blinking near the ceiling and realized that it was some sort of general warning. *Oh shit.*

I jumped up and started toward him, but he dove for cover in the nearest room, and I heard the door lock. Ignoring him, I headed back to gather the others. We'd lost all our advantage of surprise, but too bad. We couldn't leave that girl on the chopping block, not with the Demon Gate opening.

The door opened, and Camille and Morio raced out, followed by the others.

"Should we head out?" she called.

I shook my head. "No, they have another girl prisoner; she's still alive, but my bets are she won't be for long. I think she's providing lunch for a demon they appear to be summoning."

"Then let's get a move on," Roz said.

I turned and headed back for the amphitheater, the others keeping close to my heels. As we neared Duane's prone body, there was a sudden rush of shouts, and the stairs were filled with men. They'd left their cloaks behind, apparently, and there looked to be a good twenty or thirty of them. Some were a lot older than college age. Dante's Hellions' roster seemed to include a healthy alumni.

"Freakin' A," Camille said. "Spread out, and let's get busy."

I'd expected us to slaughter our way through the group, but I got a nasty surprise when I found myself battling one of the Hellions. It only took me moments to register that he, too, was a vampire. Oh shit. They weren't *all* human. At least not anymore.

He'd been around forty when he died, that much was apparent, and he was in damned good shape: average height but above average build with way too much muscle for comfort and a hungry, red gleam in his eye. As I engaged him, my fangs extended, and I gave a little hiss as we circled one another.

"She a problem, Len?" a voice rang out.

"She's a vampire, too!" he shouted back.

Damn it. Now *everybody* knew I was a vampire. I closed in on him with my usual spin-kick but something went awry. Len seemed to be anticipating my move, and he leapt back. Unbalanced, I fell forward, and he leapt on me. Down we went, rolling on the floor, a flurry of snarls and hisses.

The sounds of clashing metal, fireworks, and shouts all filtered through my anger-soaked mind. I tried to focus, to gauge just what kind of threat this dude was.

I was holding Len at bay, so he wasn't stronger than me. In fact, he was using all of his strength to keep me from lunging at him, but he couldn't quite manage to throw me off. So I had more force than he did. He also had a couple of wounds on his throat, which told me that he'd either offered himself up as a soda pop for some other vampire, or he had been attacked. Was he weak, then? The wounds had to be fresh; they'd have healed over if they'd been more than a few hours old, they were so small.

"Bitch—just who the hell are you?"

The question echoed from off to my left. Had to be aimed at Delilah or Camille, unless one of the dudes here got off on calling men *bitch*.

"Your worst nightmare!" Camille's voice came thundering through the crowd. Original maybe not so much, but there was a loud explosion, and the hall filled with smoke. I prayed she hadn't sent herself up in flames again. As my opponent reared back, startled, I seized the opportunity and decided to deal with him the way I'd dealt with the ghouls. I broke his neck. Wouldn't kill him but—

"Hey, Roz! Stake! I need a stake!"

Before Lenny boy could react, Roz was beside me, stake in hand. He plunged it into Len's chest, and my vampire buddy went buh-bye in a cloud of dust and ashes. I leapt to my feet, looking around to calculate the mayhem we'd gotten ourselves into.

Four of the men were on the ground, choking, singed. I glanced around for Camille, hoping that she hadn't got caught in the backlash. She was in a corner, kneeing some dude in the balls. He groaned and toppled—she was damned good with that knee—as Delilah rushed by, chasing one of the men with Lysanthra, her dagger. He was screaming and covering his head.

Two more were on the ground, bloody red shirts attesting to the fact that they'd never take part in another frat house party. Vanzir had backed my old friend Larry up to the wall, and as I watched, he lashed out with one hand and without so much as a blink, Larry dropped. What the hell had the demon done to him? Morio, on the other hand, had changed into his full demonic form and was towering over a group of five of the men, who looked scared out of their wits. One of them had pissed his pants, that much was apparent by the odor wafting through the air.

"Round them up—bind and gag them—" I started to say, thinking we could hand them over to Chase, when a sudden hush fell over the area. My words vanished into the abyss. One moment I was speaking, and the next, I couldn't hear a word I was saying. I looked around, confused, and saw the same bewilderment on everyone else's face.

A movement from the stairwell caught my attention. In fact, *everybody* was looking at the figure emerging from the gloom. He was cowled like the others, but there was something menacing about him: a dark glamour that the others lacked. Even Len the vampire had lacked the sense of brooding power behind this cloaked figure.

He waved a hand, and all the other members of Dante's Hellions fell to the floor, facedown. What the . . . ? They acted like he was some sort of god.

Oh shit. Was he? Was he a demon they'd managed to summon before we could stop them? But though demonic energy clung to his aura like a rodeo rider on a bucking bronco, it wasn't emanating from him.

As he approached, we formed a battle line. Camille glanced at me and tried to say something, but no words emerged; no sounds filtered through the passageway at all.

And then the figure let his robe fall open, and I saw that it was a carbon copy of Harold, only older. Harold's father? No, too young. Maybe an uncle? He was geeky looking, but the brilliant fire that flashed in his eyes told me he was far from stupid, far from safe. The slow hand of death enveloped his aura like the cloak he wore around his shoulders. *Necromancer*—he was their death mage. And he was adept but careless. The energy rode him, rather than the other way around.

And then Camille pointed, and I followed her gesture. Around his neck hung a pendant. A gem of swirling blues sat centered in the silver filigree: a diamond-faceted, round cabochon of aquamarine. The energy that spilled from the gem made me want to sink to my knees. And then I knew what Camille knew, what Delilah was realizing. He was wearing a spirit seal. Our enemy possessed the fifth spirit seal, and he was aiming directly for us.

CHAPTER 25

I backed up, wondering if he knew what the spirit seal was. Was he in league with Shadow Wing? He closed in on us, his gaze dancing from Camille to Morio. He must sense the death magic that they'd been working with. Oh shit, if he thought they were a threat—and they were—he might target them first. I raced over toward Camille, intending to jump between her and the necromancer, when he waved his hand, and all of a sudden, I couldn't run anymore.

I dropped to the floor, hitting hard on my knees. If I'd been alive, I probably would have shattered a kneecap. As it was, if there was any breakage, it would heal up by tomorrow. As I struggled to pull myself to my feet, I realized that some magical force was holding me down. I pushed against the energy, but it wouldn't let me up.

A glance at the others told me that Camille and Delilah were also caught by the spell. Rozurial was pushing against it, slowly trying to make his way forward. Vanzir had disappeared. Had the spell killed him? Morio had turned back into his human form and—like Roz—was struggling to move at about half speed.

And the man who was holding us down headed directly

for Camille. Shit. Double shit. A look of fear raced through her eyes. Morio managed to slog forward a couple steps, but then, at a wave from the necromancer's hand, he landed on his knees, too. Roz was still moving, though. One excruciatingly slow step at a time.

The man walked through the haze of magic without missing a beat. He put one hand on Camille's wrist, then lifted his other hand and brought it down across her face. Hard. She gasped—or would have if she could have made a sound—and her head fell forward. He tossed her over his shoulder, turned, and headed toward the stairwell.

As I watched him go, a haze of anger and thirst welled up, and I felt my fangs descend. He was a dead man, but not before I made sure he felt every single step toward oblivion.

Roz continued to crawl forward, pulling himself toward the stairs an inch at a time. Delilah and Morio were struggling but still frozen. All the members of Dante's Hellions were also paralyzed.

A moment later, the energy began to lift. At least for Roz, Delilah, Morio, and me. The rest of the Dante's Hellions were still down for the count. As I struggled to my feet, I heard Camille scream.

Morio reared up, fighting off the residual effects of the spell, as he shifted back into demonic form—all eight feet of his incredibly scary, beautiful self. He lunged toward the stairs just as Roz broke out of his slow-mo struggle. Morio bumped into Roz and almost knocked him down the stairs but managed to catch the incubus before he went tumbling headfirst.

Delilah and I raced forward, pounding on the heels of the men. As we entered the amphitheater, I skidded to a halt. The Demon Gate, which had been forming when I first caught sight of it, now glowed with a manic raven-black energy. A swirl of stars shot through the inky blackness, and then I saw one star growing larger, heading our way.

"Fuck! Something's coming through the gate!" I glanced around, frantic to find Camille. There she was—on the altar stone next to the elf. The necromancer had slapped her in a set of iron cuffs. She was moaning as the sizzle of smoke drifted up from her skin. Oh yeah, he was *dead*.

Morio and Roz headed down the stairs. I took a shortcut, leaping over the rail to land in a low crouch near the foot of the altar.

"Let her go. Now." I stood, staring at the necromancer, who laughed.

"You want the girl? Or you want the elf? You can only rescue one at a time, and by that time, Shadow Wing will have feasted on the other, and the sacrifice will be complete."

Shadow Wing? No—he couldn't be coming through the gate! Not the Lord of the Subterranean Realms.

"You're insane—he'll kill us all!" I realized I was screaming at him, blind panic welling up. We were all dust motes compared to the demon lord. He'd bring his army through the gate and rip the world apart.

Morio didn't bother saying a word. The next thing I knew, he was standing next to the necromancer and, with the full force of his power, backhanded the man in a swipe that should have broken the neck of any other FBH. But nothing happened. The man reeled back, quickly catching his footing. He turned to Morio, a dark look clouding his face.

"You are a nuisance." He raised one hand and began muttering something in Latin. At that moment, Vanzir appeared from behind one of the terraced shelves and tackled him, taking him to the ground.

I leapt forward and grabbed the iron cuffs holding my sister captive. I could bend them. My hands would sizzle, but because I was a vampire, I'd heal, where she would sustain permanent damage if she touched them too long. Pure steel wasn't as much of a problem. Cast and wrought iron were torture.

Camille was trying not to cry, but I saw the welts rising on her skin as I pried the cuffs apart and set her free.

Vanzir was wrestling with the necromancer. He managed to land a sound blow on the man's nose, and the guy suddenly went limp. I tossed Vanzir a grin.

"I love you for that!" I yelled as I freed Camille and pulled her to her feet.

"I'm holding you to that," he shouted back.

I turned to free the elf, but at that moment a loud noise

from the Demon Gate stopped me. I didn't want to look, but I had to. If Shadow Wing was coming through, we'd better pray for backup, because the world was doomed.

As the shooting star hurled through the gate, Camille leapt to her feet, despite the pain on her face. Morio raced to her side, and Roz to mine. Vanzir yanked the spirit seal off the necromancer's neck and tossed it to Camille, who shoved it down her bra and drew out the unicorn horn. Delilah shifted, taking her black panther form, and I wondered if the Autumn Lord would be here, fighting with us, too.

"Put out a call for Smoky," I yelled to Camille.

She nodded, closing her eyes. The magical bond that joined her together with Morio and Smoky would allow her to reach him, to send a message that she was in trouble, that she needed him.

I cracked my knuckles, waiting. Sounds from the hallway told me that the vanguard of the Hellions had finally shaken off the spell, and they were either running away or pressing against the bay window. Boy, were they in for a shock. If it *was* Shadow Wing, they'd be the appetizer in his first meal of a million.

Steeling myself, I wondered if this was the end. Delilah rubbed up against me, and Camille pulled in on my other side. I wrapped my arm around her waist.

"Can we win? If it's him?" I whispered.

She shook her head. "No. Not with just us. Not unless we have help. Not unless . . . not unless the gods are on our side. Hey," she swallowed a lump in her throat and turned to lift my chin so I was looking into her eyes. "We've had a good run. We've fought long. We've fought hard. Father's proud of us. And if we have to go down, why not go down fighting the biggest badass around?"

And then a thunderous crash sounded in the amphitheater, and the gate split wide open. We stared into the abyss, waiting.

The inky void cracked like Humpty's egg, and in a wash of blinding light that wasn't really light but rather energy, the mother Karsetii slid through. She was huge and fully healed, and I could feel her terrible hunger from the energy that coiled around her.

But none of that mattered.

She might be huge and healed and hungry, but she wasn't *Shadow Wing*, and that was our saving grace.

A noise behind us startled me. Damn. The necromancer was up and awake again. Vanzir lunged at him, but this time he was ready and sidestepped the dream chaser.

"Great and mighty Shadow Wing, accept my offering! I bring you a sacrifice. I bring you the shining soul of one of the elves." He lunged past me, his dagger raised as he aimed for the elf's heart.

"No!" I jumped, catching him around the waist and tossing him toward the Karsetii. He screamed as the hive mother hovered in front of him, and a clone split off, tendriling its long suckers toward his skull. As the demon child reached for him, the necromancer vanished.

I jerked around, looking for him. Where the hell had he gone? I couldn't see him anywhere. But then the realization that we had a healthy, hungry demon facing us who was ready for lunch yanked my attention back to the matter at hand. We'd better put her out of business for good, or we'd all be on the menu.

As I turned back to where the Karsetii waited, I could feel it watching us, deliberating. A whistling noise rumbled through the amphitheater and a few whiffs of mist appeared as Smoky stepped out of the Ionyc Sea. He took one look at Camille's wounds, and his eyes narrowed.

"Who did this?"

Roz was busy unshackling the elf. She'd passed out. There wasn't much we could do for her right now. "A necromancer— must be one of the Hellions. The Karsetii's back, and we're going to have to go after it."

"Where is he? The wizard?" Smoky was set to kill, I could see that much.

Camille touched his arm. "The demon first, or it might go after Delilah. Please?"

He glanced at the Karsetii, then gently brought her hand to

his lips, kissing her fingertips. "As you wish, my love." With a glance at the rest of us, he said, "I can carry three of you over to the astral. Roz, can you and Vanzir manage Delilah?"

Before they could answer, the Karsetii suddenly veered to the right and headed out another door that lead farther into the underground labyrinth.

"Shit! Where the hell is it going?" I took off, racing toward the door. "Come on! We have to keep that thing in sight before it hives off a bunch of clones." As I pounded through the door, the others followed.

The winding corridor led us in a spiral downward. Whoever had created this labyrinth had certainly spent time and money on it, probably long before the house had any neighbors close enough to wonder what the fuck was going on.

Up ahead, I could barely see the tail end of the Karsetii as it zipped along through the air, like a squid through water, pointy head aimed toward some unknown destination. Along the way I caught sight of several doors leading into what looked like various laboratories. I was beginning to feel like we were in one of the fifties B-grade SF movies Delilah watched during late-night marathons on the SF Fans Channel—*Robot Monster, The Island of Dr. Moreau, Beginning of the End, Them!*—all the old movies I'd learned to love.

I was running so fast that a sudden corner caught me by surprise, and I skidded, taking the curve too sharply. As I landed face-first against a wall, I realized that the passages were no longer compacted dirt but shored up by stone and brick. I bounced off the wall, shook my head, and sped up.

Ahead, about twenty feet forward, the passage opened out. Head down, I raced through the entrance and found myself in a large chamber that appeared to be carved out of solid stone.

The man-made cavern was so vast I could barely see the other side. Natural stone pillars had been left at strategic spots throughout the chamber, no doubt to act as load-bearing columns. Illuminated by lights strung along the ceiling like many caverns open to the public, the center of the chamber housed what appeared to be an opening into the earth with mist steaming out from it.

Around the chamber, scattered tables sat waiting for use, filled with beakers and Bunsen burners and various jars of one sort or another.

I blinked. We really *had* stumbled into the mad scientist's lair. A metal table near the largest research station had several bodies strapped to it. I could tell they were dead, because they were a shade of blue no human should ever be unless they were Picts wearing woad. Electrodes were strapped to various points on one of the bodies; the *only* body that looked even relatively normal.

The other corpses were in various shades of transformation. An indigo ooze covered one of the bodies—oh shit!

"Viro-mortis slime! The aggressive variety. Be careful," I called back to the others. The slime was actually a colony of creatures that attacked and absorbed flesh.

Delilah let out a "Gross!" and slowed down.

"Where's the damned demon? And that wizard?" Smoky stalked around the room, seeking out his prey. Every table he came to he overturned, sending beaker after bottle after jar smashing to the floor. Fumes rose as chemicals sizzled in volatile puddles.

"Better hope none of those goes boom when they touch each other," I said, but at his glower, I backed off. The necromancer better pray I got to him first. As rough as I planned to be, Smoky's attack would be far, far worse.

"There—another door!" Camille shouted. Delilah and I followed on her heels, the boys right behind us.

We entered another chamber, equally as large but bereft of any tables or signs of human intrusion. I felt something prickle at my shoulder and jumped, whirling around. There was nobody there except Delilah, and she was an arm's length away.

"Something touched me," I said.

"A shade? Ghost?" Delilah glanced around nervously. "I don't feel the Karsetii. Either that or it's just been ignoring me. Maybe you managed to sever its connection to my soul earlier."

"I don't know." Again, a brush to my left, and I jumped. I backed up, moving toward her. "Something is in here with us. Camille, can you feel anything?"

She closed her eyes, flanked on either side by Smoky and Morio. "Demonkin. I can sense the Karsetii somewhere near."

"More than that," Smoky said. "I sense something from the Netherworld here. Undead—and whatever it is, it doesn't feel happy."

Shit. So we were facing an astrally based soul-sucking demon, a necromancer who was powerful enough to stop us in our tracks, and now—somebody fresh in from the Netherworld. Delightful. Lovely.

"We should just nuke this place and be done with it," I grumbled as something brushed against me again. "That does it!" I whirled around and lashed out in the general direction that the touch had come from. "Show yourself, you fool! You want to fight, then come out and fight!"

But it was no demon nor shade that slipped out from the shadows. No, we found ourselves facing a throng of at least thirty young women, most of them Fae; some appeared to be human. Every one of them wore a haunted look, and they were all naked, with holes where their hearts should be.

"Oh cripes," Camille said. "They're victims of that damned bunch of perverts. Looks like Dante's Hellions have been busy over the years." She bit her lip, staring at the mournful crowd of spirits surrounding us.

"What now?" Delilah asked, a pained expression on her face. "Can we do something for them?"

"We can kill their murderers," I said, growling.

"Doing that *might* set them free," Morio said. "But first we have to take out the necromancer and the demon."

"Okay then," I said. "Let's find the Karsetii and send it packing for good."

Vanzir pointed toward a dark splotch against the opposite wall. "Look—the necromancer. He's hiding behind a camouflage spell."

Morio squinted. "You're right." He lifted his arms and uttered a loud yip, then something I couldn't understand, and a green fire raced from his vulpine fingers. The fire enveloped the dark sphere cloaked among the shadows near the granite. As it sparked and dissipated, so did the shadow cloaking the necromancer. He was hunched against the wall, trying to hide, and when he realized we were looking straight at him, he straightened his shoulders and began searching frantically through his pockets.

"I don't know where the demon is, but I know where my dinner is," Smoky said, and with a roar, he streaked past us. Before the wizard could stumble or even shout, the dragon had slashed across his chest with one taloned hand, eviscerating him neatly and cleanly with one swipe. The wizard clutched at his stomach, his intestines spilling through his hands, as he looked up at the scowling white figure that towered over him. Slowly, he fell to the floor with one short grunt.

Smoky reached out with the toe of his sneaker and flipped him over. The necromancer didn't react, simply rolled with the kick, and from where I was standing, I could smell the fresh blood, and my fangs descended.

"Now, for the demon," the dragon said, returning to us, ignoring the body of the wizard. "I can feel the creature; it's here, in this room, but on the astral, waiting for us." He held out his arms. "I can take the girls. Rozurial, can you and Vanzir manage Morio?"

They nodded. Delilah, Camille, and I crowded into Smoky's open arms, and again, I closed my eyes, partially to blank out the shift—which I was discovering made me queasier each time it happened—and partially to drown out the smell of blood, which was setting up an entirely different type of reaction in my stomach. Queasy and thirsty don't mix that well.

As we shifted to the astral, I could feel the demon's energy intensify. Smoky was right; the Karsetii was waiting for us. She must be smart, I thought. Or at least cunning. I'd been wondering if the hive mother was sentient or just some horrendous beast from the depths. Now I could feel a sense of malevolence that only comes with true intelligence and understanding.

We'd have to be ready to move, I thought. The minute we stepped onto the astral, that beast would be on our tail, and if this was the same one we'd fought before, she was back, bigger and stronger than ever.

Touchdown. I could feel the ground before I could see anything, and then Smoky opened his arms, and the mists of the astral took over. I jumped to one side, Camille and Delilah to the other.

To our right, Vanzir and Roz appeared, Morio standing between them, looking distinctly unsettled. He was an Earth-bound demon—nature spirit—and traveling to other realms that weren't grounded in the physical seemed difficult for him.

We fanned out, taking up positions without a word. Camille yanked out her unicorn horn. I wondered how many more times she could use that before it would need refreshing. As if reading my mind, she glanced over at me.

"This will be it. One more big blast, and I'll need to wait till the new Moon so I can recharge it."

"Make it count, then," I whispered, looking for the demon.

Where was she? I could feel her. The hive mother's energy was everywhere. The very air of the astral reeked with an electric charge. I moved closer to Roz, who stood to my right. Delilah and Vanzir hesitantly sidestepped to the left. Camille, Morio, and Smoky moved forward. Together we formed a triangle, keeping watch in all directions.

"We can't let her go this time. She's stronger than she was before. Which means her power is growing." Morio's voice was lower when he was in his demonic form.

"Watch Camille, though," Vanzir said. "The demon's going to sense the spirit seal and go after it. That thing is like a beacon out here screaming, *Come get me, come get me!* If we had dared leave the witch over Earthside, we should have probably done so."

"Not while I'm around," Smoky rumbled.

And then Camille gasped and pointed. Through the mist, a sparkling net of orange lights appeared. They were like a web surrounding the inky black form of the Karsetii as she broke through the boiling gray clouds, headfirst, aiming directly for us.

"There she is!"

"Everybody ready?" I poised, ready to strike out.

Delilah held out her silver dagger as Morio pulled out a silver sword. Vanzir raised his hands, and wavering cords began wriggling out of them. Smoky moved off to one side, and within the blink of an eye, shifted to dragon form. Rozurial pulled out a set of what looked like brass knuckles, but they were silver.

"Okay then," I whispered. "Let's get this over with. Bring it on."

The Karsetii moved forward, and we were into the fray.

CHAPTER 26

The Karsetii hiccupped—at least that's what it looked like—and two clones emerged from the side. Shit. How were we going to avoid them while going after the central beast?

"Ignore them," Vanzir said. "They can harm us, but not as much as the hive mother."

"Light hurt it before. I suggest we try light and fire," Camille said, holding up her horn.

"Yeah, but let's try to weaken it first. Then you can fry her butt to kingdom come." I motioned for her to move back. "Get out of the way, and let us take a crack at her."

Roz held up his hand. "Everybody stand back. I brought reinforcements."

"What?" I asked, cocking my head to the side as he flashed open his duster with an exaggerated grin. He pulled out several small round reddish globes. They looked familiar but—

"Firebombs!" Camille stared at them greedily. She always lit up when Roz brought out his explosives, and I was beginning to wonder if my sister was a little bit pyro, but now was not the time to inquire.

"Yeah," he said, a gleeful look on his face. "Firebombs." He breathed on one and then tossed it at the demon. There

was a sudden flash, and I remembered where I'd seen them
before. He'd used one to destroy a newborn vampire when we
were after my sire. Oh yeah, the boy had some hot tricks up
his sleeves. Or at least in his pockets.

The firebomb exploded into a ball of flame as it flew toward the Karsetii, a shower of sparks raining in its wake. I
jumped back just in time to miss getting kissed by one of the
burning cinders. The demon screamed and dodged to the
side, but the firebomb grazed it as it passed by. A whiff of
smoke and burning flesh spiraled up as the flame burnt into
the inky black skin of the Karsetii.

The clones zeroed in on Roz, charging at him through the
mist. He let loose with another firebomb as the Karsetii turned
my way and began her attack. It was eerie to watch, a jet-
black squid flying through the air, with a head that looked
like a giant brain. Yeah, this was how I liked to spend my
nights, all right.

Remembering that she'd figured out my strategy before,
this time I dodged to one side but instead of attacking, I leapt
toward her as she passed, landing on her back. Shit! Wrong
move! A series of electric shocks ran through me, and I
couldn't let go, even though I tried. She was frying me—
electrocution by default.

I tried to say something, but I was shaking so badly with
the current that amped through me that I couldn't get a word
out of my mouth. Just then, Vanzir dove over the top of her
from the other side, grabbing me and taking me with him to
the ground as she continued her forward motion. We went
sprawling, and he landed on top of me. A light flashed through
his eyes.

"Normally, I'd enjoy this," he whispered, "but we've got
monsters to kill. You'll have to give me a rain check."

I pushed him off me and leapt to my feet, still slightly
stunned by the amount of juice the demon had circuited
through my body. Vanzir blew me a kiss and took off at a
dead run, heading toward the back of the Karsetii. He'd covered about four yards when it spun around, then barreled back
toward us.

Holy shit, she was determined to make us her bitches!

"Look out," I yelled as I dove out of the way.

There was a loud noise, and the ground shook. As I pulled myself out of the rolling mists and glanced back, I saw that Smoky—in his dragon form—had drop-kicked her as she zoomed past. The Karsetii was now a good twenty yards away. But though the kick had sent her flying, she didn't seem all that hurt, because she was making a beeline back toward us, this time with her suckers first, tentacles ramrod straight, looking ready to force themselves down Smoky's throat.

In a movement more graceful and quick than I thought possible, Smoky soared into the air, spiraling up out of her reach. The dragon was in his element, I thought, as he dipped and hovered over us, his wings soundlessly gliding on the astral currents. The mist followed his wake, providing a motion trail of swirling smoke, and I stopped, struck by the sheer beauty of the beast.

Vanzir leapt up. Out of his hands shot the spiraling tentacles that were his attack. He aimed them toward the demon, and they wriggled forward like pale, fleshy worms dug up from some nightmare garden. They landed against the brain sac and dug in, and it was then that I could see the tip of one of them as it wavered in the astral breeze. It reminded me of a lamprey, with a circle of teeth that latched onto its victim.

Vanzir's cords caught hold and drove themselves into the demon in a frenzied, hungry dance. I heard Delilah retch. She looked horrified, staring first at Vanzir, then at the demon, as if she didn't know who to root for. I caught her gaze and shook my head, mouthing, "Knock it off." We couldn't afford to alienate Vanzir, nor could she afford to be squeamish. This was what the Karsetii had done to her. She should be grateful she wasn't dead from its attack.

As Vanzir began to source energy from the creature, Morio raced in, back in his human form, silver sword drawn high. He landed a sharp stab on the back of the head, and the creature writhed. That seemed to shake Delilah out of her revulsion, and she joined Morio, her dagger out and plunging into the head of the demon. I couldn't wield silver, but I landed a good solid kick under the eye.

The Karsetii lashed out with one of its tentacles, catching

Morio in its fury. It didn't grab hold of him but launched him back, sending him flying through the mist to land on the ground near Camille.

As she knelt to help him, Smoky bellowed out, "All clear," and we all jumped back, Vanzir recalling his tendrils like a power cord rolling back into the vacuum.

Smoky belched, and a great ball of fire rolled out of his mouth, streaking down through the sky to land atop the Karsetii. The hive mother shrieked in pain as the clones shifted position and slammed back into the central demon, renewing her from the drain Smoky's attack had inflicted.

"She's healing herself," I yelled out.

Roz threw another firebomb, and it landed on her as she whipped around in his direction. That one had to smart; he managed to hit her right above the eye. The noise was horrendous as she roared, charging him like a mad bull.

Delilah rushed forward, chasing the demon. The Karsetii's head was pulsating. Something about music soothing wild beasts crossed my thoughts, but I pushed it away. I had my doubts whether Brahms's "Lullaby" would settle the hive mother down for a nice long nap.

I was right on Delilah's heels. Kitten was a damned good fighter, but she wasn't much of a match for this creature. But she surprised me. She launched herself from a running start, flipped head over heels through the air, and as she landed, found herself close enough to take a good, long swipe at the Karsetii.

"Lysanthra!" she called out, and her blade hummed and began to glow. I skidded to a halt. Maybe I hadn't been imagining things. Maybe the blade had some form of magic locked within it that I hadn't seen before. Camille had been trying without any luck to get her own silver blade to wake up, but Delilah had apparently nurtured hers into quite a handy friend.

The silver took on a reddish sheen as steam wafted off of it. What the hell? That was weird. As Delilah plunged it into the demon, raking it down the Karsetii's side, the steam took on form and substance, looking for all the world like a winged sprite. But there, the resemblance to the willowy forest creatures ended, and the sprite opened its mouth to show huge, misty teeth and fastened itself like an eel to the demon.

"Holy hell," Camille said. She'd helped Morio to his feet, and they, too, were staring at the unfolding scene. "What the fuck is that?"

"You got me," I said, then shook myself out of my surprise. The demon was wailing now, so loud that it hurt my ears, but she was still aiming for Roz, who was running like a bat out of hell—or an incubus on the run from an irate father, I thought cheerfully as I sped up and managed a spin-kick right in the place Delilah had wounded it. The sprite—or whatever it was—was no longer visible, but the wound hadn't closed and, in fact, it appeared to be growing wider. Whatever the dagger had done to the Karsetii was having an impact.

Rozurial whipped around and yelled, "Stand back!"

I dropped to the side; he didn't have to tell me twice, especially when I knew he was carrying firebombs. As I rolled and came up in a crouch, covering my head, sure enough, an explosion rocked the area, knocking me forward a good three yards.

Twisting, I saw the Karsetii shift directions. She was headed my way now, and her eyes had taken on the gleam of a wounded wild predator. Most of her tentacles were either scorched or had been blown to smithereens. Whatever Roz put in those little goodies of his worked wonders.

I scrambled to my feet and took off. Crazed demons were nothing to mess with, and though I thought I could land another blow on her, it was about time for Camille to do her thing with the horn. Or at least I hoped she was ready. I was about to suggest that she get her butt in gear when I tripped over some protrusion coming from the ground.

The astral plane was rife with rocks and odd twisted trees and so forth, so much that newcomers often mistook them for their counterparts on the physical plane. But here, the doppelgangers were often actual creatures—or at least sentient in a way that the originals weren't. Whatever I'd tripped over scuttled away in the boiling mist that covered the ground.

Oh shit. I glanced over my shoulder. The Karsetii was gaining on me fast. The hive mother appeared to be stronger

when she was wounded—at least she was more aggressive—
and I struggled to my feet and headed out at a dead run again.
But her tentacles reached me first—the two that were still intact, that is. They caught hold of me and lifted me up. I
glanced at a third one that was sniffing me out, hovering all
too near my head.

Then, as if she hadn't found anything to her liking, the
tentacle dropped away, and I felt myself being whipped
through the air. Before I knew what was happening, she'd
launched me to the side. The world went spinning around me
as I careened head over heels toward the rising mist. I was
going to hit and hit hard. Thank the gods I was a vampire. A
broken bone would heal, a busted artery wouldn't do much in
the way of damage. Just so long as I didn't land heart-first on
a jutting piece of wood or in the middle of a bonfire, I should
be okay.

As the ground wheeled up to meet me, I found myself facedown in the mist, landing with a harsh thump. Thank the gods
again. There was nothing beneath me but the astral landscape,
sans tree roots, rocks, or boughs. But the landing jarred me so
much I could barely move. I winced, pushing myself up to a
seated position. Nothing broken. Nothing seriously wrong.
Not even the wind knocked out of me, since I didn't breathe.
The shock of hitting hard had stunned me, but as I shook it off
and stood up, I was ready to jump back into the fray.

I whirled around, looking to see where the demon was
now. There—heading toward Camille and Morio. Roz was on
her tail, pulling what looked like another firebomb out of his
pocket. Delilah was making tracks right behind him, and
Vanzir was speeding in from the side. The sound of wings
whooshed overhead, and I glanced up in time to see Smoky
bearing down on the Karsetii.

Smoky let loose with a fiery blast, scorching along her
back, then pulled up sharply and veered to the side. The
Karsetii slowed. Not much, but enough to tell he'd hurt her.
Roz reached her and tossed one of the firebombs into the
wound Delilah had given her, which had split wider still. And
that's when I realized what her blade could do: The wound
was continuing to grow; it hadn't stabilized. That meant that

the Karsetii wouldn't be able to heal up from it right away, even if she managed to suck the life energy off one of us. If we could do enough damage, we could actually kill her.

Camille had the horn out, and she frantically waved me off. I skidded to a halt and began to backtrack, looking for cover. Roz and Delilah split off to the side, and Vanzir joined Morio, flanking Camille's other side. I could hear her chanting something, but I didn't stick around to find out what. I had to find cover. Light or fire—it didn't matter. The horn had proved its ability to magnify power, and I didn't want to be around when it shifted into high gear.

At that moment, I felt talons clutch around my waist as Smoky swooped down and carefully caught me up in his claws. He flew up and away, with me dangling between his front feet, and I stared at the mist-covered ground as we beat a retreat from Camille and her horn o' death.

Smoky zeroed in on the ground and dropped me gently into the mist before landing. Within the blink of an eye, he swiftly morphed back into his human shape and opened his coat. I dashed into the offered shelter without a second thought. This was getting to be old hat: my brother-in-law saving my butt from my sister's wayward powers.

Grinning, I pressed against him. No dirt, no blood on his spotless white clothing, as usual, but he reeked of testosterone and dragon sweat. As he enfolded the long drape of his trench around me, a flare lit up the sky. I could see it even from within the darkness of his coat. There was a screech, and then Smoky whispered, "She got it. My girl got the demon."

Then he tensed. Oh shit, had the magic backtracked onto her? Camille could kill herself if one of her spells, magnified by the horn, backfired onto her.

As soon as it was safe, he opened his trench coat, and I stumbled out. We both took off at a dead run, but then— blink—he was in dragon form again and snatched me up, carrying me as his wings beat a tattoo toward the smoke that was billowing out from the area where Camille and the demon had been standing.

I watched the ground disappear below me, anxious. Was she okay? Was the demon dead?

As we neared the area where they'd been, smoke rose to meet us, and boy, did it stink. Burnt flesh. *Shit.* That better be demon flesh, I thought. Smoky spiraled to the ground and let go of me, then shifted back into human form, and we raced through the gray clouds to see what the aftermath of the blast had left behind. Coming in from the sidelines were Delilah and Roz. We joined them and plunged into ground zero.

I heard coughing. A woman coughing.

"Camille? Are you okay?" Delilah was waving her way through the soot-laden air. "Camille?"

"Here, we're over here," came a familiar voice, and I relaxed.

"The hell with this," Smoky said and stepped back. Once again he stood there in dragon form, but this time he beat his wings to a steady cadence, the rush of air clearing the smoke from the area. As it cleared, we saw just what havoc Camille had managed to wreak.

She was sitting there on the ground, looking exhausted, covered in soot, ashes, and some sort of jet-colored goo, which I strongly suspected was demon guts. Morio and Vanzir were crouching next to her and they, too, were slathered with the slime. There was no sign of the demon, at least not anything big enough to worry about. Fist-sized chunks of the Karsetii were scattered everywhere, unmoving, dead to the world.

Camille gazed up at me. "We did it. We killed her."

"You still have the spirit seal, right?" I asked.

She stuck her hand down her bra and nodded. "Yeah, it's safe and secure."

"Then I guess we're done here. We just need to go back and mop the floor with Dante's Hellions. And destroy that Demon Gate spell before they summon something else through." I glanced around. "I guess we should get moving. Anybody sense any speck of life left within the hive mother?"

Vanzir knelt and picked up a large piece of the dripping demon. I tried not to grimace. Somehow, that just seemed so very nasty. He sniffed it, then closed his eyes. After a moment, he tossed it to the ground and shook the slime off.

"No. She's dead and gone."

"Hopefully, it will be another two thousand years before another one of those things comes out of hiding," I said. "Okay, let's get back to Harold's house and put a stop to this ever happening again. Even with their necromancer dead, want to make a bet they'd figure out a way to keep the gate open?"

"Either that, or bring in another necromancer. What will seal up a Demon Gate?" Camille asked, looking at Morio.

He frowned. "If we had another necromancer on our side—a skilled one—he could take care of it with no problem. We can probably negate it, since we've been working with death magic, but to really put it out of commission, we need someone who can create them in the first place."

"What do you mean? You mean they might have a chance to recharge it after you guys take it down?" I wasn't too clear on the mechanics of spellwork in the first place, and I certainly didn't know much about death magic.

Morio sighed. "Not exactly. When a magician creates a Demon Gate, he isn't just casting a spell. He's actually ripping open a doorway to the Subterranean Realms. Or he's supposed to. In this case, the dingbat they had working with them accidentally opened it to the astral plane instead of the Sub Realms. That's why he attracted an astral demon. But once that door has been opened, it's not easy to close. You can't just turn the spell off. You actually have to be able to force it shut and mend the rips in the etheric plane. We can do a fix on it, but neither Camille nor myself has the strength to close a gate that's been opened by an adept necromancer."

"Well, shit. What are we going to do?" Delilah said, standing. She held out her hand and pulled Camille to her feet. Smoky and Rozurial were frowning, and Vanzir just looked pissed.

"I know." I smiled. "It may take a bit of cajoling, and we may end up having to bargain our way into getting him to do it, but I know who we can ask."

"Who?" Smoky said. "Camille's not making any more bargains."

"Not like the one she struck with you, huh?" I said pointedly, laughing at him. He glowered, but I just shook my head. "Don't get your smokestacks in a dither. I'm thinking about

Wilbur. You know—Wilbur, who owns Martin the ghoul? Our new neighbor? I'll bet you anything he's powerful enough to fix this little problem."

"Of course," Camille said. "Anybody who can raise a ghoul to the level that Wilbur did with Martin is bound to be able to open—or close—a Demon Gate."

"So what next?" Rozurial asked. "Do we go get him or—"

I shook my head. "No, we have to stop the Hellions from bringing anything else through first. Then we ask Wilbur to pretty please do his thing. If he wants money, we find a way to pay him money. If he wants a dead body or two for more ghoul friends, we procure him a few corpses. Whatever it takes."

"Then I guess we have our plan," Delilah said.

I nodded. "Yeah. We're about to put Dante's Hellions out of business for good. Then I suggest we raze their house to the ground and fill the tunnels with concrete."

Vanzir grinned. "I can do better than that for you," he said, but he wouldn't say another word about it as we headed out of the astral, back to Hell House.

CHAPTER 27

◄─◦✦◦─►

We'd left the amphitheater in chaos, and as we stepped off the astral, I saw that things had only gotten worse. The elf, whom we'd left unconscious, was back in her manacles, and the scattered lot of young men in sneakers and jeans had gathered around the altar. Without their robes, they looked far less menacing. Harold was at the head of the altar, and the Demon Gate glowed, wide open behind him. He was chanting something in Latin.

"Trying to call up another big bad?" Camille said, stepping forward. "Don't even think about it."

Harold glared at her. "You have our soul stone. Give it back, or we'll take it by force. It belongs to the High Priest of our order, and he'll destroy you when he gets back."

"Your High Priest is lying in the lower laboratories, gutted like a fish," Smoky said. "I'd advise you not to expect reinforcements."

"No matter. I'll take over," Harold said, barely blinking an eye.

I stared at him, amazed he even had the balls to speak. "Get a clue, dude! Your uncle was just killed, and you don't even care. We destroyed the demon you summoned. Is it that you delight in being dense, or were you out to lunch when they were handing out brains?"

"Bugger off, vampire," he said, sneering. "Or I'll haul out a toothpick and dust the floor with you."

I leapt forward and backhanded him away from the altar and away from the elf. He went flying back to land on one of the circular tiers of the amphitheater. "Cocksucker! You've murdered so many women only the gods know the number, and yet you stand here, telling us to butt out?"

As I stomped toward him, he leapt up and quickly back-flipped away from me, landing on his feet, his hands out as he Bruce Lee'd me with his index finger.

"Bring it on, Daisy. We might look like a bunch of geeks, but we took a clue from the Evil Overlord List. *We can fight.* So either back off or prove what you think you've got going for you."

The sneer in his tone grated on me, almost more than the cocky look in his eyes. This boy was bucking for an etiquette lesson, and I was the woman to teach it to him. I sped up and was nose to nose with him before he realized I'd even moved. Obviously, Geek Boy wasn't used to dealing with vampires. Before he could say a word, I grabbed his head and yanked it to one side, stopping just short of breaking his neck.

"You feel that, babe? You feel how strong I am? You have any idea of how little it would take for me to snap your scrawny neck and send you into oblivion?"

I leaned over him and let my fangs extend, letting all my anger for Sabele and Claudette and the other women spill to the surface. "You're the kind of whack-job pervert that I eat for dinner. You got it? I suck your kind dry and leave the hollow husks for the rats to find. Any reason I shouldn't do this to you? Any goddamn motherfucking good reason?"

He struggled, but one move of my index finger to his neck, and he stopped. *The pressure must be incredibly painful,* I thought. *Maybe I should make it just a little worse.* I pressed harder—just a fraction, but enough to make him groan. He'd pass out if I exerted any more force.

I glanced at the other members of the group. There were thirteen of the original pack left here, and they were waiting for a sign from Harold as to what to do. Duane was there, nursing what looked like a broken nose. Damn! And I thought I'd broken his jaw.

Duane took a step toward me, and I shook my head. "One more step, and your lame Pooh-Bah gets it. Seriously. Back off, or the minute he's dead, you're next on my list."

Smoky, Morio, Vanzir, and Delilah moved to fence in the remaining men. Camille managed to free the elf again with the help of Rozurial, who handled the iron cuffs for her. Camille gathered the girl up—she was a wispy thing—and carried her to the side, laying her down on the floor. She glared at Smoky until he crossed to her side and offered his trench to cover the unconscious girl, then returned to cage in the idiots we'd managed to corral.

I eased up on Harold's neck as his pulse began to fade. "Now, you're going to tell us *everything*: how many women you've killed, you're going to give us a list of your membership, *just all sorts of good things*. Or we'll kill you. All of you. One by one, in the most painful manner we can think of."

"You . . . you wouldn't . . ." he started to say, but I yanked my shirt up, forcing him to look at the scars lacing my body.

"*Ding!* Sorry, wrong answer. Look at me. I was put through torture you can't even imagine before I was killed and turned into a vampire. I'm *not squeamish*. I know how to give as good as I got. You understand me?"

With a slight hiss, I leaned into his face and unmasked my full glamour, both vampire and Fae. Harold went limp in my hands, a puddle of cooperation. I reluctantly let go of him—I really wanted to mess him up—and he scrambled back.

"On your knees," I said, deciding that if I couldn't play executioner—at least not yet—I would make him grovel.

He fell to his knees, whimpering. The other men stared at him, then at me, and their eyes went wide. They began to back up, but the boys and Delilah herded them back into place.

"You killed Sabele, didn't you? You stalked her, kidnapped her, and sacrificed her to the demons?" I wanted to hear him say it aloud. "And Claudette, the vampire?"

He sucked in a deep breath, but when I shook him, he answered. "Yes! I did it. Sabele wouldn't give me the time of day. She wouldn't look at me. So I decided she'd become a sacrifice. She was out for a walk, and I grabbed her. She begged us for her life," he said, his face twisting with a manic smirk. "She begged us, on her knees, naked."

"What about Claudette—the vampire?"

"We thought she was Fae at first. We invited her over and found out she planned to make a meal of us. So we managed to trap her in a ring of garlic and silver. We had no choice— we had to stake her."

I closed my eyes. So Harold *had* been interested in Sabele. Even if she'd returned his attention, he'd probably have ended up killing her. And Claudette had been hunting them, yet she became the hunted. Too bad she hadn't succeeded.

"How long have you been summoning actual demons?"

Harold blinked, and the smirk slid off his face. "We never managed to attract their attention until my uncle started studying necromancy with the sorcerer last year. This is the first time the Demon Gate really worked for us. Before, we just burnt the hearts of our sacrifices and offered them up to the demons."

"Who started the order?" I asked, even though I already knew.

Harold whimpered again but said, "My great-grandfather. He belonged to another tradition before he left England. He updated it and decided to take the group in a different direction. A more forceful one, he said. He found the soul stone, and people began following him. He passed it down to my grandfather, who passed it down to my uncle. But the lodge was still a pale shadow compared to the level to which I've taken it."

"Why did he pass over your father?" I tipped his head up, gazing at the pulse beating under his neck. I was thirsty, terribly thirsty.

Harold swallowed. "My grandfather said my father was weak. He said I was strong enough to handle it, though."

"Where did your great-grandfather get the spirit—the *soul* stone?"

He shook his head. "I don't know. But my uncle realized that it was more powerful than anybody thought. I don't know how he knew. And then a year or so ago, we found out about Shadow Wing—"

I stiffened. We'd heard them invoke him. Here was our chance to find out what was going on. I poured on the glamour. "Who told you about Shadow Wing? Tell me everything."

Harold choked on a sob then said, "We met a couple of drunken demons in a club downtown. They told us about the coming invasion. My grandfather sacrificed young women to the devil, but we decided that it might be better to offer them up to Shadow Wing in exchange for our lives when he broke through and took over. We figured we could live under his rule and maybe be part of his court. And it just seemed logical to offer Fae and elf women instead of humans. So my uncle learned to create a Demon Gate, and we used the soul stone to invoke Shadow Wing . . ."

"Yes, your uncle," I said, frowning. "Your uncle was an *idiot*. You didn't invoke *Shadow Wing*, you moron, you called in an astral demon who had no connection to the demon lord, and that is the *only* reason you're still alive. Shadow Wing would have crunched your bones for lunch. Your uncle was a sloppy necromancer. Just who taught him his magic?"

With a faint lick of his lips, Harold said, "Rialto, a sorcerer originally from Italy. In exchange for my uncle's daughter."

I closed my eyes, trying to force back the bloodlust from overwhelming me. "He paid the man with his daughter?"

Harold nodded. "She's twelve. Old enough."

Old enough? I forced myself to take a long, deep breath and counted to twenty before I asked, "One last question. Does Rialto live in town?"

He gasped out a breathless "Yes" and gave me the address. And then I couldn't take it anymore. I fell on him, savaging his throat with my fangs. There were no words that could stop me. Camille and Delilah knew it, and so did our friends. They didn't even try.

I ripped at his flesh, making it hurt, making it as painful as

I could, then lapped the blood quickly, forcefully, without offering him the sweet bliss of communion. He screamed, dying beneath my fangs. As I leaned back and squatted on my haunches, eyeing the other men with a perverse sense of pleasure, they took a collective step back.

Delilah started to say something, but Roz touched her arm and shook his head. She let out a long sigh and nodded.

I stood up after a moment, leaving the blood to stain my chin and the front of my shirt. I wanted them to fear me. I wanted them to piss their pants thinking I was coming for them next. One did—Duane. The stench of urine rose to attract my attention.

I walked up to him and smacked him full in the face, finishing the broken nose I'd started earlier. He moaned and began to cry, but it wasn't enough, so I kneed him. Hard. He went down shrieking. If I was correct in the amount of force I'd used, he'd never father children. He'd never be able to even attempt it.

With a faint smile at the rest of them, I turned to Camille. "If you don't get Chase over here, I'll finish the rest of them off. I'd dearly love to, but I suppose we should give him his due."

Camille looked at the men and shook her head. "They know too much. They know about Shadow Wing. We can't let them talk. I don't know *what* to do with them, to be honest."

"Do we play judge, jury, and executioner? They were all party to the murders here. We've got rapists and sadists here, too. You can bet they would have watched the elf girl die without lifting a hand. I don't know what the answer is. You want them taken care of, I'll do it," I said. "I can take them out without remorse."

Delilah interrupted us. "Hand them over to Tanaquar. They were trying to summon Shadow Wing, so they're our enemies. We found the spirit seal in their possession. Prisoners of war, I say. Even if the demon lord didn't know they existed, they were trying to enlist in his army."

I flashed her a brilliant smile. "You are a brilliant and wonderful woman, Kitten. What do we do about the house?"

Vanzir spoke up. "As I said, leave it to me. Once you seal

the Demon Gate, I have friends who can help. The house will burn to the ground in a fire so fierce it will destroy any evidence left behind. So hot that it easily could have incinerated anybody caught in the flames. No one will ever know these boys are still alive."

Camille nodded. "Let's do it. Smoky can take me back to the house. We'll fetch Wilbur and bring him here, while you get these men ready for transfer through the portal. I'll run up to the Whispering Mirror while I'm at home to let the OIA know to expect incoming prisoners."

"Sounds good. Go for it," I said, thinking that this was one operation I was glad to mop up and get over with. I'd rather fight a Karsetii any day than humans who had gone so wrong, so bad. Somehow, it was easier to face demons when they looked like monsters rather than the boys next door.

While Camille and Smoky were gone, I sent Roz and Delilah upstairs to bring down anybody who might be hiding, and to lock the front door. To forestall a mutiny by our prisoners, we drugged them all with sleeping pills we found in one of their bedrooms. I sincerely hoped it was the last sound sleep they'd ever get. Delilah looked a little queasy after ransacking their bedrooms. She dumped a large tin of Z-fen on the ground at my feet and a number of homemade videotapes.

"Chase is going to want to see these. He won't ask too many questions after he sees what the guys were doing here." Her voice was a whisper, and I glanced in her eyes. She was close to shifting, but I sensed Panther was hanging out in her aura rather than Tabby.

"The girls?" I asked softly.

She nodded. "Yeah. They filmed their rituals. Bad. It's *really* bad. Vanzir is right; this place needs to be burnt to rubble and then burn the ashes. There are a lot of ghosts walking these halls, Menolly. A lot of pain attached to this place. All the spirits down there—the women. Can we set them free, or will they haunt this land forever?"

"I don't know. How could something this evil go on in

secret for so many years? I don't get why none of them ever let anything slip."

Delilah sighed. "Mutual protection. War stories. It's easier to keep a secret if you share it with your buddies and make them part of it. Everybody had something to lose, and none of them wanted to end up in jail or on death row."

She wiped her eyes. "I really think they believed Shadow Wing was going to protect them. People can rationalize anything if they want it bad enough. Sometimes I just want to turn into a cat and never come back. It would be so much easier . . ."

I wrapped my arm around her shoulder. "Easier, yes, but we need you. And besides, we'd miss out on dissing Springer and his freaks. Come on, think of it this way: now these wing nuts won't ever be able to kill anybody again. We couldn't stop the murders they already committed, but we've stopped any more from happening. And the elf—we saved her life."

Delilah glanced over at the girl, who by now had returned to consciousness. Morio was looking after her, and Roz had managed to find some sort of painkiller in those voluminous pockets of his. She would be okay, though she was severely injured. We'd take her back to Otherworld with us when we took the boys through to hand them over to the OIA.

"I guess you're right. We can't win every battle. And we found the fifth spirit seal." She sighed and wandered over to join Morio.

I settled myself on the altar, waiting for Camille and Smoky to return. Roz joined me, sliding an arm around my waist. I leaned my head on his shoulder. He kissed my forehead, and I didn't shake him off or pull away. For once, I actually welcomed the comforting gesture.

I was feeling much the same as Delilah, even though I wasn't about to let her see it. I was her tough little sister, the one she relied on to remain ready to rock when she felt vulnerable. I wasn't going to let her down by allowing her to see how shaken this whole mess had left me.

"I take it you're going to hunt down Rialto once we're out of here?" Roz leaned close to whisper in my ear, but he seemed to sense the general mood and refrained from nibbling.

I nodded. "You can count on it. I hope to the gods that the girl is still okay. If she is, I'll get Nerissa in on this to help place her in a foster home, someplace far away from here. Either way, Rialto is toast."

"Let me come with you. I'd like to pay the pervert a visit myself," he said. "Vanzir promises he and his buddies can take care of this place, including the tunnels, without torching any homes nearby. I just thought you'd like to know." Roz shook his head. "I hate this. I'm an incubus. Sex is my forte. But although I seduce, I've never once—*ever*—raped a woman. And I never will."

"I know you haven't," I said. "And it's more than that . . . it's the whole sacrifice-the-woman-to-the-monster bullshit. Where do these horndogs get that? Bad late-night horror flicks?"

"Hey, it's not just the movies," Roz said. "What culture hasn't had a deity require a living sacrifice? Monsters are only one step away from the gods."

"And that's why I hate the gods," I said. "I can do quite nicely without their interference."

"As can I," Roz said. Knowing his background, I knew he wasn't just mouthing platitudes. Zeus and Hera had left Rozurial and his ex-wife up shit creek without a paddle, ruining their lives and changing them for eternity.

Just then, Camille and Smoky stepped out of the Ionyc Sea. Camille looked sleepy, as did the man Smoky held in his other arm. It was Wilbur, all right, and he looked more confused than anything else.

After about ten minutes, both Camille and Wilbur were over their exhaustion brought on by the trip through the Ionyc currents. We explained to Wilbur what we needed him to do, showing him the Demon Gate. We didn't mention Shadow Wing or anything that had gone on except for the fight with the Karsetii.

He examined the portal, grimacing as he watched the stars stream through the inky void. "Whoever opened the gate is the same one who created those ghouls, by the way. Sloppy work. There's no fundamental direction keyed into the gate."

I had no idea what he was talking about, but he seemed sure of himself. "Can you dismantle it?"

Wilbur nodded. "It shouldn't be hard. The whole magical signature is warped; whoever did this has been tooling around in some dark, dark areas." He looked over his shoulder at me, his brow creased. "Whoever did this has one sick soul."

"Doesn't matter. He's dead, and now we need his dark deeds to disappear with him." I frowned. "You raise ghouls, you work death magic, and yet you find this repulsive? Isn't that a little out of character?"

Wilbur laughed, sharp and short. "Death magic has its place. Don't judge me until you find out everything I use it for. After all, you're a vampire. Aren't you supposed to be out sucking somebody's blood?"

I snorted. "Touché. You've got me there. Okay, what do you need to fix this? And then forget you ever saw it?"

He stared at me for a moment, then arched one eyebrow. "It might be nice to get to know my neighbors a little bit better." Leaning in, he whispered, "I've never done a vampire before; I hear you can make it hot as hell."

I backed up a step. He wanted me to fuck him in exchange for closing the Demon Gate? "I'm no whore." Camille had slept with Smoky to help us gain valuable information, but she'd wanted to sleep with him. That was different.

Diplomacy wasn't one of my strong suits, and we weren't here to play games. He'd do it our way or else.

"Listen," I said, closing in on him. "Just seal the gate. You'll seal the gate because you have pride in your profession. You'll seal the gate because you don't like sloppy work like this, and you know what havoc can happen. You'll seal the gate because I'll break your neck if you don't do it. And you'll seal the gate because I promise you, we *will* find the freak who taught the man who did this and take him out of commission."

Wilbur rubbed his chin, then broke into a faint smile. "You girls aren't the pieces of T & A I thought you were. Good enough. All right, I'll do it. Looks like an interesting situation," he added, glancing around.

I glanced at the Demon Gate, then back at Wilbur. We'd have to find a way to wipe his memory after he finished, but I wasn't about to say aloud what I was thinking. "You ready?"

He nodded. "I need some privacy and—that one—the Jap." He pointed at Morio.

I winced. "He's Japanese, not a Jap, you moron. And he's a youkai-kitsune who could gobble you whole for dinner if he changed into his true form. Be polite. You have no idea what caliber of people you're standing among, except for the cretins snoozing it up on the floor."

Wilbur shrugged. "Whatever. I need his help. He knows enough about necromancy to give me what aid I require."

We carried the remaining members of Dante's Hellions into the hallway, while Morio stayed behind.

When we were out of Wilbur's earshot, Camille asked, "Just how are we going to make sure he keeps quiet about this?"

I frowned. "I hate to do this, but Vanzir, can you get into his dreams and eat his memory of this? He's a wizard so—"

"Wizard, witch, mortal, it doesn't matter. As long as he's asleep and not sequestered in a warded area, I can slip into his dreams." Vanzir looked pained. "I never thought I'd have to feed like this again, but I suppose my talents are useful in situations like this."

A hungry look washed over his face, and I remembered what he'd told us. He'd tried to quit stealing life force and memories from people, but then Karvanak, the Rāksasa, had forced him to feed. And now we were doing the same. I let out a little groan.

"I wouldn't ask, except . . ."

"Except a lot rides on him not remembering anything he hears or sees. All right. But you'll have to knock him unconscious." He gazed down at me, then lifted his hand and barely grazed my chin. "I'll do it for *you*, and I'll do it to thwart Shadow Wing."

I nodded, lightly biting one of his fingers as it passed my lips. "Thank you. We've all been forced to do things we don't like in this war."

"Look," Camille said, pointing toward the bay window overlooking the amphitheater. Wilbur and Morio were doing something, all right, because the inky black gate into space suddenly exploded in a white-hot flash that had us all dropping to the floor. As I slowly came up from my crouch and peeked through the window again, the room had cleared. Wilbur and Morio were standing there, and the Demon Gate was gone.

"A few more things, and we're done," I said softly. "I'll go get Wilbur."

Vanzir nodded. "I'll be waiting."

It didn't take long then. A quick knock on the head, and Wilbur went out like a light. Vanzir spent fifteen minutes on the astral, and when he returned, he promised that Wilbur wouldn't remember a thing from the moment before he opened the door to find Camille and Smoky standing there.

We found the keys to the van sitting outside the house and carted the men out to it under the cover of darkness. I ran back into the tunnels to retrieve Sabele's remains and Claudette's clothing. Dawn would break in a couple of hours, and by the time I returned, I was exhausted, as was everyone else.

When we lumbered into our driveway, Yssak and a group of Des'Estar Guards were waiting for us. They took the frat boys into custody and followed Camille and Morio to Grandmother Coyote's portal, where they transported them back to Y'Elestrial. Camille and Morio went with them to visit Queen Asteria in Elqaneve and give her the fifth spirit seal for safekeeping. They also took Sabele's remains with them and the wounded elf.

Vanzir headed out, taking Roz and the van with him. "We'll take care of the house in the next couple of hours," he promised. "You have my word."

I looked at the two of them and gave him a tired nod. "Thank you. Thank you both for all of your help."

Smoky made sure everything was all right, then headed up to Camille's room after dropping the still-slumbering Wilbur back at his house.

Delilah and I sat there, a bowl of chips on her lap, Maggie on mine, staring numbly at the television.

"I'm not sure what to tell Chase," she said.

"We can't tell him about taking those men back to Otherworld. He's on our side, but what he doesn't know, he doesn't have to worry about." I frowned. "Give him the videotapes.

At least he'll know that whatever happened, it was the right thing to do."

Delilah thought about it for a moment, then let out a long sigh and shrugged. "Yeah. I guess. We have four spirit seals. Shadow Wing has one. If we can manage to keep the other four out of his hands, we might be able to push back the threat and win this war. But with a new demon general in town, things are going to be a whole lot harder." She stuffed a potato chip in her mouth and rested her head against the back of the sofa.

"I know," I said. "I know." I glanced out the window. "First light's coming. I'm heading to my lair. With a little luck, nothing horrible will happen today."

Delilah shook her head. "No. Just a hell of a big house fire that's going to burn all inhabitants to ashes."

And then she took Maggie and cuddled her, watching the flickering images on the screen as I dragged myself to bed. I started to pray for a dreamless sleep but remembered I'd turned my back on the gods. They wouldn't have listened, anyway.

CHAPTER 28

Three nights later, the night after the full Moon, we decked
ourselves out in high gear and headed toward Woodbriar Park
to witness Tim and Jason getting married.

The frat house was a memory. It had burned to the ground
without so much as a timber left. Whatever portals to the underground bunkers there were had been cleanly sealed so that
the fire department never even suspected they were there.
And though there were questions—How had the fire raged so
hot it consumed every speck of bone and flesh?—the answers
were scarce, and the case would go down as unsolved.

Chase had viewed the tapes. He knew what we'd been up
against. And he wasn't asking any questions. Vanzir was good
to his word. Whatever they'd done had left a very clean path
leading directly down a dead-end road.

As we sauntered toward the chairs that lined the wide,
neatly trimmed lawn, I looped my arm through Camille's.
She was wearing a plum-colored floral halter dress that barely
contained her boobs, but she looked perfectly attired for a
summer wedding where there would be a drag queen revue
for entertainment—a gift from Tim's old colleagues. She'd

draped a silver and black lace shawl around her shoulders and was wearing stilettos with laces that wound up her ankles.

"How do I look?" I asked, nervous. This was the first time that I'd worn something that publicly showed my scars, and I felt mildly queasy.

"I've told you five times. You look gorgeous. What does Nerissa think?"

Nerissa had been pushing me to quit being so self-conscious, so I'd chosen a pretty green dress that skimmed my knees. While it had a bolero jacket, and I was wearing knee-high boots, the dress still showed more than I was used to.

"Nerissa thinks she looks lovely," the werepuma said, sweeping in from behind me to plant a long, leisurely kiss on my lips. I settled into her embrace, welcoming the warmth and safety it offered. "Camille, Delilah, you both look gorgeous. Now, I'm going to steal Menolly for a moment, if I may." She pulled me to one side. "I miss you," she said.

"I miss you, too," I said. After a moment, I added, "I slept with Roz." We'd promised—no secrets.

"I know," she said. "He told me. He wanted me to know he wasn't trying to horn in on my territory. He any good?"

I grinned then. "Yeah. You should try him out sometime. He's fun," I said, but then hesitantly added, "but he's not you."

Nerissa's eyes glowed. "Nah, he's not my type. Too flashy. But baby, you are." In a rush, she said, "I need you so much, Menolly. I want to make love to you all night long. Can I stay with you tonight? I brought some new toys I know you'll like."

"Of course you can." A shiver of anticipation raced up my spine. "All night—just you and me."

Thoughts of her golden skin under my fingers sent me reeling, and all I wanted to do was strip off her clothes and sink my tongue into that golden core of hers that I knew so well. I stared at her breasts as they swelled under the thin summer shift, and my fingers itched to reach out and caress her.

"I can hardly wait till this is over," I muttered. "I'm happy for Jason and Tim, but you just don't know the things you do to me, woman."

"Good." She smiled, arching her back lightly. "Now we're even. I can't even look at you without wanting to tear off your clothes. Come on, let's get to our seats before they start the ceremony."

As we headed up the aisle, looking for the others, I said, "I'm thinking of changing my hairstyle. At least for special occasions."

I didn't mention that the thought made me nervous. I'd braided my hair the day after I returned home from the OIA therapy center, one year after I'd been turned. The locks had never been out of the their braids since then.

"I'd love to see your hair down," Nerissa said. "A cloud of burnished copper . . . yes, it would be lovely."

We scooted in beside Delilah and Chase. Delilah grinned at us. She was done up in a rose-colored silk tank top, a pair of pale pink linen trousers, and she'd traded her clodhopper boots for a pair of ivory flats. Chase gave me a little wave, still looking subdued. He was dressed in Armani. Camille, Smoky, and Morio were one row up, along with Iris and Maggie.

The rest of the seats were filled with FBHs, although I saw Sassy and Erin sitting on the other side. A niggle of guilt washed over me. I should be over there with them, but then again, the less Erin depended on me over the coming months, the sooner she'd be able to function on her own. Learning the life from another vampire was one thing. Living with your sire could create an unhealthy bond if it went on too long.

A buzz ran through the audience as Jason took his place at the altar. He was dressed in an exquisite tux with a pink vest, and he looked stunning. To his right stood another man, as dark as Jason but a few years younger, and I guessed it might be his brother.

The officiate took her place at the podium. As the music started, Jim Croce belted out "Time in a Bottle," and Tim began to walk down the aisle. He wore a black tux, and his shirt was as blue as his eyes. He was followed by three brides-maids—it was hard to tell whether they were women or men in drag—but they wore tasteful silver dresses and carried bouquets of red roses and white carnations.

As Tim joined Jason at the altar, I thought about love. I thought about the possible pairings in the world and how rare and wonderful it was to find someone you could share your innermost self with. While I didn't know if I'd ever have that, for now Nerissa was my companion. And for now, what we had was enough.

I turned my attention back to the ceremony. The officiate was speaking.

". . . love—it's all about love. We come together, we create our families, we choose our mates out of the desire to form a life together. Love takes many forms, wears many faces, but when it's real, when it touches your heart, you will know it and—with hope—embrace it. Love is stronger than hate, love is stronger than anger. Love is stronger than all artificial divisions that exist in our world. But love must be nurtured and carefully tended . . ."

My thoughts turned inward again. Harish had loved Sabele, and she'd been stripped away from him. I'd held his hand when we told him we found her remains and he cried. Rozurial had loved and seen that love tragically ripped out of his life. Mother had crossed to another world for love. Camille's love encompassed three men—her heart was so open and embracing. Delilah was caught between lovers.

Was love permanent? Perhaps. Love could be killed, love could be torn asunder. But the one thing that couldn't happen to love was for the essential *will* to love to be destroyed. And no matter what evils lurked in the world, that would forever be true.

As Jason kissed Tim, we rose to our feet cheering, and I felt bloody tears well up in my eyes. I dashed them away using the crimson handkerchief that Sassy had loaned me and turned to Nerissa. She leaned down and kissed me.

"A kiss for love," she whispered. "Now let's go congratulate the grooms."

CHAPTER 29

The next night was Litha, the summer solstice, and our atten-
dance was required—as both emissaries for Otherworld and
relatives of Morgaine.

We were in our best ritual wear. Camille's tattoo on the
back of her left shoulder that marked her as one of the Moon
Mother's daughters glowed with a silver light. She was wearing a long, strapless dress that swept out from her waist into a
wash of sparkling gauze.

Delilah was dressed in her finest tunic and leggings, with
Lysanthra strapped to her leg. The black scythe tattoo on her
forehead glimmered with streaks of orange fire.

I'd opted for a long, crimson dress and for the first time in
years, my hair shrouded me in a cascade of curls. I still wasn't
sure about the new me, but at least for tonight, I'd wear it down.

The gathering of Earthside and OW Fae was on a thousand-
acre preserve that the Fae Queens had bought northeast of
Seattle. The land was a haven of fir and cedar, oak and maple
and huckleberry, and winding blackberry vines. Situated
among the foothills of the Cascades, it was easy to find and
yet out of the way enough to avoid being swallowed up by the
cities.

I knew the Fae Queens were actively buying up as many smaller parcels of land around the central preserve as possible. Titania was in the process of moving her barrow to the land, and soon Smoky would be free from her meddling. He was so grateful he'd agreed to attend the gathering along with Camille and Morio.

While the werepumas had opted to stay home, Chase had accompanied Delilah, which I found slightly perturbing. The detective didn't realize how dangerous it could be for a human to hang out in Fae central. Of course, a couple ambassadors from the mortal world were here, too—officials from several governments who had first been set up to deal with the incoming visitors from OW. Now they found themselves sharing their own world with Earthside Fae, and the balance was shifting again.

FBH pagans and witches had petitioned to join the gathering, and a select few had been allowed, but for the most part, those attending were Seelie and Unseelie blood, and the dryads, floraeds, sprites, and sylphs. Naiads and undines lounged in the lake along with the selkies of the Puget Sound Harbor Seal Pod.

The trees here had been woken up, I thought as I wandered around the perimeter of the vast lea in which we all stood. The trees, the land, the lake situated on the land—they were all sentient and aware. From every corner and niche the nature spirits were watching us, vibrant and joyful and feral and dark. The summer solstice was the shortest night of the year, and we were balancing on the cusp of a new era.

Tonight, the Fae Queens would officially ascend to the throne. I glanced over at the stage where the crowning would take place. Queen Asteria was there, and beside her stood our father, who had come over as an ambassador for Y'Elestrial. Feddrah-Dahns was there, an emissary from the Dahns Unicorn Herd, and several other regal presences were hanging out with them.

A loud trumpeting filled the air, and I wandered over to the court where Delilah and Camille were talking in low tones with Father. He gave me a quick kiss on the cheek.

We'd had a little time to talk since he arrived, and for the first time, I suspected he meant what he said. He'd accepted me as I was, vampire and all. He was a handsome man, and part of me, remembering Jason and Tim's wedding, wished that he'd look for love again. Mother's death had hit him hard.

"Menolly, I'm glad you're here. Before the crowning, Morgaine has something to say to you—to all you girls." He stepped back, a frown on his face. I could sense that he wasn't happy with whatever it was, but he remained silent.

Morgaine swept up, a cloud of lavender and silver, black and indigo. As Queen of Dusk, she'd be ruling over the time between daylight and night, and her court would run under the perpetual twilight.

"Good, you're finally here," she said, looking at all of us. "We have to talk before the coronation." Her nephew Mordred joined her, scowling. He didn't like us—any of us—that much was clear, but he inclined his head in a haughty, polite manner, and let out a little huff.

"Have they decided yet, Aunt?" he asked.

"Decided what?" Camille asked.

Morgaine ran her gaze over us. "You girls stand between worlds, as do I. Only you stand between three worlds—the world of mortals, the world of *Y'Eírialiastar*, and the world of the Earthside Fae."

It had been some time since we'd heard the Sidhe name for Otherworld, and her use of it took me by surprise for a moment.

Morgaine noticed and smiled. "The humans' word for your world cannot begin to encompass the beauty there. I give it due honor."

"I wouldn't go that far," I said. Relative or not, no matter how distant or close the connection, I didn't trust her. I never had, and I never would.

She let out a small sigh. "You must make a choice to-night."

"Choice? What are you talking about?" Camille asked.

Morgaine's smile turned cunning, and I took a step back. She wasn't on our side. She wasn't on anybody's side but her own.

"I offer to you seats in my court. You are my flesh and blood, no matter the centuries that passed between our births or the fact that you were born in Y'Eírialiastar and I was born Earthside. We are still kin, and I offer you the title of princesses in my court."

She glanced up at Mordred. "Mordred is my heir apparent, but should he not produce a child of his own, you would be in line for the throne of Queen of Dusk. Camille first, and then Delilah." She turned to me. "While I can offer you a seat in the Court of Dusk, I can never offer you the chance to rule, since you can no longer have children."

Camille and Delilah gasped, but I just studied Morgaine, wondering what the catch was. "What do we have to do for this honor?"

Morgaine winked at me. "It's very simple, my girls. You renounce Y'Eírialiastar and pledge yourself Earthside. You resign all your commissions over in Otherworld—except, of course, those that bind you to the gods—and you take up duties in my court." She leaned in close. "You would still be fighting the demons, but for me. For us. For *all* the Earthside Fae."

Without missing a beat, I shook my head. "I'm not playing," I said. "Thanks, but no thanks. I'm loyal to my duties, and I'm loyal to my home and the Court and Crown who now rules the city."

Camille glanced at me, worry filling her eyes. She looked back at Morgaine, and I could tell she was choosing her words carefully. "You offer us a great honor, Queen of Dusk, but we regretfully must decline. Would you willingly accept someone into your court who broke old oaths and allegiances without just cause? Could you ever *really* trust us?"

Mordred smoldered, but I detected a hint of relief in his sweat. He didn't want anybody in line to take over from him.

Delilah shook her head. "No. We can't accept. But we're here to honor you and the others and to celebrate the unfolding of a new era."

Morgaine stared at us darkly, then turned. "Never forget what I offered you. The offer stands for a time, but if you choose to take it after tonight, the price will go up. Think it over before saying no. You have until sunrise."

As she swept away, followed by Mordred, we looked at one another.

"Wherever that damned woman goes, trouble follows," I said. "We'll have to watch her carefully."

"I think the Supe Community will find itself splitting as the Earthside Fae join the Courts of the Three Queens, leaving the Weres and vamps to themselves." Delilah let out a long sigh. "All we can do is watch and wait and hope to hell Morgaine never gets her hands on one of the spirit seals, because you know she'd be up to no good with it."

"I think . . . I think I finally agree with you," Camille said sadly. "The coronation is about to begin. Shall we watch?"

Delilah shrugged. "Might as well. Let's go join Father and Queen Asteria. I feel safer around them."

I swung in beside her and wrapped my arm around her waist. "What's that?" I asked, feeling a hard bottle pressing against me from the pocket of her tunic.

She shook her head, grinning. "Nothing you need to know about." I stepped to the side and waited until she'd gone on ahead, then quietly looked at the bottle I'd fished out of her pocket. I stifled a shout. The nectar of life: the elixir that would grant a mortal extended life. One bottle of this down the hatch, and Chase would live almost as long as a full-blooded Fae.

As half-Fae, we'd be offered the nectar at some point to extend our lives, providing the Court and Crown was willing to allow us the privilege. But Delilah had to have stolen this. Nobody in their right mind would just give it to her. I stared at her, wondering whether to say anything, when Camille gave a little cry as she opened a scroll one of Father's messengers handed her.

"What is it?" I said. "Are you okay?"

She nodded as her eyes teared up and a smile broke out across her face. "It's a message from Trillian. He's alive, he's okay, and he'll meet me in Otherworld in the autumn, to come back home with me. There's a truth spell cast on this parchment, so I know it's not a lie."

In the bustle as Morio and Smoky joined us, I slid the bottle back in Delilah's pocket. Whatever happened with

Chase would happen regardless of what I said or did. We'd sort it out later.

As the trumpets sounded again, and the Queens of Morning, Dusk, and Night knelt before Queen Asteria to receive their crowns, I tried to block out worries about demon lords, Fae politics, and human hate groups.

The world overflowed with beauty in life, in death, in all stages in between. There was *so much beauty* around us—hideous beauty and beauty so brilliant it made my eyes water.

Titania was taking her vows, reclaiming her throne as I picked a solitary red rose from a bush and brought it to my face, inhaling deeply. Sometimes we had to put aside our worries and focus on what was right in front of us. Sometimes we had to let go of our fears for the future and live in the now. Sometimes even a vampire needed to stop and smell the roses.

CAST OF MAJOR CHARACTERS

The D'Artigo Family
Sephreh ob Tanu: The D'Artigo sisters' father. Full Fae.
Maria D'Artigo: The D'Artigo sisters' mother. Human.
Camille Sepharial te Maria, aka Camille D'Artigo: The oldest sister; a Moon witch. Half-Fae, half-human.
Delilah Maria te Maria, aka Delilah D'Artigo: The middle sister; a werecat. Half-Fae, half-human.
Arial Lianan te Maria: Delilah's twin who died at birth. Half-Fae, half-human.
Menolly Rosabelle te Maria, aka Menolly D'Artigo: The youngest sister; a vampire and extraordinary acrobat. Half-Fae, half-human.
Shamas ob Olanda: The D'Artigo sisters' cousin. Full Fae.

The D'Artigo Sisters' Lovers and Close Friends
Bruce O'Shea: Iris's boyfriend. Leprechaun.
Chase Garden Johnson: Detective, director of the Faerie-Human Crime Scene Investigations team (FH-CSI). One of Delilah's lovers. Human.
Chrysandra: Waitress at the Wayfarer Bar & Grill. Human.
Erin Mathews: Former president of the Faerie Watchers Club and owner of the Scarlet Harlot Boutique. Turned into a vampire by Menolly, her sire, moments before her death. Human.
Henry Jeffries: First a customer at the Indigo Crescent, then part-time employee. Human.
Iris Kuusi: Friend and companion of the sisters. Priestess of Undutar. Talon-haltija (Finnish house sprite).
Lindsey Katharine Cartridge: Director of the Green Goddess Women's Shelter. Pagan and witch. Human.
Luke: Bartender at the Wayfarer Bar & Grill. Werewolf. Lone wolf—packless.
Morio Kuroyama: One of Camille's lovers and husbands.

Essentially the grandson of Grandmother Coyote. Youkai-kitsune (roughly translated: Japanese fox demon).

Nerissa Shale: Menolly's lover. Works for Department of Social and Health Services (DSHS) and is running for city council. Werepuma and member of the Rainier Puma Pride.

Rozurial, aka Roz: Mercenary. Menolly's secondary lover. Incubus who used to be Fae before Zeus and Hera destroyed his marriage.

Sassy Branson: Socialite. Philanthropist. Vampire (human).

Siobhan Morgan: One of the sisters' friends. Selkie (wereseal) and member of the Puget Sound Harbor Seal Pod.

Smoky: One of Camille's lovers and husbands. Half-white, half-silver dragon.

Tavah: Guardian of the portal at the Wayfarer Bar & Grill. Vampire (full Fae).

Timothy Vincent Winthrop, aka Cleo Blanco: Computer student/genius, female impersonator. Human.

Trillian: Mercenary currently working for Queen Tanaquar. Camille's alpha lover. Svartan (one of the Charming Fae).

Vanzir: Indentured slave to the sisters, by his own choice. Dream chaser demon.

Venus the Moon Child: The shaman of the Rainier Puma Pride. Werepuma.

Wade Stevens: President of Vampires Anonymous. Vampire (human).

Zachary Lyonnesse: Junior member of the Rainier Puma Pride Council of Elders. One of Delilah's lovers. Werepuma.

GLOSSARY

Calouk: The rough, common dialect used by a number of Otherworld inhabitants.

Court and Crown: The *Crown* refers to the Queen of Y'Elestrial. The *Court* refers to the nobility and military personnel that surround the Queen. Court and Crown together refer to the entire government of Y'Elestrial.

Courts of the Three Queens: The newly risen courts of the three Earthside Fae Queens: Titania, the Fae Queen of Light and Morning; Morgaine, the half-Fae Queen of Dusk; and Aeval, the Fae Queen of Shadow and Night.

Crypto: One of the Cryptozoid races. Cryptos include creatures out of legend that are not technically of the Fae races: gargoyles, unicorns, gryphons, chimeras, etc. Most primarily inhabit Otherworld, but some have Earthside cousins.

Demon Gate: A gate through which demons may be summoned by a powerful sorcerer or necromancer.

Earthside: Everything that exists on the Earth side of the portals.

Elemental Lords: The elemental beings—both male and female—who, along with the Hags of Fate and the Harvestmen, are the only true Immortals. They are avatars of various elements and energies, and they inhabit all realms. They do as they will and seldom concern themselves with humankind or Fae unless summoned. If asked for help, they often exact steep prices in return. The Elemental Lords are not concerned with balance like the Hags of Fate.

Elqaneve: The elfin lands in Otherworld.

FBH: Full-blooded human (usually refers to Earthside humans).

FH-CSI: The Faerie-Human Crime Scene Investigations team. The brainchild of Detective Chase Johnson, it was first formed as a collaboration between the OIA and the Seattle Police Department. Other FH-CSI units have been created around the country, based on the Seattle prototype. The FH-CSI takes care of both medical and criminal emergencies involving visitors from Otherworld.

Great Divide: A time of immense turmoil when the Elemental Lords and some of the High Court of Fae decided to rip apart the worlds. Until then, the Fae existed primarily on Earth, their lives and worlds mingling with those of humans. The Great Divide tore everything asunder, splitting off another dimension, which became Otherworld. At that time, the Twin Courts of Fae were disbanded and their queens stripped of power. This was the time during which the spirit seal was formed and broken in order to seal off the realms from each other. Some Fae chose to stay Earthside, others moved to the realm of Otherworld, and the demons were—for the most part—sealed in the Subterranean Realms.

Guard Des'Estar: The military of Y'Elestrial.

Hags of Fate: The women of destiny who keep the balance righted. Neither good nor evil, they observe the flow of destiny. When events get too far out of balance, they step in and take action, usually using humans, Fae, Supes, and other creatures as pawns to bring the path of destiny back into line.

Harvestmen: The lords of death; a few cross over and are also Elemental Lords. The Harvestmen, along with their followers (the Valkyries, the Death Maidens, for example), reap the souls of the dead.

Ionyc Lands: The astral, etheric, and spirit realms, along with several other lesser-known noncorporeal dimensions, form the Ionyc Lands. These realms are separated by the Ionyc Sea, a current of energy that prevents the Ionyc Lands from colliding, thereby sparking off an explosion of universal proportions.

Ionyc Sea: The current of energy that separates the Ionyc Lands. Certain creatures, especially those connected with the elemental energies of ice, snow, and wind, can travel through the Ionyc Sea without protection.

Melosealfôr: A rare Crypto dialect learned by powerful Cryptos and all Moon witches.

The Nectar of Life: An elixir that can extend the life span of humans to nearly the length of a Fae's years. Highly prized and cautiously used. Can drive someone insane if they don't have the emotional capacity to handle the changes incurred.

OIA: The Otherworld Intelligence Agency; the brains behind the Guard Des'Estar.

Otherworld/OW: The human term for the UN of "Faerie Land." A dimension apart from ours that contains creatures from legend and lore, pathways to the gods, and various other places like Olympus. Otherworld's actual name varies among the differing dialects of the many races of Cryptos and Fae.

Portal/Portals: The interdimensional gates that connect the different realms.

Seelie Court: The Earthside Fae Court of Light and Summer, disbanded during the Great Divide. Titania was the Seelie Queen.

Soul Statues: In Otherworld, small figurines are created for the Fae of certain races and magically linked with the baby. These figurines reside in family shrines, and when one of the Fae dies, their soul statue shatters. In Menolly's case, when she was reborn as a vampire, her soul statue re-formed, although twisted. If a family member disappears, the family can always tell if their loved one is alive or dead if they have access to the soul statue.

Spirit Seals: A magical crystal artifact, the spirit seal was created during the Great Divide. When the portals were sealed, the spirit seal was broken into nine gems, and each piece was given to an Elemental Lord. These gems each have varying powers. Even possessing one of the spirit seals can allow the wielder to weaken the portals that divide Otherworld, Earthside, and the Subterranean Realms. If all of the seals are joined together again, then all of the portals will open.

Supe/Supes: Short for Supernaturals. Refers to Earthside supernatural beings who are not of Fae nature. Refers to Weres, especially.

Triple Threat: Camille's nickname for the newly risen three Earthside Queens of Fae.

Unseelie Court: The Earthside Fae Court of Shadow and Winter, disbanded during the Great Divide. Aeval was the Unseelie Queen.

VA/Vampires Anonymous: The Earthside group started by Wade Stevens, a vampire who was a psychiatrist during life. The group is focused on helping newly born vampires adjust to their new state of existence and to encourage vampires to avoid harming the innocent as much as possible. The VA is vying for control. Their goal is to rule the vampires of the U.S. and to set up an internal policing agency.

Whispering Mirror: A magical communications device that links Otherworld and Earth. Think magical videophone.

Y'Eírialiastar: The Sidhe/Fae name for Otherworld.

Y'Elestrial: The city-state in Otherworld where the D'Artigo sisters were born and raised. A Fae city, recently embroiled in a civil war between the drug-crazed, tyrannical Queen Lethesanar and her more levelheaded sister, Tanaquar, who managed to claim the throne for herself. The civil war has ended, and Tanaquar is restoring order to the land.

Youkai: Loosely (very loosely) translated: Japanese demon/nature spirit. For the purposes of this series, the youkai have three shapes: the animal, the human form, and then the true demon form. Unlike the demons of the Subterranean Realms, youkai are not necessarily evil by nature.

And now . . .
a special excerpt from the next book
in the Otherworld series
by Yasmine Galenorn

BONE MAGIC

Coming soon from Berkley!

"Run! Get the hell out of here!" Morio pushed me toward the iron gates.

I didn't ask why. I just took off for the opening, avoiding the metal as I darted past the wrought iron spikes. Nearing the steps leading out of the mausoleum, another shout from Morio stopped me and I whirled around. He'd dropped his bag containing his skull familiar and had pulled out a pair of curved daggers, one in each hand. A wedding present from me, but he wasn't taking any time to admire the carved antler handles.

No, it was show-and-tell time.

Two people with long, shuffling strides were headed his way. Or rather, two *bodies*.

"Can you cut off their heads?"

Morio snorted. "Oh sure. I can just zip on in and lop off their heads with these babies. Get real, woman. We've got our work cut out for us."

"Hey, life would be easier that way," I called out, but he had a point. It wasn't that he couldn't fight. In fact, Morio was an incredible fighter. But we were facing one teensy-weensy problem. Our opponents weren't exactly alive. They were already dead. And dangerous.

One of them was just what he looked like—so much dead meat on the hoof. Normally, returning a zombie to the grave wouldn't be much of a problem—they were shambling brainless monsters. No brains meant less of a challenge. But we'd made one teeny mistake. His companion was all too aware of our intentions and was whispering something under his breath.

That we'd accidentally chosen a demon's corpse to experiment on didn't help matters. Neither did the fact that we'd summoned a spirit into the body, and that the spirit knew how to use magic. Oh yeah, we'd fucked up royal.

As I raced back to his side, Morio leapt into the air, spinning with a kick that landed square on the chest of the first corpse, sending the creature reeling back. The zombie thudded against the wall and slid to the floor. It was still moving, though. If we'd done our job right, it would be back in action in a moment. And it looked like we deserved an A+ for attention to detail. The zombie was struggling to push itself up off the ground.

"Cripes. *Now* our magic works," I said, torn between being proud of our work and wishing we weren't so damned good. I ran through my repertoire of spells, trying to think of something to help. We had to reverse the summoning spell but in the meantime, what could freeze an angry spirit waltzing around in a demon's body?

Morio sliced through the air, catching one of the creature's arms. He managed to carve off a long strip of the flesh and I grimaced as the chunk o' demon fell to the floor. The zombie reeled as Morio punched him in the jaw. He knocked him back a few steps, but barely put a dent in the monster's speed.

Oh, this was *so* not how our experiment was supposed to go.

Quick, quick, what could I use? Fire? No, the damn thing was demon and there was a good chance the body was still immune to flame. But what about lightning? I grinned. Electricity just might work.

I thrust my arms into the air and closed my eyes, summoning the Moon Mother, calling down the lightning. A storm was on the way, so the bolts didn't have far to travel.

The lightning instantly responded. I could hear it crackling from about five miles away as the clouds raced in, carrying it to me. As the energy began to swirl around my hands, I felt it thicken, shrouding me like a fog. The power soaked into my pores and entered my lungs with the rising mists.

The energy coiled like a snake at the base of my tailbone and began to ascend through my spine, prickling me like a thousand needles, the pain sharp and exquisitely sensual. A rush of desire rode on the back of the bolt—sex and magic were integrally combined for me. I sucked in a deep breath as the spell took over, then arched my back, arms open wide, and pointed my palms toward the demon's body.

Morio glanced at me and I heard him mutter *Oh shit,* his look one of stark terror. He jumped back, striking the demon with a final kick and then cartwheeled out of the way. As soon as he'd cleared the zombie, I spread my fingers and let the energy stream out of me. It reared up, taking the shape of a dragon, and dove for the demon, arcing with ten thousand amps.

The spirit we'd invoked shrieked and fled the body as the carcass fell to the ground. I dropped to my knees, my gut aching like a son of a bitch, but when Morio shouted, I glanced up just in time to see the bolt of lightning coil, then reverse directions as it raced straight toward me. I screamed and raised the horn of the Black Unicorn.

"Deflect!"

The Master of Winds residing within the horn rose up and as the bolt came crashing down, he thrust his sword in front of me. The lightning fastened onto the sword and followed the trail leading to the air Elemental's body, harmlessly passing through him as it grounded into the floor. I scrambled back from the blackened spot on the concrete not two feet away as Morio carved up the second zombie into pieces small enough that it couldn't bother us.

"Well," I said, leaning against the wall, all too aware that I'd barely skipped out on becoming toast. Again. "We can add this one to the list of *thou-shalt-nots* we've managed to accumulate. Whose bright idea was this, anyway?"

"So we made a mistake in choosing our host. It happens." He shrugged.

"It happens? How on Earth did we manage to end up with

a demon's body and *not know it*?" I stared at him for a moment and he gave me a sheepish grin. "Oh good gods, *you knew.* You knew we were invoking the spirit into a demon's body and blithely told me to go ahead with it. What the hell were you thinking? Are you insane?"

"I thought you'd figure it out," he said, laughing. He looked like he was enjoying this fiasco just a little too much. "We're still alive so I consider it a success. And if you hadn't chosen a mage's spirit to invoke, we wouldn't have had a problem. If you'd chosen just Joe Schmo's ghost, then he wouldn't have been able to use magic and we could have controlled him. Can you imagine what a demon zombie could do for us on the battlefield? Hard to kill, hard to take down. Goblins, trolls, even other demons would have their hands full fighting him."

I blinked. "So now it's *my* fault?" He laughed again and I sputtered. "You didn't tell me who to call from Dial-a-Ghost. I just randomly chose somebody. I didn't know he'd been a mage—"

"Camille, babe, it's okay. No harm, no foul. We're dealing with it, so it's all good. Now, get a move on, woman. We still have to banish the spirit back to the Netherworld." He pointed toward the wall of the mausoleum.

There, a ghostly white shape hovered almost close enough to touch—the spirit we'd summoned into the demon. But the phantom couldn't do anything now that we'd blasted it out of its host. The mage had practiced Earth magic when he was alive, so he couldn't attack from beyond the grave unless given a body through which to work. And I'd just blasted his vacation home to smithereens, well beyond what Demons R Us could fix.

I dusted off my skirt, which was now beyond the place where anything but a lint roller and a lot of detergent could help.

"Fine. Where to?" I limped over to Morio, my knee aching. I'd bruised myself pretty good when I dove to avoid the blast.

"Are you hurting?" He wrapped his arm around my shoulder and leaned in to give me a long, luxurious kiss. Morio might be on the slender side, and he wasn't the tallest of my lovers, but oh Mama, he had one hell of a hot body.

"Not so much that you couldn't kiss it and make it better," I whispered, pressing against him as my fingers traveled to his nether regions. I brushed my hand against the front of his pants, inhaling deeply as I felt him harden behind the loose material.

"Stop that," he whispered with a grin. "We've got work to do."

"I need you," I whispered back. Magic and cheating death were two of my favorite aphrodisiacs. Combine the two and I was ready-to-rumble, tear-off-my-clothes, break-the-bed horny.

"Patience. Patience," he said, nibbling my ear. "When we get home, Smoky and I'll give you what you crave, love."

I danced away from him. "Then let's get this wrapped up. The sooner we're done, the sooner the two of you can play a duet on me." I loved both of my husbands. And together, they could do a number on me that sent me into orbit. Sex had become a cornucopia of delights and once Trillian, my alpha lover, returned, I expected to be the happiest woman in both Otherworld and Earthside.

"It's a deal," Morio said.

Laughing, I followed him out of the mausoleum. Spirit dude wasn't tagging along behind us for a change. In fact, he was hanging back, looking right and left as if he was trying to decide which way to vamoose.

"What about the ghost? He's kind of a must-have during the ritual."

Morio shrugged. "Don't worry. He'll be there. He can't refuse."

As he spoke, the spirit slipped around the corner into a narrow hallway that led farther into the Wedgewood Cemetery mausoleum. We watched as he disappeared from view.

I shook my head. "Does he really think he can get away that easily? He has to know that the only reason he's here is because we summoned him. And *because* we summoned him, he's magically bound to stick near us until we're done with him. Or give him another body to roam around in."

"Maybe he's an optimist," Morio said. "Come on, let's get outside and send him back to where he belongs." He shivered as a blast of cold air hit us. "We can't be expecting a frost yet—it's not even the equinox."

"Autumn's already here," I said. "Trust me. And winter's going to be a doozy."

As we slipped out of the mausoleum, a wash of moonlight splashed across our path. The wind was rising but the wind chill made it feel colder than it was. The temperature barely kissed forty-five degrees and the scent of moisture hung heavy in the air. The storm was coming in fast, and before the hour was over, I knew we'd be facing a downpour as the early autumn rains hit Seattle.

I inhaled a long, slow breath to steady myself as the rich scent of loam and moss washed through me, buoying me with the magic rife within their essences. The Earth mother had been speaking all evening, the slow, steady pulse of her heart tripping a steady cadence beneath my feet.

We traipsed back to the altar we'd arranged on a stone bench behind a patch of rhododendrons. A few yards from the mausoleum, the rectangular dais rose about eighteen inches off the ground. On the left side of the bench Morio had placed a black pillar candle, and on the right—an ivory one. Their flames flickered in the steady breeze. In our absence, wax had puddled down the sides to form rings at their bases on the granite slab. Oh yeah, that was neat and tidy. *Note to self: Next time, bring candleholders.*

Beside the black candle rested an obsidian dagger, its blade gleaming in the soft glow from the candle flame. The hilt was carved from a yew branch and a nimbus of violet light gently pulsated around the blade.

Next to the ivory candle stood a crystal chalice filled with dark wine. It looked like blood but was actually a robust merlot.

"Well, well, well, the demon brat and the Faerie slut finally remember me and come waltzing back. I thought you'd never get your asses back here," a faint voice said from one of the branches of the rhododendron. "Where the fuck have you two nincompoops been?"

I grimaced. The skeleton was all of twelve inches tall. Perched on one of the rhododendron branches, he was holding on to the leaf next to him. Grandmother Coyote had loaned him to Morio. The creature was actually a golem of sorts, created from bits of bone and then animated and given a sense of intelligence. Whether she'd made him, or found him, I didn't know. And I wasn't going to ask. Pry into the private affairs of the Hags of Fate? Not so much.

"Shut up, Rodney." Morio frowned. The miniature miscreant was a smart-ass. And foulmouthed at that.

"You want my help or not, you bitches?" Faint bluish lights glimmered in his eye sockets and he sounded a little bit overexcited.

Morio thumped him lightly on the skull, almost knocking him off the bough. "Chill, little bone man. So, did anybody pass by while we were inside?" Morio glanced at me, and by the look on his face, I could see he wasn't all that thrilled about Rodney's help, either.

"Watch it!" Rodney steadied himself. "Nope. You're home free."

Morio grinned. "Good. Back in the box." He held out a carved wooden box that looked for all the world like a miniature coffin. The lid was open and the inside was lined with thick purple velvet padding.

"Fuck a duck." Rodney let out a long huff. "Do I *have* to?"

"Yes," Morio said.

Rodney slowly lifted his middle finger and flashed it at us, then lithely leapt into the box, laid down, and the light faded from his eyes. Morio flipped the lid shut and locked it.

"I don't like to look a gift horse in the mouth, but I have a feeling Rodney's going to end up on the junk heap before long." I poked the box with my finger. "You think Grandmother Coyote would be offended if we gave him back?"

Morio gave me a long, lazy smile. "You want to be the one to ask her?"

Backtrack and avoid the steely teeth at the end of the road. "No, no . . . just put him away for now. We'll figure out what to do about him later." I wondered if we could cast a mute spell on him. Washing his mouth out with soap wouldn't help. He didn't have a tongue or taste buds.

As Morio stashed the box in his bag, I stared up at the sky. The wind was rustling through the leaves, sending a handful whirling to the ground. They were changing color fast this year. Autumn was on the way, and it was coming in with a heavy heart. I sucked in another deep breath and felt the rush of graveyard dust fill my soul. Oh yes, the Harvestmen were on the move already.

Morio motioned for me to take my place at the altar. His dark eyes sparkled with flecks of topaz, even as my own violet eyes were flecked with silver. We'd been running magic thick and fast for days now, accelerating our practice, trying to hone our spells before we faced the new demon general that Shadow Wing had loosed upon Seattle. Once we found the lamia, we'd have our work cut out for us. She was lying low, hiding out, and none of our contacts could place her or the half-demon wizard we suspected had gated her in, but eventually she'd make her move and we had to be ready.

As I stared at my husband, I realized that he was looking older. Not old, but wiser, stronger, and more world-weary than when we'd first met. Hell, we'd *all* aged, if not in looks, in spirit.

Morio wore an indigo muslin shirt and matching pair of loose pants, and his outfit was belted with a silver sash, off of which hung a sheath protecting a serrated blade. His jet-black hair was smooth and shiny, loose from its usual ponytail. My ritual garments complemented his own: an indigo low-cut gown that swept the floor. It was loose enough to move in, formfitting enough not to hinder me. Belted on my right side hung my silver dagger. On my left—the unicorn's horn.

He paused, finger to the wind, then nodded.

"So we just repeat the summoning spell, but in the opposite pattern, along with the Chant to Dispel?"

"Right. Go ahead. Since you did the actual summoning, you should be the one to banish the spirit."

I leaned over the center of the bench, across which was spread a smooth layer of salt and rosemary needles. Picking up the obsidian blade, I focused on the energy and traced the salt-drawn pentagram in reverse, then circled it widdershins to open the pentacle. "*Suminae banis, suminae banis, mortis mordente, suminae banis,*" I said, while focusing on banishing the spirit we'd summoned.

The energy swirled through my body, through the blade, into the salt and herbs. There was a sudden silence as the wind dropped and the air grew thick. Above the center of the altar, the ghostly form appeared and, with a slow shriek, vanished from sight, sucked into a spinning vortex. I sealed the spell with a violent slash, severing the energy that had opened the gate to the Netherworld. There was a swift *pop* and the portal disappeared.

"Nifty! It worked. Not quite as powerful as opening a Demon Gate, but hey, at least this time I didn't set loose a dozen wayward ghosts," I said as the clouds broke wide, loosing thunder and lightning and a flurry of hail. As the candle flames sizzled and went out, the rain began to pour, soaking us to the skin.

"Think the universe is trying to tell us something?" I watched as the rain washed away all evidence of the salt and rosemary.

Morio let out a long sigh and picked up the candles, emptying the rain that pooled in their center. "Come on, we've got two zombies to clean up after. And after that I just want to go home, take a long hot bath, and then . . ." He paused, giving me a suggestive look.

"And then you're going to jump my bones and make me a happy, happy woman," I finished for him.

He cocked his head to one side and winked. "Oh yeah," he said. "And make myself a happy, happy man."

M192AS0209